GREY RONIN

THE AWAKENED BOOK 3

MATTHEW S. COX

DIVISION ZERO PRESS

Grey Ronin

The Awakened Book 3

ISBN (ebook): 978-1-949174-28-1

ISBN (print): 978-1-949174-29-8

The Awakened Series

CONTENTS

WISE MASTER FROWNS

Dutiful Japanese men stood in the courtyard of the Noro-Shimura Officeplex, their faces expressionless. Eight identical figures in black suits, shoulder to shoulder in front of the main entrance, formed a wall. Three shorter men, an elder flanked by two younger associates, waited a short distance in front of them. Cloth fluttering in a mild breeze overpowered the stillness everywhere else. Two hundred meters past a field of grass and cherry trees, the city of Kagoshima appeared devoid of life.

The elder took a step forward and peered over dark glasses. A surge in the wind sent waves over his immaculate grey hair a second before he reached to the katana on his left hip.

Cloudless sky glowed an unnatural shade of electric blue, lit by a sun hidden somewhere behind the silhouettes of skyscrapers. White cherry blossoms danced in the wind, drifting in whorls over red brick hexagonal tiles. The Eight moved in unison, their heads tilting as their eyebrows notched upward. The same jagged stripe of reflected sunlight slid across eight pairs of sunglasses. A gust drove a flood of petals against the face of the building, a pink-and-white wave crashing upon black glass. The men on either side of the elder drew their blades, filling the air with the hypersonic wail of active vibro-katanas.

A set of gloss white samurai armor—without a wearer—stepped from behind a fourteen-foot tall carved onyx rendering of Takeshi Noro, CEO.

Orange-yellow energy seeped from the edge of the phantom's ornate katana, peeling off like smoke as the figure moved, casting a soft glow over the armor.

At a gesture from the elder, The Eight moved as one to surround their opponent, spreading around him in a ring.

The armor advanced, pivoting its left shoulder forward as it took the blade in both hands. Shimmering light wavered in the high-polish helmet. Ten paces from the elder, the samurai halted, empty helmet staring past a curtain of falling cherry blossoms. A rushing sound of energy from its blade drowned out the wind.

A voice emanated from within the hollow armor. "I recognize the honor of your attempt. However, the inevitability of your failure renders this a pointless exercise. Noro-Shimura's transgression demands my response."

"So, this is the great Saitō Mamoru," said the elder. "I am not impressed. Let us see if the legends are true."

The Eight closed in, drawing blades, all moving in unison.

Fuming energy around the samurai's katana intensified, rising. White-orange flames lapped at the air.

"I wonder"—Mamoru flexed his knees, lowering his stance—"would your courage remain if you knew the veil would not protect your life?"

The elder and his two companions glided backwards, sliding twenty feet in a few seconds, disturbing the cloud of cherry blossoms. Mamoru sprang at one of The Eight. His blade trailed an arc of phantasmal light as the edge passed through a body without a sound. The man convulsed before staring into the distance, confused. A second later, the body split in half along a diagonal cut from hip to shoulder. The upper portion slid off, shattering on the ground as though it were made of glass. The rest fell backwards, landing with a *clank*.

"Kill him," said the elder.

His two associates raised their blades, which condensed into formless metallic lumps for an instant before growing into pistols.

Mamoru spun to the left as the men fired, swiping his blade across in front of himself. A cloud of bullets hung suspended in the air as if trapped in gelatin an arm's length away. The projectiles twisted in place, pointing wherever the seething katana directed. Mamoru made a grasping gesture at nothing and shoved his palm towards one of the remaining Eight. The bullets appeared to vanish as they returned in an instant to normal speed, shattering the man into a waterfall of onyx chips.

Gloss black fragments scattered across the courtyard, consumed by bands of white light that devoured them with a shrill squeal. Mamoru glared at the men on either side of the elder. Neon blue dragons, sinuous serpents as big around as a child's arm, emerged from the barrels of both pistols, hissing and spitting violet flames. The men seemed to battle for control of their weapons, and the elder charged.

Six identical men joined him, attacking in a simultaneous flurry of screeching vibro blades. Mamoru held his katana to his chest, the spine against his helmet, and submerged into the ground.

Seven swords crossed in empty space with an angry wail of hypersonic steel.

Mamoru gazed up at a ceiling of glass, which used to be the ground, overlaid with a hexagonal pattern matching the tiles. The elder spun in circles, sword raised, unable to tell where he had gone. The six identical men stood motionless, staring straight ahead. Mamoru glided to a spot a few feet behind the two unique men, who still fought the miniature dragonlings, and willed himself to ascend. He burst upwards through the tiles. Red stone slabs the size of dinner plates exploded skyward in a plume of dust and soil. They slowed and hung suspended as Mamoru sailed among, slicing open the back of the man on the left as he flew skyward. The operator screamed, arching his back from pain. The serpent protruding from his weapon sank tiny fangs into his throat, emitting a cute trilling noise as diaphanous whiskers threaded around the man's neck.

As if time rewound, the detonation of tiles and dirt collapsed back to form perfect, unbroken courtyard.

The elder whirled about, raising his katana, and charged. Mamoru rolled out of the top of his leap, descending with a downstroke at the other gunman, who remained occupied with his mini-dragon. Mamoru landed with a peal of thunder, his boots sending light-filled cracks racing across the bricks. The second operator collapsed to the ground, screaming past gritted teeth as cyan grid lines spread over his warping body. His dragonling bit him over the heart, wriggling until it forced its head inside.

Both men convulsed as the outline of brains glowed within their heads.

The elder came in with a rapid slash, which Mamoru turned with ease. His counterattack found only air as the old man slid sideways as if blown by hurricane. The elder attacked again, but Mamoru parried with enough force to bounce him off the onyx wall of the Noro-Shimura Officeplex tower, cracking the glass.

"You insult me, Goji-san," said Mamoru. "Your feeble attempt to strike me with outdated viruses is a sign of disrespect—or incompetence."

Goji's eyes faded to fields of white static. Sensing tendrils about to emerge from the ground to snare his leg, Mamoru stomped his boot. His command triggered a buffer reset in the network node, killing Goji's trap soft before it finished loading. The six identical men blinked in and out of existence for a few seconds. As the effect of the reset faded, they converged on him with jerky, robotic motions.

Mamoru frowned. "These defense programs are little more than children's toys. You should humble yourself before your superiors, Goji-san."

He triggered a bogging program, which hammered Goji's interface deck with millions of connection attempts per second, all of which aborted after one data packet. Cyberspace rendered the software assault in the form of Mamoru summoning an army of two-foot tall green-skinned oni dressed as caricatures of samurai. The little goblins assailed Goji with bows, raining a limitless hail of arrows at him.

The six remaining defense programs advanced. Mamoru slid to the side to prevent them from surrounding him again. Damaged brick rippled like liquid wherever his boots passed, and became whole a second later. Two of the program constructs charged. Mamoru deflected the one on the left while leaning to the side enough to avoid the other. Before the construct could withdraw, Mamoru grasped it by the face with his free left hand. Software in the image of a man went rigid as threads of white energy spread out into its skin from the samurai's fingertips. Light shone from its eyes and gaping mouth for several seconds, fading as it fell to its knees, looking exhausted.

The man with the dragonling sticking out of his chest picked himself up from the ground and ripped it out. It emitted an adorable cooing noise as he crushed it into fragments of ethereal blue glass. With a snarl, he lunged, a katana forming in his hand, held low to the right. Mamoru moved his right leg to the rear. He backed away and faced the circling man as he rounded his weapon in an upward slash. Mamoru smashed the attack aside, sending his opponent flying face-first into the building.

Chirping and trilling, the remaining dragonling gnawed on the throat of the other operator, who lay on the ground convulsing and foaming at the mouth. Goji stooped by the fallen man, and pulled the little program out of him, crushing it into a fading cloud of sparkling iridescent flakes.

Another construct came at Mamoru from behind, sword in a wild overhead grip.

Simple in design, the program attempted a brute-force disconnect, which cyberspace animated as a reckless charge. Mamoru's katana blurred as he thrust it to the rear, impaling the faux man's heart. The construct gawked at the steel penetrating its chest as blackness consumed it from head to toe. Scintillating white energy leaked from cracks racing outward from the wound. In seconds, the body crumbled from Mamoru's blade, a broken glass statue.

The construct Mamoru had grabbed took a position at his side, eyeing its former brethren with an emotionless stare. Its black business suit changed from cloth to liquid, and morphed into samurai armor.

"You have succeeded only in making my task easier, Goji-san," said Mamoru.

His reprogrammed construct ran at the elder. While his minion kept his living opponent busy, Mamoru whirled into the duplicates. He cut down two more and seized another by the throat. Seconds later, that construct changed into a black samurai. Only two defense programs remained hostile. The identical men circled Mamoru as their altered brethren squared off against the elder and his one active subordinate. Blades rang against each other as viruses and counterprograms ran through the wiring of the GlobeNet, each assault on a firewall represented by the crossing of swords.

With a wail of resignation, the convulsing operator reached toward the sky and vanished in a burst of cyan pixels.

A deep frown twisted Goji's face. "What have you done? Futoshi has logged out, but he will not wake."

Mamoru's laugh echoed from the empty helmet. "I told you, the veil cannot shield you from me."

The constructs attacked in unison. Mamoru hurled his katana to the side, where it floated, and caught each of their swords in his open gauntlets. Steel met armor with a plastic sounding *clack*, rising to an ear-splitting shriek as he closed his fingers around the hypersonic blades. Swirls of azure light shimmered at his fist, and the weapons went silent.

Mamoru roared. The seething energy from his hovering katana streamed to his body and engulfed him. Serpentine wisps of amber luminescence leapt across his shoulders and spiraled down his arms, riding along the swords to his foes. Each construct gritted its teeth and tried to force its way forward, but Mamoru held fast. Red glowed beneath their skin as the energy tendrils impaled them. Two katanas shattered, sending random cracks of disintegration racing up their arms, reducing both bodies to a scattering of onyx fragments on the wind.

Deleted.

Mamoru waited, casting a half-interested glance at the elder and remaining operator dealing with the reprogrammed constructs. He reached a hand in the direction of the debris before him and thought lines of program code into being. A lingering echo of the defense constructs from the node's neural memory gave him a blueprint to build on. Chips and shards rose airborne, spiraling in an obsidian whirlwind that came together in the shape of two men. With a final flare of light leaking from cracks, the effect of a glued-together vase faded and left two ebon samurai whole. Both bowed in deference to their new master.

Mamoru pointed his blade at the network defense operators. "Your efforts, though futile, are worthy of respect."

The white helmet tilted backwards as Mamoru gazed up at the Noro-Shimura tower. Clouds raced across blue sky reflected in seamless windows, billowing and gliding as if time moved at fast forward. His target hid high in the network, and knew he was coming. Mamoru held his arms out and launched upwards, skimming inches away from dark windows and his mirror image. Both living men screamed in frustration as he took flight, but only for a second before their attention returned to the rogue constructs.

Ringing sounds of crossing blades receded into the distance below. Mamoru ascended in a blur, passing several stories of virtual building every second. Energy pulsing within the monolithic tower thumped like a beating heart in the back of his mind, leading him to his target. The white samurai glided to a halt outside the building at an impossible height, too high to perceive the men below him.

Shimmering threads of blue and orange pierced the distant clouds, intercontinental uplink conduits carrying thousands of petabytes of data every second, a sight only GlobeNet admins were *supposed* to see. Mamoru glanced at one, a pipe six feet across, made of an uncountable number of bright orange fibers, shifting and swaying as light coursed down its length. Images sprouted up around it, like a primitive animal raising spines to ward off a threat: images of objects, people, sporting events, Vidphone calls, and games. All the information within the circuit bared itself to his mind. He looked away, uninterested, and touched one hand to the opaque jet window. A smattering of white-pink cherry blossoms gathered on the glass, giving him pause until the wind took them.

He widened his stance, as if his boots found footing on an invisible surface, and grasped the blade in both hands. With a low growl, he thrust the tip into the window, twisting it back and forth. At first it stalled, sparks and flashes bursting from where the point touched. Mamoru disregarded the ear-splitting cry of steel on glass and commanded the network to yield to his will.

It obeyed.

The onyx surface turned magma orange around where the katana sank in. Mamoru leaned on the blade, grunting as though he forced it into a block of dense gelatin. Millimeter by millimeter, the edge vanished until the tsuba above his grip met glass. A noise in his throat grew to a roar. Brilliant light radiated from his helmet and the seams in his armor. Glowing white cracks splintered out from where the blade had pierced. Seconds later, the wall burst apart in a rain of foot-thick black chunks that fell out of sight.

Blue sparks lapped at the rough, smoking edges of a deep hole. What had appeared from the outside as the glass windows of an office tower now resembled three-foot thick stone walls. The GlobeNet used so-called 'dark matter' for things intended to be indestructible: network boundaries, node walls, and terrain features. Mamoru glided through the opening and let his weight settle on his feet, standing amid smoke and the scent of burned graphite.

Inside, the network space rendered in the image of an office: dark carpeting, dim lights, and a messy workstation where a slender man swiped at holographic tiles, a lunatic grasping at shiny trinkets.

The programmer shrieked, spinning in his chair to face the white samurai emerging from the dust. "T-that's impossible! Only the Sages can change dark matter! Even Minamoto couldn't afford to bribe them!"

"You are a fool, Imura-san. The Sages are not mystical." Mamoru drifted closer, raising his sword. "They have no greater innate talent over this false reality, only superior tools."

The man's body went stiff as his back arched and a matrix of cyan gridding lit his closed eyelids from behind. Mamoru blurred to a streak, seizing the man by the neck. Pixilation and static washed over the emaciated figure for several seconds before he sagged limp and opened his eyes.

He dug his fingernails into the armrests, cowering from the vacant eye sockets in the frowning samurai mask. "H-how..."

"Did I pull you back in?" Mamoru flung him from the chair, face first to the ground. "You did not think I would come all this way only to have you disconnect as soon as I arrived, Imura-san? Where is your respect for a guest?"

Imura rolled on to his back, holding an arm over his face. "Please, Saitō-sama, we can find an arrangement. The data—"

"Is already gone." Mamoru waved his katana, causing the man to scoot away from the seething vapor. "Minamoto-Heika demands retribution. Did you expect to infiltrate the network of Matsushita Electronics Corporation without repercussion?"

"Jiro? What is going on?" A man's voice crackled out of the desk. "The logout aborted."

The programmer whimpered and glanced at the desk, seeming as if he wanted to beg for help from the outside, but could not bear the shame.

Jiro Imura crawled across the office until he huddled against the wall and gathered his knees to his chest, shaking, crying. "I did not conceive the idea. Make an example of my supervisor. It was my job. Like you, I must do what I am told."

Mamoru held out his left hand, grasping at the air. Imura shuddered and screamed, cringing as he fought an invisible force. He floated into the air, grasping at cabinet handles, frantic swiped knocked small objects to the ground. The man rotated to face the white samurai, tears streaming from his eyes.

"You failed. I am doing your supervisor's work."

Imura flailed and kicked, helpless as Mamoru thrust the blade into his chest. The man stared at the glowing fumes peeling from the metal, as if the sight of a sword impaling his heart was so beyond plausible he couldn't believe it.

Mamoru's mind reached across cyberspace, following the connection from the impaled man to his login point. The electronic path unfurled in his thoughts. He flew along an infinite maze of blue on blue lines, emptiness and power, memory and hardware. At the distant end of glittering azure, a silver box etched with circuit lines and green light hovered over a pedestal. Small dots of white climbed the virtual stone, up and over the device before they zoomed off along the floor.

As many entered the cube as left: the entire chamber swarmed with signals.

Mamoru entered the M3 systems interface port of a cyberspace deck, the software shadow of a metal plug in a socket—the other end connected to a human mind. One solitary impulse, a glowing star the size of an orange, repeatedly bounced away from the box, denied entry.

Imura's continued attempt to log out, a command no longer recognized by his hardware.

Mamoru told the machine what it must do.

The emerald light leaking out from cracks in the cube flickered and turned dark. Violet lightning surrounded the pedestal, crackling and lapping at the ground. Somewhere in the real world, a fatal jolt of electricity entered a brain stem, ending the life of one of Noro-Shimura's mid-level infiltrators. The beautiful corridors of azure light faded to black, the darkness followed Mamoru's receding point of view until he was again standing in the virtual office, holding the weight of Imura's body impaled on the katana. The corpse twitched once and hung limp for a moment before it blew away, black sand carried off on an imaginary wind. Mamoru lowered his arm, frowning at the carpet.

Why was this necessary? This will fail to deter others. Minamoto demands a show of strength, but they will not stop. He tilted a sword that did not exist, gazing at a reflection of overhead lights that also did not exist. Jiro Imura *did* exist—or at least he had. On the other side of Japan, a body sagged in a chair with smoke leaking from its dead mouth, eyes bulging with shock and fear. Mamoru bowed his head, thinking on how the man had begged for his life.

"Coward." Mamoru pivoted on his heel and walked to the hole. He glanced back at the empty chair. "Worthless."

The samurai armor came apart at the seams, disintegrating as he released his hold upon the virtual world.

INCENSE—KYARA AGARWOOD! INVADED THE TRANSITION, FOLLOWED BY the feel of hard wood beneath Mamoru's knees. His sense of *being* the machine gave way to a momentary nothingness in which his consciousness existed neither in the net nor his body. His senses went from muted to extreme. Even delicate silk raked across his flesh with the teeth of sandpaper. Warm electronics beneath his fingers seemed hot enough to cook on. The edges of the vent fluting tugged at his skin like razors. A creak, inaudible to most, ran through the floor like the string of a yumi under tension.

The scent of tea came on with a rush of sickening intensity, lessening as his awareness settled back into his living body. Mamoru opened his eyes to the rice-paper walls of his dojo. Thin, dark-stained slats divided sliding panels in neat squares. Pale wood floor ran wall to wall, surrounded by rich reds and browns, and a dozen ceremonial weapons mounted on the wall. He looked down at his hand atop a slab of technology alien to its surroundings. A sleek, featureless bar of black plastic—the Matsushita Corporation Oni series cyberspace deck—rested on a squat table in front of him. He folded his hands in his lap as a red and white kimono crept into his peripheral vision. Toes peeked out from the hem. Her posture betrayed nervousness.

"The tea is appreciated, Ayame-chan."

The young woman stooped to set the cup on the corner of the table. Mamoru's gaze flicked to the little red light blinking at the front of a snug metal choker, a round cord as thick as a finger. She bowed and pulled away without turning her back. Once at the door, she bowed again until her forehead almost touched the floor.

"Saitō-sama, will you desire food?"

Mamoru sipped his tea, not answering for the fifteen minutes it took him to finish it. The girl waited without moving or making a sound.

"That is agreeable. However, I must speak with Ishikawa before I eat. Have my meal ready in one half hour."

"As you wish." She bowed again, stood, and drifted out of sight.

He stiffened, placing his hands on his hips. "Terminal, outbound. Ishikawa, Reiko, Majordomo to Minamoto-Heika."

Holographic snow appeared before him, stretching to a rectangular pattern four by three feet. Soon, an interface filled in around the stern face of a woman in a black executive's suit. An NSK news feed scrolled across the bottom, a constant stream of kanji detailing gains and losses in the endless inter-corporation battles both virtual and real. Already, word of his work had reached the world. Her glower softened at the sight of him, tinted by the faintest hint of affection.

Mamoru bowed from the hip. "Ishikawa-sama, it is done as asked."

2

WHISPERING ONI

Mamoru sat back on the cushions to allow Nami to collect his empty dishes. A year or so Ayame's senior, she was the daughter of a director in the research and development arm of Matsushita. Unfortunately, the man had attempted to steal secrets to sell to another company. Minamoto ordered him executed. Because he had refused the honor of seppuku, his daughter had lost all status. By order of Minamoto Akio, CEO, she became a pet to be assigned to anyone he favored.

Nami started to walk away, but Mamoru cleared his throat. She froze in mid stride.

"Is there honor in winning a battle you cannot lose?"

The woman tensed, a conflict of emotion on her face. "I-it is not my place to say, Saitō-sama."

"Humor my curiosity."

She brought her sock-clad feet together, head bowed at the tray of dishes, gaze at the floor. "You wish for me to say if you should feel guilt over killing a man."

Mamoru did not move or blink, his expression blank as a statue. "To slay a man from such a distance a rifle could not reach him. To kill one who could not defend himself against me."

Nami paled. "M-Minamoto-h-heika demanded his death. It is not your guilt to feel."

His head lowered a touch. "Minamoto-heika also demanded your station. Was that just?"

She kept silent.

Despite the explosive around her neck, he could not bring himself to think of her as one of the lower classes. Her father's lack of honor could not be blamed on her. Some part of him disagreed with his warlord, a part that he had not listened to in many years. The woman had two years completed at the university, and would have been more useful to the company as an engineer. Because of her father's treachery, Minamoto had declared her entire family nonexistent.

"That is all, Nami-chan."

He allowed himself a trace of a smile as she walked to the door and slipped out.

His other servant scrubbed the floor at the far end of the hallway, pushing a large white cloth back and forth. Ayame came from the outlying area, somewhere north of Tokyo. *Iwafune, perhaps?* Her parents were either farmer peasants or simple laborers. He had asked once, at a loss for anything to talk about, but could not recall. Their daughter had been in the wrong place when a handful of samurai wanted to get out of the city and enjoy nature. They got drunk, lecherous, and caused an incident with her. As much shame as she felt at her status, the way she behaved around Mamoru left him no doubt she knew any other owner would be far worse. Still, she shied from him whenever they were close, as if terrified he would demand what she had refused the samurai. He looked back in her direction, finding the hallway clean and her gone. He sat, hands on his knees, meditating on the matter of honor. Minamoto had ordered the man dead. The shogun's orders are absolute, yet he felt shame.

Ayame crept through the doorway, white obi rustling as she approached. She halted at his side, hands folded and bowing.

"Saitō-sama, the water is ready."

Mamoru offered a simple nod. She scurried away as he stood and stretched. He started for the door, but paused to glance at the window. A sense that someone he could not see was in the room with them came over him. His eyes narrowed to a squint as he surveyed the area in search of a ninja in a sneak suit. Muscles in his back tightened as a patch of thicker air slid around him. A cloud of chill swam by and condensed, becoming heavy in the distinct feeling of hands pressed on his back. He whirled to the rear, hand on his blade, and adopted a combative stance.

"Who or what is here?"

No reaction came.

After a moment of tense quiet, he backed out of the room and went down the hall to the bathing chamber. Ayame and Nami waited, facing each other in front of a bamboo-paneled square tub. Steam and scented oils swirled in the thick, humid air. He paused at the door to send a suspicious glare down the hall at the darkness. Sight and sound said nothing was there, though another sense said something—someone—was.

A step forward put him between the two women. He raised his arms and they removed and collected his haori, folded it, and set it to the side. Next, they undid his belt and removed his hakama. They folded it, and set it to the side. Mamoru removed his undergarments and stepped into the bathwater, turned to face the door, and sat in the center on a tile-covered block. Water lapped at the base of his ribcage, alive with whorls of vapor.

Both women undid their obi and let their kimonos fall to the ground, leaving them naked save for the metal cords around their necks. Ayame's face reddened and her normally fluid motions became rigid.

She wonders when I will take her.

Each day that passed without rape seemed to make her more and more anxious it would happen tomorrow. With any other owner, it would likely have been a daily occurrence. Ayame's dread had the air of a girl younger than her true age, so timid and meek. She had defied once, and wound up a slave for it. *So close to broken.* Mamoru frowned. Neither of these women appealed to his desires, especially Ayame. *Too passive, too vulnerable.* He stared at the ripples in the water at his stomach. *My touch would shatter them like porcelain flowers.*

Nami, on the other hand, seemed open to the idea of sleeping with him. In spite of her initial shame, she often skirted the boundaries of etiquette in being warm to him. *She wishes to marry back to a position of status.*

Both women entered the water at the same time. Ayame barely managed to stifle a squeal at the heat. Nami slid close to him with an eager glint in her eyes while the other girl tentatively sank to her neck and sat on the bottom. He caressed them as they set about the task of bathing him.

Ayame remained stiff, sponge at arm's length and the rest of her body as far away as possible while she washed his back. The younger girl stared into Nami's eyes, which bore a curious mixture of pleading and resentment.

Nami knelt in front of him, unashamed as she ran the soap over the front of his chest, leaning her body against his legs under the water. Something in her eyes still held a glint of independence. *Does she still think she is in control?* Mamoru concentrated on keeping his own body from reacting to her proximity. *Perhaps she is.*

"Nami-chan, I am curious. If I was an ordinary man, you would have tried to kill me by now, yes?"

Ayame gasped, clutching the sponge to her face to muffle the sound. For a moment, all was still except for the random *plonk* of droplets falling from bodies. Nami's gaze fell to the water, fear or guilt looked alike.

"No, Saitō-sama." Her eyes trembled.

"Do not deceive." Mamoru picked at her explosive choker. "I see the way the anger fills your eyes every time you address me. If not for this, you would have at least run away."

Ayame shivered.

"I cannot defeat you, nor do I believe I will survive long enough to be rid of it."

He glanced at Ayame. The emotionless expression scared her, and she resumed working the rough sponge over his back. Her enthusiasm created a surge in the water that lapped at Nami's chest. Mamoru brushed her cheek, and ran his hand down to her breast.

"You desire to try, do you not? My touch makes you bristle with shame." Nami looked away. "It is fortunate you fear death more than you despise being owned."

"We are fortunate you are such a kind master, Saitō-sama," whispered Ayame. "I am grateful to be in your home."

Nami gathered her arms to her chest, both hands clasping at the front of her electronic restraint as she picked at it with her thumbnail. Ayame leaned up out of the bath, holding the sponge over Mamoru.

"I am sorry, Saitō-sama." She squeezed the sponge to rinse his hair.

Mamoru closed his eyes, allowing himself to enjoy the warmth cascading around his head.

Nami fidgeted with the ring around her throat. "If I go outside without you near me, I will die in five minutes." *Flick, flick.* "If you so order it, I will die." *Flick.* "If Minamoto Akio desires it, I will die." Nami's voice came without fear, a rabbit's breath louder than Ayame's sloshing. "No, Saitō-sama, I do not wish to die." She looked up at last, meeting his gaze. "But, I would kill you to return to the life I once had if I thought it possible."

Nami stiffened, expecting punishment. Ayame dropped the sponge, unable to look at either of them.

Mamoru smiled. "You have strength, Nami-chan. If I am to take a wife, she must be strong. I find no allure in the petals of a shrinking violet."

Her head popped up, face a mask of shock. Nami rose from the bath and eased herself close to his lap. The woman's expression was unreadable. *Is this true affection or an attempt to earn her freedom?* He leaned back, offering no protest as she rubbed her body against his. Ayame, now crying, continued to bathe him as Nami rose from the water and kissed at his neck. After a few minutes, Nami reached down and grasped his cock. She leaned forward, asking with her eyes.

Mamoru nodded.

She lowered herself onto him. It was not her first time. For a few minutes, they moved as one. Ayame's quiet sniveling to the rear did not help the mood. A chill washed over the water, threads of fog moved in serpentine whorls above the surface of the heated tub. Mamoru's eyes snapped open; a presence was with them—one that did not belong here.

Nami's dutiful undulations came to a shuddering halt as she arched her back and threw her head to the rear while emitting a confused moan. Mamoru clutched her hips as her body succumbed to spasms, grunting from the uncomfortable tightness trapping him. The fit lasted for a few seconds, after which she slumped over and dug her nails in his shoulders. Her head flew forward, shoulder-length black hair tossing a spray of water. The sultry-eyed grin she wore held no trace of respect or deference.

She stared into his soul as if she owned him.

"Hello, Mamoru," she said, in English, and resumed moving up and down.

Something had changed. Mamoru tried to stop her, but his body refused to obey. Ayame jumped, seeming startled by the shift in language. Nami had gone to the university. Knowing English was to be expected, but to speak it to her owner was a dangerous affront.

Nami leaned in to kiss him, but he held her back. She pressed forward, causing him to slide off the block seat. Ayame scooted out from behind him and swam to the side. Water splashed over the edge of jade tiles as they rode the wave to the rear wall. He came to a halt with only his head above the surface. Ayame crawled to the opposite corner and curled in a ball, trying to hide her entire body behind the small sponge. Nami pressed against him, aggressive, strong, and in no way herself.

She didn't stop.

Mamoru flailed at the slippery tiles, lost in the throes of his body's natural urges. He leaned back, the cold ridge of the tub at his neck. Nami raked her fingernails down his chest and howled as she writhed up and down. When she stopped shuddering, she bent forward with her hands on his shoulders, pinning him. He looked up at a face shrouded in darkness, but for the glint of her eyes and the blinking red dot on the detonator.

"Twice? My, my. You've been holding that in for a while, haven't you, Mamoru?"

At Nami using his given name, Ayame muffled a squeak with the sponge.

He lay there, exhausted and spent, unable to form a coherent response as she continued to squirm on top of him. Nami draped herself over him, kissing at his cheek, chest, and neck for a moment before she glanced back at Ayame.

"Oh, dear. I'm afraid I've startled your other pet. Do you have a moment to talk?"

Mamoru squinted at her, mesmerized by the blinking light at her throat. "Who are you?"

She stretched up, running her hands down his chest until they stopped on his stomach. He grunted as she shifted about. "Someone who knows you are wasting your talents here."

The sense that this was no longer Nami did little to dim the physical reaction of his traitorous body. "I am a samurai in the service of Minamoto Akio, CEO of Matsushita Corporation."

"You are as much of a slave to him as these women are to you. Would you like me to encourage the meek one to satisfy you?"

Mamoru lifted her off and pushed her to the side. The water muted the shove to a glide, leaving Nami sprawled neck deep at his side. He sat up. The look Nami sent at Ayame made the other girl cower.

"No," he said, matching her English. "I do not find weakness attractive. Her situation… I could not."

Nami tucked her legs under herself and stroked his chest. "Yet you allow yourself to be controlled by an ordinary man?" She rolled her eyes, muttering off to the side. "Oh, calm down Nami."

"You are Oni." Mamoru grabbed her arm and flung it away from him. "I can feel you are not natural."

Ayame seemed to pick one word out of the English—oni—and shivered.

"Mamoru Saitō, you are one of us. We must help each other." Nami moved up to her knees. Stomach deep in the water, she drifted toward him with her arms lax at her sides.

"Keep your distance, oni." He held his hand out. "I shall not suffer to hear any of your deceit. Be gone from my house."

A haughty laugh, distinct and British, belted out of her. "Oh, Mamoru, you do not even know what you are."

Mamoru raised his hand, index and middle finger raised, thumb hooked. He sat up, and clapped his hands together. *Kami, I beseech you to banish this oni from my domicile.* He clapped again.

Nami folded her arms. "Are you trying to pray me gone?" She rolled her eyes. "*We* are the new gods, Mamoru. Your ancient traditions cannot—"

"Go!" He pointed at the wall. "I shall speak no more with the voice of the damned."

"Bloody simpleton," mumbled Nami. Her eyes rolled back in her skull. She swooned to the side and collapsed under the water.

Ayame screamed. Mamoru held out a hand to her in a reassuring gesture, earning a pensive stare. Nami sat bolt upright, shaking. As realization dawned of what she had done, she curled up and blushed at the tiles.

"Forgive me, Saitō-sama. I could watch and feel, but could not move." She shivered with disgust. "It was as though someone had taken my body away from me."

He growled in his throat and moved to a sitting position, elbow on his knee and rubbing his mouth with two fingers. At the look on her face, he grunted and waved at her. Nami slid backwards to the edge of the bath and got out. Ayame followed. They took clean, white towels from a shelf and held them for him, standing naked and dripping. Mamoru sat still for some minutes, trying to understand what he had seen.

Neither woman moved. Sensing they would wait there until they tended to their required duties, he stood and exited the bath. The paradigm shifted: Nami could not look at him while Ayame risked eye contact. The young woman seemed finally at ease around him.

They dressed him in his nightclothes, donned their kimonos, and left the room.

"Ladies," he said, causing them to freeze three paces down the hall. "Visit the shrine before you sleep. Something not of our world stalks us."

"Yes, Saitō-sama," they said in unison.

3

THE WARLORD BECKONS

Mamoru Saitō stood silent in his dojo. At the sense he was alone, he lifted the deck from the table with reverence often reserved for a katana and carried it to a shelf between two suits of ancient armor at the center of the long wall. After pushing the wheeled table below it, he removed his white haori jacket and let it fall to the floor. His hair tickled at the small of his back as he walked bare-chested to the center of the dojo.

"Begin."

Holographic adversaries appeared. Fist-sized black orb bots emerged from portals in the ceiling and hovered about, ready to deliver a crippling shock should one of his phantasmal opponents strike him. The first ten figures appeared alone, followed by pairs, later three, four, and five at once.

He drew on his inner power, focusing mental energy into his body. For this, strength would be a waste of effort, so he concentrated on speed and dexterity. Wisps of white light peeled from his shoulders, flickering on the walls of his private sanctum. His movements increased in speed, taking down wave after wave of illusory opponents as though they stood still.

At first, the apparitions moved at the pace of normal humans. After fifty kills, the computer simulated cybernetic augmentation. Rather than veritable statues, these opponents moved as if in slow motion. Two dozen kills later, his body glistened with a fine layer of sweat. The orbs had yet to go off even once, causing the computer to cheat.

It sped up time, sending ever-faster waves of adversaries. Slow motion became normal time. Eventually, enemies too fast for him to keep up with grew overwhelming, and one punched him. While the hologram did no damage, the blue flash of a spark struck him in the chest, knocking him to one knee. This allowed the other seven to hit him. The look on his face from eight simultaneous shocks drew a woman's laughter from the door.

"End," he wheezed on smoky breath.

Mamoru sat up, about to bark at the person invading his dojo. When he realized it was Reiko Ishikawa, Majordomo to the CEO, he leapt to his feet and rendered a deep bow. He swallowed his alarm at being snuck up on; too focused on the cheating computer, he had not *felt* her presence.

Though he *should* have.

"Ishikawa-sama, welcome to my home. My apologies, I did not hear the Vidphone."

She acknowledged his bow with a mild one of her own. "It did not ring, Saitō-san. I let myself in."

"Of course." He retrieved his haori and wore it open down the front. "To what do I owe the honor of your call?"

"Minamoto-sama wishes to speak with you in person as soon as you are able to."

"I will leave immediately."

Reiko started to fade away, but snapped back to full solidity. "Clean up. I will meet you on the roof in thirty minutes."

Violet eyes gleamed, a perfect match to her high heels.

Her hologram vanished.

🐾 ✤ 🏮 ◉ 🗿

BLACK COAT FLUTTERING BEHIND HIM, MAMORU STOOD AT THE EDGE OF HIS building's roof, squinting at the glimmering expanse of plastisteel towers growing out of ground clutter. The early morning sun rising to his rear reflected back in blinding smears of orange. Poor areas appeared as stains throughout the silver city, darkened by the lack of signage and ad-bots. A peculiar mix of seawater and industry scented the air, drawing his gaze to the east and the ocean. Sparkling lights defined the silhouette of Shōrishima, the artificial island a shade larger than Hokkaido. Its bulk was a mere shadow, drowned by the glare from overhead.

He closed his eyes and braced as a hovercar crested the roof to his left. A blast of wind whipped his clothing as the limo rotated into place on the landing pad. Mamoru pivoted on his heel, striding up to the car as an eager man in a dark uniform scurried around to open the door for him. He removed the katana from his belt, holding it across his lap as he sat.

Inside, none of the sounds of Japan broke the tranquility. Gone was the rush of the wind and the distant whirring of thousands of flying bots. Even the occasional scream of someone being attacked in the alleys could not pierce this shell of opulence.

His seat put his back to the driver and left him facing Reiko. She was tall by conventional standards, a trait that had started rumors of her having a western ancestor somewhere in her past. No one had proved it yet—not for lack of dozens of rivals trying—which was why she retained her high position with Matsushita. The tinted windows turned her deep-plum jacket closer to black, like the rest of her suit. Only a silver Matsushita emblem on her lapel broke her wraith-like outline.

"You honor me, Ishikawa-sama." Mamoru bowed.

"I needed to get out of the office for a few minutes." Reiko's slender fingers curled around a triangular glass. Sake by smell, martini by appearance. "Minamoto values your service, Saitō-san."

He raised an eyebrow. *She would never address me such in front of him. A gesture of respect, perhaps?* "It is a privilege to be in his service."

Reiko sipped, staring through the clear vessel at him the whole time. Feminine, yet dangerous with the political power she wielded. Few women could kill with a flick of their eyes, and she was one of them. "Tell me, Saitō, for what price would you seek a new master?"

Mamoru did not flinch. "It is by Minamoto-heika's grace that Kutaragi-sensei took me under his wing. What is a man without honor?" He glanced out the window at passing black glass towers and food vending pagoda-bots. "My blade is not for sale."

She smiled. "Minamoto-sama will be relieved to hear that."

He pondered her meaning for a moment, but dismissed it. The way she looked at him made him uncomfortable, as if he were a bit of sashimi she debated consuming. No one else in the service of Matsushita could equal him, inside or outside the GlobeNet. A serious frown curled his lip. This woman would have him as a personal guard, wiling away each day inside an office attending to her every need. He thought of Nami and Ayame, of the blinking red light, and adjusted the collar of his haori jacket.

MATSUSHITA CORPORATE CENTER SAT IN THE HEART OF TOKYO, AN enormous obsidian leaf-shaped building rising from a nest of smaller structures. Viewed from the air, the complex resembled either a high-tech flower or an angry alien hive—depending on one's mood. Reiko had said little for the last fifteen minutes of their flight, content to wear a smile he did not trust while sipping her sake. He could not take his gaze off her eyes. Her irises shifted in an endless cycle from violet to blue to teal and back again.

She drinks it cold... like her blood.

The hovercar set down amid a cloud of fog that smelled as frigid as it felt to walk into. He emerged from the vehicle and followed her. Reiko's high heels *click*ed across rain-soaked plastisteel turned amber by the daylight. Mamoru studied her legs, perfect calves shrouded in a haze of grey-black nylon. The woman had to be close to forty, but thanks to nanotech surgery, she looked to be in her mid-twenties. Pleasure dolls would be jealous of her. Reiko glanced over her shoulder as if aware he appraised her beauty. She narrowed her eyes, but her lips curled to a perilous smile.

I wonder how much she spends on body work?

A thin walkway led from the landing pad down to an automatic door. Two men in dark suits flanked a gleaming glass façade bearing the Matsushita logo: black on black, matte on gloss. Neither man felt *right*. Two voids where the normal sense of being in the presence of a human did not exist. AI dolls, Minamoto's outer ring of security—immune to telepaths.

He passed them without acknowledgment, entering a polished wood walkway leading past holographic gardens full of flowers, trees, and birds. At the end of the hall, he followed Reiko around a corner and down a short flight of stairs to a rice paper wall. Another pair of men in gleaming black Dragon Chitin powered armor stiffened at their approach. The nine-foot tall samurai pulled Nano-bladed naginata to their shoulders with a loud *clack* as Reiko approached. Lime green light from their visors glimmered upon the transparent blades. Mamoru followed Reiko, but the driver and Reiko's bodyguard did not attempt to enter.

Akio Minamoto sat at the far end of a sixty-meter long office beneath a twenty-foot square tapestry bearing the Matsushita logo. He perched like a warlord on cushions by a low desk, surrounded by ten holographic display panels. The screens made his fancy dark grey and white kimono glow. His silvering hair was in a tight bun, and cold eyes observed his approaching underlings with an unblinking stare. Behind and to his left, a woman in a midnight blue kimono knelt. Mamoru looked away from the blinking red light at her neck, below a white-painted face of unreadable age.

The intangible screens collapsed to thin lines and winked out at a dismissive wave of Minamoto's arm.

Mamoru stopped ten feet from the dais and rendered a deep bow. "Minamoto-heika, you give me great honor by your summons." He knelt and sat back on his heels before bowing a second time, forehead almost to the floor.

Akio gestured for him to sit up. "Saitō-san. You have handled the matter of your recent assignment with utmost efficiency. It is with that same efficiency I expect you to fulfill another need."

A doll dressed up like a geisha brought tea for Akio and his guests. Mamoru looked over the thin lines at the corners of its mouth and the gold kanji glittering around its irises. *Sub-sentient, no awareness of its existence.* He studied his lap as the remembered sound of Ayame sobbing herself to sleep echoed inside his mind. *There is no need for indentured servants.* He nodded out of reflex at the doll as it handed him tea. *We have machines.* The electronic girl did not speak, nor did anyone else until it disappeared back past the curtain from which it entered. Resignation came over him.

He blinked hard. *They were not given to me to be maids.* He swallowed the tea, hot enough to hurt. *It is the way of things.*

Mamoru bowed again. "To function as an extension of your will shall bring me great contentment, Minamoto-heika."

Akio Minamoto extended his arm to the side where a holo-panel opened in midair. Tiny lights blinked beneath the skin at his left temple from a wireless implant. A dull crimson field crossed by black gridlines appeared. A sleek combat aircraft rendered in wireframe before it filled in to three dimensions. Long and narrow, it had forward swept wings close to the rear of the craft and backward-slanted canards on either side of the cockpit. Two large tailfins angled upward on either side of narrow vectored thrust ports. Small spots of clear glass along the leading edges of the wings gave away the position of laser weapons, and the lines of modular ordinance bays traced along the belly.

"Noro-Shimura is developing an attack aircraft under the project designation Fūjin," said Reiko before taking a sip of tea. "As a further message of our disapproval for their electronic infiltration, we intend to possess the Fūjin."

Mamoru addressed Minamoto. "You shall have it."

Reiko smirked. "You will obtain the appropriate design documentation, performance evaluation data, and return their completed prototype to us."

"They are conducting flights from their facility on the northern coast of Shōrishima," said Akio as the screen switched to a map. "I do not expect you to fail."

"Noro-Shimura may as well have given you their prize as a gift. The island is not of Earth. It is one great machine that shall bend to my desires, Minamoto-heika."

Reiko flared her eyes, a scolding glare for grinning in front of the CEO. Akio responded with a curt nod and brought his cup to his lips. The three sipped their tea in silence. Mamoru found himself glancing out of the corner of his eye at the live girl in the blue kimono. His heart skipped a beat at an instant of momentary familiarity peering out from beneath the white face paint. She sensed his glare, but suppressed the reflex to make eye contact. *No, cannot be. She looks too young.*

"I am grateful for your hospitality, Minamoto-heika." Mamoru bowed.

"Go, and do as you are tasked." Akio Minamoto put his hands on his knees, gazing imperiously at the doors in the distance.

Mamoru stood, bowed one last time, and strode to the exit.

4

SLEEPING CRANE

Bands of holographic red light pulsed over the clear capsule as it slid upward along its magnetic track. Mamoru faced the city, head down, ignoring a handful of advert-bots that clustered about for seconds at a time. As soon as one relented, another swooped in as he glided up from the shadows of Tokyo. Harsh late-morning light glared from silver towers, destroying most of the projected advertisements and casting deep shadows beneath the great buildings. Distant clouds held his attention and he lost himself in the sensation of flying until the elevator stopped at his floor. Ninety-three stories above ground, he gazed out over the shimmering plastisteel, fluttering awnings, and clouds of fog—his master's domain.

He was proud to serve Akio Minamoto.

The elevator doors parted with a chime and a hiss. Mamoru kept his imperious stance for a moment longer, before striding with purpose past a shallow garden ringed in rose-hued bricks until he reached the central chamber. A right turn brought him home, one of only three apartments on that floor.

Ayame and Nami waited a short distance inside the entrance. Hands folded before them and eyes downcast, blinking lights at their necks synchronized. Red ringed Nami's eyes. *Unusual.* He paused in front of them and she diminished under the weight of his gaze. He shifted towards Ayame.

"Prepare my things for a two day journey. Set out my light armor as well."

Ayame bowed. "Yes, Saitō-sama."

Once she had gone deeper into the residence, he spoke in a soft near-whisper. "Nami-chan, I do not doubt that some manner of oni was responsible. Do not fear my displeasure. I do not think less of you for what your father has done." He lifted the front part of the explosive restraint on one fingertip. "Or because you must wear this."

Nami shuddered, shying away from him at the reminder of her station. Mamoru let the metal slip from his finger and drop against her throat. She looked up, making eye contact, frozen with a new wave of fear. Mamoru did not glower. Even after a year of this new life, refusal to accept slavery remained in her eyes. Every stare, every action, carried as much defiance as she could get away with. Of course, she metered her rebellion. Too much, and he might cast her out. Any other master would be worse.

Mamoru thought of the way Reiko smiled at him. This woman before him was in no different a place than he, except his collar was invisible.

"Nami-chan," he whispered. "Please prepare me a light meal."

With a gasp, she leaned back and cast her gaze back down. Mamoru shied away from the look on her face and went to the bedroom, where Ayame had set out a black bodysuit covered with thin armor panels. As he entered, she bowed her head. Ayame assisted him out of his jacket and hakama pants and held the armor up while he put a leg in. It lacked the ornamentation or protective ability of Dragon Chitin. Its primary purpose was to remain unnoticed while offering modest protection. Normal clothing fit over it, and it did not hinder mobility. She fussed with him, like a mother dressing her son for the first day of school. She pressed a hand to his shoulder to hold the armor closed over his chest and squeezed the control button at his neck. The MolWeave fastener sealed, drawing the material tight around his body from hip to shoulder, as though it never had a seam at all.

He wondered if the ancient ones would consider this current task beneath his station. Stealth, theft, infiltration—those were not the way of a samurai. They were the way of a corporation, and he was its instrument. Ayame helped him dress in a dark, button-down shirt, pants, and long coat that made him look less a relic from the 1400s and more like a westerner. When she circled around in front to secure the buttons of his shirt, Mamoru clasped her trembling hands.

"Your fear is unwarranted. I shall not fail."

She stared at her toes. Mamoru swallowed an upwelling of contempt at the timidity that he assumed had been beaten into her before she was presented to him. Some of the ancient ways were better off left behind. He found himself timing his breaths to the red dot at her throat.

"Ayame-chan. You are afraid of the kind of master you will be given to should I fall."

She shivered as tears wet her cheeks. "Yes, Saitō-sama. You are kind and treat me well."

He tightened the armor about his forearms, one after the next. "This task I undertake for the glory of Matsushita Corporation is but a triviality. There is not a man in this nation who can best me."

"Yes, Saitō-sama." She bowed.

Katana in hand, he went to the dining room where Nami had laid out a bowl of rice, seafood soup, and several pieces of sashimi. The woman stood in silence while he ate, focusing on speed rather than enjoyment.

Mamoru nodded his approval when finished and she cleared the dishes, returning with his travel case.

"Nami-chan. I shall be absent for at least one night, perhaps two. Until my return, you are responsible for this house."

Nami bowed. "I will not disappoint you, Saitō-sama."

WITHIN THE MATSUSHITA PREFECTURE, MAMORU WORE HIS KATANA outside his coat. Citizens averted their eyes and scurried out of his way as he walked the several blocks to a monorail station. Ocean salt mixed with a wisp of udon soup and the occasional whiff of overpowering cologne in the air. Mamoru jogged up the moving steps to the elevated concourse where a thick wall of bodies had formed awaiting the tram. At the current hour, a modest crowd of university students and those on later-starting shifts waited near the track. Whispers spread, alerting them to his approach. Like a congealing jelly recoiling from a caustic substance, the commuters split apart, forming two masses each crushing themselves to get away from him. This offered a channel through which he moved to the yellow and black striped line. No one looked at his face, no one spoke to him, and none dared come within six steps. Even beggar children kept their distance.

A pair of company security officers in gloss white armor approached, the one on the left eyed his katana while the other examined a datapad. Mamoru ignored them. Some seconds later when his identity flashed on screen, both men paled and bowed.

"With respectful apologies, Saitō-san, we did not recognize you."

Mamoru grunted. "Mmm."

Several minutes after the security officers moved away down the concourse, a tram arrived in a flurry of billowing clothing and flowing hair. The crowd shuffled back in the wind, but pressed in as soon as the maglev came to a full stop. All around him, bodies squeezed against each other in a rush to board before the automated system sent it on its way. Mamoru stepped past the door, free of the weight of a commuter crush, and took the nearest open seat. The bench was large enough for three, but no one dared.

With his eyes closed, he focused on the monorail. His body grew heavy and his sense of self melted away. The gasp of people nearby preceded a hush. They saw the light of his *chi*, manifested in the form of ghost-fire along his arms. Reality reoriented itself as he projected his consciousness into the machine. He became the tram, brushing aside the automation and assuming control. Internal lights flickered and cut out, causing a stir among the occupants. His perception stretched forward, becoming a rigid body lying on its belly in a confining tube. Every component became known to him as if a new part of him he could move: lights, brakes, fire suppression system, magnetic impeller—even climate controls. The tram leapt forward at his desire for motion, a reflex as innate as walking.

After the initial oddity of slithering wore off, he picked up speed and sent a mental feeler over the wireless into the Tokyo Metro network. Up ahead along the route, switch paths changed to his whim. The passengers became restless as the first stop shot by without pause. By the time the tram missed four stations, the twinge of a hundred hands pushing the emergency brake raked like needles along his back. A minor nuisance he found simple to tune out.

His monorail picked up speed, rushing past station after station with enough force to suck people onto the rail in its wake. He leaned with the turns, altering the flow of the magnets to prevent the cars from disengaging the rail. After disregarding another seven stops, the metal serpent plunged down a tunnel that took it out under the ocean. The passengers pounded on the glass windows, making him cringe. Mamoru, the great serpent, cringed as a gut full of angry mice swallowed live clawed at his insides.

The resplendent beauty of the ocean dulled the crowd's anxiety. Fish swam through clouds of kelp amid scintillating shafts of sunlight that tinted everything blue. A long, straight section of track carried them for about twenty minutes before the Shōrishima interchange appeared in the murky distance. The sub-oceanic installation sat near the edge of the continental shelf, a large complex of buildings that even contained a hotel. Mamoru clutched at the brakes, his hands and feet warmed to the point of pain as he brought the tram to a halt within a large chamber.

Mamoru released his connection to the machine. The change felt as if his soul peeled up from the rail, shrank to human size, and slapped back into his body. A minute later, every door along the side of the tram opened, providing access to the platform. While dozens of confused people stared at their surroundings, Mamoru bounded to his feet and slipped out before they could close. Within seconds, the normal automation resumed control of the monorail, and sent it back where it should have gone.

Myriad sounds echoed in the cavernous space, from the unending thrum of air handlers to the frantic murmurs of technicians attempting to figure out what happened with the tram. Mamoru inhaled the fragrance of the ocean tinted with the ozone flavor of high-powered magnets. The large commuter station had only a few dozen travelers waiting for a scheduled arrival, all of whom stared in various stages of standing up, wearing idiot-faces at the tram that had arrived and left almost right away.

Most who worked on the artificial island lived there. The commute was expensive and only three prefectures had a direct tram connection, forcing people to travel through the territory of a rival company to get there. Executives could reach it via hovercar; however, if tensions flared, they ran the risk of being shot down.

Shōrishima was often tense.

The artificial island started as a project undertaken by the Nippon Shōgyō-Kumiai, a trade consortium that facilitated commerce between a fragmented Japan and the rest of the world. However, the Japanese State Defense Force had co-opted it. Largely a bystander in the day-to-day micro-wars between corporations, the JSDF instead kept its watchful attention turned outward. Non-aggression treaties with the UCF emerged from pre-war friendships, though the Allied Corporate Council had made no secret of its jealousy. With Russia so close, they were ever on edge.

The NSK built the artificial land mass and the JSDF moved in. Both thought they ran the show. A tentative agreement left the consortium responsible for policing, while the JSDF kept to themselves, doing whatever they wanted. Street fights between factions were common, drunken brawls taken to the next level in an endless battle for perceived dominance. At least, that was the case if the soldiers didn't pick the wrong NSK operative to harass. Sometimes, JSDF personnel vanished.

The NSK blurred the boundary between merchant, police, and organized crime. Any one of those terms fit them, depending on their mood.

A holographic poster bathed the area in flickering pale light, its recorded voice congratulating tourists for visiting the pinnacle of technological innovation. Cartoon schoolchildren sprouted like plants from Shōrishima's surface, proclaiming it Victory Island. Victory over the gods who had given the Japanese people such limited land as well as victory over Mother Nature. Many felt it arrogant and waited for the day the ocean took her back. Mamoru looked away from the banner with a grumble of distaste. He agreed with them.

He was one of the few who held a great deal of respect for the old ways and the spirits. For many, Japan had adopted ancient traditions in costume alone as a way of solidifying a national identity. He *believed* in the spirits. Taunting the Earth was a dangerous idea, and he did not intend to remain in such a place any longer than necessary. That thought brought him to a brisk stride towards the eastward end of the concourse, closest to the yawning maw of the deep ocean. A pair of JSDF troopers with thick rifles held across their beige-armored vests loitered by a bank of vendomats, two steps to the left of an ominous black counter.

A female doll in an all-black jumpsuit, plain save for the silver dragon-in-a-circle logo of the NSK, offered him a preprogrammed smile.

"Greetings," she chirped, "How may I assist you?"

"When is the next transport to Shōrishima scheduled?"

Her head tilted to the side, smile widening, eyes never pointing away from his face. Mamoru found comfort in the Class 1 doll's gaps, the way they behaved at once so close and yet so far removed from human twisted at his gut. If the artificial island was an affront to Mother Nature, dolls were an offense to the gods.

"It is due in seven minutes. Would you like to reserve a seat?"

Impolite. So Western. He released a silent sigh. *It's just a machine.* "Yes."

♬ ✻ ▦ ◔ ▧

THE SUBMERSIBLE SHUTTLECRAFT VECTORED AWAY FROM THE UNDERSEA station. Pale blue sand soon gave way to infinite darkness as the continental shelf receded. Over the next half hour, it cruised farther out to sea, staying well underwater.

A pleasant chime preceded an artificial girl's voice. "Attention passengers: Shōrishima should become visible any moment now forward and left of the shuttle. We will be docking within ten minutes. Please begin preparations to disembark at this time. Your seats will automatically reset to default position in five minutes. Enjoy your stay in Shōrishima."

Mamoru's eyes shifted left, gazing through a ghostly image of himself at the ocean. A wide patch of shadow lurked ahead, defined by sunlit water where the enormous machine did not block the silvery "sky" of the ocean surface. The shuttle descended in a gradual turn. Colored lights blinked in the murk, gleaming across the back of the occasional fish curious enough to get close. The blurry forms of gargantuan pillars faded in from the murk, mammoth pylons two hundred meters square that stretched ninety stories below sea level. Five such towers reached to the depths, arranged at pentagonal points around the disc-shaped island. Each contained a massive number of propulsion systems, superconducting batteries, water purification systems, and dangerous packs of gangs and squatters with nowhere else to go.

Shōrishima had the capability to move around the globe; however, the AI who controlled everything kept it geostationary. Koemi, as she had been personified, had become a mascot to those who lived there. Somewhere between cute little sister and fearsome goddess, her likeness was everywhere on the artificial island. Holo-panels around the cities broadcast her daily show and sometimes let citizens talk to her. The NSK had made her a media star. Koemi merchandise was ubiquitous, although her smiling face varied in apparent age. Toys, clothing, and accessories most often depicted a likeness of her in the tween range, with varying degrees of cute based on who the product was intended for. In some places, dolls and artwork depicted an older Koemi, sometimes as wizened as twenty years old, but they were not the sort of places respectable people went.

Few things worried Mamoru Saitō. However, a sense of unease crept over him as one of the great pylons drew close. Below the metal island, a vast undersea world existed in which an army of technicians constantly labored to keep systems operational. So many things could fail, and hundreds of thousands would die if this abomination sank. He looked away from the coral-studded beams and girders and rubbed the bridge of his nose. Despite his gift, he did not fancy trusting his life to technology. Space travel made him even more nervous; here, at least, he might be able to swim. In space, one flaw in a suit, one crack in a visor, and all the skill and training in the world with his blade meant nothing.

"Attention everyone, we are on final approach to the central docking station." A ripple of mechanical thuds ran down the rows as seats reset to the default position. Several travelers who still slept jostled awake. "We will be arriving within two minutes."

Mamoru gazed into the murk. The undercarriage of the great metal beast slid by, unsettling him even further. Deceleration pushed him forward in the seat a few seconds before gravity intensified. Fragments of vegetation, trash, and fish slid down past the window as the ship's motion changed to a vertical ascent. Metal walls blocked off the view, and the ambient light outside grew brighter until a break of water washed over the hull. Streaks of white glare made him turn away as the ocean receded via unseen pumps. The shuttle creaked as its landing struts absorbed its weight. A massive elevator lifted it several meters and a heavy *clank* ran shook the hull as a wheeled boarding tunnel connected.

Here in the NSK-controlled center, his station with Matsushita meant little. People did not defer to him or move out of his way. This was a neutral area where no single corporation had any more power than another. It was a necessity of doing business. If the NSK refused a company, it effectively cut them off from the outside world, an irrecoverable loss.

He had not yet come to terms with his feelings at being 'just another man standing on line' by the time he reached the check-in station. Mamoru smiled, kept his head down, and walked through the scanners and past four security dolls. Nothing beeped, and the automated guards did not react to him.

Mamoru did not want them to.

The atrium behind the security station held a hexagonal vertical shaft twenty stories high. A clear dome protected it from the weather, but allowed in natural sunlight. Great hanging plants descended from the rafters, bedecked with flowers at random intervals. The sense of living foliage afforded him a moment of peace as he savored the fragrance of orchids.

Moving among dozens of cart vendors selling anything and everything a business traveler could want, and many things they would not, Mamoru boarded one of the elevators that expressed to the surface. Sharing it in close proximity to a dozen others who had little care for his rank left him wearing a sneer by the time the doors opened. Outside, a cool breeze carried the scent of the ocean, metal, and teriyaki. A small crowd gathered by a barefoot teen girl clad in dingy rags and a metal headset with glowing teal lights. She sat cross-legged in the square, surrounded by an array of holographic panels with shifting geometric shapes. Her hands moved as blurs, swatting, picking and waving at them, creating an ethereal mixture of electronic flute and bell-toned music. An anklet of bells added the occasional highlight as she tapped her foot. Her music had a primal, spiritual quality that felt wholly out of place on a metal island or even in this century. Mamoru looked up at the hanging garden, letting the sound lift his soul to a space removed from era. She connected him to the Kami and he found himself almost meditating on his feet.

When the urgency of his mission returned, he walked past her with a slight nod and waved his NetMini by a device she had set up to receive donations. The girl smiled and bowed as much as she could without missing a note.

The southern end of the terminal square held a taxi station. A few minutes after he hit the button, a tiny white car with one seat and eight-inch wheels rolled up and stopped. The egg-like body split, the entire front half swinging open. Mamoru settled in and put his hand on the interface panel as the car closed around him. A polite male voice emanated from a few inches behind his head.

"Good afternoon, honored guest. To where—"

His arms swam with vaporous white energy and he *knew* the taxi. Like forcing his hand into a bowl of hot noodles, he reached into the program code. Words and symbols flashed across his mind as he reordered them, inserting new programming as his brain demanded. The car would not ask him for identity, payment, or record anything that went on during the journey to Noro-Shimura territory. Five minutes after the ride ended, his custom programming would devour itself.

"Begin route," said the voice.

His tiny conveyance lurched forward, zipping around people and obstacles. Mamoru shifted and squirmed, trying to find comfort in a seat that was little more than hard, cloth-covered plastic.

♌ ✳ 🎴 ◔ 🜨

THE TINY CAR MEANDERED AMONG PEDESTRIANS DOWN A NARROW STREET not much faster than a man could walk. On either side, age and weather gradually divested the plastisteel buildings of their stucco facades. The illusion of land unsettled him. Had he not seen the underside of the engineered island, he would not know miles of water stretched out below instead of earth. Tattered cloth awnings flapped and fluttered on the faces of tall apartment buildings, some bearing the weight of poor children at play. A minute later, the car whirred to a halt at the corner of a long, three-story structure that made only a passing attempt to conceal its modernistic nature. The front end rose amid the whirr of electric motors, allowing him to get out.

The *thump* of the car hatch closing startled hundreds of seagulls from the roofs around him. One red tile slid loose, breaking on the ground. The sound echoed in both directions, stalling childish laughter from a half block away. Eyes, some visible, some hidden in shadow, watched him. With his case in his left hand, he went around the rear of the egg and onto the porch of the Tenki Hotel. Three teenaged thugs eased themselves from benches and formed up in his path.

The audacity of it raised his eyebrow. *Noro-Shimura is too lax. They do not embrace tradition as they should.*

A boy, maybe seventeen, got in his way. "What's in the case, old man?"

"It is fortunate for you that I am a guest here. As a gesture of good faith to Noro-Shimura, I shall afford you the courtesy of a warning before I kill you for your insolence." Mamoru brushed his coat aside to reveal the handle of his blade.

"Oh, big man has a knife." The punk waved his hands back and forth in front of a taunting face.

The other two mocked his gesture, pulling their shirts up to expose the handles of pistols.

Mamoru bowed his head in a grim nod. His left hand released the case. He grasped the katana as *chi* flamed down the length of his arms. Slow motion took the world as his power channeled inward, accelerating his body and mind. Energy spread from the hypersonic oscillator in the handle across the edge as he drew and attacked in one motion.

His upswing severed the four fingers of the thug's waving left hand; the downstroke took the fingers off his right. The katana slid into the scabbard before the first finger separated from the hand. He bent at the knees, catching the handle of the briefcase an inch before it hit the ground. Patches of white energy rolled over his arms as he stood, wrapping about his torso and fading away. Mamoru's perception of time returned to normal. The punk stared in horror as his fingers scattered on the porch. Blood rushed over what remained of his hands. He screamed, shaking his limbs.

"Defy me again, and it shall be your heads," said Mamoru, his face and voice devoid of emotion. "I have killed commoners such as yourselves for no reason other than to test the sharpness of my blade. Consider yourselves fortunate that I do not wish to attract undue attention to my presence here. It is only by my distaste for paperwork that you still live."

The two on either side of the wounded punk gawked at each other, having showed no reaction until after the blade was already put away. They shoved their stunned friend out of the way and let Mamoru pass without another word. *Such disrespect. I should have killed them all.* He left them to gather the severed fingers and entered the lobby. A living girl, maybe twenty, looked up from the front desk. Her broad smile faded a notch or two at the sight of blood droplets on his cheek.

"I humbly apologize for those criminals outside. My parents do not have enough wealth to gain the favor of the security patrol." She dabbed his cheek with a tissue.

He felt more at home. "Mmm."

"We are honored to have a prestigious guest in our humble hotel, sir." She bowed after tossing the tissue in a basket under the counter. "For how many days do you require a room?"

"One week, though I may not spend much time here. Please, keep the reservation in my name even if I seem to have left."

She nodded, pushing a small device on the counter around to face him. "The rate is eighty three credits per night."

"That is acceptable." He held his NetMini over the reader, touching his little finger to the scanner. The program was easy to influence, generating credits from thin air even simpler. The InterTrust Commerce Facilitation Corporation could detect such monetary manipulation easily, having spent years perfecting the virtual currency system. Though such an insignificant sum would cost the ICFC more to investigate than he had generated.

The clerk glanced at her terminal. "Thank you, Haruko-san." She bowed again. "Your NetMini is coded to room 8 on the second floor. If anything is not to your liking, please let me know."

Mamoru acknowledged her with a slight bow and ducked through a dull green door at the rear of the lobby. The stairway was clean, much to his surprise. Thin carpeting the color of jade lined the upstairs hallway. Hand-drawn images attempting to recreate old-style Japanese art hung every few paces along cracked white walls. Several patch marks covered sword gouges and the occasional bullet hole.

Room 8 was modest, as he expected. A small bed, holo-bar, attached bathroom with autoshower, and a tiny balcony were unimpressive even for the paltry price, but at least clean. He swiped his finger at the wall panel to lock the door, removed his coat and shoes, and set the case on the nightstand. He climbed onto a twin-sized Comforgel pad and sat cross-legged, placing his sword in front of him. Mamoru inhaled until he could hold no more air, and let it leak out his nostrils. He would meditate and wait for the sun to go down.

A RATTLE DISTURBED THE STILLNESS WITHIN HIS MIND. MOST WOULD NOT have discerned the subtle metallic noise as anything more than the wind worrying the balcony railing. Mamoru sensed the disharmony of the effect—the rhythm was out of step. He sat with his back to the glass, watching light move in reflection on a framed painting of Mount Fuji. A figure, all in black, rose up over the edge of the patio. The person hovered still in the air, balancing all their weight on their arms for over a minute as they brought their knees to their chest to get their feet over the railing. Gradual movements drew less attention. With excruciating slowness, the indistinct figure lowered slender legs to the floor and waved the strain out of its arms.

A professional. A woman.

Supple black material covered her face, concealing her nose and mouth, with individual opaque lenses over the eyes. Mamoru opened his eyelids a millimeter more, letting a small bit of *chi* sharpen his sight. The figure crept to the patio door, unaware he had noticed her. *Soft boots, sneak suit, small sword on her back. NSK ninja.* Mamoru remained still as the woman made short work of the dive hotel's crude security system. She slid the patio door open only far enough to slip through and pulled it closed.

"To what do I owe the pleasure of your company," he asked. The sound of creaking knuckles made him smile. "A request of Imura's family?"

She recovered her nerve and widened her stance, arms folded over her chest. "We are concerned at your presence here, Saitō-san. There has not been an assassination request filed with us."

"I am no assassin, Sadako."

For the second time, her knuckles made noise.

"You forget me so soon, Kuroyama Sadako? Was it not you the NSK sent at our request to test the security at the Matsushita tower? I remember your voice."

Her arms fell slack. She slouched ever so slightly as if trying to conceal it. The head covering melted like liquid, receding into the metallic neck of her suit. The woman's face was round and as cute as her emerald eyes were deadly. Thin lines traced across her temples and down the left side of her head, millimeters in front of her ear, as if drawn on by a pen two shades darker than her skin. Sadako scowled at the balcony railing, her head whirled at a speed that flared her short bob.

"I would suggest you should feel no dishonor at failure, but your kind knows little of such things."

"My kind?" Her arms folded again. "You really believe in that whole samurai/ninja rivalry, don't you? Both of us work for corporations that like to play dress up. It's ancient history."

"Is it?" He opened his eyes all the way, wearing a subdued grin. "Tell me, if that is the case, why are none of your kind in the direct employ of any corporation other than the NSK?" She opened her mouth, but he kept on. "It is a nod to the old clans."

"That is irrelevant. It is the way of the establishment." She advanced a half step.

"So, you have come here to inquire as to who I intend to kill?"

"You did appear to take great care in your infiltration of a competing company's section of Shōrishima. I am to ascertain your intentions."

"I am an instrument of the will of Minamoto-heika. If you wish to know the nature of my presence here, seek an audience with him."

Sadako advanced another step. "You are not above the protocols, Saitō-san."

"You should return to your clan. It would be unfortunate for me to perceive you as an impediment to my duties."

"Oh, is that so?" She narrowed her eyes. "You don't have a scrap of augmentation. It wouldn't even be a contest."

"It is the purview of lesser beings to construct ladders on which to stand in order to reach the height of their betters." Mamoru focused his power, moving from the bed to her side in the span a blink. She twisted away, but was too slow to avoid the gentle touch of a sheathed katana at her neck. "Impressive. Few manage to move before I strike. However, the metal poison in your body weakens your *chi*."

Sadako stared at him. Her gaze tracked the tickle of a bead of sweat descending his cheek. She sprang away, her back to the wall and one hand on the blade at her shoulder. A curious mixture of fear and anger dueled in her eyes for a moment before simmering down to annoyance. Her fingers slipped off the rubberized grip of her ninjato, letting her arm hang at her side. Sadako's posture seemed at ease, but her expression did not. Indignation, anger, and sadness swirled.

Mamoru crossed the room to the reassembler, moving his katana to his left hand. He set an empty cup inside the machine, closed the door, and typed at the console. The reassembler whirred to life, generating a drink from OmniSoy slime.

Sadako flattened her palms against the wall. "Only a fool turns their back… or makes tea in a 'sem."

"You are not here to kill me, nor are you capable of defeating me if you were." He removed a sad attempt at green tea from the device and sipped it, grimacing. "I am not in this part of the city to put an end to any liabilities. Your association's business interests are safe. Matsushita does not intend to infringe on your livelihood. If we require a problem eliminated from the real world, the NSK will get our money."

He sipped the tea again, wincing as if he'd forgotten how bad it was. She stared at him as if searching for some other path of debate, or waiting for him to say something else. After several minutes in silence, she crept to the patio door and let herself out. Sadako hesitated on the balcony, glancing over her shoulder at him with a hint of sadness in her emerald eyes. The liquid material devoured her strange longing stare as it engulfed her head. Mamoru turned the teacup in his hand, mesmerized by tiny floating fragments. Her stare, covered by onyx lenses, bored into his chest for a moment before she turned away.

He set down an empty cup as she vaulted the railing and dropped out of sight.

AN HOUR PAST DUSK, MAMORU LEFT THE HOTEL AND FOLLOWED THE ROUTE he had memorized in the hours spent waiting. He traveled on foot, blending with the shadows as best he could. Stealth was not his forte, though even a novice could vanish in the narrow alleyways of north Shōrishima. The occasional vagrant took notice of him, but any that would beg or steal could not react to him in time to catch his eye. A mazelike series of streets and passages shifted from the cool fragrance of the ocean to the stifling presence of sewer and back again. He emerged from the last alley onto a perimeter beltway, which ran around the entire island. No vehicles or people were in sight, as he expected. This road was limited to official use due to its proximity to the water as well as the ease with which one could traverse multiple separate corporate territories.

A quick jog across traction-coated plastisteel brought him to a chain link fence twenty feet from the edge. The sea wind came in gusts, ripping the air with a shrill whistle that chased away the reek of the city. After a glance to each side, he stilled his mind and focused on his body. A tingle of *chi* ran down his legs. Once certain of his amplified strength, he vaulted the fence. With nothing but open metal around him, he sprinted to the edge and crouched low.

He gazed down past sixteen stories of metal panels, protruding pipes, and catwalk to the ocean below. It reminded him of an old video game he'd played as a boy, before Matsushita. For a moment, he stared at the dangerous path, hearing long-forgotten electronic music play in his head. A lifetime ago, all he'd wanted to do was play games.

The air came alive with electronic sensors, teasing at senses no normal human possessed. Mamoru stilled his thoughts and chose not to exist to them as he crept along the edge to the where a catwalk offered a landing point ten feet below. The rumble of a six-wheeled armored vehicle echoed from the west, from where headlights announced the passage of a JSDF patrol. He slid over the side, dropping to the catwalk with a *clank* drowned out by the wind and sea.

A series of grated walkways and ladders took him along the path he had traveled two dozen times in cyberspace that afternoon. The simulation was true to life save for a few patches where weather eroded holes in the metal. Two hundred meters over and forty-six feet down, he reached the conduit he had selected hours earlier and touched one finger to the laser security grid. Every circuit, every logic gate, and every line of program code unfurled within his consciousness. Spiraling threads of words and numbers unraveled and wound together again. For ten minutes, the security system would ignore all faults in this shaft.

Mamoru moved through the laser grid and the alarm paid him no heed. The ventilation duct forced him to crawl, but provided a direct route to the hangar. Noro-Shimura kept their project hidden below the surface. He crawled into the metal beast, pausing where a patch of light shone on a grime-coated ceiling. A slatted hole at his knees opened to an enormous chamber below.

A rush of juvenile excitement came over him at the sight of the sleek matte-black warbird. Not since he was a boy had the anticipation of new technology gotten under his skin. There, amid a small group of workers in bright fluorescent green jumpsuits, the Fūjin slept.

His trip home would not take him below the sea.

5

FOX IN THE HENHOUSE

Mamoru emerged from the ventilation shaft, lowering himself into a maintenance closet. The first opportunity to exit the duct without a dangerous fall had taken him farther into the facility than he had expected. He fixed the lay of his blade under his coat, and stepped out at the midpoint of a polished steel hallway. After a quick left-right glance, he doubled back in the direction of the hangar. Employees of the Noro-Shimura test facility seemed to disregard him, taking his imperious gait as a sign of belonging as well as being important enough not to antagonize. One advantage he had was no one expected an infiltrator to be so brazen. NSK ninjas always tried to stay out of sight at all costs.

Before he could play with the shiny toy, he needed access to the file system. Mamoru leaned forward as he walked, searching for a direction that appeared to be offices. The company had been smart enough to make the interior version of the facility different in cyberspace. All he had to go on was a sense of which way led towards the aircraft bay. An educated guess brought him to a corridor lined with doors labeled with names and job titles, each by a floor-to-ceiling window blocked by vertical blinds. He ducked inside the second office on the left, easing the door closed behind him. A lingering presence of unagi hung in the darkened space, reminding him he had not eaten since morning. Discarded trays from delivery food sat in the waste bin at the edge of the desk. Mamoru frowned. The cleaning staff had not yet made it this far.

A minor annoyance.

Creaking leather and springs of an expensive chair protested his weight in the otherwise silent room. Mamoru placed his katana across his lap and grasped the terminal by the edges. A holographic panel began to roll like a window shade through the air, but stopped halfway and broke apart to snowy pixels. The essence of the machine flooded his thoughts and drew his consciousness from his body. Gravity lost meaning. Darkness became light, and silence became a rushing cascade of sound fading from deafening to imperceptible. For a fleeting instant, the perception of being an immobile object on a desk paralyzed him. The blinding glow dimmed, leaving him floating in the middle of the cyberspace version of the same office. Gloss white samurai armor reflected in the window, empty save for a dark amber glow where eyes should be.

Mamoru moved out of the small room and flew down the corridor, several inches off the ground. A local connection to the network made him feel as though he ran at a hundred miles per hour in bursts, at least triple what he could do remotely. At the end of the hallway of offices, he stopped at a T intersection, with a door on the facing wall. Mamoru thought about the network map and his brain absorbed the information as rapidly as the terminal assembled it. He went right, heading for the control nodes that governed Noro-Shimura's defense systems. The installation had a pair of high-output amplified laser batteries, larger cousins to the weapons on board his target.

The Fūjin was fast, but it could not outrun light.

Thin lines of brilliant blue glow surrounded a series of plain, brown doors, as if they held back a torrent of unstable plasma. He raised his arms to the sides, able to discern the relative security of each one by how hot it was. The strange ways his brain interpreted information from cyberspace never ceased to amuse him.

Mamoru halted at the lone silver door in the passage, about forty yards from where he had turned. He extended a hand and pressed the fingertips of the samurai glove into the metal. Ripples spread out from the points of contact, reflecting from the doorframe as if he had broken the tranquility of a pool of mercury. Luminous cyan grid lines shimmered through the waves, flickering wherever the surface moved. Streams of program code unwound in his mind, reshaping at the speed of his thoughts. A standing wall of liquid silver sank straight down to the floor. He stepped over the last few inches, entering an expansive chamber with four six-foot tall amethyst crystals.

No one had wasted any effort to make this digital space resemble anything in the real world. Black walls glimmered with edges outlined in bright cobalt blue. Waist-high barriers encircled the base of each crystal, with a small gap facing the center of the room that allowed a strip of yellow light to connect from the floor beneath the hovering shards to a whirlwind of energy at the center of the room. A slab of onyx stretched from the floor, the upper portion bent backwards to form a console interface out of ethereal holograms.

A swarm of tiny black fragments emerged from the left side of the room, spiraling over themselves like a cloud of locusts. The mass coalesced, taking the form of a man in a suit with sunglasses, a rifle, and a frown. A defense construct circled him. The look of confusion on its face a representation of its logic routines attempting to reconcile Mamoru's identity. The disorientation lasted only long enough for Mamoru to unsheathe his sword. The program's default response to unhandled exceptions was to attack.

In cyberspace, the security man aimed and fired globs of green plasma. Somewhere, deep inside a computer core in reality, the system attempted to disrupt Mamoru's connection. The initial barrage, the bolts flying over Mamoru's head as he somersaulted behind one of the podium terminals, an animation translated from a simple attempt at a forcible logout.

As Mamoru had not *logged in* in the sense a computer could understand, the attack missed. He leapt from cover, sailing in an arc that brought him close to a ceiling that now seemed to be thirty feet high. A streamer of energy trailed the katana as he raised it overhead. The construct raised its weapon to aim, but moved too slow. Mamoru crashed down on it, one strike splitting the virtual man from head to gut. Shimmering radiance erupted from within the body rather than gore, interspersed with black circuitry lines.

The construct lost its grip on the rifle, which disintegrated to loose chunks of silver before it hit the ground. Mangled digital howls grew loud as it staggered backwards, clawing at the air. It shrank inward, about to fall to its demise. Mamoru lunged and drove his left hand into the false man's gaping chest, grasping a rotating crystal icosahedron where the heart should be. Intense white light erupted from the eyeholes in the white samurai's mask. Streams of letters and numbers spread out across thin air as if written on an invisible cylinder that surrounded them, stretching upward to the ceiling. Mamoru pulled it back from the brink of automatic deletion. Before the network could purge the damaged program, he modified it. Corrupted routines vanished, replaced by new code written at the speed of thought.

The horrendous gash closed around his glove.

Mamoru drew his hand out, turning his palm flat with the spinning crystal sphere above it. A hole large enough for the 'heart' to return to the body remained open. Tiny sparks connected the crest of the samurai helmet to the program core, adding function and feature. It spun faster, turning from blue to red as he upgraded the software from grade six to eight. Nothing on this network, except for their most secure data vault, would be able to stand up to it. Satisfied, Mamoru exhaled, and the crystal glided backward, enveloped by digital flesh as the cavity sealed.

Shapes moved through the construct's body, sliding under the black suit. The cloth changed texture from fabric to painted metal. Gaps appeared as the imitation clothing stretched and reformed as samurai armor.

Sweat ran down Mamoru's neck in the real world from the exertion. Destroying the thing would have been faster and less tiring, but having a virtual ally would ensure success.

The digital samurai slammed its right fist into the palm of its left hand and bowed at the waist before taking its place at his side. Mamoru glided to the podium, using it to access the CPU core represented by the large floating crystals. Brilliant flashes of lightning sparked within the massive gems. From here, he forced his influence over the security routines and altered them to disregard his presence on the network. He did not create a false user, nor did he turn the anti-intrusion system off.

He did not exist.

With that done, he left the CPU room and blurred down a maze of hallways leading to the high security area of the network. What virtual reality represented as a set of glass doors with a multi-barrel rotary turret on either side was in fact a stringent authentication routine capable of burning out and damaging the deck of a would-be intruder. His modification to the security software prevented the system from noticing his approach. The virtual guns did not fire.

The white samurai approached the entrance, standing between the idle weapon mounts. He looked the barrier up and down and leaned to the side, allowing the rewritten construct to move up. Its core was still native to the network, and by proximity, it caused the door to open. Mamoru grasped the helper program by the shoulder. Tiny threads of light seeped from his fingertips into the ebon armor as he let it pull him down a featureless hospital-white hallway.

A partition barrier between the hallway and the node beyond appeared to be a modern electronic door. Mamoru brushed his fingers over the code panel, compelling the security routine to shut down. The door opened, revealing a chamber rendered in the image of an ancient temple built somewhere high in the mountains. Twelve-foot tall octagonal obelisks of grey stone stood in a ring around the center of a space coated in red bricks. Creeping vines and moss adorned everything. Cyberspace simulated a pleasant breeze and the smell of trees, as well as the sounds of chirping birds.

Each pillar was three feet thick at the base and tapered to angled points. On the flat faces, glowing light emanated from kanji carved in the stone. Every symbol bore the name of a file in storage. The touch of a finger dragged the symbols down the surface, cycling one at a time to access files too high to reach.

Mamoru smiled.

Many deck jockeys found such anachronisms annoying. Mamoru's mundane contemporaries at Matsushita preferred things to look logical: file cabinets, drawers full of data tiles, or modern wire-framed shelves packed with easy to search contents. This room distracted him for a moment with its serenity.

"Go. Disable the anti-aircraft batteries. Destroy their control constructs and block any who would use them. When I am ready, open the doors. Once the Fūjin is clear, conceal yourself deep in the memory banks and await further orders."

The black samurai rendered a sharp bow and left.

Mamoru wandered the obelisks, reading their faces, circling five before halting at the sixth. He traced a finger over the ancient-looking writing, causing the glow within the symbols to intensify. Amid a cone of light projecting out of the kanji, an ancient paper scroll appeared and unfurled. The contents of a terminal screen rendered on it as if drawn by ink and brush. Precision details in the schematics of the Fūjin were the only break in the illusion.

A man spoke from behind, calm, deep, and with authority. "I do not know who you are, but I cannot allow you to access that data."

"I must commend whoever created this node. It is peaceful. I did not sense your approach."

"I am Koga Daisuke of the Noro-Shimura Information Security team. All egress from our network is shut down. You cannot flee."

Mamoru chuckled. "You dishonor me with your lies." He spun, facing a man in a blue and white haori jacket and baggy black hakama pants. Tall, thin, with long hair down to his knees, he carried a long bo staff. "Tell me, Koga Daisuke, are you proficient enough to know that I did not access your network from the outside?"

The staff shifted in Daisuke's grip. A dark crimson dragon appeared from the black, painted down one side of the weapon. "My deception was an attempt to resolve this without violence."

"You seek to stall so your forces may locate me outside. That, I cannot allow." Mamoru's thumb flicked the katana an inch out of the scabbard. "I find no honor in a contest I cannot lose. You may leave."

Daisuke stepped back, bringing the staff level. "I am the master of this network. This is my domain."

"Your domain shall not shield your life from me. I will not offer again."

Swirls of blue energy coalesced around Daisuke as he activated various combat softs. Before any could complete their startup sequence, Mamoru surged forward as a blurry white streak. The meeting of katana and staff rang out like thunder over the rolling mountains below the shrine. Even the stone obelisks shuddered under the weight of the noise. Daisuke sailed backward, headfirst through the air like a man-shaped noodle. The ghostly traces of his combat programs trailed after him and dispersed.

He hit the ground on his shoulders, flipping over and sliding on his chest for several meters before coming to a halt in a cloud of dust. Mamoru leapt at him, driving the seething blade into the stone a split second after Daisuke rolled to the side. The administrator staggered away, left hand guarding his face with the staff held behind him. His eyes widened with astonishment for an instant before his fear faded. He spun the staff over and brought it down in a powerful slap against the floor. A wave of orange energy peeled from the tip, rushing at Mamoru with building light.

Mamoru strode past it, as though it possessed no more solidity than smoke. "An interesting technique, Koga-san, and your first mistake." His body stretched in a smear, a rapid sideways strike, which Daisuke deflected at the cost of being knocked ten feet away. "You cannot burn out an NIU that does not exist."

Daisuke's eyes hardened. He twisted the end of his staff and withdrew a long, straight sword. Once clear of the lower portion, the edge curved to take on the shape of an odachi, larger cousin to the katana. He dropped the staff scabbard and took a two-handed grip as he moved with a cautious circling gait.

"How is it possible that you are here without a neural interface? Surely, you do not expect me to think you are using a senshelmet?" Daisuke spun with a midair feint, plunging the now-glowing blade into the stone floor.

Around Mamoru, six long dragon's heads made of blue light leapt from the ground, biting. He slashed at two, cutting his way out of the ring. One snaked in as he whirled about, sinking its virtual fangs in his left forearm. Its green eyes flared as it chewed. A torrent of meaningless data surged through the terminal, overloading the ingress buffers and grinding its CPU to a near-standstill. A miniscule slice of Mamoru's mind still receptive to the real world detected silicon smoke.

The flash of pain came unexpected. Mamoru's concentration faltered for an instant, long enough for two other dog-sized heads to bite him on the calf and thigh. Mamoru cringed at the sharp pinpricks of more circuits burning out. Without the vulnerability of a metal wire connecting his brain to the device, he was safe from the most lethal attacks—but the terminal wasn't so lucky. Effort spent on forcing changes to the incoming data left him staggering in cyberspace.

Daisuke took the opportunity to leap in with an overhead swing. Mamoru ignored the teeth in his virtual flesh and brought his katana around in a crescent arc. The *clang* of metal echoed from the distant mountain. The odachi's long reach prevented Mamoru's instinctual counterattack from scoring. The administrator launched attack softs from multiple remote terminals, which kept Mamoru from attacking his deck in retaliation. His attempt to step into the swipe tugged teeth deeper in his left thigh as the tip of his blade missed Daisuke's throat by a finger's width. A low rumble started in his chest and became a bellowing cry half made of rage, the rest satisfaction at encountering something near a challenge. His armor flared with peeling energy vapor tinged red as it wafted in thin wisps.

Daisuke backpedaled as Mamoru slashed through the dragons with one fluid spiral. He stalked after the administrator who paled at the dozen tiny holes in white armor sealing. With a desperate shout, he raised his blade and lunged. Mamoru swatted the incoming sword to the left, spinning through the defense and countering with a horizontal slash. Daisuke flung himself over backwards, feet on the ground, legs bent at the knee. The katana sailed over his chest, missing by inches. He floated up, driving a kick into Mamoru's chest that launched him against one of the obelisks.

Fire burned through his skull, the desk terminal overheated, filling his senses with the smoldering reek of melting plastic and the crackling agony of burnt chips. The workstation did not have the same hardware protections as a deck, and would cook itself under the weight of Daisuke's onslaught. Mamoru's consciousness receded from the net into the machine. A plane of onyx ground stretched to infinity, consumed in the distance by a rolling avalanche of white squares, the roar of the consumption deafening. His living body shuddered in place as he focused on neutering the incoming viral code. The wall of onrushing chaos slowed as he disassembled the enemy program. Enormous razor-sharp slabs broke apart as snowflakes that scattered, harmless, on the smooth ground.

He returned to cyberspace, on his side at the base of a pillar. Despite the tremendous crash and cloud of dust, neither stone nor samurai seemed injured.

"What is the meaning of this?" Daisuke asked of no one in particular. "That should have destroyed you."

The white samurai armor unraveled to a wireframe model drawn in lime green. It crumpled into a sphere and stretched vertical. Mamoru reformed in three dimensions on his feet, blade low and to the right. He raised his sword, a slight nod conveyed his respect, and he charged. Katana and odachi clashed in a series of strikes, virtual steel ringing out against the soft cry of the wind. Daisuke attacked his opponent's connection; each swing of his blade symbolized a burst of data. Every defense reflected the software's failure to disconnect the samurai from the network or fry a deck. Mamoru laughed to himself, this man did not even understand he was inside the building on a hardline terminal.

With each meeting of steel, Mamoru's sense of his opponent's technology grew clearer. Their duel paused after thirteen stalemates, each man orbiting his opponent at a cautious distance. Were Mamoru's avatar capable of doing so, it would have smiled.

"Impressive, Koga Daisuke. Nishihama Warlord decks are quite rare and expensive."

Daisuke shuddered as his eyes widened. "H-how could you—"

Mamoru's body stretched to a smear, anchored between two copies of himself. One where he stood and a second, which appeared nose to nose with the administrator. Daisuke's attention had not left the more solid looking Mamoru that remained a few paces away. Realization of his error paled his face. He shuddered and glanced down at the katana through his chest. Patches of cyan light ran up and down below his skin, over his face. The odachi fell from his grasp with a *clank*.

"My connection is local, Koga-san. Your obfuscation was focused outward, not against your own terminals."

"T-terminal?" Daisuke gasped, his voice modulated as if coughing up nonexistent blood. "Y-you are using a terminal?"

The duplicate Mamoru wrenched the blade out and withdrew along the connecting light ribbon, merging with the original. Daisuke cradled the hole through his body, from which random fragments of glowing matter crawled. He fell to his knees, trying to look angry despite his helplessness. Crackles echoed in Mamoru's mind. The distant pinpricks of burned chips in the administrator's deck brought him satisfaction. He snapped his blade into its scabbard with a sharp *click* and returned to the obelisk to gather the data he had come for.

"Finish it." Daisuke gasped and collapsed to his knees. "You have bested me"—he coughed—"in my own network, n-not even using a d-deck. I am unable to stop you from looting our most valuable project. Spare me the dishonor of seppuku for my failure."

Mamoru pulled at the glowing kanji. An ancient scroll extruded from the obelisk through the carved symbol, which faded as soon as it came loose. One by one, he extracted the data related to the Fūjin, and stacked scrolls in the crook of his left arm. "Koga Daisuke, you should feel no dishonor in this defeat. You could no more have stopped me than you could stop rain from touching the ground."

"Shizuka-sama will not see the situation in those terms. If you have Black ICE, I request that you spare me the disgrace of failure."

He set the last scroll at the top of the stack, finally spinning to look at Daisuke. "You did not fail. Failure implies the outcome was at any point in doubt."

Mamoru lifted his gaze to the carved wooden roof, reaching out across the GlobeNet with his mind. The room blurred, becoming an impressionist painting. Color ran liquid to the floor, leaving the walls black and glassy. Forms shifted, and the area took on textures and designs—the network representation of the Matsushita Corporation research data center. Tables, desks, and chairs sprouted from the ground, changing from onyx to wood or steel. White tiles drew in across the floor, rising and becoming three-dimensional. One by one, employee avatars appeared, images mimicking their real-world appearance. Mamoru manifested as an egg-shaped mass of blinding light, causing four women and three men to shield their faces until it dimmed.

Out of respect for Minamoto's decree, he discarded his samurai form for his true self. Without the influence of the Noro-Shimura node, his armload of scrolls took on the form of standard silver data tiles. At last realizing what happened, the lead researcher approached and offered a polite bow. Mamoru felt a sense of power from the fear in her eyes as he handed over the tiles. His sudden appearance had worried them all. The Sages went to great lengths to block 'teleportation.' If the monitoring authority noticed, they could cause problems. Even a company as powerful as Matsushita viewed the Global Internetworking Group as a threat.

Mamoru faded away, his voice lingering after he was gone. "Be at ease, Fujiwara-san. I am but a ghost amid the wires."

THE SENSE OF IMMOBILITY GAVE WAY TO THE TOUCH OF SMOKY AIR IN Mamoru's lungs and a nagging pain in his arm. Burned electronics soured his throat, making him cough despite his best effort to resist. He lifted his hands from the smoking ruin of the desk terminal, fingers frozen in their claw-like posture for several seconds before they yielded to his desire to move. He grasped at his arm where the dragon had bitten him, rubbing tooth-shaped bruises under his clothing—the downside to his talents. Becoming the machine let him share in its pain.

He looked up as the office door opened. One of the cleaning staff, a Class 2 doll made in the image of a teen girl, froze in shock. Thin lines ran from the corners of her eyes to her jawline, molded plates formed an innocent face. Blue glowing irises reflected on cheeks of porcelain white. Dark grey metal peeked through gaps on the insides of fingers and around the wrists.

Mamoru vaulted the desk on chi-boosted muscles, seizing the doll by the wrist. The fake girl offered a meek stare. The self-preserving nature of its basic AI attempted to capitalize on a cute appearance. He pulled it into the office and put his other hand on its cheek while forcing it back against the desk. From the moment he touched it, he shared in the debate raging in the doll's CPU. It had found him in an office as though he belonged there, but he was unrecognized. The imitation girl was afraid he would harm it, and offered no resistance as his mental command triggered a shutdown sequence. The doll slumped in a heap.

After easing the inert body over the desk, he retrieved his blade and sprinted down the corridor to the hangar bay. Workers ran screaming in random directions as he leapt hose bundles and dodged carts. One man ran at him with a large tool, attempting to wield it like a club. Mamoru evaded the clumsy attack with ease, cracking his opponent across the bridge of the nose with his sheathed katana. The man hit the ground dazed, with blood gushing through his fingers. Mamoru ducked the wings of the Fūjin and leapt onto the left forward canard by the cockpit. He crouched and put a hand on the aircraft's skin, reveling in the sense of advanced technology. Armed guards scrambled toward the door of an elevated booth. Fire suppression systems went off without warning, flooding the upper catwalk area with great clouds of rolling fog. The reprogrammed construct was with him.

Mamoru gathered a sense of the machine before him and opened the canopy. He climbed in, stashed his blade beside the seat, and fastened the harness. Security forces fumbled their way through the mist. A few aimed at the aircraft, but seemed hesitant to damage something so valuable.

He sealed the canopy dome, cutting off the frantic shouts outside. The scent of new technology filled the air in the small space, but he did not have time to bask in it. On either side of the seat, strips of black glass glowed dim with the silhouettes of embedded displays and holographic controls. Mamoru set his palms on the smooth surfaces and closed his eyes. White energy washed over him.

He became the Fūjin.

Component systems linked as extensions of his body: his legs were engines, his arms wings, his eyes sensors, cameras, and radar. Within seconds, Mamoru the man ceased to exist. Mamoru, the great predatory bird of plastisteel and carbon fiber opened his electronic eyes.

Engines came online hot, creating a surge of thrust that flung carts and debris away from him. A crack of darkness split the shining silver wall before him. Enormous hangar doors drew apart, opened by the black samurai still loose on the network. Taps plinked across his back as the Noro-Shimura soldiers shot the plane, their rifle slugs unable to pierce its composite armor panels. On the scale of war machines, the Fūjin's armor was thin, but to mid-sized rifles, nigh impenetrable.

Mamoru thought about standing. Thrusters whined, lifting the craft several feet off the ground, where it hovered as the landing gear retracted. He felt off balance, as if standing on a giant rubber ball. The plane shifted left, right and forward as he acclimated to the maneuvering system. As soon as the doors parted to a sufficient width, he burst forward. His startled cry began over the communications system but ended in reality. The shock of sudden acceleration broke his concentration and left the Fūjin flying like an unguided missile in an arc towards the waiting ocean. Mamoru clawed at the featureless armrests, hitting several controls by accident that launched countermeasures and armed weapons. Flares erupted in the night sky, expanding to the shape of burning wings behind him. Error messages flashed *No Target* on the heads up display. The waves grew closer.

He forced himself to be calm, tuning out the crash warning beeping that hammered on the edges of his brain. Mamoru closed his eyes to avoid the sight of the water rushing up at him. An urge to lean away from the ground tilted the plane skyward twenty meters from a salty, wet demise.

The Fūjin streaked out over the North Pacific Ocean trailing two thin tails of cerulean light from the main engines. He thrust his chin into the wind, turning and climbing. Below him, small waves highlighted by the moon rippled through the black. His panic faded, replaced by a sense of freedom and power as he edged past Mach 3 with little effort.

I am Fūjin. I am the wind.

6

DRAGON STRETCHING WINGS

Flying was not an entirely new sensation for Mamoru. He had embodied the systems of hovercars many times. Possessing a military combat aircraft capable of orbital flight provided an altogether different level of exhilaration. Where the hovercar handled like a brick dangling by a string, the Fūjin had the grace of a hawk and talons to match. The slightest inclination to move yielded major turns and rolls, leaving him with the feeling of ice-skating while drunk.

Weapons ran like threads of adrenaline through his arms, wires from the central power system to the laser cores embedded in the wings. The impulse to use them had no human analogue, as men did not possess any natural mode of attacking from a distance. Alone over the ocean, he played until he figured it out. Brilliant yellow lines, three per wing, turned long trails of seawater to steam. Empty internal weapons bays where missiles and bombs would go took on a presence like hunger.

A bizarre feeling came over him, alien to his mind, which attempted to convey information. He pondered the odd notion of a presence creeping up on him until he realized he had a sixth sense—the radar system. Another aircraft approached from the direction of Shōrishima. The warplane's internal systems identified it as an older atmospheric fighter craft half the size of the Fūjin. A nagging tug in his mind rang out from a different sensor and became knowledge the other pilot was angling for a targeting lock.

He thought of speed, and his new body obeyed. His stolen craft surged ahead until his face burned. Mamoru backed off, unprepared for the heating effect of Mach 8 flight on the aircraft's outer skin. Perhaps the plane could withstand it, but the feeling of roasting alive prevented his finding out. Designed for space superiority as well as atmospheric warfare, the engines were capable of speeds sufficient to escape gravity. Such velocity, in Mamoru's untrained opinion, might destroy the craft if used at too low an altitude where the air was thick.

With no experience regarding military aircraft, he had little idea of his pursuer's capabilities. He had no faith in his newly dried wing feathers, and feared going up against a seasoned pilot would make him feel helpless. Mamoru did not relish the thought of being on the receiving end of a one-sided conflict, so he committed to fleeing. The objective was to obtain the Fūjin for Minamoto-heika, not to seek glory in the skies. He risked more speed, pushing to the limit of his tolerance for burning. Maneuvering felt different at that velocity. The air had gone from gossamer to a viscous substance that fought against every motion he attempted. Pain pierced his shoulder as he tried to turn. Fearing the wing about to tear, he leveled off.

The other pilot, his fighter unable to keep up, slid off the outer edge of his strange, inhuman senses, but Mamoru continued course and speed for another few minutes. His heading pointed him south toward Kyushu, home of Kurotai Electronics. If Minamoto wished to keep the Fūjin, having it appear that a third party stole it would prove an advantage. However, he expected the Fūjin to exceed Matsushita's production capabilities and desires. In all probability, they would sell it back to Noro-Shimura as a lesson not to trespass again.

Mamoru was pleased with himself. His existence guaranteed the sovereignty of his master's network. No mere deck jockey, deprived of the ability to use *chi*, could hope to match him. Aglow with confidence, he cut speed to a casual subsonic cruise and turned west. He overflew Japan and circled back to approach Tokyo from the west.

Ocean waves zoomed below him, crests aglow in the light of a full moon. When the darkness of land replaced them, he slowed further until the wind slipped from the wings and the aircraft stood on its thrusters. Below three hundred miles per hour, the wings did not provide enough lift and the craft handled like a hovercar.

Navigation systems appeared as massive holographic panels floating in front of him out over the countryside. A course plotted itself at his desire, and he followed the dotted line to the high-rise maze of Tokyo. Some streets proved too narrow for the Fūjin to fly level. For those, he rolled the craft ninety degrees to one side or the other. The nimble fighter, even this slow, danced like a ballerina through the confines of the city.

Several camera bots and a handful of hovercars followed him to sate their curiosity at the strange sight. Matsushita Security Forces pulled up on either side, red lights flashing atop their hover patrol cars. Voices flooded Mamoru's mind; he had embodied the craft, and with it the communications system.

"Unknown pilot, you are in violation of Matsushita Corporation airspace with a military craft. You are to divert course immediately out of Tokyo airspace."

"Unknown simpleton, I am Saitō Mamoru acting on the order of Minamoto-heika. You are to stand down."

A moment of silence passed.

"*Gomenasai*, Saitō-sama," said the voice on the comm.

Mamoru swung the plane flat as the narrow street gave way to a major highway. The security cars drifted apart, becoming an escort instead of a pursuit. Mirror finished buildings created the illusion of three planes flying abreast. Windows wobbled in his wake, advert bots spiraled in the jetwash, some colliding and falling to the street, while others went careening through windows. The thrill of flying succumbed to the sense of confinement at the limitation of the machine's vision. Mamoru raised his nose and climbed, the burst of thrust sent several cars sliding off the road as he headed to the center of the city.

Vectored engines swung forward, slowing the Fūjin to a halt within twenty meters of the Matsushita building, where it hung in space. Lit by the city behind it, the plane's reflection met him head on in the black glass. *This is an apex predator.* He stared at it, fixated by the canopy glass flooded with white light, *chi* fires shimmering over his body.

The sight of it made him tired, and the plane drooped. This was a complex machine and the effort of embodying it had drained him. With a grunt, he heaved his avian form skyward. The aircraft cleared the roof and glided over the edge toward the landing pad. Reiko and two men, one of whom wore a black flight suit, cringed away from the harsh winds as the combat craft landed and powered down. Mamoru disconnected his mind from the machine and sat in quiet stillness for several minutes.

When he recovered the energy to move, he pushed the canopy release, took his blade, and climbed out.

Reiko met him at the bottom of a short metal staircase connecting the pad to the roof. The man in the flight suit bowed and moved past him.

"Minamoto-heika is pleased."

Mamoru showed no emotion as he waited for the roar of the departing Fūjin to fade. "As he has commanded, I have done."

7

VISITATION

Mamoru knelt on cushions at the low table. The fragrance of soap lingered in his nostrils as the memory of women's hands continued to massage the fatigue from his muscles. Clattering behind him announced the arrival of dishes on a tray. Timidity in the approach told him it was Ayame. Bright pink fabric covered with embroidered orchids filled his peripheral vision as she approached and set the meal before him. The scent of the bath clung to her still-wet hair. She hovered close enough for the heat of her body to warm him.

He took hold of her delicate wrist as she went to stand, gliding his thumb across the back of her hand. "Did you have a suitor?"

A tremble ran through her. "N-no, Saitō-sama, I am y-yours."

One tear patted on the tatami floor.

"I mean before you were convicted of assault."

Ayame drew in a breath. He expected the usual insistence that it was all lies, but all she offered was a sigh.

"Before you were abducted."

She froze. Mamoru moved his thumb over the vein rising out of the back of her hand.

"Y-you believe me?" She fell to her knees. After a moment, she gave him a terrified look for having addressed him with such causality. "Forgive me, Saitō-sama. No, I did not have a suitor. I was dedicated to my studies. My family is not wealthy. I did not wish to remain a peasant farmer."

He released her hand and gathered a bundle of soba noodles on chopsticks, which he dipped in a bowl of dark sauce. "Such a desire does not match your frightened exterior."

Ayame folded her hands on her lap, silent.

"Indulge me. Speak your mind without fear." He continued to eat.

Hanging hair hid her eyes. "Saitō-sama, you are a samurai in the service of Matsushita. You have the right of *kirisute gomen*. You can kill any of lower status who displease you. I am below even the status of commoner. Each time the sun rises, I wonder if this will be the day I am killed or made to lie with you." She turned her head away. "I know you desire a strong woman. It was my hope that by being weak, you would not make me do things."

Mamoru finished his mouthful and took a sip of tea. "Did it not worry you that acting too meek might fill me with such contempt that I trade you to another?"

"Yes, Saitō-sama. That is why I am frightened. No matter what I do, bad will come of it."

"It is unfortunate that they chose you. The security forces receive compensation for providing servants."

Ayame sniffled. "Can you help me prove it was false?"

Mamoru smiled and brushed the hair from her face. "So, this is what you are like without the burden of a slave's subservience."

She hooked two fingers on the metal ring about her neck. "Please, Saitō-sama, help me."

He dipped more noodles and devoured them, thinking of Reiko. "Our circumstances do not differ as much as they appear to. All things are as Minamoto-heika desires. I shall not be the pebble that startles his koi."

She covered her face with both hands, emitting a tiny squeak.

"You may weep."

Ayame did so.

When she quieted and sat upright, he stood. "I am many things, Ayame-chan, some less pleasant than others. Cruelty, however, is not one of my vices. Your *sentence* is short, is it not?"

She bowed her forehead to the floor. "Yes, Saitō-sama, eight years."

They will find a reason to deny her release. They always do. Perhaps at least that I can alter. "As long as you are of my possessions, I shall not force myself on you. See to it that you remind yourself that any other owner would not be so kind."

Ayame bowed a second time. "Thank you, Saitō-sama."

HOLOGRAPHIC PROJECTORS FILLED HIS DOJO SPACE WITH IMAGES OF A ZEN garden, complemented by an artificial wind that made it seem as though he were outside. The illusion filled in around him in the form of an old wooden porch and roof. Mamoru knelt at the center of the room, attempting to bring stillness to his mind, though he continued to see Nami staring into his eyes. The woman who gave herself to him in the bath was something else.

He let the air out of his lungs with a strained breath and adjusted the lay of his hands on his knees. What had befallen her was more of a tragedy than poor Ayame, for Nami had belonged to the higher social order. She had the mind of an engineer and was skilled at business, diplomacy, and the byzantine mess that was corporate law.

Her father's betrayal had angered the CEO. To fall from such great heights to the lowest strata of society was unthinkable. A weak person would have quietly ended their life. It would have seemed cruel for the warlord to order her killed directly. *Perhaps that was Minamoto's desire.* To that end, had he been too kind to her? Did Minamoto want someone to treat her so harshly that she preferred death to a life of servitude? While he debated between admiring her spirit and the possibility that he had disappointed his master, a sense came over him that he was no longer alone.

He heard no steps, nor smelled another. His right arm crossed to the katana at his hip as he stood, ready to draw. A slow pivot allowed him to survey the garden, finding nothing out of place. He started to kneel once more, but froze as the sand moved in a spiral. Pure white grains rose into the air as though an invisible tornado had erupted from the ground. A man's shape formed out of the whirling chaos, changing from white sand to shimmering metal. Wing-like projections of violet energy spread out below platinum struts connected to the back of a human figure composed of suspended ingots of gold.

The overall shape hinted angelic. Its hooded face was hollow, containing only two points of red light. Ornate armor formed of thousands of individual bits of precious metal drifted to the edge of the porch.

Mamoru knew this was a hologram, but it felt as if someone was in the room with him. The presence that AI dolls lacked, this had.

"Ahh, Mr. Saito. It is a pleasure to finally meet you," said the golden angel, in English.

Once his eyes acclimated to the glow, Mamoru lowered his arm. "Who are you? How did you infiltrate our network?"

The figure's shoulders bobbed with laughter. "It was as simple as a holovid call. There is much we need to discuss."

"What do you want? I have all I need here. There is nothing you can offer me."

"Oh, but there is. You do not even know what you are." The entity glided around as if pacing. "Mamoru Saito, you are one of a number of exceedingly rare individuals. Those who hold power over this world seek our elimination." Golden light shimmered over the dark wood of the porch as the figure drifted. "You are no slave, Mamoru. Every one of them is beneath you."

"I am a samurai of—"

"Yes, yes." The angel held up a hand. "How quaint. Samurai? You do realize what year it is, do you not?"

Mamoru narrowed his eyes.

"Your countrymen have a flair for the anachronistic. I never understood why some societies cling to ancient ways. Evolution is the destiny of humankind. Those who resist waste their efforts. You, Mamoru Saito, are one of The Awakened."

"Saitō." The figure's eyes turned searing as Mamoru corrected his pronunciation. "What is this awakened?"

"Do you think it common for a man to be able to control a machine by simply touching it?" The figure shifted, gliding closer. Energy wings fluttered with the sound of a dozen blowtorches. "Have you ever flown a military aircraft before? Such things take years of training, yet you did it by simply becoming the device. Fascinating."

Mamoru drew his blade, shouting, "How do you know of our private affairs?"

"I know much you do not, Mamoru. You are psionic."

"Kutaragi-sensei taught me how to use my *chi*. True samurai listen to their inner self." Mamoru tapped his fist to his chest. "I draw on that energy."

"What you so adorably call 'chi' is how your culture has defined a phenomenon the rest of the educated world refers to as psionics. Powers of the mind, my boy. You possess two skills which are both quite strong." The shimmering hood tilted forward and back as the figure appraised him.

The katana thudded point-first into the ground, slipped from his hand. Mamoru stumbled under a passing spell of light-headedness.

"Interesting. It seems your talents feature in equal prominence. You are a kinetic adept, Mamoru. Most psionics focus their abilities outward. Telekinetics for example, can move objects with their mind. Pyrokinetics create fire. Your power turns inward, making you stronger, faster, and tougher. That is why you made a fool of that"—he chuckled—"ninja girl."

Mamoru leaned on the wall, his gaze hardened by worry.

"Sadako," said the figure. "You admire her, but cannot respect her lack of honor. Oh, and Mamoru, forget the knife. This is, after all, only a hologram."

He glanced at his katana. "How can you know this?"

"Feel free to take a swipe if you must, you cannot kill light." The angel held his arms to the side as if offering not to defend himself. "Your ability over machinery and technology—some have dubbed it with the awkward moniker 'technokinesis' or the even more droll 'mechanical aptitude' is quite impressive. I prefer to think of it as a refined form of electrokinetics. Your brain can process voltages at the most precise levels, far short of the flashy bolts of lightning people expect from the term. The talent is sufficient, however, to allow you to link your consciousness with machines and do things that no mere pilot, driver, or cyberspace cowboy can."

"Why are you telling me how my *chi* works? I know these things already. Your strange terms do not change what I can do."

The angel laughed, a sound radiating condescension. "Do you honestly envision the ancient monks focusing some quasi-mystical chi nonsense through circuitry and cyberspace? You are part of the next step of the evolution of man, and we must help each other."

"I do not need your help. His majesty, Minamoto Akio, provides all I need."

The figure groaned. "You know not how much it pains me to hear one of my own kind refer to a lesser being as 'majesty.' That man is a relic of fading genetics. He is not even psionic, much less Awakened." The angel's golden arm extended toward him, palm upraised, wings spreading. "I offer you the chance to be far greater than anything you will find on Earth. Minamoto is an ant."

"My loyalty lies with my warlord, and my sensei. I am honor bound to serve them."

The figure's grand pose faded. "There are forces at play who seek to destroy us. You are not at all subtle in the use of your talents. Soon, the governments of Earth will become aware of your existence. They may simply destroy you, they may dissect you to understand how you work, or they may attempt to turn you against us. If you do not join us, Mamoru Saito, you become a liability I cannot afford."

He waved the katana through the holographic form. "Your threats are as empty as your body, golden man. I do not believe in your lies, demon."

The visitor laughed again, a deep, haunting sound that rumbled as though it echoed through the entire building. He leaned forward, mirth evaporating in an instant. "Until we meet again, Mamoru."

The angel flew toward the center of the rock garden, arched his back, and burst into thousands of points of light. Mamoru lowered the katana. At a wave of his left hand, the hologram projectors switched off and the room was once more a darkened dojo. He squinted at the Matsushita Oni deck at the center.

"Someone will pay."

8

SENSEI

D ust particles swarmed through a narrow cone of light, lofted by a single breath. A tiny wooden stick, an inch long, hovered before Mamoru's eyes in the grip of tweezers. He dipped a brush with his left hand and brought the harsh scent of chemical glue to his nostrils. Bristles parted over the length of the wood, coating it with clear liquid. With great care, he lowered it in place among thousands of its kin. Two taps with the tweezers aligned it smooth with the rest of the miniature wall.

Mamoru sat up and away from the model of Edo Castle covering an entire dining table, taking deep breaths now that he would not damage it. He glanced to his left, at a datapad bearing a schematic drawing of the old structure. He took another stick from a plastic-wrapped cube of ten thousand and leaned forward to paint on the glue. The faint *ssssh* of the sliding rice paper door behind him announced the arrival of one of his women, who hesitated at the entrance.

Mamoru dipped the brush in the glue. "What do you require, Nami?"

"Ishikawa-sama is on the vid for you." She stepped into the room and slid the door closed behind her, dropping her voice to a whisper. "How did you know it was me?"

He painted the stick, and set the brush across the shallow bowl of glue, whispering as he aligned the miniscule building block with where he wanted it. "Your breathing is slower, more confident than Ayame." With the bit of wood settled in place, he sat up and away from the model. "She takes air in short breaths, a mouse afraid of making too much noise lest it be noticed." He set the tweezers down, dropped the brush in a cup of solvent, and covered the glue.

Nami walked up behind and to his right. "It is beautiful, Saitō-sama. How long did it take you to build such a thing?"

He turned his head toward her, gazing down. Her nervousness was visible in her toes' grip on the floor. "Kutaragi-sensei suggested it two years ago. A task such as this holds infinite tedium and imparts no tangible reward."

"Then why do it?" She shifted to the right, gazing at the immense model.

Mamoru stood. "It centers the mind and nurtures the soul. Inner calm is the gate through which one taps their chi."

She flinched, keeping her stare on the castle of matchsticks. "I would not mind if you wished to lay with me, Saitō-sama." Nami pulled at her kimono, a narrow gap in the fabric revealed nothing on beneath it.

"You wish me to take you for a wife." He caressed her cheek with the back of his hand before sliding his fingertips down her neck to the explosive metal ring. "And be rid of this collar."

Nami looked away, a mask of shame on her face. "I…" Tears formed at the corners of her eyes but did not fall. "It is a choker." She touched her fingers to the front of it. "Collars have rings for a tether."

"How would you know such things?" Mamoru flashed a devious smile that lasted for an instant. He pulled her robe closed. "A tether need not be physical to be effective. Tell me, Nami. Do you seek my affection for its own sake, or simply release from your shame?"

She let her arms drop, limp. Her fingers teased at fists as her face cycled through several emotions. After a moment, she dared eye contact. "I am not a slave. What my father did was shameful, but I had nothing to do with it. I would accept a place as your wife to be thought of as a person again and not a piece of property. You are an honorable man, Saitō Mamoru, and I would not regret a life with you."

Mamoru remained silent until the presence of fear showed on her face. Many a samurai would have killed her for such an outburst. *Perhaps she would not mind that.* "You are honest if not foolish." He hooked a finger through the band and tugged her closer.

Her eyes widened and she pressed herself against him, trembling. "Saitō-sama, I beg you, don't pull at it. It may go off."

She does not desire death. Mamoru lowered his arm. "I shall attend to Ishikawa's call."

Mamoru slid the door to the side and left the room. Nami's silhouette on the white paper wall fell to a kneeling pose. He paused outside, listening as she recovered from teasing death. He wore an expression of contempt on the walk to the main room, wondering how any honorable man could derive a sense of empowerment from instilling terror in the defenseless. The idea that Minamoto could chafed at his nature.

A phantom presence surrounded his neck as he rounded the corner into the living room, where the upper half of Reiko Ishikawa floated above the Vidphone.

He did not speak until after he had approached and rendered a bow. "Ishikawa-sama, forgive my delay. I had matters within my house that demanded attention."

Reiko lifted an eyebrow and flashed an irritated scowl. "We have experienced another intrusion, Saitō-san. The network operations team is unable to pinpoint the source. I ask that you succeed where they have failed."

She thinks I was with Ayame, as would I in her place. Such things are expected. Why else did Minamoto give them to me? "I will begin my search now." He bowed.

Reiko offered a slight bow in return, and hung up.

Mamoru crossed the room to the inner hallway where Ayame, clad in a red kimono, scrubbed the floor on her hands and knees. His attention gravitated to the silver ring about her neck wobbling back and forth with her motion. *Each of us is owned by our fate. How fragile a man must be to need such a thing to elevate himself. My lessers have machines for this. This serves only to remind the girl of her place.*

Ayame, noticing him, glanced up and sat back on her heels. "Saitō-sama, is the floor clean to your satisfaction?"

"No."

Redness appeared around widening eyes. Her lip quivered. She leaned back, as if about to erupt with tears.

"Busy yourself with a task that does not bring you so low to the ground. Floors should be left to bots."

He left her there, in stunned silence, and sought the quiet of the dojo. The air still held a trace of a presence, a reminder of the golden visitor. Mamoru put a hand on his blade as he strode into the room and knelt before the deck. His mundane senses assured him he was alone, though a feeling nagged at him that he was not.

"Nami," he said at a volume a touch shy of a shout.

She appeared at the door within seconds. "Yes, Saitō-sama?"

He gestured to his side. "Sit."

The woman approached in a rapid shuffling gait, and took a place on the cushion next to him with her legs off to the side.

"I do not feel at ease, Nami-chan." He placed one hand on the deck. "I am about to send my thoughts to the electronic world. I will not be aware of what goes on here."

She bowed, unable to suppress a hint of a smile at his affectionate address.

"My *chi* will manifest itself as light on my arms. Do not fear. However, if you see anything else you cannot explain, pull my hand away from the device and I shall wake."

"Yes, Saitō-sama."

He stared into her eyes, ignoring the sporadic red flash from her throat. No deceit lingered there. Perhaps her deferential politeness came from gratitude for his trust rather than fear for her life. If she wished to harm him, this would be the perfect time. Nami grasped his forearm with both hands, trembling as if ready to pull him away from the machine at a second's notice. She risked a full smile.

He closed his eyes and surrendered his awareness to the machine.

Her grip tightened as the cool aura swept up his arms, the fires of his *chi* burning visible. Once more, the momentary sensation of being an immobile block came and passed. When he opened his eyes, the white samurai hovered inside an empty dojo. Mamoru held up his left forearm, gazing at the polished enamel, a blurry reflection of his empty helmet. The weight of her hands had gone, lingering only as a memory.

He focused on the Matsushita network, reaching out as if to open a door. A swipe of his arm pushed open a panel of reality, creating a portal to a bright corridor. On the other side, six men in plain black suits waited for him, bowing as he drifted through. Points of heat teased at the back of his brain as the deck's processors struggled to compensate for the rapid change in virtual location.

The youngest glanced to his rear and back at him, worry and awe on his face. A familiar look for the new guy. Before he could ask Mamoru how he teleported, their manager spoke.

"Welcome, Saitō-san. I am deeply ashamed at our inability to find this intruder and honored by your assistance."

Mamoru pressed his fist to his palm and returned a half-bow. "What have you discovered, Nakamura-san?"

"An unknown entity gained access to our network approximately forty-five minutes ago. We picked the intrusion up at the GlobeNet interlink node masquerading as a Vidphone connection. My team has completed an assessment of all critical data storage nodes and can find no evidence of access. As far as we are able to discern, it appears to be an ordinary Vid call."

"What reason do you have to suspect it is more than it appears?" asked Mamoru.

Tense silence hung in the virtual air. Nakamura searched for meaning in the gleaming patches of reflected light crawling over the samurai's armor. When no answer came, Mamoru leaned closer.

"Deepest apologies, Saitō-sama. The connection passed straight through to the desk of Minamoto-heika. Such a route is not only private, it requires a direct transfer from Ishikawa-san. She has no recollection of doing so."

"Continue monitoring the data storage. This feels like a diversion." Mamoru glided down the corridor to an elevator.

The doors snapped closed and open again in the blink of an eye. The transition from the virtual ninetieth floor to the lobby occurred in a nanosecond flash. A reception area of white tile and polished black marble columns spread out before him where the network simulated the fragrance of hyacinth. Thirty some odd people milled about. The dull murmur of conversations lent believability to the illusion of a room. They were all program constructs, false shells inserted like plants to make the environment appear natural. This room represented the connection between the Matsushita network and the GlobeNet, flagged as a public area. Any traveler in cyberspace could walk right in, guided by helper constructs that spawned whenever a guest arrived.

Mamoru approached the mannequins and reached into their code, searching each in turn for any trace of tampering. Letters and numbers spiraled out as he touched them, forming a column of glowing symbols winding upward until the strings broke apart and faded away.

A woman in professional attire came through the front door, glancing at the vaulted ceiling and glass-walled corridor on the third floor. Amid a flurry of blue light, a pleasant looking older man with salt and pepper hair and a slight beard formed. Personality analytics measured the prospective client, and predicted the highest chance of sale to a fatherly presence. Mamoru ignored her and the resultant conversation about a large electronic component deal.

As soon as the woman mentioned she was a purchasing agent for Timmons-Orben Hovercars sniffing around for a contract potentially worth billions, a live agent in a grey suit added himself to the conversation and walked her towards a private conference room.

Mamoru reached out and stuck his fingers through the glass of the front door. His awareness extended in to the blackness of memory buffers. Unlike Nakamura's team, he searched by feel. Thoughts begat action; the machinery reacted to his desire. He peeled a shimmering thread out of the glass, stretching it between both hands while examining it.

It represented a digital recording of an incoming connection to Majordomo Ishikawa's desk that had not passed through the normal operator first. He pulled at the strand, stretching it out and unraveling the bits through his consciousness. The face of the virtual visitor from his dojo, the angel, filled a nonexistent screen in his thoughts, followed by the emotionless face of Reiko Ishikawa lit by his golden radiance. Reiko did transfer the line to Minamoto, after which the energy distorted. Mamoru attempted to glean the substance of it from a dozen pools of buffer memory scattered throughout the network, but recoiled from a strange onrush of power that overwhelmed his mind.

The white samurai glided away from the doors, holding his helmet in both hands and letting the connection thread dissipate. He shook off a jolt as though the information blast had physically struck him in the head. Something squeezed about his left forearm. Mamoru smiled and caused the deck to project a holographic screen back in the real world, bearing the message: "I am fine. Keep watch."

He thrust his fingers once more through the glass, gathering a countless mass of azure data strands that appeared like an illusion outside. One at a time, he sifted through until he found the same thread. Rather than attempt to travel its path to Minamoto's terminal a second time, he sent his efforts in the other direction.

The Matsushita corporation lobby disintegrated around him as his perception squeezed forward and condensed, becoming a tiny orb of blue fire racing along the wire. Tokyo fell away below him and took on the form of a glimmering map of dark sapphire scored with lighter lines pulsing with signals. He glided down the path, now as wide to him as a road. At a pace of hundreds of virtual miles per hour, he shot through ninety-degree turns and bridge gates, entering border routers that looked like massive halls packed with thousands of similar light-balls queuing up by dozens of out-paths. Thousands of simultaneous Vidphone conversations echoed around him, fragments of words, laughter, faces, and shouting. The path led him to Shinjuku city, and its starport.

Mamoru slowed as his little energy sphere entered a cavernous chamber where tens of thousands of similar pathways wavered in the air like udon in broth. Each connected to an enormous amethyst crystal projecting a beam of white energy through a hole in the ceiling.

He leapt up from the link thread, resuming his samurai form. The CPU crystal still dwarfed him, rendered at a size equivalent to a nine-story building. He floated to its surface, basking in the fuming warmth of processing power depicted as a wall of amethyst fire.

"Who are you?" he asked.

In response to his question, the object shimmered. No voice spoke. As was the nature of his gift, he read the machine and its purpose. The crystal represented a massive neural-net processor handling routing algorithms and data resequencing for a high-speed interplanetary transmitter. Subroutines appeared and vanished, streams of lime green letters and numbers whirling about in midair. The concept of control code referencing the 'quantum entanglement' that facilitated the faster-than-light speed communication formed in his thoughts. Millions of holovid calls, emails, messages, and cyberspace connections passed through this processor on their way to a structure that resembled an inter-dimensional gateway at the top of the vast chamber overhead. Glowing emerald energy drifted in clouds within a great circle of bronze and gold, inscribed with runic characters meaningless to him. The walls of the enormous vault appeared to be damp stone covered in moss, set with medieval torches. Flashes appeared here and there in the churning green as it devoured the incoming stream of data.

He frowned at the overdone graphics, no doubt inspired by that 'Monwyn' craze spreading through the commoners. Mamoru had little patience for such wasted effort in design; this construct was a visual representation of the instantaneous echo of information to the opposite point on Mars. A simple opening would have sufficed.

Quantum... something: pairs, nonlocality, teleportation... The machinery enabled data to travel between two fixed points with zero time, though the interpolation that translated data between the planetary network and the preprocessor for the faster-than-light link added a perceptible delay to anyone inside cyberspace. For infiltration or gaming, Earth-Mars latency was severe to the point of prohibitive. An action initiated on Mars could take thirty to forty seconds to happen on Earth. While a master might make it into a poorly maintained network with minimal security under those conditions, no one should be able to infiltrate Matsushita's network from another planet. The thought struck him as more laughable than using a senshelmet for serious hacking.

He didn't trust what effect such a gateway would have on a cyberspace presence like his, and backed away. The people who designed the data bridge never imagined anyone could project their *chi* into the network, and he didn't feel like gambling his soul on technology that defied the laws of the known universe... at least to the point he understood them. For all he knew, it would tear his ghost from his body or split him into two people.

The more he thought about it, the deeper his frown became.

"Impossible. Perhaps I am not as alone as I believed myself to be. Only a wielder of *chi* could have accomplished the infiltration over such a link in real time."

Mamoru gazed up at the roaring inferno of energy above him and scowled. His adversary was on Mars, and should not have been able to breach their network. If another existed who possessed a similar gift, they were a threat. For the sake of Matsushita's secrets, and for the glory of Minamoto's favor, he would have to find them—even if it meant going to Mars.

He focused once more on his company's network, and sent himself there.

BLACKNESS GAVE WAY FIRST TO THE CALMING SOUNDS OF THE OCEAN AND attendant seagulls. Next came a cool, salty breeze, followed by the feeling of wooden boards beneath his feet and a world of blank light. The wraparound porch of his sensei's home in the countryside drew itself in, first as black lines, then a real-looking object. The house came next, followed by a countryside drawn in as green spread out over white, racing to the distance where mountains erupted beyond the haze of morning fog.

Ichirō Kutaragi emerged from a set of double sliding doors, which opened on their own and closed behind him. The man seemed younger than when Mamoru had last seen him, though the hair that hung to his waist was still steel-grey. Every fold of his flare-shouldered haori jacket lay perfect, every embroidered black orchid where it always was.

Mamoru shifted his image to appear as himself and knelt. Since his death, his old mentor had appeared on several occasions in cyberspace. At first, he believed it to be an AI created to replicate the wise old master, at Minamoto's insistence. Lately, he was not so sure of the truth of it. The essence of the entity held a strange quality he could not quantify, beyond the nature of a self-aware program.

"Kutaragi-sensei, it is my utmost desire that I have not disappointed you."

Ichirō waved him to stand. "Saitō-kun, you are about to suffer a storm not of your own making."

"Is this the work of the oni?"

Ichirō chuckled. "What threatens you is no oni, Mamoru. It is a man as mortal as you are or I once was. I cannot guide you anymore. You are no longer a boy."

Mamoru let his gaze fall. "I understand, Sensei. I do not fear them."

"This threat is external to the company, though it has dropped a venomous serpent in your bed." Ichirō moved past him to the railing and stood in silence, gazing out over the fields.

"Nami?"

The wind fluttered Ichirō's dark hakama pants, billowing like a skirt about his legs. "No, though they may manipulate her as well. You must promise me, Mamoru, you will not accept what is about to happen to you as a mark on your honor."

"What do you mean?" Mamoru's eyes widened and he rushed to his former master's side. "What threat is there to my honor?"

"A stone does not disturb a pond unless a man hurls it into the water. Which is responsible for the ripples that mar the surface, the stone or the man?"

"The man," said Mamoru without hesitation.

"Indeed." Ichirō glanced back at him wearing a trace of a smile. "A foolish man would blame the stone."

"What—"

Ichirō vanished amid a brief cloud of white light specked with silver numbers. When no trace of his mentor remained, Mamoru approached the railing, searching for understanding amid the wavering grass-covered hill. In the distance, a false village dotted the endless greenery. Small children giggled and ran through the field in pursuit of a bouncing dog. Birds seemed to hang still in the air, wings outstretched to ride the oncoming wind. This was how he remembered it.

If not for his former master's warning, the scene might have brought him peace.

9

HONOR BOUND

Ayame's fingers teased at the deadly choker. She sat on cushions the same dark blue as her kimono, eyes downcast. A gentle breeze kicked up by the air system made the sky-colored obi at her back flutter. She kept her gaze away from Mamoru, staring at her bare feet. Nami faced her from the opposite side of a square, black table, eating dry soba noodles in silence. Ayame had not yet taken a bite.

Mamoru sipped the last of the broth from a bowl of udon soup and set it down. He glanced to his right at Nami, and seconds later, to his left at Ayame.

"What is on your mind, Ayame-chan?"

Her hand froze; two fingers and a thumb in contact with metal, reflecting the flashing red light. "Forgive me, Saitō-sama. I do not wish to die."

"You expect to run away?"

"No, Saitō-sama. I fear"—she released her grasp on the choker and let her hands fall to her lap—"that it may malfunction."

"What if I were to tell you they were stunners rather than explosives? You are young, pretty, and valuable. Why would they risk losing you to such a gruesome death?"

Ayame faced forward, head down. "To make an example for others."

Mamoru frowned at the shivering woman, thinking for a moment of his parents. Like her, their weakness allowed others to harm them. If

Ayame were stronger, she would not be his property. He stalled his thinking. She was here because she tried to resist the drunken samurai. Had she been weak, they would have had their way with her and left her be. His face darkened with a frown. *If she survived. They broke her anyway.* Ayame risked a glance, making eye contact for a mere second before cringing away. The sadness in her eyes tightened his throat and sent his gaze to the window.

"Ayame-chan," he said, near a whisper. "You must eat."

She gathered her chopsticks and bowl, pushing the noodles about for a moment before lifting a smidgen to her lips. Mamoru found himself unable to watch, wondering where this sudden pity for someone so pathetic had come from.

A tone chimed through the apartment, followed seconds later by the shimmering face of Reiko Ishikawa appearing ten paces to their right. She looked frightened and confused, two emotions the majordomo never showed.

"Mamoru, listen to me. You must leave right away."

He placed his hands on his hips, a guarded stare at the lack of politeness. "Ishikawa-sama, what—"

"There is no time to explain. Something has happened to the Shogun. He has ordered you killed for trading our secrets to Kurotai. I know you would never betray us, and he expects you to die by seppuku to recover your honor. Please, Mamoru, do not consider fleeing a loss of respect. I... can't remember any of it. I think... He could not even say which secrets you are to have given away. None of this is within tradition."

Ayame and Nami gasped. Both covered their mouths with their hands. Ayame burst into tears and muttered about what horrors a new owner would inflict on her.

"I find this unamusing, Reiko. I have had no contact with Kurotai. The connection was a Vidphone call to your terminal. Did you transfer someone to Minamoto?"

"I-I don't recall." Reiko's eyes glazed over. "I remember hearing the chime and... gold."

"Someone has influenced him." Mamoru narrowed his eyes. "I must find the man who throws the stone."

"What does that mean?" Reiko's eyebrows scrunched together. "If I am seen warning you... Please don't do anything foolish."

Her hologram vanished.

His servant girls looked at him. Fear was evident on Nami's face as well, though she concealed it far better than Ayame. *Minamoto demands my death. I should...* Ayame's weeping intruded on his thoughts. His honor required obedience, but how casually had his beloved shogun cast him aside. *Do these women deserve the result of my death? I am only the stone. My honor is my own. This is false. An oni has forced Minamoto against his will.*

The sounds of people approaching made Mamoru stiffen. Neither girl reacted.

"Do you trust me?"

Ayame stopped whimpering; red-ringed eyes stared at him. Nami nodded once.

"Yes, Saitō-sama," whispered Ayame.

"Then do so."

Mamoru stood as the front door opened. A short, thin man in a black suit entered carrying a small case, flanked by a pair of taller men in gleaming white armor with rifles. A shadow drifted along the rice paper wall as an armored figure took position at the far side of the apartment, beyond the dojo. Another entered through the window at the right.

Company soldiers to either side raised their weapons at him from twenty meters away. Mamoru remained standing with his back to the three closer men.

"Saitō Mamoru," said the man in the suit. "It is with great sorrow that I have come." He walked up to within arm's reach and held up the case. "You know why I am here. Minamoto-heika has discovered your treachery."

Ayame whimpered, staring down at her toes. Nami tentatively reached across the table to touch her, but did not have enough nerve to move.

"I understand why you are here, Moriyama-san." Mamoru spoke in an even, emotionless tone.

Moriyama opened the case, rotating it to present a plastisteel wakizashi lying alongside a white enamel scabbard covered in golden dragons. A cloth wrapped the weapon at the midpoint, positioned such that an embroidered black Matsushita symbol rested along the blade.

"We have brought Omura-san to act as your second," said Moriyama.

Footsteps at the door announced the arrival of a man a decade Mamoru's senior, clad in modern composite samurai armor. He stopped in the doorway, thirty feet away.

Mamoru waited for the plastic clicking of the samurai's motion to cease. "These two have been exemplary servants. Allow me a moment."

Moriyama nodded.

With his foot, Mamoru nudged the wheeled table out of the way and motioned at the women to move to him. Sniveling, Ayame stood and drew close. Nami followed suit without a noise. He held their heads to his chest, savoring the scent of their floral shampoo and the warmth of their touch.

"Remember your trust," he whispered, and slid his hands under their collars. He made a fist right at their throats, grasping the thick front part.

Ayame's legs shook. Her fingers clutched his shirt both as a plea for her life and so as not to fall. It was not unheard of for a disgraced company samurai to take his slaves with him in death. Nami went rigid and closed her eyes. Ayame whimpered, too terrified to even beg.

"Moriyama-san," said Mamoru.

"Yes?"

"I am but the stone."

"Wha—"

Mamoru forced his *chi* to overwhelm the mechanisms in his hands. The electronics bowed to his will. He jerked his arms down, snapping the explosive restraints away into limp cords. Power flowed through his body as he accelerated himself. He twisted and flung his arms to the sides, hurling the metallic noodles at the more distant soldiers.

Flexible explosive cord wrapped over the helmet of the man on the left, and coiled about the neck of the man on the right. Both soldiers had barely begun to react to the motion when the effect of Mamoru's influence on the electronics faded and the charges detonated. Their bodies ceased to exist from midway up the chest; pieces of arm spun to either side as the majority of their torsos splattered to the wind. The women's panicked screams occurred four seconds after the explosions. Nami caught Ayame as the younger woman fainted.

Mamoru continued rotating, emitting a battle cry as he drove his fist into the chest of the soldier to Moriyama's right. His fist cracked through the composite armor chestplate, which splintered to shards around his now-bloody knuckles. In Mamoru's accelerated state, the sound resembled a boot crushing glass wrapped in cloth. The man flew backwards, red spewing from his nose. Mamoru's left hand caught the ceremonial wakizashi as he followed the momentum of the punch and whirled. Moriyama squealed, holding the case up as a shield. Mamoru funneled power through his body, amplifying his strength. He smashed his right foot across the helmet of the remaining soldier, crushing it like an egg and launching the lifeless body into the wall. At the same instant, his left hand came down and plunged the blade through the case.

Moriyama's pants turned dark and wet—the tip of the wakizashi hovered millimeters from his heart. Ayame snapped awake, clutched her bare neck, and screamed again. Her body lapsed into shivers, evidently overwhelmed by a collision of terror and relief. Omura drew his katana and stalked in as Moriyama collapsed to sit on the floor, still staring at the blade that almost killed him.

"Omura-san, our master has been poisoned. You are a respectable samurai, and so I offer you the chance to leave with your life and honor intact."

"You know I cannot defy Minamoto-heika's order even if his sanity may be in doubt. Because I do not believe you have betrayed us, I shall not cut you down like a peasant dog. Retrieve your weapon, Saitō Mamoru. "

Both women squealed. The reason for it washed over Mamoru a second later in the form of a frigid patch of air that seemed to move as if alive. He rendered a slight bow to Omura and started to walk toward his weapon, but stopped as the man shuddered.

Omura howled, losing his grip on his blade and grasping his helmet with both hands. He collapsed to his knees and shivered once more before standing again.

"S'okay, luv," said Omura with a British accent. "I got this lunk. You should get out of here before the other soldiers arrive."

"You." Mamoru pointed. "The oni who took Nami."

Nami clung to Mamoru from behind, now trembling as much as Ayame.

"Sweetie, you don't have enough time to worry about what plane of hell I came from right now." Omura winked in an unsettling feminine way and flicked his fingers at him. "Get going. Go on, sod off. You'll find your way. I'm trying to be nice here and spare you the trouble of killing a decent man. Now, move."

Mamoru growled low in his throat, but moved to the rack that held his vibro katana. After affixing it to his belt, he ran to the dojo and stuffed his deck in a bag he slung across his back. On his return trip through the living room to the door, he stopped. Nami and Ayame held each other, looking terrified and not having moved. A trail of urine led to where Moriyama cowered in the corner, still clutching the pierced box. Mamoru stooped to grab the cloth that had been around the blade meant for his suicide, wiping fragments of armor and blood from his knuckles.

"You are both free. Go."

The women stared at him.

He gestured at the door. Lights shifted as an unseen aircraft circled the building. Nami and Ayame continued to cling to each other, shaking in stunned silence. Nami appeared close to vomiting and the younger girl gawped at what her collar had done to one of the soldiers. Her fingers pulled at her throat. *Damn.* Mamoru stomped over, seizing a wrist in each hand, and dragged the women behind him to the elevator. Several floors passed in silence before Nami whispered.

"I am sorry, Saitō-sama. I was afraid—"

Ayame looked at him with a blank expression. "That… was around my neck."

"I do not own you now, woman. I am no longer samurai. I am ronin. Until I find the man who threw the stone, I have no master. Both of you are free to leave."

Nami gave him a perplexed look. He brushed her cheek with his hand, pale blue and lit by passing bands of light from their descent.

"What will we do now?" Nami gathered his jacket in two fists. "They will come after us. We stand out dressed like this."

"What more do you wish from me? I have already freed you from your bondage."

Ayame looked up with the face of a little sister begging her brother for help. Mamoru let his head sag forward and loosed a heavy sigh. When the doors opened at the lobby, he again took hold of their arms and ran. The sound of three people running barefoot over faux marble tiles brought the din to a halt as everyone looked up to watch them. A light rain fell outside, misting around passing cars and keeping pedestrians' heads tucked low in their coats.

Mamoru parted the crowd like a plow, dragging Nami and Ayame behind him. Between his speed and the wet ground, the women stumbled in a perpetual state of almost falling. He ran through the neon-soaked streets of inner Tokyo, beneath the *whirr* of advert bots and the occasional hovercar. Several blocks from his former home, he halted at a street corner where the congestion showed signs of thinning. Clouds of fog drifted low over the near-standstill ground traffic here. Rain-soaked pavement glistened blue-white in the moonlight. A lone advert-bot passed overhead, low, trailing a spray of holographic cherry blossom petals as it tried to sell cosmetics.

Ayame pressed herself to his back, teeth chattering as she shivered.

Rain had soaked through all their clothes. She grabbed at her neck again, legs wobbling. No longer able to hold it in, she leaned to the side and retched.

"Hey, which way is the theater?" shouted a man.

Mamoru squinted at him, a thirty-something in a modern outfit that made his haori and the ladies' kimonos seem like artifacts from a bygone era.

"I do not know," he said, and pulled the girls into an alley.

They splashed through puddles, some as deep as their shins. Ayame mewled in protest at the pace. Nami gasped, too out of breath to complain.

Two streets down, Ayame pulled back and sniveled. "Saitō-sama, you are hurting my wrist."

He continued, slowing to a modest jog out of the alley to a sidewalk in a middle-class shopping district. After taking cover under the awning of a noodle house, he eased them to the wall and released his grip on their arms. Ayame rubbed a bruise where he had held her. Nami did as well, but smiled at him.

"Come." He trudged a short distance to a store where a number of older teens loitered.

The street toughs leered at Ayame and Nami until they saw the katana. Acting as though they would not have done anything, they un-leaned from the wall and rushed away. Carrying such a weapon meant he either had station enough to kill them or was crazy.

He lingered in the doorway until the thugs went out of sight around the edge of the building, chased by an advert bot looking to sell beer. The door hissed closed behind him as he walked amid the glow of a dozen holographic girls around the ceiling. The two-foot tall figures modeled the latest popular clothes for 'normal' people, those not of the upper class. Ayame and Nami stood a few steps in from the door, soaked and shivering. Mamoru put a hand on their shoulders and turned them to face rows of garments.

"Find clothing. Take whatever you need not to stand out. Put it on right away, be quick."

A younger girl behind the counter, not yet eighteen by appearance, smirked at him through a veil of hot pink hair. She jerked and bobbed as if in the throes of a mild seizure, to music fed into her brain. "You gonna rob me?"

"No," he said, not looking at her. "I will pay."

The women hunted through the racks, both confused and muttering. Ayame seemed not to know her way around big city stores, and Nami had grown up with people to shop for her.

Mamoru took a grey long-sleeved shirt from a rack and folded it over his arm atop plain black pants. "I would have thought the two of you would welcome the return of your freedom with more enthusiasm."

"Do you need any assistance, miss?"

Nami glanced at the pink-haired teen who had snuck up on her. She shot Mamoru a look brimming with gratitude. The girl speaking to her as if she were a real person again hit home. He offered a slight bow, snagged a pair of dark sneakers from a shelf, and went to the back.

Mamoru discarded his wet anachronistic clothes, changing in the rear of the store by the door of the lone dressing room, unconcerned with the clerk watching. Ayame and Nami, each with an armload, walked up behind him as he secured a row of click fasteners down the left side of his new shirt.

"There's only one room," said Ayame.

Mamoru grumbled. "You can both fit. You've been bathing together for a year."

Ayame blushed, eyes down and whispering, "But, I am no longer a slave."

Nami pushed her toward the door and dropped her bundle, peeling her clothes off with only the cover of a freestanding rack of sweaters. "Use the room. He is right. We do not have time for modesty."

The clerk's face flushed to match her hair as Nami stripped, and she hurried to the counter. Mamoru followed, waiting as the girl tallied the items.

"Thank you, sir. The amount comes to 2466 credits."

Mamoru swiped his NetMini over the device, which chirped as he paid. White light surrounded his hand as he concentrated on masking the transaction from anyone who might be searching for his electronic identity. The clerk squeaked at the sight.

"May I see your 'mini, girl?"

She stared at him, no longer bopping to the unheard music. "Um…"

"Calm yourself, child. I mean you no harm."

The girl swallowed and held out a small oval device shaped like a white cat's head. He chuckled at it and concealed it between his palms. Eyes closed, he sent his consciousness through the Nippon-Shisei communications grid. In the deep dark of the GlobeNet, far out of reach of Matsushita or even the JSDF, he kept a stash of credits. Pointers to accounts left orphaned by careless operators he had collected over the past several years. Both arms crawled with luminous energy wisps. When he slid his hands apart, the little device showed the girl's balance at a hundred thousand. She backed up against the wall, knocking a few small boxes of jewelry off the shelving. He offered it atop an outstretched palm. She gathered her hands to her chest and gasped, shaking her head as if she could not believe her eyes.

Mamoru held the NetMini closer to her. "Tell no one of our presence here."

The clerk bit her lip and ventured a timid nod, accepting her device.

Ayame and Nami emerged from the back, now dressed in modern attire. Both had opted for pants rather than skirts or dresses, and loose-fitting tops in subdued colors. Mamoru fussed with the katana, unable to get it to sit right on his new belt.

THE TRIO MOVED THROUGH THE CITY, DRIFTING AMONG HUNDREDS OF people dressed in modern fashion. Cloaked in their new designer anonymity, they reached the western outskirts where the dense city showed signs of fragmenting to suburbs. Mamoru stopped, squinting at the long downhill street crisscrossed by hundreds of ancient, suspended wires running between four and five story residence buildings. None of them were used anymore, except by birds. Everything was wireless, but no one wanted to pay to remove them.

"You do not need to follow me. You are no longer owned."

The women exchanged a glance, a silent rock-paper-scissors carried out in their eyes.

"We cannot simply return to our lives. Nami has no family left, and Matsushita knows her face. The wretched beasts who made up lies and arrested me are the security men for my village. They will know me if I return." Ayame paused, overcome by the urge to cry. "I cannot go home."

Mamoru stared at crows clinging to a bouncing wire. "I am unable to watch over you now. I must find the one responsible."

Nami interlaced her fingers with his. "You have taken a great risk by helping us. I do not wish to think what might have become of us if you had left us there." Nami shivered. "I am in your debt. I am ashamed to ask for even more help…"

"Please, don't leave us here," whined Ayame, at last succumbing to tears. She balled her hands to fists, trying to hold it back. Moments later, she reined in her emotion and stared at him. "Please forgive me for showing weakness."

Mamoru looked away from her. As much contempt as he held for such displays, her childlike face softened his reaction. *There is no honor in harming the helpless.* He squinted through the crisscrossed power lines at the fading sun. After several minutes of silent contemplation, he loosed a breathy sigh before resuming his walk with a change in direction.

"This way."

Beneath a steady stream of advert bots, they trudged for several blocks. Ground traffic had lightened at this hour, making cross streets dangerous. Mid-level workers wealthy enough to own personal vehicles raced through the narrow passageways in an effort to find a place to park before their neighbors took their favorite spaces. Twice, Ayame came within inches of being hit.

Mamoru took a left, passing rows of stacked apartments full of people at the upper end of poor. He found Nami's expression of awkwardness at their surroundings amusing. *How soon she remembers the person she was.* At the end of the street, he approached the decaying remains of a factory abandoned decades ago when its usefulness migrated to Shōrishima. That decision he had approved of. The *real* Japan, the natural Earth, was for people—not factories that poisoned her.

He ducked through the broken front gate and stepped around puddles of rainwater in the courtyard as he led his companions into the dripping darkness of a former automobile plant. Shadows cast by the arms of dead manufacturing robots kept Ayame close to his back. Their footsteps echoed through the cavernous darkness, drawing attention to how quiet it should be there. Mamoru stopped at the door to a foreman's office which contained a cot and small lavatory. Both women jumped at a sudden scraping of metal interspersed with menacing electronic growls.

A small spotlight danced across the floor twenty meters away, accented by the clatter of loose bits of steel striking the ground and rolling. Ayame muffled a scream with her hands before Nami shoved her through the door. The light leveled out as a spider-bot the size of a compact car pulled itself out of a mound of scrap metal and parts and stood on eight articulated legs. It jittered, as if it had been a long time since it needed to find any sense of balance. Yellow paint peeled to shiny plastisteel in spots, black bands ran the length of each leg as if such a thing needed stripes to warn of danger. It shook itself like a wet dog, throwing off bits of debris from the pile in which it had slumbered.

On the front end, a shroud of armor guarded a single glowing red eye that narrowed with focus at Mamoru. A pair of industrial lasers, once used for welding and cutting, emerged like chelicerae from hatches on either side, trained on him.

"Attention: You are trespassing on the property of Mits—"

The room became a smear of blurry color as Mamoru accelerated himself to a sprint that brought his hand in contact with the enormous spider. It wobbled, its voice processor stalled by confusion at such rapid motion. Before it could select another course of action, Mamoru plunged his mind into the machine's computer core.

He gazed through its eye at his own face, an image tinted in green and banded with narrow lines. The bot contained a sub-sentient artificial intelligence capable of reacting to situations and making decisions, but lacking self-awareness. Psionic fingers spread through its digital essence, moving it like dough. Mamoru massaged and twisted, rewriting its control modules at the speed of thought.

Moments later, his consciousness returned to his body and he stepped away. Ayame and Nami, two heads peering through the doorway, oohed at the incandescent fog peeling from his arms and shoulders.

"What is that?" asked Ayame.

"What did you do?" asked Nami.

Mamoru stilled his mind, letting the glow recede. The patrol bot settled on its legs in a nonthreatening stance, the laser arms folded back against the body. It followed him like a dog to the office.

"I cannot stay here. The security forces are looking for me. You will be at risk if you remain in my presence. Stay here for two days. This machine will protect you. I will send you food as soon as I am able to, as well as take care of your record, Ayame-chan."

She hugged him, though he remained stoic. Embarrassed, she backpedaled and sat on the small bed, still grinning.

"Nami…" He studied her face. "Your father was well known here. I cannot alter the memories of men."

"Take me with you?" Nami pressed herself against him, hands on his chest. "I would stay with you if you will have me."

Mamoru stood still. "You flatter me with your devotion. For the time we have been together, you have sought my favor to escape the disgrace of your fallen station." His hand moved to her cheek, thumb brushing below her eye. "You are strong, Nami. You do not need to offer yourself in exchange for freedom any longer."

She looked down.

"I will create a life for you in another prefecture. Once my affairs have been settled and your fate is no longer at my whim, you will know if these are your true feelings."

"You think I am manipulating you?"

"I do not know what to think. My world is broken, Nami-chan. Oni walk the Earth and plague my affairs. My shogun has disavowed me, and those I once considered allies seek my death based on lies. The two of you do not deserve to be caught up in the storm that approaches."

"Mamoru, I want to know your body while I am in control of my own." She kissed the side of his neck. "It is not only men who have desire."

"There is no time, and it would be rude to Ayame." He guided her to sit on the cot next to the other woman. "I must leave before we are discovered here. Perhaps you will still feel this way when our circumstances are different. Stay here. Remain inside and out of sight until I send word."

Nami rested the side of her head against his chest. "Please proceed with caution, Mamoru."

He felt no insult at her use of his given name, and almost allowed himself to believe her words genuine.

Ayame slid from the cot to her knees. "Thank you, Saitō-san. You have given me back my life."

Mamoru returned her bow and squinted through rows of assembly machines. Outside, Tokyo's lights glimmered as smears of color on grimy windows.

Now, I must take back my own.

10

WHITE ONI

I n the darkness of an alley a few blocks from Hachiko Square, Mamoru paused to catch his breath and think. A hundred and sixty meters away, the giant holographic visage of Akio Minamoto dominated most of a silver-windowed tower. Eerie shadows elongated through the crowd as the thirty-foot tall Shogun gazed down at his subjects with eyes the size of train tubes. What once had seemed grandfatherly, now struck Mamoru as condescending. The grand figure he once admired now seemed like a clueless old fool. He clutched his fist to his chest, shaking with anger. How could he be cast aside so easily after such loyal service?

Certainly, even Minamoto understands there are none other like me.

A feeling of being watched had nagged at him since he left the old factory. He flattened his hand over the spot Nami had last touched on his chest. Unfamiliar emotions swam through his mind. *What did she want?* For as long as he could remember, life possessed a certain order. He had superiors and he had subordinates. Nowhere within any of it did emotion dwell. Even Kutaragi-sensei had never shown much of anything resembling love for a son, merely pride in an exemplary student.

Nami's eyes lingered in the shadows, earnest and pleading. Had she expected him to change his mind? He stared at the phantasm of memory, unable to understand why his heart pulled him from logic. Mamoru scowled at himself. He had allowed Moriyama to walk away. The man had done no wrong. He was as honor bound as any of them to follow Minamoto's decrees. His presentation of a ceremonial blade was a gesture of respect. Mamoru could not kill him for it. Believing some external force poisoned Minamoto against him offered a small amount of comfort from the disgrace of rejecting honorable seppuku.

Mamoru closed his eyes and pictured a fist-sized rock splashing into a pond, startling koi.

Nonetheless, Moriyama witnessed the women leave with him. Ayame would be overlooked. No one would care about an unimportant peasant girl from the suburbs. However, Nami's disgrace came at the direct command of Minamoto. Freeing her was tantamount to defying the shogun. That issue he would address in due time. Perhaps gratitude at ridding his master's mind of whatever oni touched it would forgive such a transgression. If Minamoto demanded Nami's return, he could lure her back—she trusted him. Mamoru thumbed the handle of his katana, unable to avoid imagining her betrayed expression as a new bomb was placed around her throat.

Why do I feel such shame at the thought of obeying my warlord?

A hollow rattle of metal echoed off the walls, startling him. A vagrant half a block down sifted through dumpsters, singing. He staggered by in a drunken lope, intoxicated to the point his sake-laden breath overpowered the reek of trash. Mamoru studied the darkness. The sense that someone watched him continued, yet nothing had shown itself. Once the fatigue of walking across the better part of Tokyo faded, he slipped into the crowd, still thick even close to midnight.

A few blocks from the factory, he had appropriated a long coat to hide his sword. The shame of having to conceal his katana twisted at the practicality of it. In his current attire, it would attract too much attention. He walked among the commoners, by appearance, no different from one of them. Anonymity had not been something he often enjoyed. At the same time it felt as alien as it did reassuring. Citizens paid him no more attention than they did the hundreds of advert-bots floating over their heads.

Mamoru crossed the square beneath Minamoto's imperious frown and exited on a street heading northeast. A crowd massed at the corner, waiting for the signal to change. Four security officers at the center of the intersection scanned the crowd, not an uncommon sight. Their full-face helmets eased his nerves, and he concentrated. The wisp of white light dancing across his arms drowned in the neon glow of commercialism.

The closest officer tapped the side of his helmet twice, paused, and slapped it. Mamoru's mirth fell to ice as the man took the helmet off. He looked away and down, moving with the crowd when the light changed. One of them shouted as the group reached the far side, making him glance back. Four figures, beige armor over dark blue jumpsuits, shoved their way through the trailing mass of people. A man flew to the ground, two women followed. A little girl sailed off her feet, screaming for her daddy. The shriek of a woman shoved to her knees came a second before the *crack* of a rifle on face, and an angry father landed unconscious next to his wailing daughter.

Out of instinct, civilians dropped where they were, shielding their heads with their arms in hopes of avoiding unwanted attention. The helmetless man pointed at Mamoru, the only person aside from the security forces still standing.

Mamoru ran, ignoring their commands to halt.

Low-born fools. They will derive pleasure from this. He snarled as he took a corner. The security force often bristled at the samurai's authority. When a rare opportunity such as this presented itself, they adored every minute of it. The officers rounded the building in pursuit as white radiance burst around Mamoru's entire body. Boosted by his *chi*, he leapt six lanes of traffic, causing a few cars to collide as their drivers gazed in awe at the fireball sailing overhead. His pursuers hesitated only a few seconds before they shot the tires out of enough vehicles to dam the flow. Screams rose in the night as citizens dove to the ground, begging for their lives.

They usually warn first. These fools are chasing promotions. He maintained his focus, pushing his run up past forty miles an hour as he zoomed through a series of cross streets. After stumbling to another alley, he collapsed against the wall, out of breath.

Minutes later, the helmetless security man appeared around the wall. "Mamoru, wai—"

The vibro katana passed through the armored chest plate before his brain could process the officer had spoken English.

Glowing vapor seeped out of the man and coalesced in a blanket of fog that swam around behind him. Blood sprayed out of a diagonal cut from left shoulder to midway down his right side. The officer's upper body slid from the rest and clattered to the street. Blood seethed and bubbled along the length of his vibro blade, crimson boiling off to gleaming metal in seconds, filling the area with the scent of burnt meat.

Mamoru's eyes widened as the mass of phantasmal energy roiled about for a few seconds before it took on the shape of a nude woman about six feet tall. She stumbled to her right, thigh-length lemon blonde hair swaying behind her. From height alone, she would stand out in Tokyo—even without skin the color of snow.

She found her balance and glared at him. "Bloody hell. Now I'm going to have to find someone else to wear."

Several people passing the mouth of the alley stopped to gawk at her.

He held the katana out, pointing it at her. The sight of her eyes, black onyx gems, stole the words from his mouth.

"You are rather difficult, Mamoru." She walked toward him, unconcerned with her lack of clothing. "When will you understand that I am trying to help?"

"You are the oni who took Nami." He shook the blade at her.

"I'm no demon, sweetie. If I was, that would make you one as well. We are more alike than you know." She glanced over her shoulder at the crowd. The appearance of her eyes changed lust to fear. "Do you like what you are staring at?"

Most of them ran, screaming.

She leaned back with a haughty laugh. Mamoru backed away.

"Don't tell me you are afraid of a woman, hon?"

"You are unnatural. No shame. No respect. Go back to your hell."

"Call me Aurora." Her hips swayed as she exaggerated her strut towards him. "Oh, don't back away. You need me."

"I do not need you." Mamoru lowered the blade, muttering under his breath. "Kami, take this oni from my sight."

Aurora tapped her foot. "For an intelligent man, you are a superstitious fool. Your abilities are not magic or some ancient mystical 'chi' nonsense. You are psionic. Your Shinto gods aren't going to pop up and whisk me off to some dreary hell. Stop looking at me like that. I thought you preferred your women confident." She folded her arms. "Besides, we've already more or less snogged."

"What is... snogged?" Mamoru raised an eyebrow.

She laughed to the point of crying. When she recovered, she blew a kiss at him. "Don't tell me you've forgotten already?"

Mamoru closed his eyes. "Don't mention that again. Nami was—"

"Thinking about it for weeks." Aurora made a dismissive wave. "Look,

I enjoy pushing people off center. I thought it would be funny to watch you squirm. But in all seriousness, I am here to help you. Exactly how do you expect to get yourself out of Tokyo alive? You'll do no one any good dead."

"Why should I tell you? How do I know you aren't working for Minamoto?"

"Well, first of all, I'm not Japanese. Your society doesn't trust outsiders enough to give them any power or responsibility. Second"—she waved her hand over her nakedness—"I'm a bit underdressed for a formal event."

I must get to Sapporo. He glanced at the open alley, beckoning him to run.

Her eyes narrowed as a trace of an amused smile formed. "What's in Sapporo?"

Mamoru backed up to the wall. She leaned against him, pinning him, straddling one leg. He could not help but study her curves. A woman taller than him, even by an inch, did something to his mind that left him speechless. Despite his best effort, he found himself staring at her breasts.

"You can touch them if you want, but I don't think you'll have enough time to enjoy it." She winked. "At least they'll buy you some time."

Before he could say a word, she whirled about to face the street. The three remaining security officers skidded to a halt, gawked at their dead compatriot, and aimed rifles at Mamoru.

Aurora struck a raunchy pose and jiggled her chest. The men did a double take, giving Mamoru the opportunity to move before they could fire. He roared, and the flame-like glow peeled along his arms. The alley smeared around him as he charged. In a flash of screeching plastisteel, the vibro-katana split the center man in half from crotch to skull. The other two broke to run, but the next managed only a step before the katana took his head.

The strange woman laughed again and arched her back before she vanished in a spectral haze that trailed after the remaining officer. Mamoru pursued until the man fell on all fours, clutching his chest and screaming. The odd seizure kept Mamoru a pace behind and to the left, katana held vertical.

"Would you mind not killing this one, luv?" Her accent emerged in the man's voice as he wobbled back to his feet. "I'll attract less attention wearing someone."

"What manner of oni are you?" asked Mamoru, adjusting his grip on the katana.

"I hope you're not going to be this difficult all the time." The officer, drenched in sweat, slung his assault rifle over one shoulder. "I told you already; I am psionic. As are you. Since Minamoto has declared you kill-on-sight, I imagine you need to get out of this prefecture as soon as possible. I've come to help. I'd rather not bother with asking, but I'm not fluent in Japanese and can't make much sense of what you are thinking."

"You are... inside that man?" Mamoru mumbled a self-protection prayer to the Kami. "I am not the same as you."

"If you tell me what is in Sapporo, perhaps I can be of more assistance?"

"It is the center of the prefecture governed by Yoshida-Nakano Corporation."

The officer adopted a decidedly feminine posture as he contemplated. Mamoru looked away. "They make hovercars. Is that all you need? There are plenty—"

"No. Their ways are similar to the West. Their laws are not bound up in the traditions of old." Contempt dripped from his voice. "Yoshida-san thinks it backward."

"It *is* backwards. You would be far safer with us, outside of Japan."

"I do not trust what you offer." He relaxed, sliding the katana into its scabbard.

Aurora's puppet followed as he strode off. "I'm trying to save you some time, Mamoru. You'll wind up in the West soon enough. Why can't you accept that I am a friend?"

He walked, not looking back at the entity following him. "There is no help you can give me. You cannot understand."

"A bit of a hard head, aren't you?" The possessed security man grumbled. "Awright then, suit yourself. I'll see ya in a couple of weeks."

A moment later, a shrill man's voice shrieked commands to drop the katana and wailed for backup. Mamoru glanced over his shoulder. Panic-stricken hands fumbled to bring the assault rifle to bear. Past the officer, a barely visible presence receded off down the street. Mamoru lunged, shoving the rifle down with one hand while smashing the other into the officer's helmet. Frustration and anger erupted in a brilliant flash of energy along Mamoru's arm. The security man sailed backward ten meters before he hit the ground and slid to a halt against a parked car with an echoing *whump*.

Mamoru gazed at his bleeding hand, once again studded with flakes of bullet-resistant plastic. He frowned as the strange woman's words echoed in his thoughts. *Psionic? Hmfh. I can't read minds. What does an oni intend to do but trick and deceive?* Some of the fragments fell out of his fingers as he clenched his hand into a fist. At the sound of sirens, he sent one last distrustful glare at the empty sidewalk and ran.

🐗 🕯 🎴 ⚪ 🗿

A DOZEN SECURITY OFFICERS CHASED MAMORU DOWN THE HUNDRED-METER long escalator to the subterranean tram system run by the Nippon Shōgyō-Kumiai. Citizens ignored the disturbance, heads down, walking as though nothing at all went on—unless one of the participants collided with them.

As the NSK guards at the main doors braced to stop him, Mamoru tapped his power. Everything fell into slow motion as he pushed himself out of the realm of human ability. The black jumpsuits seemed to freeze in time, their arms rising as if to command him to stop. He ran through, leaving them staring at the spot where he was before he blurred. Inside, he weaved among dozens of bodies twisting about in slow turns to see what all the shouting was.

Mamoru kept the pace for six seconds, long enough to go from the entrance to the security checkpoint by the boarding platform. He let his mind rest. The clamor of the crowd rolled over him as the perfect silence of accelerated existence faded. Advertising jingles, squealing children, a thousand conversations, and the now-distant shouts of the security forces left him disoriented. He fell onto a bench between two potted bamboo plants. A five-inch orb bot hovered about, watering them.

There, he sought stillness. He tapped another part of his mind, withdrawing to a state of meditation as he forced his breathing to even out. He did not move as the security team arrived. Their full-face helmets reflected the ceiling lights, stripes of intense white crept over glossy beige. Mamoru fixated on the camera dots at their temples that fed pass-through view screens.

Soldiers glanced at each other and turned in a circle. A moment later, they split up and ran off in different directions. When he could no longer hear them, Mamoru made his way to the checkpoint at a slow gait so as not to disrupt his concentration. Two women and a man in NSK jumpsuits sat behind the checkpoint station, staring at screens linked to a massive walk-through scanner. A large screen on the far wall presented a digital recreation of everyone as they went through, calling attention to cybernetic implants and any weapons.

Mamoru ducked through the sensor tunnel, dragging his fingers along the dark glass inside. *Be a good boy and pay no attention to me.* None of the three security people looked up from their screens.

Mamoru strolled to the tram, head down and mind racing.

COFFIN

Within the dingy streets of downtown Sapporo, Mamoru walked among a mass of people that could have existed in the West. They spoke Japanese, though much of the formality was absent. They dressed in the clothing of other cultures, listened to the music of other places, and few respected anything but money, the latest fad, or the newest designer narcotic. Even the smells that rolled by carried shame. Hamburgers, pizza, Indian spices, and other things all with the cloying undertone of OmniSoy.

At least, despite the incessant bump of careless shoulders, he was safe from Minamoto's misplaced wrath. To go after him here, they would have to contract through NSK. It was foolish to hope he would be safe for long. Minamoto's influence could affect the whole of Japan, despite his direct power being limited to the area around Tokyo. Mamoru did not care about building a new life here… all he wanted was enough time to repair what had been done.

Yellow-bordered green kanji flickered in the air up ahead, threatening to go dark at any moment when ancient wiring gave out at last. Tanoshī Yoru Economy Hotel, according to the sign, stood at the end of a U-shaped street filled with dirt-covered, shoeless children. Laundry fluttered in the air from an adjacent high-rise tower, the lack of electricity apparent by the darkness within. Torn barricades around the door indicated the building as condemned, which meant the hundred or so families that lived within it squatted.

Some of the kids noticed him, attracted by his clean, untorn clothing and general lack of grime. He walked past them to a dark, dusty space full of the smell of over-salted ramen. Hospital green overwhelmed the room, elevating the concept of drab to an art form. Yellowing plasfilm posters adorned the walls of a short entry corridor: missing kids, ads for off-Earth jobs, people looking for work. A dozen or so cheap tables occupied the center of a section set up like a restaurant. Left and right of the entry, stairways led to the upper floors. Two old men played cards at one of the tables, a few prostitutes clustered at the opposite side. A middle-aged woman busied herself behind the counter, disinterested in anything going on outside of her immediate vicinity.

Mamoru walked among the empty tables, sending a casual glance to the roof forty stories above. A central shaft about the same size as the dining area allowed a view of thirty-nine floors of coffin-sized beds. A handful of the children from outside followed him at a safe distance. The most forlorn, wide eyed, and dirty led the way. He approached the counter, standing under the flickering shadow of a ceiling fan.

"Yeah?" asked the hunched figure.

He did not respond until the woman looked at him. "I am in need of a place to sleep."

She squinted, annoyed at the disruption of her routine of nothingness. "By the night, by the week, or by the month?"

"I will start with a week."

The troll threw a glance in the general direction of a NetMini reader and fiddled with a terminal. "Two hundred an' forty."

Mamoru took a credstick from his pocket, and swiped the tiny three-inch device over it, causing a chime. No one looking for him would notice an untraceable transaction here. The presence of small bodies getting too close made him whirl. Five children jumped back. "You shall find my pockets contain nothing of value."

They offered well-rehearsed pouts. One girl surreptitiously pulled on her tattered dress to accentuate her bare shoulder peeking through a rip.

"Nabeyaki Udon." He glanced back to the troll. "For them as well."

A little boy broke away from the end of their group and ran to the door.

She flung her arm out, pointing at a dented silver appliance, an old atomic reassembler. "What do you think this is? I got shrimp or chicken."

"Shrimp." Mamoru grumbled, squeezed buttons on the credstick, and swiped it again.

"What the hell?" She slapped the terminal twice, not believing what she saw.

"That should be enough to feed the little ones about to flood in the door." He leaned toward her with a face of iron. "See that you do. It would be unwise to cheat me."

Cherubic faces smiled at him, though he did not stay to bask in their gratitude. After receiving his bowl of OmniSoy noodles, disposable chopsticks, and a bed assignment, he went upstairs. On the sixteenth floor, he left the switchback staircase in search of bunk 16-82. With the shape of each level being identical, and square, he needed only to follow the narrow corridor until his number came up.

The sleep chambers were stacked three high, some had their awning-like doors propped open while their occupants sat with dangling legs. A few people ran merchant stalls out of them, selling cheap electronics, quasi-legal drugs, performance enhancing derms, and holo-vids from artistic to pornographic. One even had an inventory of handguns and knives. A scrawny teen girl with bright pink hair, cat ears, and nothing else on, sat on the edge of a sleep pod, painting her toenails the same shade as her hair. Panties, a torn skirt, other clothes, and trash sat piled up against the foot-end wall inside. She looked up as he passed, and gave him a wink that said she was for hire.

An emaciated man rounded the corner. Too many nights sleeping in alleys had stained his clothes, and his eyes were unfocused. He waved his arms as if flying or swimming, and made sputtering engine noises as he wobbled past, oblivious to Mamoru's existence. A used, yellow autoinjector dangled between the fingers of his left hand.

He ignored the lot of it until he found his bed, mid-level along the wall near the front right corner. The wireless fob the creature behind the desk gave him beeped as he waved it by the handle, and the door creaked up with a pneumatic hiss. The space offered barely enough room to sit up, being about eight feet long and about as wide as needed to lie down in. A thin Comforgel pad lined the bottom with a chintzy plastic-foam pillow at one end. The inner wall contained a tiny common-use terminal with basic access to the GlobeNet.

That would be all he needed.

Mamoru set his weapon inside, followed by the Matsushita Oni deck. After removing his coat, he tossed it over the pillow and sat on the edge to choke down the pitiful excuse for food. The thin broth tasted like fish salt more than shrimp, and the noodles were mushy. One small squiggle of whitish matter floated in it, supposedly a shrimp. It had the consistency of a rubber band, and about as much flavor. The only good thing about the meal was that it had been convenient.

The cat-eared girl, not bothering to put anything on, walked up to him and struck a pose. A bright pink cat tail swished around her legs. "Hey, handsome. Wanna play?"

Mamoru didn't look up from his soup. "How much for you to cease pestering me?"

"Huh?" She twirled her finger through her hair and bit her lip. "I'm eighteen."

He set his chopsticks in the bowl and removed a credstick from his coat. A mere C7813 remained, but to her it would be a fortune. She had the reflexes of a cat, catching it as soon as he tossed it at her. Mamoru resumed attending to his soup, disappointed she didn't have to go chase it. The girl gawked at the figure on the display. When she started to crawl into his bunk, he palmed the top of her head, holding her back.

She grabbed his wrist, trying to pull his hand down. "What? You're not supposed to pet me."

"Go buy some food. I did not pay you for sex." He twirled a mouthful of noodles around the chopsticks, and ate.

The girl stared at him for a long moment. Confusion gave way to shame. Her tail dangled limp and straight. Her eyes reddened. She bowed. "Thank you."

"Mmm." He busied himself with his meal, half aware of the girl racing back to her bunk and getting dressed.

Expensive silence.

When the soup was gone, he reclined and pulled the hatch closed, careful to secure the lock. With one hand on the deck at his side, he sneered at the dull green metal above him. This tiny chamber was not his dojo.

He wanted to go home.

THE WHITE SAMURAI GLIDED DOWN A DESERTED STREET TOWARD A FAMILIAR factory. Indistinct shadow figures drifted past him wherever the citywide surveillance system detected a person. None of the random debris or decay existed in this world. Glowing yellow barriers cordoned off the facility. In the entry gate, a large yellow triangle with rounded ends and silver edges bore a black exclamation point, rotating above a redirection notice that the company had moved to Shōrishima. He disregarded them, entering what appeared to be a furnished and functional reception area.

A young woman wearing a plain black skirt suit materialized in the middle of the room, in front of a wooden counter. She bowed.

"Many apologies, sir. Our production operations have been relocated. This GlobeNet site is no longer maintained by Mitsubishi."

He walked around the program construct, which followed and recited a litany of offers of information. She stopped when he passed through a door at the rear of the lobby, and vanished a second later. Up ahead, a shimmering green orb floated through the virtual mock-up of the factory floor. Deep within the sphere, a hole offered a glimpse at the real world. Mamoru reached out, cradling the glowing presence in his hands. He drew it closer to his face until he slipped through the opening. His vision blurred to monochromatic green crossed by raster lines. Status readouts at the corners of the square view displayed statistics about temperature, battery life and cutter status.

The transition through the wireless control interface was tiring. His session in cyberspace felt as if he'd been inside for an eternity. He acclimated to the sensation of having eight limbs, and pivoted his borrowed body until he found the door to the small foreman's office. Murmured voices from behind the door made him pause. Nami and Ayame talked about their lives before. Mamoru, the giant metal spider, slouched and listened.

Ayame spoke of her grandmother and how the woman kept a small garden full of cats. She had two small brothers. Nami consoled her, saying little about her past life other than she was ashamed of what her father had done.

One metal leg rose up, extended forward, and knocked. The women fell silent. A minute later the handle pivoted and the door pulled open an inch. Nami peered out, startled by the sentry robot so close. She froze in place, knuckles whitening on the doorframe.

"Nami," said the robot, projecting a crackling version of Mamoru's voice into the world. "It is me."

Fear evaporated from her face. She pulled the door wide open. "Saitō-san? It is very late."

"I am pleased to see you are in good health." The arachnid

shifted, pointing one leg at the exit. "I have ordered you both clothes, food, and some things to help you leave Tokyo. Delivery bots should be arriving here within minutes. There is a new NetMini. I have created a PID for you under the name Hokama Kiyomi."

Nami reached out and touched the spider bot. "Kiyomi?" She blushed. "I am grateful for your compliment."

"The account has enough credits to allow you to establish yourself in Sapporo. I have altered records and made you owner of a respectable apartment. The details are in the 'mini."

She leaned her forehead against the machine. Mamoru's vision fogged from her breath. "Oh, Mamoru, when will you return?"

Ayame appeared in the doorway, wiping tears from her eyes.

"I do not know, Nami-chan. Perhaps when I am finished you will no longer need to wear the name of another."

"I am proud of the name you have given me. I am no longer burdened by my father's shame. Please, do not be reckless."

"Saitō-san, what of me?" asked Ayame. She moved up to Nami's side, and they held each other.

Two women who would never have crossed paths, as close as sisters. The large robotic spider shifted to Ayame. "Your detention records are gone. You should have no trouble returning to your family. I located surveillance video of the incident that portrays your encounter with the security forces in a different light. If your name crosses their network again, a dormant program will transmit it to the GlobeNet. The loss of honor would be irrecoverable. I have ensured they know this and will not bother you again."

Ayame fell to her knees, whispering for her grandmother, mother, and father.

Delivery bots floated in through the window. A short train of hovering machines left a pile of boxes outside the office.

Nami, now Kiyomi, rendered a formal bow at the car-sized robot. "Mamoru, you are not like them. You showed us kindness beyond what our station deserved. Please..." She stepped back, gazing down. "If you will not forget Minamoto now, please find me when you are at peace with who you are."

Ayame wrapped herself around one of the machine's legs, hugging it. "Yes, yes. Thank you."

"This robot will protect the two of you as long as you remain here.

Kiyomi-chan, leave Tokyo as soon as you are able and do not return. Ayame-chan, be good to your family. I must go now."

Mamoru ceased concentrating. The rectangular green window filled with Nami's face pulled back and sailed into the infinite black. His consciousness rubberbanded backward through the electronic world and crashed into his meat sack of a body. The reality of his miniscule living space flared in around him, the resplendent glory of dull green-tinted plastisteel and the stench of sweat. His work in the net had taken four hours of virtual time, a little more than one in the real world. Exhausted, he allowed the soothing warmth of the Comforgel pad to take him as the distant sound of happy children downstairs carried him off to sleep.

THE SCENT OF AUTUMN FILLED MAMORU'S SENSES. SOMEWHERE BEHIND him, the shrill laughter of a little girl tore the silence, filtered through the thickness of a dream's fog. Pain spread over the side of his head. He lifted his face from the leaves in which he had fallen and moved to his knees, cradling his head in his arms. Blue hakama pants stepped into his peripheral vision. Out of instinct, he leapt away as a wooden bokken struck the ground where he had once been.

The startled cry of a young boy, tinged with anger, came out of him as he staggered backwards, glaring up at a man cloaked in an odd familiarity. *Is that my father?* He rubbed the side of his head, cringing as he touched the spot where a strike had sent him face-first into a pile of leaves, the result of his entire morning spent raking. Father relaxed his combative stance and walked away to a neutral distance.

"Mamoru, you must learn to reach deep within yourself. Your *chi* is waiting. Pick up your weapon and ready yourself."

The boy scowled at the ground. Six feet away, another wooden sword lay where it had fallen. A little girl in a black kimono laughed at him, sparkling emerald eyes half closed, yet familiar. *Sister?*

"Father, why must we live so far away from the city?" Mamoru trudged to his weapon.

"There is nothing electronic here to distract you."

"It's boring," he whined. "There's nothing to do here."

"There is nothing to corrupt your focus."

His father raised his practice sword, a stance ten-year-old Mamoru mimicked. They circled, drawing nearer.

"If you continue to lose your head in those toys, you will not uncover your true potential. Again, as before. Do not let me see you being lazy, or I'll give you another good whack."

Mamoru struggled to deflect a series of quick but light strokes as he backpedaled. When he did not counterattack, his father pressed the attack with more speed and strength. A blur of wood ended with an agonizing crack across the shoulder blades that knocked him flat. Mamoru rolled on his side, wheezing. Again, the girl laughed.

"Disappointing, boy." Father stomped off. "Get up. Again. You're not even trying to strike."

Mamoru grunted and rolled to his knees. "Every time I try to attack you, you hit me."

"He hits you when you don't attack, too," chirped the girl.

Ebon hair blew in his face as he squinted at her. She gave him a silent raspberry. His sister looked to be about two years his junior. Mamoru remembered being jealous of her not having to do this. All he wanted was to go back to their city home and enter the GlobeNet again. In there, he was as strong as a Kami. In there, he had power.

A woman emerged from the trees with a tray bearing tea. *Mother.*

"Pay attention, boy. If you want food tonight, you'll hit me once."

"This isn't fair." Mamoru grasped the bokken, leaning his weight on it as he struggled back to his feet. "I can barely move. I think you broke my back."

His father spun the wooden blade point-down, resting both hands on the end. "You are correct. This should not be a fair duel. I know you find it difficult to believe, but it should be you knocking me senseless. Tap your *chi*." He gestured at the forest. "We are surrounded by nature, where the Kami dwell. To be here is to be with them. Call on them."

"I don't know how."

The woman set the tray down near the girl. "Perhaps the reports were wrong?"

"They are not wrong." Father slid the false blade through his belt and moved behind him. Mamoru squirmed to look up as he positioned his arms in a proper stance. *He is my father. Why does he hate me so? What did I do?*

"It is the same as with your electronic toys." Father's hands slid down Mamoru's arms. "The white light will empower your body. Focus your desire inward rather than outward. Think of your muscles and bones as another machine."

Mamoru stared at his hands, clenched around a handle too large to be comfortable. All he wanted was for his father to show some hint of affection or approval. He wanted a mere scrap of the attention they showered on his sister. His fingers whitened at the knuckles as he tried to link himself to the wooden blade. There was no presence within it, nothing for his thoughts to touch. Father gripped his arms and helped him find a proper stance before moving away.

His father drew the bokken with a flip over his hand and faced him. Mamoru scowled, focusing on his feelings of resentment. Mother and sister having tea and smiling at each other brought strength to his sorrow. He gazed down the length of his sword at the trees. Father moved in, a blur in his periphery. Mamoru wanted this to stop. Anger swelled within his heart and he screamed, springing into an unexpected forward lunge.

Wooden blades crossed, though Mamoru's attack shattered his father's bokken and swatted the man to the ground. The boy's body trembled with energy and rage; blade down and to the left, he kept his head low while the fire shimmered over his shoulders. A teacup clattered onto its saucer to his left, amid startled gasps from his mother and sister. When he looked up from the grass between his toes, he caught a fleeting glimpse of luminous wisps around his forearms. Father wound up some distance away on his back with his legs in the air. Mamoru's jaw dropped as he took on a posture of concern.

"Father? Are you hurt?"

A growl became a cheer as the man swung his legs down with enough force to pull him upright, seated on the ground. "That's it, boy. Excellent!" He blinked at the cracked bokken, and tossed it aside. "I am proud of you."

Mamoru beamed. He had finally earned his father's affection.

From everywhere in the woods at once, a series of muted *pops* rang out, followed by fleshy *thumps*. Blood spurted out of his father's mouth. His white haori turned red, torn left and right by a hail of unseen bullets. Sister shrieked. Mamoru spun, but mother had already fallen over. The tea set—and the little girl—were spattered crimson.

Six men emerged from the trees with compact rifles aimed. Their skin-clinging garments shifted in a myriad of colors, making them appear as if they wore the forest. Seconds after they walked into view, the suits turned black. His sister jumped on their dead mother, wailing, screaming at her to get up. One of the approaching men fired two more bullets at the corpse of his father.

The world flashed white with rage and sorrow. When sight returned, his bokken swung with enough force to tear a man in half through the gut. His arms throbbed with pain, streams of energy wafted from them as he raised the blade again. One attacker pointed a gun at him, but another shoved him aside.

"We want him alive, fool."

Mamoru swiveled to face them. The sharp turn caused his wooden blade to fall apart. He dropped it and ran at the nearest assassin, driven by blind hatred. His scrawny arm sank to the elbow in the next man's chest, followed by a paralytic flash of agony. The wheezing man fell in a heap, alive but out of the fight. Mamoru cradled his bloody, broken hand. His anger stalled until the screams of his sister snapped him out of a daze. He sprinted for the figure who dragged her away from Mother by a fistful of kimono, failing to spot a leg sweep from another assassin that left him sliding on his chest.

Before he could get up, the high-pitched whine of a needle-gun screamed over him, and burning swarmed across his back. Pain became numbness. His muscles lost strength as he struggled with a man binding his arms.

The forest blurred into darkness.

APEX HORIZON

Mamoru awoke with the sound of his sister's voice screaming in his memory. Exhaustion spread through his limbs, and he lay staring at the ceiling of his small sleep chamber for several minutes before moving. He had not thought of her in years. Was it the little beggar girl staring at him last night that triggered the memory?

A glowing button with the kanji for "open" sat at the upper left corner of the space. He bumped it with an elbow, causing the hatch to whirr open on motorized struts. Mamoru yawned and swung his legs over the side, sitting for a moment with his face balanced in his palm. *Never have I slept in such squalor.* Chilly air rolled in, forcing the stagnant warmth out of his nest. With it came the stench of humanity, poverty, and horrible food.

He wiped a hand over his cheek before balancing his chin on his fist. His tiny room sat near a corner, with bunks on both sides. The facing wall gave way ten meters to his right, where chain link fence covered the open areas that looked out to the central shaft. Dozens of holo-panels flew about in the middle, advert bots. The distant, echoing voice of a soft-spoken woman urged people to contact the NSK for employment opportunities on colony worlds. Better to be prosperous on a new planet than live in the gutter of the old one.

A stretch worked some of the kinks out of his back and made him miss his attended bath. Eyes closed, he tried to remember how it felt to have servants bathe him. In seconds, his mind went to the face Nami made while under the influence of the strange creature. Mamoru forced the sight from his memory and ambled off toward the floor's communal bathroom.

Hot water jets inside the autoshower were a poor substitute for Nami's delicate fingers, but they still managed to ease life back into his body. He stood like a statue, staring at the fluttering grey privacy curtain until the dry cycle stopped. Mamoru frowned at the narrow confines of the tube, wondering what had become of his former home and its opulent bathtub.

After dressing, he returned to his tiny rented bed and used the wall terminal to summon real food. He busied himself by going through several warm up katas in the hallway until a silver box floated out of the stairwell and approached his chamber bearing his breakfast. He ate, seething about the golden angel, the likely source of his fall from grace.

Several men in street-weary coats covered in gang symbols came around the corner. They proceeded in a methodical search of bunks, checking for locked doors. When they found one that was, and no one responded to a knock, the shortest of their number produced a handheld device and set about hacking it open. Several of them carried handguns, which caused him to raise an eyebrow. Few CEOs allowed firearm ownership among their citizens, even one as "modern" as Yoshida-Nakano Corporation. It was possible the local security forces permitted it, or simply turned a blind eye. Either way, it was not his problem to deal with.

Mamoru finished off his food while the men looted the bunk. Annoyed at finding nothing of value, they continued opening and closing doors until they were near enough to see the black Matsushita Oni deck resting on the Comforgel behind him. The group stood idle for a moment, sizing him up.

"Nice hardware," said one with neon yellow hair.

Mamoru turned a chopstick through his fingers. "It is adequate."

On the left, one with black hair with an inch of white at the end took a step closer. "Let's have it."

"No." Mamoru gazed at the rotating utensil.

The gangers shifted and grumbled, some glancing at their displayed weapons as if questioning Mamoru's sanity.

One grabbed his pistol. Mamoru's right arm burst with energy. A flick of his finger sent the chopstick through the hand as well as the gun, lodging it in the man's hip. The now-screaming punk stared the blood dribbling down his fingers while collapsing to the ground. Captivated by the glowing light, the others turned pale.

"I have just enjoyed a restful night, a hot shower, and a pleasant meal. It would be regrettable for you to intrude on my inner harmony at this juncture." Mamoru slipped his vibro katana across his lap, still in the scabbard. "By your armament, I see you have little honor and less respect for the law. I too, do not rely on the security forces to settle my affairs." He snapped his gaze up, making them jump. "Shall we agree that what is mine is mine?"

They retreated, dragging their wounded fellow to his feet. He had worked his hand free of the chopstick, but had not been able to get it out of his hipbone. Mamoru glared as they stumbled through a door to the stairwell, waiting for one to go for a weapon again. When silence returned, he withdrew to the coffin bed and secured the hatch. Now, he had work to do.

APEX HORIZON EXISTED BEYOND THE REALM OF KNOWN SPACE IN THE GlobeNet. Stylized as the bastard offspring of a nightclub, a bar, and a temple to cyberspace, it sometimes appeared on network surveys as being located far off the western coast of South America most of the way toward Antarctica. Some had tried to reach it by navigating the virtual world using program constructs simulating aircraft or boats. It existed well removed from any area of the net where corporations had interest. None of that region had been defined beyond a basic blue-on-black grid, the bones of the net.

Those who attempted the journey were often disappointed, as Apex Horizon did not exist in physical space in the sense one would have expected. Only those skilled enough to circumvent the GlobeNet Consortium's travel protocols could get there, as to the outside world it was the size of a pinhead. Three pixels wide by one pixel tall, the entrance needed to be targeted with specificity as the landing point for a 'teleportation.' Most who knew of it described it as occupying a parallel dimension through a pinhole in a false reality.

As a boy, Mamoru had sifted through the topography of cyberspace until he found the point. The last time he visited, he was nine, but everyone there thought he was a grown man playing a child. Surely, a simple boy could not have found the place. One had to be eighteen to get implants, and no one using a senshelmet could be good enough to teleport. He doubted anyone would remember him.

With a thought, he appeared a step inside the door. Numerous denizens stopped in mid-conversation to evaluate the samurai armor now floating in their world. His avatar seemed mundane by comparison to some: soldiers, spies, superheroes, a nude elf woman, space aliens, medieval knights, and several anthropomorphic animals ranging from humans with cat ears to full-on bipedal dogs. Everyone stared at him only long enough for an opinion on his avatar to form on their faces before resuming their various activities.

Ahead and left, a topless medusa tended the bar. On the other side, down a short flight of stairs, a dance floor flashed and throbbed with lights and music. Right of the bar, a passage led to an area lifted out of a milieu of entertainment vids. Most of the avatars congregating there seemed to be rabid fans of one space vid series or another.

He glided to the medusa, but disregarded her once he realized she was a program. A drunken mutter emanated from the people near that side of the room. Recreational softs stimulated the same neurons as alcohol, creating a sense of inebriation that lingered as long as a person remained plugged in. Mamoru took the passage to a room designed in the image of a nonexistent starship's interior. No one that caught his eye seemed like a reliable source of information.

"New faces… or the lack thereof, are rare here."

The woman's voice came out of nowhere, silky and alluring.

"I am looking for someone," said Mamoru as he whirled around.

Golden eyes glimmered with unearthly light, set in a face of dark crimson. White fangs flashed through an impish smile. Draconic wings flexed as she studied him, accompanied by the swishing of a long, thin tail tipped with an onyx barb. A few scraps of tattered black leather clung with no apparent support over her breasts. The rest of her clothing consisted of a loincloth no wider than a hand, draped over a silver chain belt. Aside from the dark red skin, her features looked European.

Mamoru frowned at cute little horns protruding from her temples. "Your subroutine is ineffective on me, woman. Your software cannot affect the pleasure centers of my brain."

With a demure glance to the side, she stepped back. "I am Naamah, and this is my home."

"Your name is not unfamiliar to me. Word of your elusiveness has reached even Japan."

"Yet I know nothing of you." She looked him up and down. "You do not even seem to exist here."

"That is because I have instructed the system to disregard me."

Naamah's eyes gleamed, excitement tinged with anger. "No one has ever been able to defeat my security protocols before. Who are you?"

"I am"—he hesitated. He expected this woman to be foreign due to her use of English, and spoke his name in western order—"Mamoru Saitō."

She cocked an eyebrow. "That's it, no fancy nickname? Can't say I've ever heard of you." Black clawed fingernails scraped down his chest in a playful swipe.

He caught her wrist and concentrated. Naamah's smile lasted a few seconds before she tried to pull back, but could not get away.

"You are linked to four decks simultaneously, which you have arranged in a multiprocessing cluster. A Titan Alchemist for your soft storage, a Nishihama Berserker, grade 9... Most impressive. The other one"—Mamoru's empty helmet tilted upward, his body not moving despite the succubus jerking at her arm—"NinTek Netspider, and a Vostochnaya Proizvodstva Oboroten."

She stumbled away as he let go. Anger burned in her eyes, but her mouth hung open with fear.

"VP does not export its hardware outside of the ACC, even to neutral nations. Between that and the route path your signal is taking, I'm going to say you're located somewhere near Chernobyl but routing through Moscow, Warsaw, and Helsinki to mask your trail. Resistance?"

Terror won the battle for her face.

Mamoru held up a hand. "I do not wish to bring discord to your life. The quarrel you have with your government is none of my concern."

"How the fuck did you do that?" Her claws extended several inches to dagger blades, while her tail thrashed side to side. "It would have taken *me* at least ten minutes of hammering to get through *one* of my barriers."

"I did not break through your barriers, Inna Markov," he whispered. "I became them. Check for yourself. You will find no trace of my passage."

"What are you? An AI? A Sage?"

"I am neither. Several days ago, someone breached the network of Matsushita Electronics using the avatar of a gold-armored angel." Mamoru held out his hand. A six-inch tall version of the entity from his dojo appeared above his palm, spinning. "In the same way that you do not see my presence here, I was unable to find his. I was unaware that there were others who possess my gift."

Naamah let her claws shrink back to fingernails. "You just invaded my systems in seconds and know more about me than anyone else in the entire GlobeNet. What is it you think I can help you with?"

"I traced the signal to the interplanetary relay. I believe he may be on Mars. My abilities in this place are not like yours. I do not possess the same degree of technical knowledge. Machines do what I ask them. Is it possible for someone to do such a thing over so great a distance and remain a threat?"

"So you are the one that's caused all the fuss in the land of the rising sun? Your former boss is quite upset. There are a lot of credits looking for you." She circled him, tracing her tail around his leg. "Pleasant Evening coffin motel? You're not so far from home." Her eyes narrowed as she made her way around and stopped in front of him. "I can help you if you promise to return the favor should I need it."

"If your request is honorable, I will help you."

Naamah's tail caressed the inside of his thigh. "You are correct. The latency on an interplanetary link would make GlobeNet infiltration and combat impossible. I know of a technique to ghostscript a session and prepare an attack in advance. It is quite difficult to pull off as the user would have no indication that anything on the target network changed between when they took the copy and when they transferred the infiltration routine to an Earth-side server and ran it."

"So you are saying this person did not have a real-time link?"

She guided him out of the center of the room, one hand on his arm. A high tech starship door parted with a hiss, revealing a hallway made of dark grey stone—something out of a medieval castle. Naamah ducked into a shaded alcove with a pair of skeletons hanging by manacles. She wound her arms through dangling chains and grasped them, mimicking being shackled.

The samurai armor clicked as he folded his arms. "I do not find your display attractive."

"Are you Japanese, or dead?" She let go of the restraints and pouted.

"I know you are not as you appear to be, and I do not care for weakness."

"What's her name?"

Mamoru glanced to the side.

"Ahh, so there is a girl."

"It is too early to derive truth from manipulation. However, that is none of your concern. Where can I find this golden angel?"

One fang, ivory against crimson, poked out of her mouth as she bit her lip. "There is only one person I know of who is both skilled enough to compromise your network from Mars and has an affectation for the angelic. He calls himself Raziel, after the heavenly keeper of secrets. He has done many things within the net that people thought impossible. Are you sure you are as unique as you claim?"

"Indeed. Where on Mars can I find him?"

"Remember you said you would help me." She leaned toward him with an aggressive wave.

"I admire the way you alter your affect to render yourself tempting. I apologize if my nature frustrates you. Yes, I will help you if there is honor in your request."

Naamah sighed and hooked her thumbs through her chain belt. "I'm not exactly sure. Couple of months back, things got shitty in Kiev and I tried to reach out to him. Most of the MarsNet doesn't even believe he exists." She leaned around him, peering at a man in a white suit in the 'starship.' He appeared to be made entirely of bronze, with visible gears turning about inside him. "Ooh, gotta go. An important friend is here. He does exist, I'm sure of it, but all I can tell you is that some of his outbound connections were marked with a locator of *Araphel*. That must be important."

She slipped away, sashaying over to the bronze man. As soon as she was within arm's reach, his aristocratic expression melted to a dopey grin. Mamoru shook his head as her software tweaked the pleasure centers of the man's brain.

"Araphel?" Mamoru glanced at the ceiling. "Well then, Raziel. It is time for us to meet in person."

PURSUIT

Creating a boarding pass for a Mars-bound shuttle was an easy diversion between leaving Apex Horizon and logging out. The difficult part fell somewhere between accepting the concept of leaving Earth and making it to the launch platform within the NSK region of Shōrishima. Mamoru had little doubt that Minamoto had arranged a contract with them for his elimination. Aside from facilitating trade between a dozen fragmented, warring prefectures and the outside world, assassination was their leading service. Traveling to their territory would all but guarantee an incident.

He hoped the shuttle's in-flight food would be tolerable.

With his blade under his coat and his deck slung over his shoulder, he left the coffin motel and walked for several blocks. The early evening air was crisp, carrying the fragrance of the ocean as well as the squeaky voice of the pink-haired anthropomorphism of the latest Yume Koujou video game console, projected from an advert bot. Forty feet above, an enormous holographic anime teen waved and greeted her fans. Mamoru moved in a brisk zigzag, weaving through the crowd at a speed sufficient to foul the aim of any sniper looking for him.

The closer he got to the business district of Sapporo, the thicker the streets were with people. Perfume, sweat, and the occasional drift of food mixed with the metallic flavor of hovercar downdraft. Less traditional than most of Japan, the Yoshida-Nakano Corporation did not regulate the sale of hovercars, much like the UCF. Anyone who could afford the cost could buy one. However, taking them out of the prefecture could prove problematic. Despite the risk, it was still his best way to Shōrishima.

Mamoru went through the heart of the city, heading for the first parking facility he could find. The attendant at the booth paid him little mind, no doubt thinking him another man who had worked late. An odd feeling ran down his spine as he slipped down the stairwell. He tugged his coat open and kept a grip on his katana.

He paused at the exit to the thirty-ninth floor, listening. A sense of malice lingered on the other side of the wall, accented by the sound of a blade sliding from its sheath. The automatic door squeaked open as he advanced, allowing the cold of the windowless space to blow over him. Drying rain collected in puddles among the columns and a handful of parked cars.

Three paces in, he spun to his right. He whisked the katana free of its sheath and bisected a black-clad figure that leapt at him from behind. The upper body sailed past him on the right while a clear-bladed Nano sword passed on his left and stuck into the floor. Mamoru pivoted, attacking a hissing coming up from the left. His blade took a Nano shuriken out of the air, shattering it on contact. Mamoru locked eyes with a second man an instant before the assassin ducked out of sight behind a column about ten meters away. A scraping sound warned him of a third above him, who peeled away from the ceiling as if the concrete had come to life. Mamoru's body glowed as he channeled psionic energy through his muscles. The falling ninja slowed, his downward stroke became a triviality to avoid. His opponent's suit retained the color and pattern of concrete, down to the water stains.

The ninja landed in a slow tumbling roll, which surged to normal time as the man's neuralware activated. Concrete texture faded to black as the man sprang at him with a follow-up attack. Mamoru parried hard enough to knock the ninja into a stagger, returning a sideways slash that passed over the ninja as he flung himself to the ground. The ninja kicked into a backflip, and a ten-inch blade sprouted through the tip of his boot from an implant known as a 'raptor.' Mamoru leaned to the right, catching his weight on one hand. The blade passed over his head.

He shoved off the floor, standing as the ninja moved in with a series of quick side to side slashes. Mamoru deflected them with ease, but realized it a ruse to occupy his blade too late. A precise kick to his arm numbed it; his katana slipped from his fingers and clattered to ground. The assassin pressed his advantage, forcing Mamoru back with two missed beheading strikes.

Psionic energy rushed through his muscles, driving reflexes to their limit and dragging the world to a near standstill. Mamoru caught the man's arm at the wrist on the next swing, grunting at the contest of strength. A soft *click* announced the raptor blade an instant before a foot flew for the underside of Mamoru's chin. Shifting his power from speed to strength, Mamoru shoved back on the arms and caught the man by the ankle in a bone-crushing grip. He roared as his body lit aflame, and swung the ninja by the leg, smashing him against the wall and then the floor. Mamoru wrenched the foot around with a splintering crunch, reducing the limb to a formless ruin, before stabbing him through the chest with his own implanted weapon.

Mamoru stumbled to the side, snarling at the twisted mess of a corpse.

A fourth figure circled to his left, at a greater distance than the others—hesitating. Mamoru ran to his katana, snatching it from the ground before blurring in a superhuman sprint past the column where the shuriken-thrower hid. He ran past him, stabbing backwards. The hypersonic blade sank into the concrete. Smoke poured from where the seething hot blade touched flesh.

The man gurgled, feebly attempting to retaliate with a set of metal blades that sprouted out through his knuckles. Mamoru grunted in disapproval, jerked the katana free, and spun through a one-handed swing that decapitated the assassin before his knees met the floor. He stood with the blade held out to the side, where the swing ended, letting blood steam away.

His senses told him one ninja remained—the one that kept distance.

"You cannot hide from me."

Stillness pervaded the thirty-ninth floor, save for the disquieting presence of the active vibro blade. He pivoted to lead with his left shoulder, holding his sword with both hands as he roamed in a circle.

"Mamoru," said a female voice behind him. "I can see how tired you are."

He froze, confident the source was far enough away not to be an immediate threat. "Sadako."

Mamoru lowered the blade, turning as her head covering melted away from her face. Melancholy surrounded her like a cloak. Sweat beaded on his face, but he did not let fatigue show in his breathing.

"You surprise me with your gesture of respect. Your kind are often keen to seek a disreputable advantage."

"I would prefer that neither of us die. I do not wish to kill you. Whatever has caused Minamoto to seek your death, his reach is far weaker outside of Japan. Any corporation in the West or the ACC would be honored to welcome you. You could even find work in China."

He loosened his grip on the rubberized handle, the vibro inducer stopped. "My intention is to find whatever has influenced Minamoto, and restore things as they should be. I will return home when that is done."

"You can't set it right. Minamoto had no more loyalty to you than any of his other tools. You were an asset in his war chest." She moved her arms up to fold them, slow enough not to seem threatening, and without looking at him. "The NSK does not know what made him discard such a powerful weapon."

"I cannot simply leave. I must avenge this insult to my honor."

"You are stubborn, Mamoru!" she yelled, at last making eye contact. "They will kill me for failing if you remain in Japan."

"When I understand what oni has influenced Minamoto, I will destroy it and he will satisfy the contract."

Sadako thrust her arms down. "It's not that simple! It is an internal matter. If I fail, my life is over. They will not make it quick." A tear gathered at the corner of her eye for a second before running down her cheek. "We are all slaves, Mamoru. All of us. If you will not listen to reason, and leave Japan for good—"

"I cannot allow this affront to go unanswered."

"Stubborn," she muttered, and reached up over her shoulder to her sword. "If you will not leave, then I would prefer a quick death at your hand to the pain of failure."

Her ninjato glowed cyan as the transparent Nano blade caught the harsh overhead lights.

"You can leave." Mamoru shifted ninety degrees to his right.

Life seemed to fade from her eyes. "There is a component inside my neural interface. If I betray them, it will release nanobots that will devour me from the inside. I have heard it takes four agonizing days to die. If you insist on remaining in Japan, you must kill me."

She leapt. He got his blade up in time to stall her attack and the next two that followed—barely. Mamoru backpedaled, all of his concentration required to defend. Sadako's technique was perfect. On equal footing, no cybernetics or psionics, he had no doubt she would defeat him. They circled for several paces before she feinted back and thrust. Point down, his katana pushed her attack aside with the sound of scraping blades. She did not attempt to oppose his strength advantage, instead yielding to the force and gaining a few paces of distance by using his defense to fling her away. Her neuralware kicked on, rendering her as an ebon blur for an instant before his kinetic psionics compensated. Her body solidified out of a smear of color, sailing at him a hair shy of normal speed. She was faster than the other ninja—higher in rank, she had better hardware. Again, Mamoru deflected the strike. Awakened kinetics pushed his body beyond the limits of cybernetics, but the advantage he enjoyed in speed she countered with skill.

They stalemated.

"The poison metal within you is impressive, but you are still slower. I did not know your kind worked so hard on technique."

Sadako narrowed her eyes. "You try to intimidate me, but I know you cannot keep this up for long. You will tire long before the wires burn me."

She slashed and advanced, he turned each strike before he bled, but suffered a few rips to his coat. Sadako faked a sword stroke and spun in the other direction with a kick. He caught her ankle, boot an inch from his face. He twisted his grip, forcing her foot away as a thin plastisteel blade snapped out from between her big toe and the next, leaving a cat scratch on his cheek. She grunted, trapped for a second.

"I had to learn or die. The NSK teaches with steel, not wood."

Mamoru threw her leg to the side and raised his weapon, still powered down.

"Why aren't you attacking? My *metal poison* does not make me tired. This will end in my favor if you hesitate."

"This is no fight, Sadako. You are committing seppuku."

With a series of lunging swipes, she forced him back. The speed disparity allowed him to keep her Nano sword at bay, sparing his katana any damage. Scraping, buzzing, angry sounds echoed over the bare concrete parking deck. It was a game of angles. A direct meeting with such a sharp edge would destroy his blade, but the hypersonic katana could also shatter the synthetic diamond if he managed to slash it on the spine. Her technique faltered with desperation, she lost focus of her environment and overextended. Mamoru's defense knocked her sword to the left in a wide arc that sliced a head-sized chunk out of a column.

"You are not really trying to kill me," he said, rasping for breath.

He backed away while she struggled to free her weapon.

"Please, Mamoru... leave Japan and do not return."

"You know I cannot."

Sadako put her foot on the column. "Then, you must spare me a horrible death."

She yanked her sword loose, and ran at him with the blade high and to the right. Ten feet away, Sadako leapt. She passed overhead in a somersault, swiping down at him. Mamoru kicked his legs forward, letting gravity take him to the floor.

Sadako is going to kill me if I don't end this now.

She recovered from the maneuver and started back at him. He rolled over and flowed to his feet, pushing his powers to the point of pain. Vaporous energy billowed across his arms and shoulders, a flickering beacon that bathed the entire area in eerie light. Sadako, even with her neuralware on, slowed as he brought his body to the limits of his *chi*. Fire burned in his lungs, every muscle felt as though it was on the verge of peeling loose from his bones.

Her ninjato came around, going for his throat. He threw his weight forward, sliding under her strike and scoring across her side with an unpowered katana.

Sadako skidded to a halt on her knees a few feet away, having lost her grip on the blade. She cradled her side with both arms, spitting up blood from a punctured lung. The blow was not mortal, given access to medical treatment, but it left her in no state capable of fighting. She leaned forward, letting a tendril of snot-blood fall from her lip. He remained motionless, sword held out, as he let his power ebb. Mamoru closed his eyes, trying to force guilt out of his heart. At the sound of his blade sliding into its scabbard, she grunted in pain and looked up.

"F-finish it. If you leave me like this, I will be forced to kill myself."

"Do not lie to me, Sadako. Your kind have no honor. This is a ruse intended to lure me close enough for some hidden poison."

"You are wrong, Mamoru." Her head sagged and she coughed up blood. "I do not wish to kill you, nor could I if I wanted to. Your power is too great. Why do you spare me? I have failed."

Mamoru remained quiet for a moment, listening to her labored breathing. She tried to get up, gasping and collapsing to the floor when her arm gave out. He moved behind her and took a knee. She lifted her chin, exposing her neck. He put a hand on the side of her head and leaned around, staring at her dark emerald eyes.

"Beautiful things should not be broken carelessly."

Blood seeped through her lips as she tensed in pain. Energy simmered along his arm as his thoughts ran through the wiring embedded within her flesh. Sadako convulsed, spitting a glop of red slime over her chin. Her arms fell away from her wound. Metal claws shot out of her fingertips and retracted an instant later. The glow faded and she slumped to the ground, eyes closed. He replaced her sword in its sheath before gathering her in his arms and carrying her like a rag-doll to the nearest hovercar.

"You would have won, Sadako, if you were really trying to kill me."

A hand on the roof allowed him to invade the electronics and open the doors. He eased her to rest across the back seat, and climbed in up front. Glow seeped over his arms while his consciousness inhabited the machine. Unlike the Fūjin, embodying a hovercars came as second nature to him. After the battle, even that small exertion hurt, but he had no time to wait. The car leapt skyward with practiced grace, slipping through the narrow gap at the west edge of the parking garage. With the navigation unit part of his thought process, Mamoru turned in the direction of the Sapporo Medical Pavilion as if second nature.

Less than three minutes later, he set down on the roof by the MedVan arrival pad. Two security officers, their dark blue uniforms unkempt by Matsushita standards, approached, gesturing as if to shoo him away from an improper landing. Mamoru caused the right rear door to open, giving them a clear view of the unconscious woman in the back seat. Their shouts summoned an attendant with a hover gurney.

"W-where are we?" asked Sadako, barely awake.

Mamoru's voice filled the cabin over the stereo. "Recover your strength. Do not fear their wrath."

The security officers put their hands on their sidearms at the sight of the 'burning' unconscious man in the driver's seat. Once Sadako was clear of the car, he jumped airborne again and closed the rear door with a roll.

APPROACHING FOUR HUNDRED MILES PER HOUR, MAMORU FLEW IN A DIRECT line to Shōrishima. As the glittering artificial island drew near, he slowed and aimed for the center where the NSK had established its domain. He landed on the roof of a residential tower within sight of the starport and disengaged his mind from the vehicle. Mamoru slouched in the seat as a penetrating ache ran up and down his limbs, one that he would know for a few days.

He drifted in and out of sleep for about an hour before he summoned the desire to move. A stray thought popped the driver side door, which rose with a weak hiss. He pulled himself to his feet and made his way to the edge of the roof, pausing to gaze out at the artificial city. The placid quiet let him release his anger and fear, and he attempted to bring calm to his mind.

The starport resembled a pink-orange basin scooped out of the metropolis, surrounded by a ten-story perimeter wall intended to divert the powerful thrust of starships. The sky over it came alive with thousands of flying specks of light. The hologram-lit city around it appeared dark by comparison. From this vantage, Shōrishima seemed quiet and peaceful, but he had heard stories of street warfare between the NSK and Yakuza.

He closed his eyes, took several slow, deep breaths, and clapped his hands twice. *Kami, watch over Sadako. Guide her to safety.* He clapped again. Cold ocean-touched air ran up the face of the building and lofted his hair. Mamoru bowed in thanks, taking it as an acknowledgement, and went to the stairs.

The starport had a modest crowd, even at this hour. Most of its traffic was cargo the NSK handled between the various corporations of Japan and points beyond Earth. With the current treaty arrangement, ninety percent of cargo leaving the country was destined either for Arcadia city on Mars or to more distant colony settlements under the protection of the UCF. All parties tended to ignore a small degree of trade with the ACC, primarily with the intention of maintaining the tenuous peace that remained on the planet of humanity's origin.

Mamoru clung to the strap holding his deck against his back as he traversed the concourse, one unassuming figure among many. He followed a handful of people through security checkpoints he did not permit to detect his katana. After a short walk through a boarding tube, he settled in a seat near the back where he had "purchased" tickets for the entire row. Added to the bag with his Matsushita Oni deck, the concealed sword escaped the notice of the flight crew.

Vigilance remained for the near hour it took to get airborne. Mamoru feigned rest, but kept a wary eye out for another visit from the NSK. He glanced out the window as the hundred-meter long craft shuddered and rose from the landing pad. When it had cleared the level of the starport wall, acceleration pushed him against the seat. In seconds, the ground fell away and the midnight blue of the sky darkened to black.

He thought about Sadako, wondering where she was within the narrow strip of light that Japan had become. His homeland receded to a speck in the ocean, which soon became a shrinking blue and white marble rotating beneath him. Sunlight crept around the distant edge, shimmering over clouds that resembled soap bubbles. Daytime at the edge was still hours away from reaching his home. For a moment, he pictured Nami's face superimposed on the Earth, the last worried look she had given him before he left the robot.

What shall I do if she is genuine?

14

KILL THE MESSENGER

Twenty-seven hours after Mamoru left Earth, the shuttle landed amid a plume of crimson dust. To his right, the city of Arcadia glistened like an immense snow globe in the Martian desert. A city as large as Tokyo blinked and flashed under a transparent multilayered dome supported by a framework of plastisteel spars.

"Attention passengers: Please note that atmospheric terraforming operations on Mars are incomplete. While some areas of the planet's surface contain breathable air, many do not. Depending on the prevailing wind conditions, air quality in the area around Arcadia city can vary from acceptable to toxic. For your own protection, RedLink Corporation asks that you follow the safety procedures mentioned in our pre-flight media presentation. We are not responsible for injury or death occurring from improper use of doors. The boarding ramp will be arriving in a few minutes and a complimentary tram will take you to the city."

He gathered his bag and took a position among the stream of passengers jockeying for position at the exit. After some time, a motorized ramp met the curved outer hull with a *thump* and a *hiss*, creating a passable seal. Inside, the air held a dry, metallic flavor that left deep breaths tasting like dirt. RedLink operated an external facility separate from the city, a sprawling shuttleport campus covering several acres that spared the logistical problems of letting huge interplanetary shuttles through the dome.

Some passengers who had elected to have their bags shipped to their hotels went right for the monorail to the city while others lurked by the baggage carousel. A handful of desperate individuals went over to a coffee and refreshments counter, rather than obtain better for fewer credits from inside Arcadia.

Mamoru followed the first wave boarding the tram, which ferried them through a sealed tube out of the network of landing pads and toward the city. Less than a quarter mile from the dome, it halted at a platform that resembled any Earthbound commuter station, except for the RedLink logo depicting a cartoon-eyed shuttle doing a figure-eight around a smiling Mars and Earth.

Towers of charcoal-colored glass and plastisteel stretched out before him, interwoven with an uncountable number of advert bots. Somewhere within this place lurked the answer he sought and his ability to return home. He disembarked, finding it strange walking on a planet with less than half of Earth's gravity. Several locals chuckled at his awkward bounding gait until he got a feel for it and headed off down the street. The Kami were present in all natural things, however, nothing about this place was natural. One out of every five or six people he passed felt *wrong* somehow, like dolls even though they appeared human. It took him more than half an hour to recall the existence of synthetics.

Two design paths intent on the same goal produced two different types of being. Dolls had rigid bodies formed of plastisteel plates sandwiched between Myofiber muscles and artificial skin. High-end models indistinguishable from humans often had living brains, the mechanical body serving as a prosthetic replacement in cases of grievous injury or disease. Military versions were far stronger and faster than any human could expect to be.

Synthetics, or synths as most called them, were almost all AIs. They had plastisteel bones, but everything else approximated "living" by virtue of nanobots. By and large, the capabilities of synthetic bodies were on par with that of humans except for being unaffected by most hostile environments.

After a brutal rebellion almost three hundred years ago, the vast majority of synthetics migrated to Mars and the manufacture of synths was outlawed on Earth. Unaffected by the lack of atmosphere, they played a pivotal role in early colonization and were rewarded by assimilation into Martian society like any other ethnicity. Intellectuals still debated if they were truly *alive* despite being made of metal and silicon. Rumor, no more than whispers, held they had discovered a way to reprogram their maintenance nanobots and in some situations could reproduce.

Mamoru thought of Nami. *What is life but finding a way to survive and adapt?*

A chance encounter with a Japanese-themed restaurant made an immediate need apparent. Fortunately, the place used vat-grown fish, identical in every way to ordinary fish other than being made in forty-pound slabs. By the time his sashimi arrived, an in-table terminal had allowed him the opportunity to create an alternate identity in the network and pad his credit statement enough to be comfortable.

While eating, he left one finger on his NetMini and searched for any references to "Araphel" or "Raziel." Only a handful of anonymous postings turned up, most of which referred to Araphel as the jewel of freedom. One entry connected it with a quasi-terrorist group that called itself the Martian Liberation Front, or MLF. A query on that term brought up thousands of entries on the official NewsNet Mars channel, ninety-eight percent of which condemned them. The handful that didn't explored their motives in a way that made them seem noble, but sorely misguided.

He absorbed the content faster than reading would allow, integrating it with his memory as he ate. The MLF had declared war on the UCF and the ACC, wanting them both off Mars. The Red Planet had been in various stages of colonization since the year 2160. Now, two hundred and fifty-eight years later, some people bristled at the rule of an oblivious government housed on another planet.

The MLF was the only link he had to finding whatever Araphel was. The context in which the postings mentioned it made him think it to be a place, though whether it was actual or virtual remained to be seen. A waiter dropped off a plate of sliced oranges and a NetMini reader. Mamoru waved the device over it, making it beep.

The waiter bowed. "Thank you, Mr. Tanaka."

"*Gochisōsama-deshita,*" said Mamoru while returning the gesture. At the confused stare he received, he put on a plastic smile and swallowed his contempt for someone who could not be bothered to learn their culture's own language. "The food was excellent."

ACCORDING TO THE ANNOYING VOICEOVER IN THE AUTOMATED TAXI,

Arcadia City was the only place on Mars where the PubTran Corporation fully integrated with the infrastructure. The recorded voice reassured him he was safe here from potentially unscrupulous living drivers who would be as likely to take him where he wanted as drive him to a dark tunnel and rob him.

The car took him through the city along a highway elevated fifty stories above the ground, driving among countless other self-driving vehicles for a touch over six miles. Advert bots cruised up to the window, soliciting support for a vote to lift the ban on hovercars. Two bots simultaneously explained he could have been at his destination in a third the time if he were the owner of an unjustly deprived modern necessity. Mamoru leaned back and closed his eyes, meditating through the occasional jostle of a lane change or turn.

"Thank you for choosing PubTran Corporation for your transportation needs. You have arrived at your selected destination. Caution: This area experiences a crime rate higher than the average for Arcadia City. Please note that PubTran Corporation is not responsible for injury or death sustained as the result of an unexpected Violence Event. Have a nice day."

Mamoru emerged through the self-opening door as it swung upward from the side of the boxy, silver vehicle. He shook his head at the whine from little ten-inch wheels as it sped off. The inanimate thing behaved as if eager to get away from this part of town. He glanced over the building at the address he lifted from the NewsNet.

Plain grey metal walls bore the scars of several laser blasts and a handful of dents from physical bullets. Beneath a thick layer of dust, the painted words *Sergeant Dean's* spread off to the right of the door. A rough-looking woman with a black metal arm leaned against the structure below the "n" in Dean, flanked by six much younger, thinner, and prettier women. All had paper-white skin. Three still showed their natural black hair, one blonde, one red, and one white. They flirted while the augmented one squinted.

He paid them no mind and went inside.

The door led past an abandoned coat check to a dusty room with poor lighting. On the left, a long bar took up the majority of the wall. Tables occupied the center, clustered about columns with small holo-bars displaying Gee-Ball matches. A few men and women in well-worn clothing, some of it camouflage, sat around watching the games while sucking down synthbeer and devouring orange wads of breaded something. Mamoru had never smelled anything like the sauce they swam in. He cringed, finding it eye watering and nauseating.

They could subdue rioters with that substance.

All the way on the right, two men who appeared to be ex-soldiers sat on benches on the rearward side of the stage receiving lap dances from girls that looked too thin to be alive.

Mamoru's arrival stopped the room for several seconds. Not only did his long, dark coat and sunglasses stand out with an appearance more upper class than this place catered to, his skin tone marked him as from Earth—a tourist. According to the "helpful information" provided by RedLink, many natives of Mars opted for cosmetic genetic modification a few generations back. What had started as a designer gimmick had become a sort of planetary identity driven by university students hopped up on coffee and idealism.

A dark haired woman in a short skirt and clingy top that bared her midsection carried another basket of the strange nuggets to an occupied table, leaned on the man sitting there for a moment of conversation before collecting an empty synthbeer canister.

On her return trip, she gestured at the room. "Sit wherever."

He approached the bar where a greying man in his later fifties gave him a perplexed stare. Spilled booze might have stained his fading Martian-camouflage pants, though one would never notice.

"You get lost, son? You don't seem like the type of guy to walk in here by chance."

"I have not come by chance. Are you Sergeant Dean?"

He muted a laugh. "No, son. I'm Sergeant Konrad, formerly with the Colonial Expeditionary Forces. Dean was our point man when I was still a corporal. Named the place in his honor. You looking for a drink?"

"Water."

He put a metal can painted with snow-capped mountains in front of him. "Water's not the cheap option. You lookin' for cheap or you actually want water?"

"The water is fine." He swiped his NetMini—forty nine credits. "Imported from Earth?"

"Nope. Them eco-heads raised holy hell about that a few years back. They came up with some cockamamie diatribe about destroyin' the Earth by stealing its water. This was manufactured in Primus by the same outfit that runs the terraformers. No contamination."

Mamoru held the can up, inhaling the scent from it. "Do you think the Spirit of Water is present within such falsehood?"

Konrad leaned both hands on the bar. "Water is hydrogen and oxygen. Whether it happens naturally or we make it, doesn't change what it is."

"Hmm." Mamoru took a sip. "It is acceptable."

The bartender smirked at him and started to wander off, shaking his head.

"Sergeant Konrad, I believe you may assist me in finding something of great importance."

"I hear a lot of things." Konrad stopped and folded his arms. "What makes you think the info's for sale?"

Mamoru took a long sip and set the can on the bar. "A pattern analysis on several hundred thousand entries in the NewsNet archives creates an undeniable relationship between your establishment and the MLF."

"Don't know a damn thing about them other than they blow shit up sometimes tryin' to make political statements." Konrad leaned closer, a grid of shadow from an overhead light spread over his face. "You think I'd still be in business if the MLF made a habit of bein' here?"

"There are some who claim they are in fact an extension of your UCF's intelligence operations. Eighty-six percent of MLF hostilities over the past two years have been directed at ACC assets. When UCF holdings are targeted, they are often deserted or abandoned already and the casualties are limited."

"For an Earther, you've got your head up Mars's ass to your shoulder. What's it to you?"

"The state of Martian government is not my concern. I seek a single man. Do you know where I can find the one who calls himself Raziel?"

Konrad stood still, though a vein pulsed thick through his forehead. "No such man, son."

Mamoru finished his water. "References are limited in the news. I found evidence indicating files had been tampered with. I imagine that was to remove connection to him. If this Raziel is a cyberspace operator, he is quite skilled."

The bar creaked as Konrad let his weight settle on his elbows and lowered his voice to a murmur. "Look, son. What I hear 'bout Raziel is that there ain't no Raziel. He's no man. He's a figment of some crazy Tí-zhèn's imagination." Muscles on either side of his neck swelled as he leaned his head up to check the room for eavesdroppers. "Just sayin' if the

MLF wanted a flag-bearer, they might talk up the existence of some supernatural shit what could be a motivational tool."

"Tí-zhèn," said Mamoru, pondering. "Your society borrows a Chinese word. I am unfamiliar with its usage here."

He glanced to his right when an empty plastic basket stained with the foul-smelling orange sauce landed nearby.

Tapping her foot, the waitress smirked at Konrad. "Sarge, can you amp up the buffalo sauce? Jimmy said it's piss weak, like the beer."

"Weak, eh?" Konrad cracked his knuckles. "I'll show him weak."

She shifted her weight.

"What rock have you been living under, son?" Konrad laughed and 'semmed another batch of what the machine called 'chicken nuggets.' A smell, more plastic than food, caused Mamoru to cover his nose. "A Tí-zhèn's someone with a bunch of cyberware jackin' them up so they're fast and deadly." He dropped the food in a basket on the bar with a rustle of wax paper, then jabbed his finger at the holo-terminal on the machine. A batch of sauce formed inside an empty bowl, the intensity of it watered Mamoru's eyes through the closed door. "More often than not, it's used to refer to a hot piece of ass boosted to hell and back."

Mamoru blinked away from the acrid steam, wondering if Sadako would qualify as a Tí-zhèn.

"On d'other hand, you got Zēngqiáng, though no one bothers saying that whole mess. If you hear someone talkin' about a Zēng on a rage, run. Usually means some guy with more metal than brains looking to make large objects into small objects with his bare hands."

"Sergeant Konrad"—Mamoru held up one hand—"While I do appreciate the advice regarding your local terminology, I fail to see the connection between this Tí-zhèn and Raziel."

"I don't know much. I only hear some rumors. There's a Ti-zhen out there who claims to talk to Raziel, says he's a proper angel. She's a real head case. Thinks she's been 'chosen by Heaven' for something big."

"You are not well practiced in the art of deception, Sergeant Konrad. However, I will respect your desire not to get involved if you can provide me a direction."

"What are you really doing here? I thought Japan was on our side?"

Mamoru raised an eyebrow. "Are you referring to the UCF or the MLF?"

"I'm too old to give a flying fuck about who pulls the strings up here. Don't matter who does it, someone's going to wind up on top. There's a man by the name of Foster who trades in merchandise of questionable legality. He's got a place inside Aperture 2, right on the courtyard. Bunch of scrap and shit outside, plenty of muscle too."

"This Foster will lead me to Raziel?"

"Can't say for sure." Konrad leaned one elbow on the bar. "You'll have to ask him that, and as far as I'm concerned, I don't know you."

AT THE NORTHEASTERN CURVE OF ARCADIA CITY, THE GATE DESIGNATED Aperture 2 afforded access to the Martian exterior. A modern-day bazaar spread through the adjacent square, two hundred meters per side. On a dais at the center, six carved stone figures raised proud faces to the stars. Three of the courtyard's edges were crammed with a mixture of warehouses, mechanic stations, restaurants and other things. To the right of the gate, a prowler dealership glowed red and blue in the castoff light from a holographic sign playing an animation of a cartoony six-wheeled vehicle bounding over a spinning planet. Beyond it, a small herd of the boxy vehicles congregated in a lot. Two were plain plastisteel-silver, one black, and three others shared the same dull crimson hue that saturated this place.

Mamoru walked among the people, heading for the northwest boundary. Dozens of vendor carts around the Founders Memorial reduced his travel to a frustrated serpentine for most of the way. Being the only person in sight with a skin tone other than chalk white drew stares of curiosity. With most of the population carrying firearms in the open, he had ceased bothering to conceal his blade. Several young pickpockets gasped as he stared them down, too stunned at his catching them to them to do anything but gawk.

Foster's scrapyard, the last building on the west wall, sat at the corner of where open space ended at city. A few square metal panels sealed off the windows, while scraps of plastic stuck on hydraulic actuators fluttered in the breeze. No lights were on inside. Out front, a yard full of stacked boxes and unidentifiable machine parts stood devoid of activity beneath a white cloth tarp bound with twine to metal posts. Light through the shifting material stretched wavering shadows from the junk—the perfect place for an ambush.

In the courtyard of Aperture 2, merchants, explorers, beggars, and orphans swarmed. Foster's yard looked like a ghost town. He scowled, moving out of the crowd to the shade of the periphery buildings thirty meters away.

Apparently, I am to have a more vigorous discussion with Sergeant Konrad.

Mamoru turned to leave, trusting the odd wariness that came over him, but hesitated.

A yelp stood out from all the other noise, somehow rising above the din of the chaos behind him. The sound came from the rear of the quiet structure. *The spirits wish me to look closer.* He emerged from cover and strode with purpose through the light crowd at that corner of the bazaar.

Overhead sunlight yellowed through the tarps and industrial chemicals tainted the air in the front yard, leaving him tasting metal and imagining grit on his tongue. He gripped the exposed handle of his katana as he drifted among large, broken machines. Some had been half-covered with plastic, while others collected piles of red dust wherever their crevices trapped it. Mamoru recalled the words of his sensei and opened his perceptions. The old man had said he could *feel* the heartbeat of malice and always knew when someone meant to attack him. Alas, he had died before passing on that skill. Mamoru relied on hearing, smell, and sight.

"Who sent you?" growled a man.

The echo led Mamoru to the side of Foster's building, down a narrow passage between it and a prowler mechanic shop. He walked sideways so his arms did not brush the walls.

"Who's your contact?" yelled a different man.

"Tell me what the target is!" barked yet another, before a fleshy slap.

"Your sister," said a young voice.

Mamoru halted at the end of the building, leaning far enough to look. Amid a yard full of more technological scrap piled in clumps, three men in dingy coats, dark pants, and sunglasses surrounded a thin boy in a baggy jacket and loose dull-green fatigues. One shook a dull green backpack at him, while brandishing a large pistol in the other hand. The other two men aimed identical weapons at the small figure. An inch of solid, clear material in place of a barrel gave them away as laser weapons.

The boy, who could not have been older than eleven, knelt between them. Unkempt black hair fluttered over a porcelain-white face streaked with crimson from his nose. Hate-filled brown eyes glared up at his tormentors as he struggled to free his hands from metal binders behind his back.

Snarling, the man with the pack punched the boy in the gut, leaving him slumped over a salvaged capacitor unit, cheek on metal with his head to the side as if on a chopping block. The boy whined and coughed, growling through the pain since he could not clutch his arms to his stomach. He looked right at Mamoru at that instant and went still. He did not seem at all close to crying or showing weakness. His stare took on a pleading quality for the second or two they left him alone. A man behind him lifted him to his knees by a fistful of hair.

"We have you on cam, you little shit. You planted the device." He shoved the kid face-first against the capacitor with a muted *thud*, before he leaned his weight on the boy's neck. "Who is your damn contact?"

Even if he wanted to speak, the act would have been impossible, as was breathing. The boy gasped and wheezed. The man crushing him slapped him across the back of the head. A weak growl emanated from the kid.

The man in front raised his pistol. "Fuck it, the little prong isn't gonna crack." The pistol chirped.

"I find it quite dishonorable that it takes three men to threaten a small boy." Mamoru took three steps forward, entering the yard. He stopped about fifteen feet away from them.

The boy sucked in a great breath when the weight released, and succumbed to a fit of coughing. At the distraction of Mamoru's appearance, he tried to leap up and run. The man behind him snagged his jacket and slammed him down on the capacitor again. He wheezed, paralyzed by the impact.

"This is none of your concern." The man who had grabbed the boy by the hair reached his left hand around behind him. "This is offi—"

Mamoru's gaze flicked to the one aiming at the boy. Psionic power flowed through body and dragged the world to relative slow motion. He surged forward, drawing the katana with a swing that took the man's arm at the elbow. His attack happened with such speed the other two had not yet moved their attention from where Mamoru stood before he charged. The man with the backpack did not have time to look over before the blade freed his head from the rest of his body.

A spinning thrust plunged the katana to the hilt in the chest of the last man. Mamoru paused for a few seconds in his accelerated time before stepping left and wrenching it out in a stroke that sheared up through the torso of the now one-armed man, beheading him. Smoke hung in the air, carrying the scent of charred meat. He flipped the blade over in his grip to let the blood steam off, and slid it with a soft click back into the scabbard.

The boy curled against the metal block, no longer able to hide his terror. Wild eyed, he gaped at the three dead men and shivered.

"Holy shit... You just like, disappeared and they all exploded." He swallowed, looked around again, and worked his way to his feet with a clumsy behind-the-back grip on the capacitor. After failing to slip his hands past his butt, the boy attempted to offer a handshake as best he could with his arms trapped in binders, while someone else's blood dripped off his face.

"Hey, thanks for saving my ass. I'm Caiden."

15

IMPLAUSIBLE DENIAL

Mamoru disregarded the boy's ungainly outstretched hand and moved to the man who had reached behind his back. He kicked the body over to see what weapon was about to be hurled at him, but found the man holding a faux-leather ID wallet instead. He squatted, picked the item up, and opened it. The face of the dead man, minus a few years, smiled at him from inside. Caiden trembled, cringing from the sight of headless corpses.

"Boy, what is MDF?"

For a moment, silence settled over the yard, save for the fluttering of the plastic awning out front and the rattle of binders. Caiden slouched with a resigned sigh and tried to blow his hair out of his face, having no greater success at that.

"Um, they're the police."

Mamoru stood, and tucked the ID into his coat. "What manner of atrocity did a small boy commit that they were going to kill you?" He scowled at the corpses. "They appeared to be thugs."

"Yeah, pretty much. Thugs, police, ain't much of a difference." He kicked one in the leg before eyeing the blade on Mamoru's hip. "That's a vibro, right? Can you cut me loose?"

"You have not answered my question."

"I was trying to break in to this shop. Guess they didn't like what I said about asshole's sister."

"I see." Mamoru pivoted on his heel and walked toward the passage he had entered from.

"Hey, wait." Caiden trotted after him. "Let me outta these."

Mamoru stopped, leaving his back to the boy. "Those men were going to kill you. Police do not usually kill thieves, even disagreeable children."

Caiden stared at his battered, laceless sneakers. Snow-white skin peeked through numerous holes and rips in olive drab pants. "I'm only a street kid. They think it's bad for tourism. I'm gonna be eleven in a couple months, getting too old to be a cute beggar, so they want to scare me off before I 'become a real criminal.'"

"Everyone in this place is a poor liar." Mamoru started walking away again.

"Come on!" yelled Caiden, jogging after him. "You can't leave me cuffed. These fuckers have a tracker in them. They'll find me again. That's a vibro sword you got. It'll take you a second to cut the chain."

Mamoru, now halfway down the passage, stopped. This time, he spun and frowned at the emaciated wretch. "A wise man once told me to seek freedom in knowledge."

Caiden shivered and took a step back.

"You are afraid of what you know. Why would I have saved your life only to kill you later? I do not expect Mars to be so different from Earth that the death of three policemen will be taken lightly."

Caiden bit his lip. "I swore not to tell anyone. It's like an oath or something."

"That is honorable."

"You're really gonna walk away and leave me cuffed if I don't tell you?"

"Yes." Mamoru moved as if to leave.

"Wait, please." Caiden's eyes glimmered with guilt and fear. "I... I'm involved with some people, but I can't say more than that. If you cut me loose, I'll take you to my contact. If he trusts you, he can tell you stuff. I really don't know much. They only let me run packages and messages. They don't tell me anything 'cause of my age."

"The reaction of those men did not seem appropriate for an errand boy."

Caiden offered a weak smile and a shrug. "Sometimes, the packages go boom."

Mamoru rubbed his chin. He reached toward the boy, poking both index fingers through the drape of hair shrouding his face, and parting it to reveal eyes. Man and boy exchanged a long stare. Despite his situation, Caiden seemed as though he could laugh at any moment.

"I suspect your urge to disappear would be strong. However, you were about to die rather than talk. If you agree to bring me to your contact, I will accept your offer."

Caiden gulped, and shook his head in an emphatic nod that sent his hair flying. "Deal."

Mamoru made a circular gesture with one finger. When the boy turned his back, he grasped the chain between his wrists and gathered a sense of the electronics within. The simplistic programming changed to his whim in under a second, and they snapped open.

"Whoa..." Caiden rubbed his wrists. "How did you do that?"

"Ancient Japanese secret." Mamoru allowed himself something close to a smile before he gestured at the bazaar. "Lead the way."

"One sec." Caiden sprinted back to the dead men, gathering their pistols and e-mags into his backpack before searching them for stray credsticks.

A twinge of discomfort ran through Mamoru at the boy's utter lack of apprehension at touching corpses.

Finding nothing else of use, Caiden closed his bag and trudged over.

"Do you expect to need those?" Mamoru smiled. "I did not know the MLF would employ one so young."

The boy froze, mouth gaping. "I-I didn't say—"

"No, you didn't." Mamoru bowed. "Consider it an educated assumption."

Caiden brushed past him. "No, they ain't for me. I'm not allowed to shoot people yet. Kendrick said if I gotta gun on me, it makes me a target."

Mamoru followed him through the square to the street. The boy walked at a casual stroll, as if he had not almost died or witnessed three men cut down in under a second. Their route took them through areas the establishment left off tourism brochures. From the back of a building abutting an alley, prostitutes of both genders gathered in clusters around men who carried themselves as if they had the authority to kill whomever they wanted.

"Syndicate runs most of the bad shit here. All those guys work for Mirek, but don't worry. They know me. They help us out sometimes since we both have issues with the MDF."

"Your movement seeks independence. If your people win, you will become the law. These men will no longer consider you allies."

Worry spread over Caiden's face. "You think they'd turn on us?"

"Without hesitation, once their interests and yours no longer align."

The boy moped for a few streets, lost amid thoughts of how things would change if the MLF ever won Martian independence.

"I am sorry for ruining your dream."

"I always thought everyone would be happy if we kicked the UCF an' the ACC offa Mars. The Syndicate isn't gonna go away, are they?"

"Unlikely. However, it would be foolish for your leaders not to expect that outcome. I am sure they have taken that into consideration. If they have not, they are inept. In that case, it is an irrelevant consideration as they will not win."

Caiden jogged ahead, swinging left to an even narrower passageway. He ran his fingers across the grime-smeared metal walls of the buildings on the left. Air handlers, pipes, and other square protrusions created dozens of shadowed spaces. Small white hands poked and prodded at panels, searching for the right one. Mamoru waited in silence. A few feet beyond a thrumming refrigerator-sized component leaking odious yellow vapor, Caiden found what he had been looking for.

A small door, engraved with, ACMA – Authorized access only.

"Who is Acma?"

Caiden laughed. "What planet are you from? It's Arcadia City Municipal Authority." He grunted in an effort to drag the door open, managing to pull it only far enough for a malnourished boy to slip through before it got stuck on the ground.

Mamoru reached over Caiden's shoulder and, with a mild boost of strength, pulled the hatch open the rest of the way one-handed. Inside, a small chamber held a ladder leading down through a square opening. The first rung lit up with a weak glow, a strip of flexible LED tape that activated with the weight of Caiden's shoe. He scrambled down it without hesitation, vanishing amid the dark. Mamoru pulled the door closed behind him and followed. The shaft amplified the clattering echoes of his sword and loose metal buckles swinging from Caiden's backpack. Without the sun to compete, the glow moving with them did not seem as weak.

Caiden jumped the last few feet to the ground, and crept away. When Mamoru reached the bottom, the boy flashed a smile and darted down another shaft, only an inch taller than he was. Mamoru stooped, glancing in either direction. Every ten meters, caged LED bulbs struggled to emit light. Some were forever dark, but enough remained to illuminate the underground corridor. Mamoru scowled at the grin his companion made at his awkward posture.

"It's not too far," said Caiden, pointing forward.

Mamoru ambled behind him, grumbling about the tight confines. Bundles of wires and pipes along the wall made the shaft seem as though it existed for maintenance access, yet a thick layer of dust coated everything. Every so often, a spark leapt from one of the weaker lights, making Mamoru twitch as if to defend against an attack. Caiden's laugh did little for Mamoru's mood.

"The city is not wise to expose its infrastructure to any who can find the door."

"All this shit is old," said Caiden, his voice phantasmal with a metallic echo. "Everything's wireless now, above ground. This stuff is all ancient. Older than you are."

"I do not consider myself old. I am twenty-seven."

Caiden stopped to evaluate a turn in the passage. "That's pretty old. You're like my mom's age." He kept going straight.

The throat-growl of an unamused samurai rumbled over distant dripping. Minutes later, the fragrance of wet dirt and moss became overwhelming. His little guide took a right turn that led to a chamber full of control boxes, fuse panels, and a workstation with long ago broken status monitors. The chair beside it had turned from red to white with decades of fungus growing on the cushion. Mamoru took a moment to stretch to his full height, feeling a modicum of pity for whatever person had been required to work here.

The boy grabbed the handle of a metal door, lifting himself off the ground rather than budging it. He backed off, kicked it a few times, and cursed. Mamoru took a step, but Caiden held a hand up.

"I got it."

Once more, he did a pull-up on the handle, kicking at the wall with squeaking shoes. A little tint of red appeared in his face before he sagged back to his feet and panted.

"How long must one live on Mars before their skin turns white?"

The boy shot him a glare that called him an idiot. "People don't turn white unless they go get modded." He held up his hands as if to show off his color. "I was born like this. It's genetic or something."

Mamoru reached for the door.

"I said, I got it. I opened it last week. It's just stuck."

He put a hand on the boy's shoulder. "Sometimes one needs to seek help."

Caiden scowled and folded his arms.

"I understand, but you are yet a boy. There is no shame in it." A frown formed as he gazed at the ashen-white face scowling at the wall. The color reminded him of an offer of help he had declined. *No oni seeks to help. What game does it play? It takes the form of a beautiful woman to trick me.* Mamoru clapped his hands twice, making Caiden jump. Without considering if the Kami could hear him from Mars, he beseeched them to guard his soul. He clapped again.

"What did you say?" The boy backed against the wall. "What language was that?"

"Japanese. I do not mean to unnerve you, but it seems a certain demon has decided to toy with me. I am merely asking for protection."

"Oh, guess people pray different on Earth. That looked kinda angry."

Mamoru grasped the door handle and focused on becoming stronger. Glowing energy shimmered down his arm, making the boy gasp. A horrendous metal-on-metal scraping sound rang out. Caiden covered his ears and cringed, gawking at the apparent lack of effort on Mamoru's part.

"Holy shit! Are you a doll?" Caiden pounced at him, stopping short of performing a squeeze-test on his muscles.

"No. I do not believe in contaminating the body with metal."

"So how the hell did you"—he glanced at the scratches on the ground—"move that door? Some kinda Kung Fu monk magic?"

The glare pushed Caiden back a step before Mamoru caught his indignation. He was a boy quite far removed from any knowledge of his culture. No offense could have been intended. "Kung Fu is Chinese, Caiden. I am from Japan." He gestured for the boy to continue, and waited for him to walk. "I have spent my life believing that I tap my inner energies—"

"Chi?"

Mamoru chuckled. "Yes." *The demon called it psionic, but I cannot hear the thoughts of others. She or it seeks to deceive me, turn me from my ways.* He bumped into the boy when he stopped short. "Why have you stopped?"

"Uh." Caiden looked up. His stomach growling was loud enough to echo.

The scent of food eked through the stench of grease and metal, entering the shaft from a hatch at the top of a ladder.

"Very well," said Mamoru. "After you."

16

NONPRESENCE

Caiden sat low in the booth, leaning against the wall while staring through the window at the street. A fog patch formed by his mouth on the glass, which thankfully looked opaque black from the outside. Mamoru had guided him by a grip on the backpack around a vendor cart selling street meat, favoring a place that offered real food. The unwashed smell that permeated the boy's clothes had not been noticeable before they entered a clean environment.

"Try not to look so frightened," whispered Mamoru. "It will cause people to ask you what is wrong and attract undue attention."

The boy scooted away from the window and sat up. "Sorry."

A waiter dropped off their orders, burger and fries for Caiden, grilled vat-grown chicken on a roll for Mamoru. The boy hovered over his meal as if he needed to defend it from thieves. Mamoru found it both amusing and pitiful. Caiden all but inhaled his food and slurped every crumb and trace of juice off the plate when he was done. Mamoru was only halfway through his sandwich.

"How did you come to associate with terrorists?"

Caiden took a break from licking his fingers long enough to mutter, "They're not terrorists."

"No?"

He crossed his arms, staring at the empty plate. "Terrorists kill civilians without caring who gets hurt. They wanna cause panic and chaos." He lowered his voice to a whisper. "The MLF goes after military targets. We're trying to protect ourselves from a corrupt government so far away that it has no idea what Mars is even like." Caiden squinted. "What are you laughing at?"

"Ancient history." Mamoru finished the last of his sandwich. "The nation you know as the UCF was once a colony of an older country. They also rebelled for their independence. I imagine they were called terrorists as well, or whatever term they used in the day."

Caiden sank in the seat, patting his stomach. When the waiter returned to check on them, the boy gave Mamoru a pleading look. After receiving a nod of approval, he ordered a basket of chicken nuggets.

"How can you eat those?" asked Mamoru, cringing at the memory of the orange sauce in the soldier's bar.

The boy shrugged one bony shoulder and stuck his tongue out. "How can you eat raw fish?"

"A fair point. So, have you been involved with these people for long?"

Caiden picked at the table, breaking eye contact. "A couple months."

"Parents dead, I imagine?"

"I dunno." Caiden glanced out the window at passersby. "I don't remember my dad at all. Mom got arrested for protesting at some mining corporation office. There was a big fight in the street with the MDF and some people got hurt. I haven't seen her since."

The waiter dropped off the nuggets, smiled at them, and walked away. Caiden kept gazing outside, ignoring the food. Mamoru sampled one of the fries that came with his meal, deciding he didn't care for the excessive amount of salt. He pushed the plate across the table.

"You can have those… potatoes? If you want them."

Hunger pulled Caiden away from his somber thoughts, and he rested his elbows on the table. He ate a nugget and two fries before looking up.

"What about yours?"

"They are dead. I was about your age when they were killed."

"Sorry."

"It does not bother me. They were too weak to save themselves."

Caiden looked up wide-eyed. "Uh, okay. That's kinda, um, fucked up." He nibbled on another piece. "I guess it's easier to deal with if you say it's their fault. I was mad at my mom too."

Mamoru frowned at the table, wondering why on a red planet they made everything else the same color. Motion by the door grabbed his attention.

"Come here, boy. Don't go in the aisle. Do it quick."

The child hesitated for only a few seconds before sliding under the table and crawling up between Mamoru and the wall. He furrowed his eyebrows when Mamoru put an arm over him, and tried to push away. He went from shoving to clinging when six MDF troops in full armor entered and stood inside the front door. Caiden seemed intent on burrowing into Mamoru's coat as white energy danced along it.

"Do not move or make a sound," whispered Mamoru as he concentrated.

Three to a side, the MDF soldiers went in two directions, searching the restaurant. Caiden stared at them, unable to pull his eyes off the red, featureless faceplates turning back and forth. When one trooper looked right at him for a long several seconds, his fingers clutched Mamoru's sleeve and he stopped breathing.

The officer looked away and kept walking. Caiden buried his face in Mamoru's chest in an effort to muffle the sound of his urgent need for air. Within minutes, the MDF officers completed a circuit around the building and converged on the front counter. It seemed a routine check rather than a purposeful hunt. They ordered coffees and to-go food.

"Why did they ignore us?" whispered Caiden.

Mamoru squeezed the boy's shoulder. He intended the gesture as comforting, but at the same time a warning to remain quiet. He waited a moment after the troopers left, in case they pulled a switchback. When he felt confident they would not return, he relaxed and the energy dissipated.

As if to distance himself from his embarrassing attack of fear, Caiden returned to the far side of the table, acting casual. He tossed his hair over his shoulder with a nod and finished off the nuggets and fries before settling back on the cushions with a face that said he could go to sleep at any moment.

"Thanks for the food."

Mamoru nodded.

Awkward silence lasted for a moment.

Caiden swiped sauce on his finger and licked it. "So, um, what the heck just happened?"

Mamoru suppressed a cringe at the sight of grimy fingernails going into the boy's mouth. He drew in a breath to explain, stalling as the concept of chi and technology seemed at odds. While one had been around since the days of the original samurai, technology was a comparatively new phenomenon. He gazed at Caiden's inquisitive look for a few minutes trying to answer the questions in his own mind first.

"I..." Mamoru frowned. "Perhaps I am psionic. I can make electronics obey me. All of those men see through their armor. Their helmets have cameras that create an image on the inside of a metal plate. I told the cameras to regard us as a non-presence."

"Neat. Psionic, huh? Can you read minds and stuff?"

Mamoru squinted, attempting it, but whatever went on in the boy's head was out of his reach. "No."

"Guess that's better then. They might not be too happy with me bringing a telepath."

"Then it is fortunate I am not a mind reader."

Caiden laughed, a bit of the boy peered out from behind the curtains of a tattered childhood. Mamoru remembered his father and the bokken lying in the leaves. His throat tightened at the memory of finally earning his father's approval, even if it happened in the last moment of the man's life.

GARRISON

C aiden walked several feet ahead, carrying a small e-lantern in a lazy two-fingered grip. Mamoru hovered at the edge of the nimbus of unsteady white light, using the long, creeping shadows to avoid tripping on the rocks that cast them. The boy moved with all the urgency of a ten-year-old on his way to school, shifting the light from hand to hand out of boredom. With each breath, the taste of Martian silt bubbled in the back of Mamoru's throat as strong as if he had licked the wall. Metallic and earthy, it raised the question of why anyone would want to live underground.

Crunching footsteps echoed in two directions through the narrow passageway. Mamoru gazed at the dark ceiling overhead, not sure which he trusted more: several meters of rock, or a clear dome of advanced composites. If either one failed, semi-breathable atmosphere would surround him—a foe he could not defeat.

"I am getting the sense your friend does not like visitors," said Mamoru.

The boy held the lantern out to the side, balancing as he traversed a short distance while trying to stay off the ground by stepping on tiny boulders. "MDF wants to kill him."

Mamoru felt uneasy at the boy acting his age. Caiden grimaced at a near-loss of balance, as if to put a foot in the dirt would harm him. Hours ago, the police of this world were about to shoot him in an alley—now he played.

"This MDF has no honor."

"They were trying to scare me." Caiden jumped down when he ran out of stones big enough to stand on. "They weren't really gonna do it." He glanced up at Mamoru, searching for reassurance.

Mamoru put a hand on his shoulder, not speaking. His grim expression needed no words. Caiden stared for a moment longer, and let his gaze fall. He trudged forward, absent any trace of boyhood distraction.

"I am sorry, Caiden. It would be a disservice to lead you into a false sense of security." Mamoru's hand tightened on the hilt of the katana as his sister's panicked screams cried out in his mind. "I believe those men were breaking their own rules. Perhaps others will not want to harm you."

"Yeah." The boy kicked small stones out of his way. "They know I could lead 'em to the MLF."

"Well, it would be foolish of them to kill you. They could not gain from your knowledge."

A knee-high cloud of dust from the punted rock flowed around Mamoru's legs.

"I guess," mumbled Caiden, regaining some of his earlier animation. "We're almost there. They're real suspicious of unfamiliar faces, especially anyone from Earth."

"As they should be. However, the doings of the governments of Earth and Mars are not my concern."

Several dozen meters of bare stone passed on both sides before the tunnel took on signs of construction. Metal panels covered the walls in patches, interspersed with side tunnels containing shattered overhead lights, metal grating floors and dangling wires. Large fragments of rock protruded through bent squares of metal barely clinging to the ceiling. Caiden ducked a low-hanging ventilation fan and stepped through a trio of two-inch thick cables suspended in a U shape. Mamoru followed, twisting to avoid tearing his coat on a jagged outcropping.

At the halfway point in the cross tunnel, Caiden stopped by a painted logo of CMMC—Colonial Mars Mining Corporation. Scrapes, pits, and gouges in the metal dated the construction to at least a century and a half. The boy rolled up his sleeve and stuck his arm through a six-inch square hole up to the armpit. His eyes searched the ceiling while he made a series of faces that led up to a satisfied smile. As soon as he grinned, a beep rang out and the wall panel hissed and retracted.

Caiden ducked through before it finished moving. "Hurry up, it won't stay open long."

The slab of inches-thick plastisteel receded far enough for a man to enter without feats of yogic mastery. Mamoru followed with haste, entering a narrow metal-walled shaft on the other side before it slid closed. A bundle of multicolored wires ran along the left corner overhead, an obvious recent addition compared to the rest of the construction. Distant murmuring voices filtered through dusty air, mixed with the fragrance of sweat, horrible food, and gun cleaner.

Caiden outpaced Mamoru as he did not have to turn sideways to fit down the hallway. He waited at the end, some thirty meters down, tapping his foot and looking between him and something out of sight with an earnest face. A shadow fell over him, causing him to flash the forced-cheesy smile of a child caught doing something they shouldn't. He pointed back at Mamoru.

A man in drab crimson military fatigues leaned around the corner. If he was not already the color of snow, he might have gotten paler at the sight of the Japanese man in a shin-length black coat.

"It's okay, Kirk. He saved my ass. Someone gave up Foster. The MDF was waiting for me inside." Caiden held up one bruised wrist and glanced down at the floor. "They were gonna shoot me. Mamoru killed all three of 'em. They were all dead before the first one hit the ground."

Kirk put a hand on the sidearm at his belt. "Earth?"

"That is correct. I mean to return as soon as I have finished my task here." Mamoru emerged from the narrow tunnel, his presence pushing Kirk back.

Groups of vertical lockers occupied the space around the walls of a small chamber between dingy bunks. Out of six, four had blown their Comforgel pads. Improvised mattresses of tattered cloth strips replaced them. On one, bare copper wire led from the contacts meant to provide power to the gel pad's climate control to a naked LED bulb hung by a loose screw over the bunk. Discoloration from where the viscous fluid had leaked decorated the ground.

Kirk backed into a table made from an old wire spool, knocking a tall, metal mug wobbling. A dark skinned man in a sleeveless T-shirt with a red-bandana on his otherwise bald head caught it with a *slap* before it fell.

"What's got you spooked?" His voice held a trace of an Earth accent.

"Kid had a close call, brought his friend with him."

Mamoru stepped out of the shadows by the hallway, rendering a slight bow to both men. Caiden hovered behind him, risking a hesitant peek at the transplanted African.

"Well now." Muscular arms stretched out as the man slid his palms flat across the table and leaned back. "What've you brought us, boy?"

Caiden went through a recitation of the events behind Foster's salvage. "...he had questions I'm not allowed to answer."

"I am Osebi," said the large man as he stood. "For what purpose have you come 'ere, to us?"

"I need information. I must find the one who calls himself Raziel."

Kirk and Osebi exchanged a glance that said 'here we go again.'

"I... I'm not touching that." Kirk held his hands up and moved to a small, dented metal case where he retrieved a can of synthbeer.

Osebi rubbed his chin, drawing his long fingers over stubbly cheeks. "Do you hear him speaking to you?"

Mamoru showed no emotion. "I do not, though I would like to meet him. I have many questions."

A glimmer of humor shone in the man's eyes, though his face remained serious. "How are we to know you aren't some mercenary or agent of Earth government?"

"I am Mamoru Saitō. I was once a samurai in the service of Akio Minamoto, CEO of Matsushita Electronics Corporation. It is my belief that this *Raziel* has interfered in such a way as to damage my employer's perception of my loyalties. I must discover why." Mamoru gestured at the wall. "I do not have an opinion about your movement or the government of Mars. What little information I discovered indicates a connection between this person and your group. I am following the only clue I have, and it led me to a scrap merchant."

Caiden shivered. "If he was an agent, he wouldn't have killed three MDF."

Osebi came around the table, giving Mamoru a head to toe glance. "Some portions of the government would not think twice about a minor collateral loss."

Mamoru offered a curt nod. "Perhaps. I am not asking to learn your secrets. I want only to find Raziel."

The stoic ebon face broke with a bright grin, followed soon by deep laughter. Kirk lost it too, sputtering synthbeer out his nose and coughing. Caiden looked as confused as Mamoru felt.

Mamoru tilted his head. "Forgive me, but I do not understand the humor."

"Hah." Osebi patted him on the shoulder. "Raziel is an enigma, my friend." The big man struggled to speak through his mirth. "One of our number believes an angel talks to her." He twirled a finger at the side of his head. "I believe you have been deceived. Raziel is a figment of the woman's imagination."

"Figments do not infiltrate corporate networks," said Mamoru. "I detected a trace which led me here."

Osebi's grin vanished to confusion. He skewed his jaw to one side for a moment. Dust flickered through a shaft of light between them. "There is something strange about you, Mamoru Saitō, but I do not think you work for military intelligence. They would not be wasting their time with angels and demons." The smile returned. "Wait here a moment."

Caiden stuffed his hands in his pockets, nervous eyes watching the room. Kirk leaned against the lockers, sipping from the plain silver can. Mamoru kept an impassive stare on the doorway Osebi vanished through. After some minutes, Caiden took a seat on one of the bunks. With the relative security of a quarter mile of stone and dirt on all sides, he shrank into the form of a frightened boy who had come too close to death. He kicked off his shoes and crawled under a blanket, staring through unkempt hair at Mamoru.

"You should keep him out of sight for a while," said Mamoru as he walked toward Kirk.

The MLF soldier slurped the can empty. "Yeah, figure that's right. They'll be looking for him now. Morons will probably blame him for killing those men."

Twenty minutes after leaving, Osebi returned with six others. Two women and four men wearing a hodgepodge of rifles, armor, and clothing waited in the space beyond the door. Osebi waved Mamoru over.

"Come, there is someone who will speak to you."

Mamoru followed, pausing among them as one of the women held a hand up. A pale native Marsborn with a stern face framed by short, black hair. Hard, blue eyes regarded him as a threat.

"You got any weapons?"

"I do not carry a firearm, if that is what you are asking. I need only my katana, which is sacred to me. I will not relinquish it, and it would be most unwise to attempt to touch it. If your person is concerned for his safety, I have no quarrel with an electronic meeting."

The resistance fighters looked around at each other, unsettled by the calm in Mamoru's voice. One sword against many rifles, and not one drop of nervousness showed. The woman glanced at Caiden and back at him.

"All right, but keep your movement easy." She took a few steps backward before spinning and walking with a stiff stride.

With three in front and three plus Osebi behind him, Mamoru traveled through a maze of metal-walled corridors. The passageway they led him to had a disused appearance, lined on both sides by pipes of varying size. Silt coated everything in a thick layer, tainting the air with the flavor of grit. *They are being cautious. A fight here would not cause significant damage.* He kept quiet, focusing on the motion of those around him in case they were the ones who meant to initiate unexpected hostility.

At the end of another hall filled with metal scraps and loose arm-thick wires, they went through a door to a dim room. Outside light flickered in from the right, chopped by the blades of a lazy ventilation fan. Behind a plain steel-grey desk, sat a middle-aged figure in olive drab fatigues and an armored vest. To his left, a man Osebi's size loomed. Dark blue plastisteel wrapped around the right side of his head, cradling the amber glow of an artificial eye made of older technology that looked nothing like a natural organ. The lens whirred as it focused. A soft pulsating glow swelled through seams in the metal of his right arm, a mechanical limb that clicked as he opened and closed his fingers.

"That's far enough," said the hard-eyed woman once Mamoru had reached the middle of the room.

Mamoru bowed at the seated man. "I am grateful to you for seeing me."

Several days of unshaved beard shifted as he rubbed his chin. "What sort of person comes all the way from Earth to ask about an angel?"

"What sort of army dangles small children before their enemies?"

The man behind the desk narrowed his stare as the air seemed to hang still. He tapped a finger on the desk, watching Mamoru for any crack in his perfect calm. When none came, he smiled.

"Caiden is a runner. He likes to help, and he's small enough yet where he can move around unnoticed. He was not supposed to show up on their watch list. I honestly have no idea why they were waiting for him. The only thing I can think of is that Foster got compromised and they grabbed the first person to show up there who didn't want to trade in junk. Odds are they had no clue."

"Those men knew who he is."

"The MDF will say things to bait you," added the metal-armed guard. "Kid doesn't know enough to keep his mouth shut. They don't know a damn thing, but they can get it out of you."

"Osebi believes you have information I need," said Mamoru. "I seek the one known as Raziel."

Pistols attached to the vest sagged as the man leaned forward. "What do you know already?"

"Very little, unfortunately. I have found reference to a place known as Araphel, and there are connections between him and your organization. Other than that, nothing."

The MLF senior hesitated for a moment. "Please understand how careful I must be. A man in my position has many lives depending on him. I may be able to help you, but I need to know beyond any doubt that you are not an agent of the government."

Mamoru shifted his weight to his left leg. "How would you ask me to do that? A favor for a favor does not seem an unreasonable request. As I am now ronin, my blade is mine to hire out."

"We have several good-hearted men and women who have been captured by the military, held in a remote encampment for interrogation and eventual execution." The man interlaced his fingers, staring at the half-globe his hands formed for a moment of silence. "If you were able to find information connecting Raziel to the MDF on the GlobeNet, you're either an AI or one of the best deck jockeys ever to live." He looked Mamoru in the eye. "If you can find that camp and help us get our people back, I will give you what you are looking for."

"We have an arrangement." Mamoru bowed.

"I'll have Osebi bring you all the information we have." The man stood, offering a handshake. "Call me Garrison."

ASSAULT

I t was by the fortunate luck of the UCF military being stingy that their holding facility occupied a bubble of stable atmosphere at the bottom of an unnamed crater a few hundred kilometers northwest of Arcadia city. A handful of field emitters kept the air within the bowl-shaped depression Earthlike. Between the city and the prison camp, the air was close enough to get by without the need for a full envirosuit.

Mamoru clung to the rear of a military transport rover similar to the civilian prowlers he had seen for sale, with the addition of weaponry. His rebreather mask tainted every breath with the flavor of rubber and sweat. Dim light shimmered along his arms as he focused on nonpresence to remain invisible to the sensors monitoring the area.

For all of Garrison's talk about danger, the UCF treated this camp as if they assumed their detainees to be low risk and low value. A tour of the facility's security system via MarsNet showed about two dozen military personnel and two medics on staff. Security appeared minimal. Most vexing of all, the prison units themselves were drop box buildings with no network connection. All he could do from remote was peer through cameras.

He extended a fragment of his consciousness into the machine to share the view of the forward-facing cameras, the same ones responsible for the driver's ability to see the outside through the armored front end. A boulder as large as the vehicle marked the point where a roadway had been cut through the crater's rim, leading to the encampment about two hundred meters away.

Mamoru induced a total shutdown of the prowler. With the crew distracted by an unexplained blackout, he leapt to the ground, hid for a few seconds behind a tire taller than him, and darted behind the large rock. Within a moment, the exterior lights came on and the vehicle lumbered forward. The ground appeared to devour it as it sank over the rim on its way to the crater floor.

For hours, he sat in the dirt and meditated. On oni, on Minamoto, on Nami, and on the golden angel. The Kami provided no insight, leaving his thoughts swirling with doubt. When he could emerge under cover of darkness, he walked along the four-foot wide tire tracks the prowler left behind. Twenty meters past the crater's rim, a holographic sign flickered, bearing a warning of a restricted area ahead where trespassers would be shot.

A quarter of the way down the sloping road, the air became thicker and gusted in a circular wind that hugged the walls. Weary of the taste imparted by his mask, he removed it, turned it off, and secured it in his coat pocket. Outside of the domed city of Arcadia, the induced atmosphere carried an odd fragrance. Some part of it was a latent chemical tinge imparted by membranous filters within the air scrubbers and terraforming machines—but the lack of organics left it feeling stale and dry compared to Earth air. Mamoru frowned, eager to be rid of this desolate place where the Kami seemed not to exist.

Energy emanated from various points on the ground in a ring formation surrounding a cluster of eight plastisteel pods. The camp looked as if giants had ordered delivery food and left the containers behind. Four of the drop boxes were long and narrow, about a hundred eighty feet long and twenty wide. *The prisons.* Indentations on the outer hull hinted at forty eight-by-eight foot cells in two facing rows.

Of the remaining buildings, the largest was the barracks pod—a square that dwarfed everything else. It formed the center of the residence area, flanked by an infirmary, a vehicle bay, and a storage building that doubled as a mess hall. All of the buildings floated four feet off the ground on spring-loaded shock-absorbing legs. A number of separate metal stairways on wheels, older and far more battered than the buildings themselves, sat by every door.

A pair of sentry guns, asleep in six-foot plastisteel cubes, flanked the approach road a short distance in front of the nearest building. Small lights blinked from the corners and they emitted a soft status beep every thirty seconds.

Mamoru squinted at a ring of proximity sensors planted forty yards ahead. The small ten-inch antennas would pick him up if he got any closer without nonpresence, but the glow of his *chi* would stand out like a flare in the night, were he to use that ability. For the first time in his life, he envied Sadako, but only a little. Sneaking around was never something he considered honorable. Even now, stealth was more for the sake of saving time.

He drew in a breath and calmed his mind. *The quarrels of Martians are not my concern. This is a step on the path to regaining my honor.* Mamoru exhaled as shame touched his heart. He pictured Minamoto's smile turning to a frown of eye-swelling rage. Despite knowing his fall from favor happened because of an outside influence, the feeling of betrayal was a wound he would nurse for years. *What has this Raziel shown to Minamoto to make him believe me a traitor?*

"You there, freeze." A voice, tinged with the crackle of amplification came from the left. "This is a restricted area."

Two men in Mars-red camouflage armor pointed rifles at him. Glimmering flecks of light danced within their visors.

"I am standing still already, can you not see that?"

"Oh, we got a wiseass," said the one on the right.

"Okay, pal—"

Mamoru's body erupted with a sheath of brilliant energy. Psionic power flooded inward, throwing him in a horizontal leap at the two silhouettes. Mamoru's eyes widened at his speed, having forgotten about the lower gravity here. He sailed forty yards in the span of a blink, landing between them in a downstroke that split the right side man open through the chest. He stepped through the swing, bringing the blade around and stabbing the other man through the heart from behind.

Alarms rang out as the proximity sensors registered his motion. Mamoru shot a glance at the emerging sentry gun and rushed forward. He skidded to a halt in front of it before it could arm, too close to the box for it to angle down and fire at him. In seconds, a hand on the side of the housing let his consciousness into the gun and it bent to his will. The sense of immobility that came with embodying the turret unnerved him in a scenario where enemies had firearms. He swiveled right until the other sentry unit lined up in the crosshairs.

The emplaced particle cannon created ripples of orange fire wherever it struck. Clusters of charged particles traveled faster than the eye, or the weapons' sensors, could perceive, resulting in an effect as though the will to attack created spontaneous detonations wherever he aimed. Two bursts reduced the second emplacement weapon to a shower of fragmented, burning chunks.

With the other sentry turret down, he chased several UCF soldiers to cover behind various buildings. Mamoru triggered at random for several more seconds before devoting his concentration to the creation of an automation construct. A small program formed within the electronics of the defense gun. The new software took over the turret, altering the friend-or-foe routine to recognize only one friend: Mamoru.

He left the weapon on autopilot and let go, jogging out of cover to the side of the main barracks pod. The particle cannon went off behind him as a thick muscled soldier leaned out and aimed at him. Mamoru boosted his strength and agility, leaping to the right as he twisted under a flurry of bullets. The soldier exploded in a shower of charred gore and orange plasma before Mamoru landed.

One hit from a particle cannon meant to disable vehicles had vaporized the soldier's torso and flung arms and head in random directions. Smoldering composite armor ash flaked through the air like snow. All around him, men and a few women cursed.

"Stay down and you will live," said Mamoru in a loud, calm tone. "I will only harm those who interfere with me."

"Who the fu—"

The electronic *whirr/whine* of the particle cannon cut the voice off with a wet, splattering explosion.

A woman's scream melted from anguish to words. "Kevin!"

"Kevin should have stayed down," called Mamoru. "Do not repeat his mistake."

He paid no mind to the angry stream of obscenities and death threats flowing out in a feminine voice, and put his hand on the wall of the barracks pod. Electronics inside the building fell under his control, locking both doors and four hatches. Another minor program came into being at his desire for it, designed to block communication with the outside world until someone found and destroyed it.

Mamoru jogged to the nearest prison pod and overrode the electronic lock at a touch. Inside, the narrow hallway glimmered with dim green light. Muffled crying, both male and female, mixed with snoring as well as nervous tapping.

"Are you MLF?" called Mamoru, a hair quieter than yelling.

All went still except for the occasional blast of the particle cannon outside reminding the trapped soldiers it was still online.

"Who the hell are you?" A man's fingers emerged through the bars of a small window at the top of an armored door.

"Your associate Garrison has arranged for your departure from this place."

Cheering, weeping, thanking of God, and banging erupted.

"Calm yourselves!" yelled Mamoru. When they had quieted, he continued. "I need you to remain in control." He raised his voice over their protests. "I have reprogrammed an automatic weapon outside. It will kill anyone other than me who walks through its field of fire."

The prisoners became quiet.

"So how the hell are we getting out of here?" asked a frazzled man.

Mamoru touched the wall. A series of heavy clunks ran down one side of the hall and back along the other as doors unbarred. Sixteen men and four women, all looking bruised and battered, emerged from tiny cells and gathered in the corridor. At the sight of fire dancing across Mamoru's arm, they all but stopped breathing. One woman did not seem to care. She shoved her way through the disoriented prisoners until she clung to a man and wept. The way they embraced left no doubt they were husband and wife.

Mamoru coughed loud enough to cause silence. "Stay here and remain quiet. Wait for my signal."

Outside, the handful of soldiers pinned behind one of the thick spring-loaded legs of the mess hall traded fire with the turret. They held weapons around the wall, using optics to aim without exposing themselves. Streams of metal liquefied from the sides of the particle cannon mechanism as high-velocity indirium rounds tore at it. Mamoru blurred to the second prison building and forced his way through the security system. This building smelled of vomit and held more whimpering.

"Attention, MLF people, it is time to leave. I am here at the request of Garrison."

As the doors clanked open in sequence, ten people emerged. They looked, and smelled, as though they had been trapped in the same clothes for weeks. Many appeared in their later teen years. All wore the heavy cloak of resignation that came with impending death. Only a handful regarded him with a spark of life in their eyes.

The portable building rocked on its springs from the force of an explosion outside, jostling the prisoners against the wall. A few fell.

"What the hell was that," asked the closest boy, perhaps seventeen.

"That was…" Mamoru looked at the wall and sighed. "Unfortunate."

THE BEAST OF MANY ARMS

F ragments of flaming debris rained over the compound as the particle cannon went off in a shower of ruptured energy cells. The weapon core was nowhere to be seen, well on its way into low Mars orbit. Mamoru hovered inside the prison pod door, listening as the sound of boots drew closer.

Three men, one woman.

Mamoru closed his eyes, reciting a silent request to the Kami in his mind—to guide the souls of these fools in the next life. The younger MLF sympathizers behind him murmured and gasped as light wreathed his arms and shoulders. When crunching gravel drew close, he let his power off its leash.

He erupted from the door, leaping from the top of the detachable stairway. A female soldier led the way up the metal steps, desire for payback clear in her eyes. Three men followed. Mamoru rushed past her, slicing her rifle in half and landing between two of the distant soldiers before her facial expression changed. Shock crept in to her rage as his blade ended the men in the time it took her to spin around.

The third man, who looked as young as the prisoners in the second berth, had his rifle sideways across his chest. Mamoru stood with the katana pointed at him. Patches of blood boiled away from the sides.

The soldier shook, terrified by the blazing glow. "W-what are you?"

"In a hurry."

"You killed my fiancée!" screamed the woman behind him.

Mamoru lunged, covering a dozen meters in an instant. He landed next to her on the stairway platform with a precise upswing that sheared the holstered pistol from her belt before she could get a hand on it. She had not yet reacted to the stroke when he pinned her to the wall next to the door with his sword at her throat. Her glare radiated anger while her body sought to recoil from the seething edge approaching her neck.

Mamoru narrowed his eyes. "Stay out of my way if you do not want me to arrange a reunion. I take no pleasure in slaying women."

She tore her gaze away from him, looking at the remaining man and shouting. "Landis, why are you fucking standing there?"

Private Landis glanced down at his untouched, fully loaded assault rifle, and back at Mamoru. "I-if I s-shoot at him, it'll go through both of you."

"That would require that you live long enough to aim," said Mamoru.

Landis whimpered and took a step back. His arms shook as he tried to force his fear aside. Even without telepathic abilities, Mamoru could almost hear the man wondering if he would be fast enough.

The female soldier screamed with rage and drove her fist into Mamoru's gut while he was distracted. He grunted. When the blade inched away from her neck, she grabbed his arms and shoved. One of Mamoru's eyebrows went up in shock at the realization she was, in the absence of his power, stronger than him. The detached porch shuddered as she forced him backward over the railing. *What kind of woman is this strong?* Energy crawled over his arms as he empowered his muscles. *I am not in Japan. This woman is a soldier. I should not have hesitated.* He pushed his strength beyond human limits and flung her at the wall hard enough to knock her senseless.

He shifted his grip on the blade, ready to finish her off. *She is helpless again.* He closed his eyes, trying to tune out the memory of his little sister shrieking as the men grabbed her. One-armed, he grabbed the trooper by her armor and hurled her at Landis, knocking them both into a tumble for several meters.

"Shit... It's a god damned doll," rasped the woman, struggling to crawl toward Landis's abandoned rifle.

Mamoru's boot was on it in seconds. She looked up at him, unable to suppress the startled scream at how he had moved with such speed. Her green-gloved fingers clutched a fistful of dirt. The anger in her expression gave way to dread as she crawled back. He was about to disregard her until her hand crept toward a knife.

The MLF prisoners came streaming out of the two detention pods, running toward the three dead soldiers. The first two grabbed dropped weapons while others scavenged armor. They overwhelmed Landis and the woman, forcing them to their knees. One of the MLF men raised his rifle at them.

"Don't," said the oldest among them. Greying hair blended with his Marsborn white skin and gave him the look of a phantom. "The MLF does not execute prisoners. We shall not become the tyrants we seek to dislodge." He moved up alongside the eager executioner, and looked down at the soldiers. "They are only following orders. Isn't that right, Sergeant Goss?"

"The bombs you set off killed thirty-six UCF military personnel. A third of them weren't even soldiers. How the fuck can you kill us then and want to spare me now?"

The younger man with the rifle edged toward the two, head whipping to the side every few seconds to give the old man a protesting glare. "They were gonna execute us."

"Their bosses were going to execute us, Kalas." The elder frowned at Sergeant Goss. "When two armies meet in the field of battle it is one thing. When an enemy has been captured, different rules apply. Your leaders would kill my men by labeling them terrorists, using fear to dissuade others from the cause. What are terrorists but those who use fear as a weapon? They care nothing for your dead compatriots, Sergeant. They want our movement broken."

"Fine. Fuck." The younger man snarled at the soldiers. "Get outta that armor, both of you."

"You're nothing more than a bunch of killers," said Goss, energy fading from her voice. "With a political agenda."

The elder gestured at his companions. "Some of these boys are sixteen. Like your brethren, they have never killed anyone, yet your commander would see them dead. Examine the motives behind your generals, Sergeant. The Martian Liberation Front is a movement of the people. A room full of politicians has no power over a planet of angry citizens."

Goss flung her armor to the ground, glaring at him. "You're delusional."

"I am sure the British thought the same of the Americans." He waved at the detention box.

"That was almost seven hundred years ago." Goss shook her head.

"I would love to debate politics and philosophy with you, Sergeant, but we do not have the time. While you wait to be let out, consider the similarities in our situation despite the centuries. Men and women hundreds of thousands of miles away make decisions that alter our lives without the slightest idea of what it is like here. They exploit us, they exploit *you*, and if you think for one second they give a Cydonian crab's ass whether you live or die, you're mistaken."

Mamoru sheathed his blade and walked away as they poked and prodded the two soldiers up the stairs of the prison building at rifle point. He went past the pounding walls of the barracks box to the prowler he had hitched a ride on. Between the first and second wheels on the left side, closer to the front, a ladder led to an armored hatch. The underside of the vehicle sat far enough off the ground for him to walk under it without stooping. It took only a second to convince the code lock to open. He ducked under a four-inch thick slab of armor plating as it strained upward on powered struts, and climbed in to a narrow corridor. A left turn past storage cabinets on each side brought him to the cockpit, where he took a seat in the driver's chair.

"Much more comfortable than the rear bumper," he muttered.

Mamoru's consciousness embodied the vehicle, leaving him with the sense he was some manner of bear. The angled nose and subtle forward tilt of the body, combined with its overall shape, felt ursine. Of the six wheels, the front and rear pair turned for steering, which required a moment of adjustment. It was far less complex than a hovercar and an order of magnitude easier than the Fūjin. He brought the vehicle around in a circle and rumbled to a halt by the former prisoners. The two soldiers were nowhere to be seen, most likely occupying the cells they used to guard.

Mamoru's voice emanated from an external speaker. "Get in."

After a mental squirm, he found the proper pattern of thought to open the rear hatch. The entire back end of the vehicle droned down on hydraulic struts and formed a ramp. Mamoru brought the suspension in close to the hull and the prowler settled low on its wheels, near the ground like a cat about to nap. Inhabiting a vehicle was a surreal experience to begin with—the addition of people inside it made it stranger.

"What the fuck?" A man's voice echoed in his belly. "Is he on fire?"

"No, I am controlling this machine." He let go of his link, and sat up in the chair as his consciousness rushed back to his body. As odd as it felt having people walking around inside him, being helpless among so many strangers was unacceptable. "Would one of you know how to operate this in the normal manner?"

"Yeah," said at least four of them.

"Good." Mamoru got out of the driver's seat. "Please do so."

IT DID NOT TAKE LONG FOR THE PROWLER'S AIR FILTRATION SYSTEM TO BOG down, allowing the interior to fill with the stifling stench of the unwashed. Despite its size, the designers intended it to house a crew of eight—not thirty-one. The liberated MLF fighters packed wall to wall in the main cargo space. The older man, Darl Ulyn, had the highest rank of the former prisoners, equivalent to a military captain. Redness had taken his face from a minutes-old argument. His subordinates wanted to keep the bulk of the supplies the prowler had brought in; however, to do that would have left most of them walking.

After weeks, and in some cases months, in detention, not one of them could have handled a two hundred kilometer hike. Mamoru disregarded much of their conversation, which consisted in large part of grumbling at the lack of sleeping berths these vehicles were supposed to have. No matter how often someone mentioned it was a cargo-converted unit, another person invariably whined about having to stand.

"Hey," said Darl, leaning through the bulkhead. "I wanted to thank you for getting us out of there."

Mamoru glanced at the outstretched hand. "It was a request of Garrison in exchange for information."

Darl chuckled at Mamoru's apparent confusion and lowered his arm. He bowed. "Regardless of *why* you did it, I appreciate it."

"That soldier had a point. Why do you attack military targets? If you are fighting a demon with many arms, it is foolish to chop off its hand. While you waste the effort to do that, its other arms will kill you. You should take the head from the beast, not break its weapons."

"Easier said than done." Darl crossed his arms and leaned on the wall. Weariness manifested as sweat tracing cleaner lines through grime-stained pores. Against his pure white skin, the dirt created the appearance of beard stubble. "I get what you're saying. We should be trying to get the military on our side, not making enemies of them."

"A campaign of truth, electronic sabotage, and diversion can be carried out from safety. The military can only oppose force."

"You're pretty sharp, son."

"I am not your son."

Darl laughed until he wheezed, and pounded a fist on his chest twice. "Sure enough you're not." He looked at the driver. "Pria, take us to grid 098, reference 22-45."

The woman at the controls whirled at Darl. Her short, black hair swished about eyes brimming with eagerness. "Won't that leave us about five kilometers away from the shaft?" Pria's complain-face relaxed to a neutral expression and then to one of understanding. "Oh, I get it. No tire marks to give us away."

Darl grumbled. "I don't even like going that close, the transponder—"

"Is dead," added Mamoru.

"Still, not to say I don't trust you, but I'd rather not take chances." Darl looked over his shoulder to the back. "Need a volunteer in reasonable health who'll drive this thing about ten kilos away and ditch it."

One man attempted to volunteer, but could not speak over coughs.

"I'll do it," said Pria. "I'm seventeen. They won't kill me if I get nabbed again."

"Unnecessary," said Mamoru. "I will deal with it."

"I thank you again, stranger."

Mamoru closed his eyes and linked to the machine.

🐗 🦅 🏛 ◌ ☒

THE PROWLER PULLED AWAY, LEAVING THE FORMER PRISONERS SURPRISED TO find Mamoru standing in the dust cloud. He strode through the billowing haze, while the six-wheeled behemoth continued on a course farther toward the north polar cap.

"It will go about one hundred sixty kilometers and veer west to throw them off."

"Those things don't have autopilot, how did—"

"That one does now." Mamoru grinned. "It is merely a matter of software."

"Hah. I never even noticed you plug in."

Mamoru raised both eyebrows. "You did not notice me plug in because I did not plug in."

Darl Ulys held his arm out to the side. "You are truly gifted, my friend. This way."

The beleaguered former detainees shuffled off in single file. Mamoru fell in step to the left of the line. Some bore bruises from interrogations that went too far, and most looked in dire need of food. Only Pria seemed in good spirits, almost chipper. She reminded him of Sadako for a moment in height and hair color, though the NSK ninja was never that upbeat. At least, not that he could remember.

Young and clueless, no wonder they went easy on her.

Walking a hair over six kilometers in thin Martian air caused numerous fainting spells and a handful of rest breaks. The prowler only had two re-breather masks, which got passed among the group. Mamoru added the one he obtained to the rotation, not eager to inhale the taste of rubber again. The air was decent enough for a healthy person to weather the trip.

Before long, a third of their number could no longer walk and those who still could carried them. When it seemed the bulk were ready to collapse, their leaders brought the group to a halt by an unassuming rocky outcropping. Darl and two other men climbed over it, searching.

"Clear," yelled a voice from within a large cleft on the southeastern face.

People backed away as a heavy *thud* rumbled the ground. Dust blasted from the rock face and the stone split along a man-made seam. Machinery groaned in protest as it pushed open a small sealed door bearing a thousand pounds of rock on long, curved hinges. The escapees went in one at a time, with Darl entering last, after waving Mamoru through.

A ladder occupied almost all of the tiny space inside, wobbling under the weight of six people. Mamoru climbed down, pausing to look up as the closing door cut off the stars. In the room below, weak chem lights sprouted up here and there, bathing the area in a lime glow. Some of the former prisoners broke down in sobs finally accepting they were free, and others tore through old lockers and boxes searching for any provisions stashed in the tunnel.

Sand and grit blasted over the assembled crowd when the other exit to the underground chamber opened. Full-density air flooded the room, bringing with it the licked-dirt taste of the Martian underground.

Mamoru grumbled at the reminder of how far away from home he was.

Darl announced a short break while those who were exhausted from the weak atmosphere outside regained strength. A man unearthed a case of silver dry-ration packs, which he handed out among the group. The married pair held each other, Pria bounced around hugging everyone, and several of the others slept. Mamoru used the time to meditate, thankful at least that the strange demons which plagued him back on Earth had thus far seemed incapable of following him.

About an hour after they arrived in the safe room, Darl called for them to move out. A short hallway led to a tunnel of dirt and rock, braced every twenty meters by plastisteel beams. They walked into the dark for what felt like an eternity, yet no one complained. With each step through familiar surroundings, their freedom became more real. Mamoru followed at a respectful distance, occasionally stooping under a damaged bracing strut. The joyous murmurings of the people ahead of him blurred in his mind as he pondered the potential value of Garrison's information.

SEEKING REFUGE

Mamoru leaned against the wall, accepting some unknown woman's offer of warm tea. It was not his usual fare, and it most certainly did not appear to be grey despite what she called it, but it would have been rude to decline. Amid the disturbance caused by the arrival of thirty brothers in arms, Caiden stirred in his bunk. Tired eyes stayed open for a second before he slumped into the ragged cloth. The boy shot upright as Mamoru took a sip of the strange tea.

"Mamoru!" he croaked, his brain more awake than the rest of him. "You're back." He staggered over, almost falling twice. "What happened? Did you have to kill anyone? Did you blow anything up?"

Mamoru guided him with one hand on a shoulder back to bed. "I will tell you in the morning. You are so tired you would not remember now. Go to sleep."

Caiden pouted, but was unable to put up much resistance, and curled on his side in bed as close as he could to the edge. He mumbled incoherencies resembling questions for a few minutes. Mamoru glanced over the cup at him, gripped by a sudden awkwardness from Caiden's obvious attachment.

He drained the remaining tea in one gulp as Osebi ducked in through a door too short for him.

"Garrison asked if he could meet with you in the morning. He is trying to accommodate those you have returned to us."

Mamoru set the cup on the table and glanced at the boy. "I suppose I, too, could use some rest. Would it be acceptable to use one of these bunks?"

Osebi waved at the room. "Aye, sleep wherever you care to."

Both of the spaces with still-functioning Comforgel pads had people in them. Mamoru let off an inaudible grumble, draped his coat on the back of a chair, and unhooked his sword from his belt. He sat on the edge of one of the lower cloth-packed bunks on the south wall and removed his shoes. The chamber was larger than the space in the coffin motel, though it lacked a built in terminal and closable door. With the katana nestled between him and the inner wall, he closed his eyes and sought the calm of meditation.

MAMORU WOKE WITH THE SENSE OF BEING WATCHED. HIS EYES SNAPPED open, startling Caiden who had pulled a chair up close to his bunk, staring him as if he were a holo-vid movie. When the child's shock faded, he grinned and held up a plastic tray.

"I made you something. You got chicken at the place, so I picked that. You didn't like the fries, so I didn't add them."

Mamoru's gaze flicked from the boy's broad grin to a lump of beige material on a bun. It vaguely resembled a fried, breaded chicken cutlet; however, it looked as if it was melting and glistened like slime. The bread, too, had a gelatinous sheen.

He made eye contact again. "Thank you."

Caiden waited for him to sit up and handed him the tray. The most frightening thing about the 'meal' in front of him was that it smelled like chicken. He shot an imperious frown, one worthy of Minamoto, at the offering. The boy laughed at the way it jiggled, as if afraid.

"Is it okay? I made it a little bit ago, but it usually takes an hour to turn back into OmniSoy."

Mamoru nodded and seized the sandwich before it could deteriorate further. Visions of servants being slapped to the floor for putting two millimeters too much sake in a cup, and other minor infractions, danced through his head as he bit down. His teeth closed around a mass of semisolid ooze with a chemical impression laced with bread, cheese, and chicken. It tasted like dense pudding flavored in ways no one had ever intended pudding to be flavored.

It brought him back to the first time Nami had attempted to prepare his food. As the daughter of a prestigious employee, she spent her entire life on the receiving end of servants' work. Absolute terror shone in her eyes as Mamoru appraised her piteous offering. Before he could say one word, she fell to her knees and begged him not to kill her. Those who had prepared her for a new life as someone's property cautioned some samurai would slay her if she committed a grievous enough mistake. He sighed, trying to put the sight of her like that out of his mind. At the time, he didn't let it bother him. Now, he felt no better than the MDF troops who had almost killed Caiden.

Nothing she ever made was as much an atrocity as whatever this thing is I am eating right now.

That night, Nami learned she was fortunate—fate had given her a kind master.

"What are you thinking about?"

The small voice dispelled his dreams of his old home. He felt a bit like a boy himself at that moment, missing the security of his old life.

"I am thinking of home." Mamoru spoke in a flat tone, bracing for another bite.

"Oh." Caiden looked dejected. "Back on Earth, right?"

"Yes." *Do not think of what this substance is.* He squinted at the boy for guilting him into eating the OmniSoy horror.

"Do you think I could go with you?"

Mamoru almost choked. He swallowed what was in his mouth and patted himself a few times. "You would not like it where I live. My society does not regard those born elsewhere as equals. They would mistake you for a kabuki actor, or taikomochi."

"Huh?"

"Look," said Mamoru, reaching out to grasp the boy's hand. "You are white like snow. People will assume you are wearing face paint." He found himself frowning at the bone thin appendage. "Your life here is cruel, but it would not improve where I am from."

"It's okay if people don't trust me there. At least they won't want to kill me." Caiden failed to produce a convincing smile through his disappointment.

"It is not fair what has been done to you, or your mother." Mamoru let go of his hand and stood, gathering his coat. "Being close to me would only expose you to more things you do not deserve."

Caiden sulked.

"I will answer your question from last night and tell you of the prison break."

He perked up. "Okay."

The boy did not notice the last third of the chicken sandwich had degenerated to a quarter-inch layer of beige ooze. While putting his coat on, Mamoru slid the plate onto the empty spool serving as a table. The retelling of the attack on the prison camp occupied the majority of the walk back to the room where he had met Garrison the other day. Mamoru did not soften the details, but confined the deaths to simple statements that spared his young follower the gore.

Caiden seemed thrilled and worried in equal parts, listening with rapt attention until the story ended. He studied the ground for a moment in silence. Several cots had been set up in the last stretch of hallway before their destination, where the weaker ex-prisoners rested. Hands emerged from blankets, eager to wave, touch, or greet Mamoru. Caiden appeared about to speak, but at the sight of the injured, he remained quiet.

Garrison looked up from the desk at the squeak of the door. Mamoru bowed again, a slight gesture one gives to acknowledge one of lesser status, to which the man nodded. The giant with the metal arm snored on a cot at the back of the office behind a teal medical curtain. Mamoru raised an eyebrow at an arrangement of plasfilm posters on the wall over the bed. Aside from one blonde, tan swimsuit model, the rest of them had images of boy-band stars, the sort of things a tween girl might hang.

Caiden saluted Garrison, who returned it.

"Welcome back, Mamoru. I had intended for you to *find* the encampment. I... I don't know what to say."

"There was insufficient time. At least half of your people would have been executed before you could have mobilized an effective strike. They considered the prisoners of 'minimal intelligence value.'"

"Still," said Garrison, walking around the desk with an outstretched hand. "That was damn fine work."

Mamoru accepted the handshake as if gripping a slab of spoiled meat. "I do not understand your society's fascination with physical contact."

"Neither do I." Garrison laughed. "I'm... I never expected such a fortunate outcome. Only six of the original squad died." He studied the desk for a few seconds, tapping his fingers. "There's so much good you could do for us here, Mamoru. I know you have affairs to settle back on the blue ball, but if you ever find yourself in need of a place to be, we would be honored to have you."

"I appreciate the offer, Garrison."

"I will give you the information you need. Would you be willing to do one more small favor?"

Mamoru's eyes did not belay his irritation. "I am pressed for time."

Garrison held his hands up. "No, no. This will not take any additional time. The place you are looking for, Araphel, is a hidden city tucked in the canyons of the Scandia depression."

Caiden edged closer to Mamoru.

"The place is dangerous... hostile. The air's good due to the downdraft from the North Pole, but it's chaotic as hell. They got all the terraforming stuff set up on the caps, and for whatever reason, the wind tears through that area, enough to strip the paint from a prowler. Makes it nine shades of hell to fly anything through there. Fortunately, the UCF thinks it's the middle of nowhere. I'd like you to take Caiden with you."

Mamoru blinked.

Caiden shivered. "Why?"

"Some sources we have inside the Defense Force tell us their commanders believe he killed those three officers."

"That's dustblow!" blurted Caiden. "There's no way I could have. I was cuffed! I'm only ten. I don't even have a sword."

Garrison leaned on the desk with both hands. "I know, Cay. It doesn't make any sense. Our friend here didn't show up on any of their video streams. They don't claim to know how you did it. They were hoping to ask you."

"If they think I killed police officers, they're not gonna try and get me alive... Even if I am only a kid."

"That's likely." Garrison pursed his lips, sending a sad stare at the desk for a few seconds. "You can't stay here. There's too much going on for any of us to look out for you."

Caiden looked up with an indignant face, as if about to launch into a justification of his usefulness, but deflated.

"I will take him." Mamoru bowed. "Since I am going there already, it is no imposition. The boy clearly cannot remain here."

Small white hands kneaded Mamoru's dark shirt. Caiden looked up at him, trying to force a smile through his fear.

"STAY CLOSE," MUTTERED MAMORU WHILE GUIDING THE BOY ALONG THE street leading to Aperture 2.

He made a sour face as he held on. "I feel like a clingy little girl."

Mamoru smiled. "You are shaking like one. You have a thin face and large eyes. If your hair was longer, you'd look like one."

Caiden glared at him, but broke up laughing from nerves. "No big deal, right? Only all the police in the entire city want me dead."

"They will not touch you."

"Uh, Mamoru… I know you're a badass and all, but they're the police. They have lasers and stuff. Your sword isn't gonna kill someone a thousand meters away."

"This city is dense. Few places afford them that sort of range." He hesitated at the end of the street, watching the courtyard.

Caiden looked up and twisted to peer behind them. "They'll be up on top of the high towers where they could see the whole city."

"Then stop looking up."

He ducked, huddled against Mamoru's side.

"You are right. You cling like a frightened girl child." He kept his face serious long enough to get the boy to scowl at him before grinning. "Do you have a credit stick?"

He rummaged through his pockets. "Yeah, one, but its only got three creds left. Can't even buy dirt with that."

Mamoru took the tiny device, closing it in his fist. He opened his mind to the circuitry within. The world around him changed, becoming a neat one-room office. A faceless mannequin sat behind a desk wearing a black suit traced with a hairline grid of sparkling green threads. On the wall to the figure's left, a round old-style bank vault door opened to white shelves. They were barren, except for three miniscule silver flakes. The other side had an enormous red button.

"Do not step past the yellow line, user. It is a violation of international law to tamper with the contents of an ICFC virtual node."

"What is ICFC?" asked Mamoru, feigning ignorance.

The faceless figure stood, head tilting as if to stare at a glowing yellow line inches from where the unoccupied samurai armor floated.

"The InterTrust Commerce Facilitation Corp—"

As soon as the information routine ran, Mamoru's right gauntlet stretched sixteen feet out to touch the mannequin's chest. The logic conundrum of him being inside without entering the node dropped its rote recitation to a warbling stutter. Cyberspace, at least the tiny slice of it within the credstick, lacked the processing power to delineate a difference between him tampering with the program and exerting his psionic power on the hardware. Ordinary hacking would have left him butting heads with a grade eight firewall represented by an invisible force wall in line with the yellow glow. The credstick's microprocessor had no exception handling for Mamoru's ability to effect alterations to program code with a thought.

The banker program construct detected *something* happened that should not; however, because the barrier remained untouched, it did not need to self-destruct. Armored fingers plunged like daggers through the now-liquid chest of the mannequin as if displacing gooey tar. The body jerked about as if electrocuted while Mamoru's mind filled with thousands of lines of words, numbers, and symbols. He *experienced* it as a collection of intent and function rather than strings of discrete symbols. Here, in the isolated safety of a credstick's virtual world, he was free from the monitoring of the ICFC. Pumping up the balance of a credstick would go unnoticed, unless he spent large sums of manufactured money in one shot.

An avalanche of silver chips flooded the vault as a blizzard of mercury raged. When he was done, Mamoru opened his eyes. Mere seconds passed in the real world. Ten fingers tried to drill into his arm.

"What?" asked Mamoru, glancing down at the lockjaw panic on the boy's face.

"Your arm was on fire. I could see it, even in the daylight."

Concern tinged his voice as he looked at the crowd. "Did anyone else notice?"

"I don't think so."

"Good."

He opened his hand. A tiny blue on blue display screen read twenty million credits.

Caiden stared, teetering on the verge of passing out. "H-holy shit. How did you do that?"

Mamoru looked ahead at the prowler dealer. "I wanted the money to be there."

"Can you teach me how to do that?"

"Are you psionic?"

"Oh, right," Caiden kicked at the ground. "Nope."

"Stay close."

"Doing the thing with the cameras?"

"Mmm."

They crept through the bustling mid-day crowd in the Aperture 2 courtyard. Workers out for a lunch break zoomed past on their way to their favorite street-meat wagon. Fumes tainted the air where they passed an artist who attracted a modest audience by creating images with physical paint rather than digital holograms. Caiden used Mamoru's body to hide from the direction of Foster's old shop, where a pair of low-ranking MDF officers out front looked about ready to fall asleep on their feet. Several head-sized orb bots floated around the alley leading to the back, their passage tracked by wide blue laser lines on the walls and ground.

Caiden peered around, and shivered at the scene.

"Perhaps it is a good thing people here have become so pale. It is hard to know when you are frightened."

He shot Mamoru a wounded look as they entered the prowler dealership. Caiden soon forgot all about his worries, fascinated by the gargantuan all-terrain vehicles. The tops of the massive tires towered two feet over Mamoru's head. Caiden climbed all over one as a pudgy man tripped over himself to rush out of the attached office space and onto the lot.

Mamoru pointed at one of the Mars-red ones. "I am in need of transportation. What is your fee for that machine?"

"That one is four point two. It's got some miles on it, couple of dings. The one next to it"—he pointed at the shiny black one—"that one's brand new outta the factory. Less than four thousand miles on it, all the latest electronics and double-redundant life support."

"In an ideal situation, I will be back within a week or two. I do not need to be wasteful. What would you charge for the use of the red one for two weeks?"

The salesman deflated, but tried to hide it.

Mamoru frowned. "Regardless of the charge for the service, I will tip you two hundred and fifty thousand credits for your discretion."

"Two weeks?" asked the man. "Rental fees are usually about a thousand credits a day, but since that's a used unit, I can let you use it for six hundred—with a returnable deposit."

"Agreed."

"Great," said the salesman with a huge smile. "I'll get started on the forms."

JOURNEY

The steady whirr of six motorized wheels vibrated through the hull as the prowler rumbled over open ground north of Arcadia. Mamoru's unconscious body jostled in the driver's seat with each dip in the terrain or boulder large enough for the tires to notice. Neither he nor Caiden had bothered to ask why the interior reeked with the overwhelming stench of cleaning chemicals.

The boy spent the first hour alternating between staring at a plastic hula dancer at the center of the console and the Navcon, while covering most of his face with his shirt and both hands. He glanced at Mamoru, no longer enthralled by the shimmering energy surrounding him, and sighed.

"Is something wrong?"

Caiden jumped from the loud voice filling the vehicle. He spent the next minute choking on fumes from his sharp inhale. After wiping watery eyes on his sleeve, he blinked at Mamoru.

"You can talk?"

"Of course." The prowler shifted with a slight leftward course adjustment.

"Why are you driving like that?"

Mamoru was quiet for a moment. "Like what? Too slow?"

"No, I mean while sleeping."

"I'm not sleeping." Internal speakers vibrated with an attempt to convey chuckling. "I am operating this vehicle with my mind."

"Oh, kind of like a wire?" Caiden poked a finger behind one ear.

"I suppose that is a passable analogy."

The boy swiveled the seat to face center and slid forward until his feet hit the ground. "You sound tired. Want food or something?"

"This is somewhat tiring. The ponderousness with which this beast lumbers is frustrating."

Mamoru brought the prowler to a halt and ceased concentrating on the mental link. His awareness settled back in to his body as Caiden appeared with a plastic carton. He accepted the offering with one hand as the other rubbed his eyes. A blast of dust shot out of the cushion when the boy jumped into his seat, a matching carton in his lap.

"Why don't you drive it like normal? It's not as tiring."

He frowned at the over-cute chibi face on the top of the pre-packaged meal as he pulled the red cord. "I am not sure how to work the controls."

Caiden pulled the string on his. "You're like, old. Don't all old people know how to drive?"

Hissing emerged from both boxes as they swelled, spewing the fragrance of instant ramen. When the sound stopped, they opened their meals and picked at the steaming broth and noodles.

This smells like the water used to clean the pots. Mamoru risked a taste, finding it on the low end of tolerable. "I had drivers."

"What, you were rich or something?" He slurped some noodles. "Well, I guess you have as much money as you want."

Mamoru waved his hand to the side, spoon stuck between his fingers. "I do not do that often. The commerce authority can track abnormal patterns. Too many credits coming out of nowhere will make them suspicious. I was a samurai in the service of a powerful man. I had two women, a respectable home, and lived with privilege outside of the law that binds commoners."

"You had two girlfriends?" Caiden leaned closer.

"Not in that sense. They were given to me by my shogun."

"What's a shogun? Given to you? What, like slaves?" He made a scrunched face.

"Shogun are called CEOs in the West." He took his time with the next mouthful of noodles. "These women are those who have lost their status as a result of criminal activity or disgracing the company."

"That's not nice… that you own people."

"It is complicated. They become assets of the company, not one man. When they are criminals, it is similar to your prison—a set amount of time to serve. Is it not kinder than sitting in a cage?"

Caiden shrugged. "So your shogun's mad at you?"

Mamoru narrowed his eyes. "This Raziel has made him so. It was not of my doing."

"Did he take your women back?" The boy stared at him as more noodles slithered up through pursed lips.

"They would have been given to another. Nami was once part of the upper class, but her father brought great shame on their family. She was strong. Ayame would not have endured." He frowned at the floor. "She is too delicate."

A smile spread over Caiden's face. "You set them free, didn't you?"

"What makes you think that?" Mamoru looked up, raising a brow. "That is no different than stealing."

"You sound sad talking about it. I bet you liked them, and you're nice."

"I am not 'nice.' Nice men don't cut other men in half as a favor to a veritable stranger."

Caiden closed the empty carton. "You're nice to me. What's Araphel like?"

Mamoru shifted the seat to face forward and looked over the controls. Two prominent sticks. "I have never been there, and there is almost no information about it online."

"Sticks are pretty simple." Caiden hopped out of the passenger seat, ducked under Mamoru's arm and stood in front of him. "Left stick sideways turns the back wheels. Right stick sideways turns the front wheels. Up and down control the speed on that side." He moved his hands through the air as if pushing invisible levers. "Left all the way forward, right all the way back and we'd spin."

"You know how to drive this thing?"

"Sorta. I've watched the fighters do it all the time." He pointed at the various readouts, buttons, and dials. Afterward, he glanced back over his shoulder with sad eyes. "You're really gonna leave me in Araphel?"

Mamoru kept a blank face despite a twinge of guilt. "I can think of nowhere safer for you. The police forces here are still part of the UCF military. If they discover you have gone to Earth, they may still pursue you."

Caiden looked down. "But, I didn't even *do* anything but get beat up. What about Japan?"

"As I said before, you would forever be an outsider there. I will do what I can to remove you from their systems, though you should still hide until those who studied your photo forget. I can do nothing to their memory."

"But, what am I gonna do in Araphel? Just be another street kid?"

"Garrison was confident that there would be someone there willing to watch out for you. He told me many in the MLF go there when they need to hide. Perhaps it would be best for you to disassociate yourself from the movement and seek a normal life."

The boy folded his arms, trying to drill through the prowler's side with his stare. "Bad people go there too, anyone who needs to hide from the law. What if it's not safe?"

Mamoru put a hand on Caiden's shoulder. The boy's lip quivered at the contact. "I am not a good role model. You, and your fellows, fight for what you believe in. You have an ideology that inspires you to risk your lives for a better world. I believe in honor, money, and status."

Caiden sniffled. "You're not as mean as you try to act. It's okay. I know you don't wanna get stuck with a kid to watch."

"I have enemies, boy." Mamoru grasped the sticks and pushed them both up.

The prowler lurched forward, pushing Caiden into his lap. He held on to the armrests to avoid being thrown to the ground as Mamoru experimented with steering and alternating throttle.

"Careful," said Caiden. "You can do a small turn by speeding up one side without twisting the wheels." When he trusted inertia not to fling him away, he held on to the sticks on top of Mamoru's hands and guided them. "Here, like this."

Mamoru furrowed his brow, annoyed at a ten-year-old talking to him like a child in need of learning. He swallowed his pride and let the boy show him. In this case, age was not a measure of experience. Some minutes later, Caiden trudged to the passenger seat and flopped down. A patch of rough stones jostled them about, though the prowler's tires took them in stride.

"I know you gotta leave me there, but can I stay with you till you go?"

Mamoru glanced at the Navcon, sliding the left stick farther up than the right to induce a mild rightward turn. "Are you hoping to endear yourself to me to the point I change my mind?"

The boy picked at the seat, not looking up. "Uh, maybe."

"Your life will be happier in this place than at my side, Caiden. I do not know what awaits me back on Earth. I am the target of assassins. If they detect a weakness, they will exploit it."

"You don't want them to use me against you."

Mamoru remained quiet.

Caiden tilted his head, attempting to hide a smile behind his hair.

22

ARAPHEL

everal hours of driving brought them over hard wind-swept ground that even the prowler's weight could not mark. The same violent polar gusts that made flying too risky wiped out what little tracks the vehicle created. Mamoru stared at a Navcon point Garrison provided, which led to a desolate ridgeline. He brought the great vehicle to a halt, though it continued swaying in the gale. Stones ranging in size from pebble to fist bounced off the hull. A few hit hard enough to cause the video display mimicking a windshield to pixilate for a moment.

"This is the location, but there is nothing here."

Caiden swung his feet back and forth for a moment. "Um. Remember Garrison said you gotta send that message."

"Right." Mamoru fiddled with the console, taking a moment to locate the communication system. He set the transmission mode to manual and forced the frequency to 777 Mhz. He held up his NetMini, displaying the note he took from Garrison, and read aloud. "Seek shelter from thine enemies among the rocks, and from the darkness watch."

Silence. They glanced at each other for a few minutes.

Caiden offered a cheesy smile and scratched his head. "Guess there's no Araphel after all. We should go back before it gets dark."

"Hey, y'all." An older male voice crackled through on an audio-only signal. Static interference worsened in time with the wind. "Just a one-man science post up in the hills. You folks lost?"

Mamoru shook his head at the notes. "Ran out of sugar, was wondering if I could borrow a cup." He muted the comm. "Who came up with this?"

"I dunno." Caiden stared into his lap, fidgeting with his shirt. "I guess they wanted something no one would ever say on accident."

"You came a long way for sugar, why'd you think I'd have any?"

Exasperation leaked through Mamoru's words. "Garrison's whipping up some cornbread."

"Fair enough." The phantom voice lost the timbre of an old man, deepening. "Come up about seventy meters ahead and face the wall."

A nudge on both sticks got them moving.

"You're getting better at driving," said Caiden.

Mamoru stopped at the designated point and glanced to his left at the ridge. Caiden made a gesture with his hands as if moving sticks—back left forward right. Mamoru copied it on the actual controls, rotating the prowler in place to bring the nose facing the wall.

A section of ridge sank inward until it went flat on the ground, revealing a large tunnel. Inside, where the wind could not reach, numerous tire tracks crisscrossed in the silt. Not wanting to chance his meager skills in tight confines, Mamoru linked with the prowler. Embodying the device made control as simple as walking, and he navigated the passage with ease. A mile later, the tunnel ended at a huge underground chamber. Nine other prowlers parked here and there around support columns of plastisteel and stone, some with crews working on them. Smaller open-topped rovers lined up near stacks of metal shipping boxes, and a handful of ATVs with oversized, fat wheels clustered on the far right.

The wall opposite where they entered was more than a hundred and fifty meters away, a smooth surface of plain Mars rock with a square tunnel cut into the midpoint. Strips of light ran through the corridor, embedded in all four corners. A large banner hung on either side of the tunnel, bearing a black field with an image of Mars at the center. Gold lettering superimposed on the planet read *Pueri Verum Martis*.

Mamoru pulled in to an open prowler-sized space, defined by a painted yellow rectangle, and stopped. An instant of desire commanded the machine to power down. He moved for the door, pausing to look when the boy did not stand.

"I will not leave you in a bad situation."

Caiden looked at him with a morose face, sighed, and stood. "Okay."

Mamoru went down the ladder first. The air smelled of lubricant and metal, as well as the ever-present taste of dirt. He cringed inside. *I'm going to be imagining the flavor of dirt for months.* Caiden closed the hatch and shimmied down the boarding ladder, jumping the last bit to the ground with a heavy stomp that echoed through the cavernous garage. Workers operating on another prowler some distance away stopped what they were doing and glanced up at the noise. The sight of a pair of new arrivals did not keep their interest for more than a few seconds.

Caiden leaned back, staring up at the blackness as the pair walked towards the entry tunnel. Mamoru cast a wary look upward, half expecting a ninja to be waiting overhead. Indistinct shapes of crossbeams, catwalks, and girders hid behind the glare of harsh lights. He dismissed it, and picked up his pace. At the sound of his steps clanking on the metal floor of the tunnel, Caiden looked down and hurried to catch up.

From the mouth of the tunnel, the distant glow of a subterranean city illuminated the walls, overpowering the feeble light from the four strips. Once in the hallway, the snapping buzz of failing electronics became noticeable. Every so often, and more common among the two ground-level lights, a three-foot section flickered. Mamoru exhaled through his nose, trying to force away the stink of fried silicon.

The tunnel went twenty meters at a slight downward grade, ending at an elevated metal platform with a waist-high railing. A vaulted stone ceiling opened into a cavernous space above one and two story buildings. Araphel, the city, stretched out before them, seven stories down from the level of the tunnel. Flickering holographic signs danced in the darkness, illuminating patches of wall with various colors. Far off, six-story structures similar in appearance to skyscrapers connected floor to ceiling. A conspicuous lack of advert bots left the streets darker than expected, save for the occasional gasping flutter of an ancient lamp. The fragrance of food, beer, and piss battled for prominence in a mild, but constant breeze.

Fortunately, food was winning.

Mamoru regarded the sight with curiosity—the absence of advert bots seemed somehow *wrong*. Caiden approached the railing to the right of a square slab elevator, of size enough to transport a light truck or car. He stood on tiptoe and hung his head out over the side. Saliva gathered in a wad on his lip, lingered a second, and fell. Mamoru cleared his throat. The boy fell on his heels, looking back with an impish smile. Mamoru pointed with a grunt and walked left toward a stairway. Once Caiden couldn't see his face, he allowed himself a faint smile. The entire frame of the stairway rattled and clanked as they descended through six switchback platforms.

At the bottom, ill-set plastisteel plates three meters square attempted to smooth out the dirt beneath them. He paused, glancing left, right, and straight ahead at the three streets leading away from the entrance. Since he'd been on mars, he'd come to expect a certain degree of grunge coating everything, but this place went beyond. Everyone carried weapons of one type or another, handguns more often than not, but rifles and even swords passed by in the crowd. Quite a few individuals had metal arms or legs, some with mounted blades. Over a few minutes of people watching, not a single person under the age of twenty-ish went by.

Caiden shivered and edged closer. "I don't see any kids."

Maybe they are hiding. He looked at Caiden, his expression adrift between loneliness, fear, and curiosity. "If I had one, I wouldn't let my child outside in this place either."

"This place is scarier than I thought."

"Not what you were expecting?"

Caiden kicked at the ground. "I dunno."

FIVE WOMEN LEANED ON A DUSTY METAL WALL BENEATH THE TRANSPARENT red glow of the word *Abaddon* traced in holographic calligraphy. Of the lot, two were topless, and none struck him as appealing. One was a little too young, one a lot too old, one looked male, and the last two were far too high. All of them winked and waved. Mamoru's gaze gravitated to the artillery on their belts rather than their chest.

This is a strange place. Even the whores are armed.

Caiden stared at breasts as they approached the building, leaning back to keep them in sight on the way through the door. Mamoru gave him a light swat on the back of the head.

"Careful, boy. People like that can be dangerous."

A short entry corridor led to a dim room. Azure light shimmered over a number of booth tables from several life-sized holograms: virtual nude dancers of both genders on round stage-like tables. A couple of Gee-Ball themed 3D games were set up on the far right, but dust said they had not been touched in a while. Mamoru squinted at the woman behind the bar: thirties, average build, her every curve revealed by a purple and black bodysuit with a sweetheart neckline. Her bare shoulders bore tattoos of thorny roses. The flowers changed color in a slow seep, darkening from bright red to violet to black, repeating in an endless cycle.

"You didn't even look at them. I guess you don't need a pross when you have your own women." Caiden rubbed where he'd been smacked, frowning. "Did you…"

Mamoru's expression hardened. *Once, but it was more like she used me…* "Our arrangement was different. They cooked, cleaned, and managed the house."

"I mean, you could have made them if you wanted to, right?"

"In terms of our law, yes." Mamoru stopped at the end of a short hallway between the door and the barroom. "But…"

"You liked one of them, didn't you? Avas used to look at my mom with the same face you're making now."

"Who is Avas?"

"Was. Some guy who was seeing my mom, but he wasn't a badass like you. He made a couple creds sellin' illegal stuff. Softs, 'lectronics, some chems. He had mom's PID in his NetMini, so the MDF dragged her in for questioning and to identify the body."

"It's possible." Mamoru walked towards the bar.

Caiden held his hands out, following. "Possible? You either like her or you don't."

"In her situation, it was in her best interest to do everything she could to make herself appealing. She could not accept her change of status. Had I taken her for a wife, she would rise in social class."

"So?" Caiden crossed his arms on the bar.

"My feelings are meaningless if hers were false." Mamoru thought back to Nami's face, pleading eyes staring through the lined display on the spider bot. "I suppose I have some hope they were genuine."

"Aww, he's adorable. Getting him started young?" The bartender leaned all her weight on one leg, hands on hips. Violet patches on her suit hinted at the shape of a lace corset. "You still smell like Earth."

"I smell nothing but dirt in this place." Mamoru gestured at the door. "The entire planet reeks of metal and dust."

She laughed. "You get used to it. Need a menu?"

"I am not here to eat."

The woman leaned on her elbows, squiggly black hair hung to the bar as she leaned forward. "Oh, that sounds juicy."

"I ran into one of your associates a short while ago near the Hollow.

Helix I believe his name was. He was convinced you could give me some information about Raziel. You are Shanna, correct?"

Shanna cocked an eyebrow and leaned back. "I'm supposed to believe Helix said anything about me?"

Mamoru folded his arms. "He became rather conversational after he got back up."

"You..." Shanna pointed at him. "You beat Helix in the Hollow?"

"It wasn't much of a fight... Lotta people lost money," said Caiden.

"Horseshit." She set her hands on her hips.

"He said you would say that. He also said that he loves some little squeaking noise you—"

"Stop!" She held up a hand. "Okay, fine. Maybe you did." Shanna fired another disbelieving glare at him. "Tell me how your skinny ass beat an aug with combat-grade limbs?"

"I desired to."

"That doesn't tell me anything." Shanna squinted, letting a sigh slide through her teeth. "Maybe I don't want to know. What are you after Raziel for? You lookin' to find God? Only people that wanna find him are either kooks or spooks, and you don't look like an intelligence agent."

"No. I wish to understand what power he holds over a man I once worked for. I must reclaim my honor."

"Reclaim your honor sounds like you mean to kill him. Good luck with that, hon. He's he's supposed to be an angel, if he's even real." Shanna waved her hand about. "You know, power of Heaven and all that. Bunch of dustblow if you ask me."

Caiden stared at an animated hologram of buffalo nibbles, all but drooling.

"The result of our meeting is up to him. I seek understanding before anything."

Shanna stared into space for a moment, a glazed look coming over her. Seconds later, his NetMini beeped and her eyes regained focus. "I gave you a nav point. Go talk to Jasden at NuOrganix. He claims to know where Raziel is. I've never seen the man. I don't even think he's real." She looked from Caiden to Mamoru. "You sure you don't want to see a menu?"

Mamoru closed his eyes and slouched. "Fine. What do you have that won't kill me?"

Shanna winked. "You'd be surprised."

23

IN THE GARDEN

According to the Nav pin Shanna gave him, NuOrganix placed their facility deep within the interior of Araphel, close to where the digging had ceased. Were it not for the stone forty meters overhead and the inescapable taste of dirt, this could have been any other metropolitan area. Residential and office towers spanned from floor to ceiling, but continued deeper into the rock below the ground level. Pro-Martian-Independence graffiti covered every surface, ranging from crude black outlines to full-color pieces depicting daggers stabbing a bloody Earth.

Caiden kicked trash out of their way as they walked down the center of a two-lane street. Mamoru expected some manner of ambush or hostilities in every shadow. *I wonder why they made the hallways look like roads. No one has cars here.*

The odor of molten plastic mixed with the eye-watering ambiance of burning thermogel. Smoke wisps trailed from the broken windows of a large building, near a shot-out sign, no longer recognizable for whatever corporation put it there. About thirty people sat around portable cooking units in what appeared to be the former lobby of a corporation. A red-haired woman bundled up in too-large coats sat on a metal shipping carton in front of a tent, exhaling into her hands to warm them. She seemed in her early to mid thirties, and stared at him as if weighing the odds of success at robbing him.

Deep azure light bathed the right half of the room, emanating from a broken wire conduit as thick as Mamoru's thigh. Broken fiberoptic strands sprouted in several layers, resembling a sad attempt at a tree growing out of the cracked metal.

On the left side, near a metal table bearing several small cans of blue fire, two preteen girls clung to a man who appeared to be their father. Mittens of tied cloth strips covered little hands seeking warmth. Their clothing appeared to be made from scraps of plastic and cloth tied on with twine, and their shoes seemed made of silver duct tape that left their toes visible. Neither girl noticed them, focusing all their attention on their imminent meal.

Carcasses rotating over the gel cans bore an alarming resemblance to rats the size of dogs. The adults gave Mamoru glares ranging from challenging to wary, which seemed to soften when they spotted Caiden. None reached for weapons.

Mamoru put a hand on the boy's shoulder and whispered, "They are as afraid of us as you are of them."

Caiden locked eyes with the only other children he had seen since arriving in Araphel. The older girl was his age, the sister about five. Their makeshift garments suggested a life even harsher than what he had endured in Arcadia. Only after they'd walked too far to see them anymore did Caiden look away from the girls.

"I'm gonna wind up like that…" He tucked his hands under his armpits and shivered. "Maybe I should go back. I'd rather be in jail. At least it'd be warm."

Mamoru sighed through his nose, without making a sound.

Other buildings had the appearance of offices, though the locals had repurposed them as living space. Narrowed eyes and brandished weapons gave him the feeling people here occupied whatever area they could find and defend. A few blocks over, tucked in a shadowy dead-end alley, a white metal wall bore the word *NuOrganix* in three-foot tall block letters. Unlike the rest of this section of town, this facility seemed to be in operation and the area relatively clean.

A pair of broad-shouldered men flanked the door, clad in pale grey longcoats. Both held full-sized rifles with boxy frames glittering with electronics. Mamoru paid them no mind as he went for the door between them.

The one on the right moved to block the entrance while the other one fidgeted at the grip on his weapon.

Roadblock raised a hand. "Hold it. I don't recognize you. This is an employee only entrance."

Mamoru offered a slight bow. "I need to visit one of your employees."

"You'll need to wait for him to leave or request a guest authorization from the corporate office."

The man with the rifle smiled. "They usually get back to you within forty-eight to seventy-two hours."

"I am afraid I am pressed for time." He held his hand up, moving it to the side as if scraping something out of his way. "Please move. I do not wish to injure anyone."

The man blocking the door grabbed Mamoru's shoulder. "I ain't gonna ask you again."

Energy simmered on the back of Mamoru's hand. He felt the presence of significant cyberware within the man touching him and forced some of his consciousness through the machinery, causing a plastisteel fist to fly to the side. The hand not on his shoulder smashed the other guard in the head. The unexpected and superhuman attack bounced the rifle-bearer off the wall to the ground, where he flopped corpse-still save for a sporadic twitch.

The still-conscious sentry gawked. "Fuck... What the—"

White luminescence flared, creeping up Mamoru's arms as it brightened.

"Aww shit..." The guard leaned away, staring in confounded fear.

The man's array of cybernetic implants unfurled in Mamoru's mind. A mental command leapt across a synapse, and the man's eyes rolled back in his head. He collapsed in place, an inert sack of meat. Mamoru stooped to touch the other one before he could recover from the punch to the head. Two seconds of concentration disabled the man's Neural Interface Unit.

"Did you kill them?" asked Caiden, failing to sound braver than he was.

"No. I turned them off for an hour. A piece of cyberware exists between their bodies and their brains. These unfortunate fools both have augmented arms and legs, which are now disconnected from their minds." Mamoru gestured at spasmodic curling of the lips, a futile attempt to growl. "I imagine they are quite angry."

"That's awesome." Caiden went to search their pockets, but Mamoru snagged him by the back of his coat and pulled him away. "Aww."

"Do not steal." Mamoru set him back on his feet. "We are guests."

Mamoru touched three fingers to the mirrored panel by the door.

Sharp lines defined azure numbers through the surface as it cycled through access codes. Digits locked in place one after the next until a five-digit sequence remained. The seal broke with a sharp intake of air that resolved to an exhalation of earthy chemical stench. Caiden pulled his shirt up over his face.

Inside, a minimalist lobby of grey and black held a reception desk positioned below a holographic rendering of the word *NuOrganix* as if formed from emerald. Flowers, vegetables, and formless meat lumps sprouted from the letters on vines, a fast-forward animation of growth. Behind it, a slender woman in her later fifties looked up with hard slate eyes. Steel-grey hair pulled back in a severe bun added to the harshness of her presence.

Mamoru covered the forty feet to her desk in an instant, grasping her wrist before she could touch the button an inch below her fingers. The fading glow over his shoulders left her speechless. He walked to the side, dragging her away from the desk on a rolling chair as he rounded the corner.

"This is not a corporate action." He released her arm. "I am here to speak with one named Jasden."

Caiden caught up, standing at Mamoru's side.

"I cannot discuss personnel matters with a non-employee," said the woman, folding her arms. Though her expression remained stony, sweat beaded on her forehead.

The boy sighed and darted to the terminal, shifting his backpack on one shoulder. His face turned shades of blue and violet from the holo-displays as patterns changed with each screen.

"That's private!" shouted the receptionist as her attempt to stand ended with a shove back into the chair. "You"—she glared at Mamoru—"he can't do that. It's secure corporate…" She surrendered to a resigned calm, tinted with worry. "They could terminate me."

Caiden looked at her. "Tell him where Jasden is. He doesn't wanna hurt the guy. We need to talk to him." He frowned at the screen. "I don't know where to look. Maybe you could try bribing her instead of threatening her?"

"One hundred thousand, on my way out… Provided you do not create trouble."

The woman squinted. "You expect me to believe you have that much?"

Mamoru flashed the credstick.

Some of the dark veins in the woman's cheek faded away. "Two and we have an arrangement."

"Done," said Mamoru.

RADIANT GLOW FROM THOUSANDS OF HEAT LAMPS POSITIONED ABOVE LONG tanks filtered through grow fluid, saturating the interior of Biosphere 4 in lustrous green light. Above them, a tall domed ceiling of black steel came alive with dozens of cat-sized spider bots crawling over dangling cables and support beams. Some had reservoirs of liquid on their backs, which they squirted into tanks while others scuttled up to the side of the growth vats and conducted tests.

Mamoru covered his nose for a moment in an effort to adjust to the overpowering reek of chemical growth medium. The teeming activity in the ceiling conjured images of a rainforest rendered in steel and rubber. Caiden seemed far less amused by the thousands of eight-legged bots and turned almost blue in the face.

Strands of translucent biomatter twisted and fluttered in the viscous green fluid, sprouting buds wherever something had started to emerge. Gauze-like sheets of nanometer-thin material, a form on which meat would grow, turned milky as cells built up in layers. Deeper in, more developed six-foot long slabs of beef, chicken, and fish floated in the substrate.

Caiden followed him down the nearest passage between tanks, gawking at the various pipes, filters, and maintenance systems keeping the growth medium in constant motion. He gazed transfixed at a warped version of his own face sliding along the tank surface. A great slab of chicken tissue moved with a muscle spasm that clanked it against the glass. Caiden jumped and grabbed Mamoru with a gasp.

"This is where food comes from? This stuff looks nasty."

Mamoru chuckled. "This is the expensive food. The presentation improves with preparation."

"I guess." Caiden stared at the floor to avoid looking at the writhing primordial ooze. "At least they don't kill real animals anymore." He looked up after a moment of quiet. "Have you ever seen a real animal?"

"Yes. There are still a few left on Earth."

Caiden's face shifted through varying degrees of contemplative expressions. "Why are they making this stuff here? Can't fly a shuttle in."

Mamoru raised an eyebrow at a rectangular block of salmon four feet long, and imagined an enormous pillow of rice under it. *I must be hungry.* "They need less security here. Perhaps the credits they save on staff offset the increased logistical complications of ground transport."

"Huh?" Caiden blinked.

"This place is so remote, no one bothers trying to steal anything." Mamoru smiled. "That piece of fish is likely half a million credits."

Caiden stared at him, mouth open, eyebrows together in a flat line. "That's stupid. Who would pay that much for food?"

Mamoru chuckled, thinking back to several 10,000 credit-a-plate functions at the Matsushita office. "It is a matter of perspective."

The corridor between vats narrowed as they progressed, their pace slowed by the need to step over an occasional twelve-inch diameter cable snaking along the floor. A hundred meters later, the narrow gap forced Mamoru sideways to slip into a central hub where more pipes and wires ran haphazardly over an ebon floor. All of it connected to a horseshoe of ceiling-high machines and computers. From here, it was obvious they stood in the center of a massive round chamber full of growth beds arranged like spokes of a wheel.

In the center of the C-shaped mainframe, a cluttered desk bore the weight of a ragged-looking man in a pale blue lab coat. His fluorescent green hair exploded from his scalp as if he'd touched an electrical line. He sat up, startled, babbling at Mamoru and yelling about intruders and security protocol. Loud metal scraping from above announced the arrival of a multi-legged Tarant: a robotic spider with a five-foot body and twelve-foot leg span. It weaved through girders on the ceiling with grace, sprouting a pair of vibro-blades where chelicerae would be. Dozens of smaller bots scurried out of its way, sliding down wires in an effort to avoid being knocked to the floor.

Caiden screamed and dove under the nearest tank, crawling as fast as he could through a tangle of hoses to get away from the thing. Mamoru stood his ground, watching it.

Jasden pointed with a shaking arm. "This is a secure area. It'll give you ten seconds to run."

"Jasden," said Mamoru, gaze locked on the bot. "I need to speak to you. I need you to tell me where I can find Raziel."

"I don't know what the hell you're talking about!" His voice rose to a near-screech.

An actuator creaked. Mamoru shimmered with energy, focusing

power on strength and speed. The metal spider pounced, diving in relative slow motion. He slipped out from under it, putting one hand on its side to guide it face-first into the floor. It swiveled to bring its deadly mouthparts around to strike, but Mamoru leapt over it in a blur of fluttering black coat. Blades collided with a spine-twisting squeal as they passed.

Jasden whimpered, scrambling through his desk for something useful. "Shit… o-o-of course they s-send a doll."

The bot lunged. Mamoru ducked under the blades and shoved the machine airborne with one arm. It seemed to hang in place for a few seconds as gravity reclaimed it. Mamoru grabbed one of its legs and swung it around, pounding it to the floor upside down. Bits of debris bounced away from the bot while damaged wireguides beneath it vomited sparks. Caiden yelped and shielded his face with an arm, coughing on the smoke of burnt silicon.

Mamoru maintained his grip on the flailing bot, and forced his will over the programming.

The Tarant squawked and beeped for a few seconds before its thrashing went still. One grey Myofiber bundle suffered a spasm, pulsating in the hollow channel along the underside of the leg. Mamoru stood, letting the robot right itself. Now calm, it rotated to face its former master, eight camera dots glowing red. Jasden shrieked, but not because of the spider.

"Drop it," said Caiden, holding a knife to the technician's throat from behind.

Jasden released his grip of a pistol, which fell with a *thunk* into a drawer. The boy kicked the drawer closed, but left his blade at the man's neck.

"A-a-at least make the boy w-wait outs-s-s-ide." Jasden cleared his throat. "He's too young. He'll b-break something."

Caiden pulled the blade against his neck and snarled.

Sweat ran in streams down the technician's face. If the sight of Mamoru throwing the thousand-pound spider around like a toy had not terrified him enough, a knife at his throat was the final nudge that reduced him to babbling incoherence.

Mamoru waved Caiden off. "A mutual friend tells me you can help me find Raziel. I do not have time for games. Your guard dog will begin destroying everything in here in thirty seconds."

Caiden lowered his knife, folding the blade closed and backing away.

Jasden slumped forward on his elbows. "You can't kill Raziel. He does so much for the movement. He's a good man."

Confusion took hold of Mamoru, though it did not show. "Raziel has information vital to me. I seek to reclaim honor that I believe he stole. A 'good man' would not be responsible for what was done to me."

"You're wrong," whined Jasden, on the verge of tears. "Raziel doesn't do mercenary work. He watches over Mars." The spider bot pivoted to face the nearest tank. Vibro-blades switched on. A sonic presence beyond the edge of hearing made the air feel strange. "Please don't. Is your 'honor' worth punishing the citizens of Araphel?"

"Dustblow." Caiden slapped Jasden over the back of the head. "You don't feed Araphel. They're starving out there... eating rats."

"We donate our extra every m-month. Ask B-Boris at the Last Resort."

"Their fate is in your hands," said Mamoru.

"All right, fine... Promise you won't hurt him?"

Mamoru shook his head. "His fate will be decided by his own choices."

Jasden gnawed on his fingers, shaking as the spider ambled up to the first growth chamber. It leaned its weight back in anticipation of a lunge.

"Couple million credits 'bout to hit the floor of... what is that, tuna?" asked Caiden.

"Wait!" yelled Jasden. "Fine."

"Ma-te," said Mamoru, barking Japanese at the bot.

The Tarant froze in place.

Whimpering, the scientist fell back in his chair, rigid and with the vacant eyes of a corpse, head to the side. "He lives near the core, several levels under the main city center. There are tunnels below that hold wires, pipes, and sewer lines. The entrance is near the Hollow, where they fight for money. At the south end, you will find a shaft once used to carry a service elevator to the reactor level before dolls replaced the crews." He tried to rub guilt off his face. "Sublevel 7. I don't have the codes."

Jasden shuddered. He raised his hands. "Please. I don't—"

"I do not need codes." Mamoru rendered a half-bow. "You have been most helpful."

He spun on his heel and headed for the exit at a brisk pace, ignoring the hundreds of dog-sized robotic spiders littered around the ceiling shifting to watch him pass. Caiden slipped the knife back into his jacket pocket and stepped over wires on his way to catch up.

Mamoru stopped at the door long enough to shout "Modosu" over his shoulder before continuing out.

The bot collapsed, and beeped as if it had rebooted itself. The sound of the Tarant racing toward them with raised weapons cut out as the door hissed closed.

IN THE PRESENCE OF ANGELS

Clouds of steam rolled through the narrow confines of the subterranean tunnels, carrying the bountiful scent of chem-treated sewage. Patches of dark ooze slid in rivulets down the walls, coating everything in a glistening layer of greasy slime. Mamoru walked through the center of a passage wide enough for a loader cart, ignoring the dozen or so offshoots barely able to accommodate a single man's width.

Pipes and hoses of various diameters lined the ceiling and walls, some labeled, others cracked and leaking. Caiden kept his shirt over his mouth and nose with one hand, waving the other arm for balance as he avoided stepping in or on anything suspicious. Even Mamoru coughed after several minutes in the eye-watering stench.

"I thought angels, like, lived in Heaven or something," mumbled Caiden. "I think we're going in the wrong direction."

Abandoned boxes and barrels littered the main corridor, evidence of the occasional maintenance project. From the look of it, none of it had been touched in several years. Careful not to disturb anything, he weaved through the junk in search of the old elevator Jasden mentioned.

At the end of a quarter mile hike, the damaged doors of his objective emerged from the darkness ahead: one tilted at an angle, the other stuck half open. Caiden ducked through the triangular hole, peering down. Unable to resist the urge, he gathered a wad of spit and let it fall. Mamoru chuckled at the echo. Both remained silent for several seconds until the distant sound of impact came back up the shaft.

"That's pretty deep," said Caiden, backing away from the door. "There's a ladder on the right. Are you gonna cut the doors out so you can fit?"

"A katana is not a utility knife. It is a sacred weapon those who cross me should feel privileged to taste."

Mamoru put a hand on the boy's shoulder and pulled him back a few steps before grasping the angled plastisteel slab. A low growl came from his throat as he concentrated on strength. Energy flared along his arms, deepening the shadows in their vicinity. His face twisted with a determined frown and his body shuddered. Bare fingers dimpled metal, drawing forth squeals of stress.

Caiden stared in awe.

With a shout, Mamoru pulled, tearing the door off its rails and flinging it into the shaft. The mangled metal sheet bounced away from the wall, trailing loose wires, and fell. A series of thunderous crashes reverberated out of the darkness, ending with an even louder *whump* as it landed flat. Mamoru swayed against the wall, out of breath and sweating.

Caiden gulped. Adoration shared space with fear in his eyes. "Uh, whoa."

"That... was quite tiring."

"You got limbs?"

Mamoru gave him an unamused smirk. "Of course."

"No, I mean metal ones. 'Ware."

"I do not." Mamoru let his head sag forward, nauseated by the flavor of the air he gulped.

"You're like... as strong as a damn doll or something."

"Only..." He wheezed. "Only for a short time."

Mamoru's breaths remained heavy for several minutes. The elevator shaft grew cloudy with a cloud of silt and dust. Once he gathered a second wind, he straightened out and filled his lungs as he stretched the fatigue out of his arms. Caiden had taken another step back and busied himself trying to make sense of grime-covered writing on a wire conduit.

"Ready to climb?"

The boy glanced over and down. "Okay."

"Making myself that strong takes great concentration and leaves me tired. Not only must I increase my strength, I must also reinforce my body so I do not crush my own bones. Concentrating on both at once is not a power I can call on in a flash of anger. Do not fear—"

"It's not you…" Caiden crept towards him. "I was thinking about what you said, about people that are after you." He stared at his boots. "I guess that's why."

"Mmm."

Caiden stared at his sneakers. Mamoru stepped on the ladder first, and descended. Apart from loose pipes and sparking wires dislodged by the falling door, the six-story climb offered no complications. An elevator cab rested at the bottom, crushed like an enormous synthbeer canister under the door, which had bent on impact. Mamoru climbed down the twisted metal and kicked through what remained of the exterior doors on that level. The boy crept down and slipped past him, raising his arm. Darkness beckoned, flecked with silver wherever metal reflected the feeble glow of Caiden's e-lantern.

A patch of red light faded in, the upper left corner of a holo-pane struggled into existence as its emitter sensed their approach. Zaps and arcs burst from the projector as it created an image resembling a sheet of glass shattered from a gunshot at its center. Enough remained to discern it as a radiation warning. Mamoru surveyed black wire-bundles running in serpentine tentacles along the ceiling of a twenty-meter long corridor. The tubes lent an organic quality to the walls. Coupled with the crimson glow, it seemed as if they trod a passage to Hell.

Mamoru ignored the warning and the ominous atmosphere, advancing with one hand on his blade. Caiden hovered close behind, jumping when another holo-panel opened without warning. A blaring voice, garbled beyond understanding, caused him to grab Mamoru's arm. The boy shied away from it, pressed against his side as they passed the unintelligible shouting. Were it not for the out of control tubes and wires that did not seem to be part of the original construction here, the aperture at the end of the corridor would've been wide enough for a prowler.

At the end of the corridor, Mamoru touched a glossy onyx panel by a heavy bulkhead door. Ten white holographic zeroes floated in midair, warped by a two-pixel tall band of left shift that scrolled up from the bottom in a loop. Caiden raised the lamp over his head, examining the wall where dozens of wires emerged from beneath a bent section of metal. Mamoru shoved a mental feeler through the electronics. After a minute, zeroes remained on the screen, but the door opened.

A thin strip of mirror-polished plastisteel formed a serpentine path among a tangle of countless segmented hoses. The open walkway led to a cone-shaped protrusion of technology at the center of an immense, round chamber. Panels of violet, white, and orange light moved around it as if sliding on invisible circular rails. The counter-rotating holograms progressed in precise increments, creeping millimeters at a time, stopping, and then racing about. Their animation gave Mamoru the impression of an ancient computer drive stuck in an endless seek routine. Thousands of wires varying in size from finger-width to as big as a man's thigh draped in loops from the ceiling, all glistening black.

At the center of it all, angled plastisteel shards collected in the shape of a twenty-foot metal obelisk, as if the will of a mad god had drawn them forth from the ground and formed them in place. Every seam and gap glowed white, pulsing to the rhythm of the machine.

Dwarfed by its size, a man hovered near the top, arms outstretched. Waist-length black hair hung from the hood of a white robe. Enormous wings spread from the figure's back, silver metal struts etched with dark circuit lines bore stylized feathers of violet light too intense for a direct stare. Wire bundles connected at the joints, shifting as the wings flexed. The entire assembly crackled with power and the thrum of machinery.

The room filled with a voice so deep it vibrated through the ground.

"Greetings, Mamoru Saitō. I have been expecting you."

The wings stretched to their full thirty foot span, the glowing shard-feathers brightened with a painful brilliance. Pale amethyst energy pulses collected along their length and slid inward until they vanished at the figure's back. With a resonant mechanical thrum, the great appendages swung upwards until the leading edges came together above his head. The struts became long, metal arms that lowered him to his feet. Caiden shielded his eyes as the searing violet feathers drew closer.

Raziel reached to his chest, pressing his palm at the center of a black metal vest striped with glowing cyan. With a click and a hiss, he detached and stepped free of his wings, standing a shade less than seven feet tall, clad in a flowing robe trimmed with gold. The angel pulled back his hood, revealing a face as white as a Marsborn. Four thin strips of metal flickering with blue lights angled across his each cheek. He lifted his head, gazing down on Mamoru with eyes like holes peering into the furnace of a violet sun—no iris, no whites, only radiance. The sight stunned the concept of words out of Mamoru's brain, leaving him staring.

Caiden ducked behind Mamoru, risking a peek around his side.

The strange man adopted a regal posture as angel's wings of gleaming silver shimmered into being from thin air, chasing a wireframe outline of blue until they looked solid and real. Holographic feathers fluttered in a breeze that did not exist.

"Something's not right," whispered Caiden. "He feels creepy."

"Tell me why you have dishonored me." Mamoru stood his ground.

Raziel brought his hands together and bowed. "You have been misled. It is true that I have visited the GlobeNet shadow realm of Matsushita Electronics, though my goal was to obtain information to assist the liberators."

Mamoru took a step closer, dragging Caiden. "Right after your visit, Minamoto-heika disavowed me. What did you show him?"

"You elevate a man that would own you, calling him 'highness?' I find that most interesting." Raziel paced to the right, as if gathering his thoughts. His ethereal wingtip brushed Mamoru without effect. "Akio Minamoto regarded you as nothing more than a tool. To him, you are a powerful weapon to wield until you are of no further use. He has discarded you with no more thought than a broken handgun. My influence is not responsible for his change of opinion."

"You appeared in my home, trying to tempt me away from him. When I refused, you connected to the majordomo's terminal."

"I have a question for you now, Mamoru. Do all who bear katana serve the same master?"

"Only a fool would assume such a thing."

Raziel glanced back with a hint of a smile. "Indeed. As is assuming any avatar with wings is mine."

"How many avatars with wings originate from Mars? How many others are there who can infiltrate Earth networks from here?"

"Falsifying route uplink paths is novice work. It is all ones and zeroes in a header stream. If I wanted to conceal my entry, I would make the intrusion appear to have come from an internal terminal, or bounced through a dozen different countries." Raziel faced him, star-eyes widening. "If I wished to hide from you, why would I lead you right to Mars?"

Mamoru squinted, weighing the logic of it. "You did not lead me anywhere. I found your true route because I am one with the system. Your masking techniques would fool an operator, but I am no mere deck jockey."

"You still control a deck, Mamoru. Some of the laws of cyberspace *do* apply, even if you are too stubborn to notice. I am aware of your nature. Why do you think Minamoto had your parents killed?"

White light shimmered along Mamoru's arms. He lunged forward, katana moving from sheath to strike in the span of an eye blink. He froze, outstretched having touched nothing. Raziel had vanished, his motion indiscernible even to Mamoru's accelerated perception.

"Your emotions get the better of you," said Raziel.

The sound drew Mamoru's gaze up. The angel hovered twenty meters in the air above him, holographic wings outstretched in a casual flapping rhythm.

Caiden gawked, pointing. The effect of moving wings seemed to mesmerize the boy.

Mamoru glared. "You know nothing of my parents."

Raziel circled, ionic downblast from thrusters in his vest sent thin blue sparks spidering along his robe. "The man you regard as father was not your biological parent, Mamoru. The woman you know as Mother did provide half of your genetic material, however, they were employees of Eisei Pharmaceuticals who volunteered for the project to create you."

Knuckles creaking on the rubber-coated handle, Mamoru angled his katana towards the floor. Caiden offered a sympathetic stare. Burning rage faded to longing as memories swam through his mind. He brought the sword up, resting the tip on his finger at the scabbard's mouth before sliding it in. Mother was pleasant to him, but doted on his sister. Father was harsh, but fair. He needed training. Father spoiled sister. Scene after scene played through his head, scattered memories from those brief ten years: the nagging want for approval, the way they looked at him. His little sister seemed to have genuine love for him, the parents... His brain found truth in the thought of being an outsider.

Mamoru stared past his shaking fist at the floor. "Are you another demon seeking to destroy me?"

"I would appreciate a lack of further hostility." Raziel glided to the ground, landing a few steps away. "Even if you ruin this shell, I will not die. It would be pointless."

"Nothing is as I know." Mamoru stood straight. *Kami, guide me.*

Raziel extended his arms to the sides. A ribbon of holographic panels seemed to race from his open sleeve, stretching out in a wide circle that surrounded them before connecting at his other hand. Caiden glanced up, attracted by a starscape of dots from holo-projectors in the ceiling. Each window filled with images of a Japanese baby in a lab. Employees in pale green scrubs and facemasks held him up, evaluated him, and measured him. One man bounced him and seemed affectionate. The worker pulled his face covering down to smile.

Father.

"Doctor Ichiro Saitō," said Raziel. "He was the lead geneticist on the project."

The screens showed his early childhood: toddler Mamoru wobbling around in front of a pregnant woman. History replayed before his eyes. Caiden watched in silence, hovering close.

"They desired for you to have a normal upbringing. He volunteered to raise you as his own."

"What does all of this mean?" Mamoru reached through the intangible screen attempting to touch the woman he called Mother.

"Ichiro wanted to find a way to extend custom embryonic modification to produce children capable of psionic ability, specifically kinetic adepts. If they could reliably create people with those talents, they could produce soldiers as strong and fast as augmented individuals, but immune to EMP and without the need for expensive doctors and maintenance. They managed a few others after you, but none matched your unique strength. All met with varying degrees of success. Your talent with machines was unintentional. Individuals with mechanical aptitude are well known in the UCF, though not one of them can do what you can."

"How do you know all of this? What does this have to do with Minamoto?"

"I am the keeper of secrets, Mamoru." Raziel offered a lingering sympathetic glance. Despite having the face of a man in his young twenties, he seemed much older. "As soon as I became aware of your imminent arrival, I gathered information. Matsushita network operatives breached Eisei's secure data vaults when you were eight. Your family had been under surveillance since."

Mamoru studied the far wall, glancing away from both Raziel and Caiden. "Father spent years trying to get me to unlock my *chi*. When I finally did, they killed him."

"Correct, and they took you for their own."

Mamoru started for the door. "I must find the one responsible for ruining my honor."

"Curious," said Raziel. His silken voice stopped Mamoru after three steps. "You suffer for the loss of respect from a man who stole your life."

"As you have demonstrated to me, they were not my parents. They were too weak to protect themselves."

Caiden gasped. "They adopted you. They were your parents… and your mom *was* your mom."

Mamoru whirled about, squinting at Raziel. "What exactly are you?"

"As I said, I am the keeper of secrets. I do not suffer your qualms about eavesdropping on my employer, as I have none."

"If you know so much, tell me what happened to this boy's mother."

Raziel gazed into the distance. "She was arrested at a protest of Benton Mining Corporation almost a year ago."

Caiden kicked at the floor, looking down.

The glow in Raziel's eyes intensified, flickering as if processing data. The same flutter repeated in the gargantuan light-wings near the roof. He swept an arm to the side, hurling a ribbon formed of holographic panes in a circle around his two guests that met his other hand. Fingers splayed and a pulse of light followed the ring. Each square went from white to black in sequence before faces appeared, rotating within.

Caiden spun in place, biting his lip as he looked at each picture in turn. At the sight of a slender Marsborn woman, purple bruise under her eye, he cried without sound and pointed. Mamoru looked away, but after a few seconds went over and put a hand on the boy's shoulder. Caiden hid his face, failing to stifle sniffles. He twitched as if to hide the shame of his sorrow, but Mamoru didn't let go.

Raziel lifted his gaze as the ring collapsed. Both sides of the holographic circle retracted into the chosen image, leaving it floating alone.

"Mara Avoris." Raziel tilted his head as if studying an unseen object in the air. "She is being held at a work camp run by Benton Mining, located in a remote region of Mars known as the Acidalian Sea."

The boy hid his face against Mamoru's chest.

"How do I get there?" asked Mamoru.

Caiden's head snapped up, mouth agape.

Raziel held his right hand up. A basketball-sized Mars appeared hovering over it, and rotated until a blinking dot faced him. "It is quite far, and the air is not amenable to life, being mostly carbon dioxide. You would need a sealed e-suit as well as enough weapons to engage a corporate security force of sixty to seventy. They do not have defense bots you could take over for reinforcements."

Mamoru glanced down at Caiden, who fought to hold back tears. "I must correct what has happened to my honor. However, I am now conflicted. I need time to think and plan. As I have no further idea where to look in regard to my own needs, I may as well return the boy's mother to him in the meantime."

"There is something I have never before seen, Mamoru. A strange presence in the GlobeNet searches for you. It appears to have an origin in the region of East City, UCF. It may be the impostor you mistook for me."

"Strange?"

Caiden pulled away enough to look at Raziel.

"Connections form with standard headers and route data that resemble an ordinary Vidphone connection. However, once the link is established, there are signal anomalies with no known corollary in any reference database. My best estimate is some manner of electromagnetic energy that has not yet been documented."

Mamoru glared at nothing in particular. Caiden gave him a desperate look.

"I believe your assault on the Benton facility would be impractical. You are not given to stealth, Mamoru." Raziel chuckled. "I know of someone who can liberate the enslaved miners without the risk of a full on assault."

"The Tí-zhèn everyone believes crazy?"

Raziel smiled. "I offer you this bargain. Owe me a favor that I may call on at my discretion, and I shall unburden you of your guilt over the boy."

"For as long as I can remember, I have done the bidding of another for no reason other than it was my duty to do so. I did not question the 'why' of any task. I did as I was told." Mamoru tightened his grip on Caiden's shoulder. "For once, I will act of my own choosing. I will repay the favor he has done me."

The angel sighed. "I do not foresee that ending well for you. Your powers are impressive, but you are not an immortal."

"You are?" Mamoru raised an eyebrow.

"I am incapable of death. If that fulfills your definition of immortal, then I am." Raziel lowered his searing gaze to Caiden. "You have made a loyal friend in Mamoru, boy. However noble his intentions are, he will only find his end there. The chaos he brings to Benton Mining may claim your mother's life as well. Do not think less of him for allowing another this task. My hand shall induce the change you cannot."

Caiden looked up. "What if he's right, Mamoru? You get tired fast. A hundred guys... I don't want you to die."

Mamoru stewed for a while, failing to come up with an effective counter argument. His hatred of ninja grew. A frontal assault would likely cause panic, rebellion, and death among those he attempted to save. "Very well. Give me the information you have on the entity in this East City."

"You're leaving?" Caiden's voice broke up.

"I told you that you would not be safe with me on my journey." Mamoru narrowed his eyes. "However, I will stay with you until we see if this Tí-zhèn is capable of bringing your mother home." He shifted to look at Raziel. "If your agent fails, I will not."

Raziel walked to the large spars from which he had descended. His holographic wings faded away as he backed up to the metal struts. They connected with the *hissing* and *clicking* of multiple interfaces linking. He rose once more to the top of his obelisk and the room filled with the light of a thousand glowing feathers.

Raziel's hood fell over a knowing smile. "She will not fail."

THE ONI RETURNS

Mamoru knelt on a straw mat, frowning at the pathetic plastic shimenawa teetering on fragile posts. The disgraceful thing was a solid piece—not woven. The chintzy simulacra of a thick rope with paper streamers threatened to fall off the kamidana he had ordered a week before. A wave of contempt bubbled up inside him, stalling his best effort to search for calm. What did he expect in this place, this East City? The best Shinto shrine they could offer: form pressed plastic and Epoxil in the image of little wooden sticks.

Whoever made this deserved death.

He closed his eyes, trying to ignore the way the West smelled. He tried to forget how everything here was fast, cheap, disposable, and utterly unworthy of any kind of pride in artisanship. Minutes passed, though the sounds of hovercar traffic outside continued to vibrate through the windows. Endless, at all hours of the day, he had not known true silence since leaving Mars a month ago. Raziel's 'hand' had never shown herself, though the boy's mother had returned alive.

A thrust of his arms forward snapped his loose, white sleeves with an audible *pop*. Mamoru held thoughts of the Kami in his mind and brought his hands together in a sharp clap before his chest.

A hollow clatter announced the shimenawa falling.

Growling emanated from his throat as his frown deepened and his eyes narrowed to slits. With great care, he retrieved the green plastic 'rope' and balanced it on its holder. The Japanese-esque box behind it mocked him with small lines left by the mold-forming process, and the logo of Triton Manufacturing Corporation—in English.

Fifteen minutes or so later, he had once more reached a state close to calm. He clapped once expecting the insulting object to fall again, but it did not. A second clap, still silence. Mamoru relaxed.

"I have decided on a path with no end."

Mamoru bowed his head. Nami glided through a daydream. For an instant, a wisp of her scent drifted by. He recalled Caiden's face the moment they entered the room full of dirty prisoners and found his mother. A boy of eleven so overwhelmed with joy he sobbed like a child half his age. The far wall changed from Mars rock to rice paper and wood. Minamoto burst through a pair of intricate red doors with gold knobs, shouting. Darkness fell over his mind. His eyes opened, leaving him alone with the pathetic shrine sitting in the path of a creeping square of refracted headlight glare from outside.

"Do I chase a ghost?"

Thick, cold air brushed past him. A cloud of amber light took on the outline of a nude female figure drifting through the room. It glimmered along the dark windows, circling him. Wispy and indistinct, the figure hovered at the precipice of invisibility. Were the room lit by more than the unending passage of traffic outside, he would not have noticed.

He drew a great breath, stiffening his posture as his eyes widened.

The cloud brightened and became opaque, as if a glass hollow in the shape of a woman filled with smoke. Seconds later, the familiar tall blonde with paper-white skin stood before him.

"Hello, Mamoru. Sorry if I am interrupting, I don't speak Japanese."

Mamoru looked away from her nakedness, leaving his hands on his knees. He exhaled at the cheap kamidana. *Disgraceful altar gets me a tainted oni.* A sideways shift of his eyes caught sight of lemon-yellow hair and white thighs as she wandered in a circle, spinning.

"This is a nice place. I won't ask how you can afford it. Bet you nicked it." She winked. "Told you that you'd wind up in the West."

If this is the will of the Kami. He clapped once again.

Aurora jumped, and raised a hand. "Easy. I'm not here to hurt you. Be back in a tick. It's a bit brassy in here."

He tracked her reflection across the front windows until she disappeared into the master bedroom. A loud *thud* emanated from the back, causing the shimenawa to fall and roll towards him.

"Sorry!" she yelled. "Hey, you know I'd normally find it rather amusing to make you uncomfortable what with me standin' around starkers. Really, I'm tryin' to be nice to you." Another heavy object fell. "Drat. 'Ang on, then. I'll repack this closet. Guess you've always had someone do this for you."

Watching the plastic shimenawa fall *again* brought his rage to the point of wanting to crush it with a fiery fist. He had stopped shaking for only a few seconds when she padded in, with one of his haori jackets draped over her shoulders. She tugged the cloth belt into a loose knot and let it the strands fall.

Mamoru shifted his gaze to her feet, pale against the charcoal carpet. Shades of orange, blue, and violet decorated her legs, wherever light from advert bots outside painted her. He looked up, over blue silk that began at mid-thigh to more white where she had left the haori open to show cleavage. His stare lingered on her eyes, onyx from corner to corner.

"Are you ready to accept that I am not some manner of demon yet?" She rested her hands on curvy hips.

Mamoru clapped once more over the shrine—after replacing the fallen shimenawa—and bowed. "I do not know any more." He let his forearms drape over his knees. "I have asked the Kami for guidance each night since I have returned to Earth, yet in three weeks' time, their only answer is you."

Aurora bit one finger while making a playful face. "Are you saying I'm some kind of gift from your gods?"

"Perhaps you are meant to lead me to that which I search for." He whirled his head toward her with a snap. "Perhaps I am meant to send you back where you came from."

Her seductive smile faded. "You've been traipsing around the east coast for weeks, Mamoru. You've given up your search for honor and you're taking freelance data grabs... I bet because you have nothing else to do. It won't be long before you have quite a name for yourself in the community. I imagine there's not a network in the world you couldn't own."

He grunted, casting a lamenting frown at the piteous shrine.

"If you're so potty for 'er, why not bring 'er here?" She shifted, reaching for the belt. "We could have another toss if you want."

Mamoru raised a hand. "No. It is a matter of my honor in the eyes of Minamoto and Matsushita. I cannot simply ignore it."

"He's ordered you killed on sight? Are you some sort of spoon? You know it was him that had your parents killed. Why do you have any loyalty to such a man?" She knelt and sat back on her heels. "He doesn't give a stuff what you are. He 'asnt a bastarding clue about us."

"When I became a samurai, I swore an oath to my station. The shogun's will is all that matters."

"If that were true"—Aurora folded her arms—"you should kill yourself. But you haven't."

"His decree is based on a falsehood. The one whom I seek has influenced him somehow."

"'The blighter's not a shogun, 'e's an executive of a corporation playing dress-up. That feudal stuff sodded off thousands of years ago. Your whole country's like a damn addled theater company playing with live ammo."

"Do not mock my culture."

She let her head sag forward and ran a hand through her hair. "Look, Mamoru… You are one of us. I know you met with Raziel on Mars. I am no more a demon than he is an angel. I, like you, am one of the Awakened. We are psionics."

"I cannot read the thoughts of others." He stood and moved to the floor-to-ceiling windows along the north wall. Hover traffic streamed by, mesmerizing patterns of light in the darkness. "Such ability would simplify things."

Like a glowing ghost, Aurora's reflection shifted behind him, drawing near. He tensed as she came up behind him, close enough to feel her warmth. Ivory fingers laced through his hair and ran down his back, alighting on his hip. He glanced away.

"Not all psionics are telepaths." She let her chin rest on his left shoulder. "It's more common among Awakened to wind up strong in one area and anemic in others. I'm not much of a telepath either. All I can get are surface thoughts… unless I hop inside someone."

"Were you born on Mars?"

"No, Essex actually, not that there's much difference." She paused to watch a passing hovercar as it wobbled out of its lane. "I suspect you're wondering about my appearance then. Awakened often have quirks. I look like this. You light on fire."

"Why?"

She gave him a helpless look. "Why do you eat fish without cooking it? It just is."

Mamoru found the darkest patch of city he could, and tried to pierce it with a stare. A huge delivery bot, as big as a trash dumpster rumbled by, rattling the windows. The hollow plastic *clatter* of the shimenawa falling behind him made his blood boil. Never before had he wished so much for the utter destruction of an inanimate object.

"You should not dwell on Minamoto. He's the same as any wanker who's got power over others and lets it go to his head. What is more important, what 'e thinks of you, or Nami?"

Mamoru bowed his head, eyes closed. "I do not know if her intentions were true."

"Forget Japan. Ask 'er if she wants to join you here. If she agrees, you will know. S'not like she's got anyfing left there either."

"I must avenge my honor first, even if I never return to my homeland." He slapped his hand on the glass, sending a shuddering wave to the wall.

"Minamoto has an idea how powerful you are. He would see you destroyed before you could be used against him." She leaned against his back, tracing her fingers around his chest. "Without allies, you will eventually fail."

Mamoru glanced to the left, through the open haori at her smooth, perfect breast. "You lack shame."

"When my abilities first showed themselves, I was a little girl. Every so often, I'd sneeze and pop out of my kit. Quite embarrassing at first. The first time I crossed over, I was terrified. I had no idea what happened. Honestly, clothing gets in my way. It's expensive to leave behind all the time. Besides, I adore making people uncomfortable."

"Cross over?"

"You believe in spirits and gods and whatnot, right? There's another world, a shadow of our own. Some psionics can project their spirit into it."

"Astral walking. I have seen mention of it." Mamoru paced away from the window, and her, heading towards the kitchen.

"Non-Awakened psionics can send their spirit out of their bodies and enter the astral realm. I can bring my whole body over, but nothing that's not part of me goes." She winked. "I can't even cheat and put something—"

"You are a ghost then?" Mamoru set about preparing tea.

She trailed after him to the kitchen, and leaned on the doorframe. "No. I am as alive as you are, but I do sometimes chat with the dead. They're not terrible fond of me though, always come beggin' for help with this or that, and I'm a busy girl."

"Why are you here?"

At him pouring two cups, she smiled. "We are rare, but in danger. As of right now, the governments of the world know little of our existence. Psionics are often treated with derision here in the UCF. Most people are scared witless of them, but a handful are bigoted and hostile. The ACC actively hunts them down and has been known to wipe out entire family lines. Britain kills the ones it cannot control. In the Middle East, they're shot on sight no questions asked. China forces them to join the military, with special 'handlers' ready to kill them if they suspect them of getting out of line. Switzerland kicks them out... too many secrets there. I shudder to think what would happen if the world truly understood us and our capabilities."

"My abilities do not allow me to do anything more than what is possible with cybernetics. In fact, the metal poison is more efficient." He handed her a cup, contempt thick in his voice. "As Sadako proved, my skill with a blade is merely *acceptable*. I am only skilled enough to slay bundles of straw that cannot move when I accelerate myself."

She turned the teacup, studying the painted bamboo. "Kinetics is not your strength. Your father was misled by his desire. You have always preferred technology." She peered at the surface of the green liquid. "You adored the quiet calm of being alone in your room with your electronics."

Mamoru stared at her over his tea for a moment before taking a sip. Without her at a sideways angle, the haori covered her chest and left him feeling less awkward. "What do you want?"

"There are a handful of us working to find a better life. None 'ave your talent. Your help could accelerate our salvation." Aurora poured sugar into her tea, stirred it, and took a healthy swig. "You're a good man, Mamoru. No matter what that Minamoto wankstick did to you, it did not destroy the good heart you've always 'ad." She gave him a consoling look. "That boy will never forget you. As Awakened, we must help each other, or they will destroy us all."

"You were on Mars?"

"No, have you ever heard of clairvoyance?"

Mamoru muttered into his cup as he sipped again.

"Yes, I 'ave watched you shower." She winked. "Might've touched m'self while doin' it."

He coughed tea all over the table. Aurora laughed. Mamoru retrieved a towel and cleaned up the mess, glaring at her the entire time. She shifted in the chair, twisting the cup in the saucer with small, precise motions.

Mamoru fell seated. "What of Nami? She is not psionic."

"I don't think it'll be a bother to bring 'er along when we depart."

"Depart?" Mamoru raised an eyebrow.

"On Earth, we will always be hunted. Archon intends to find a world where we do not have to hide what we are."

"Will she not be the one who is persecuted then?"

"There are so few of us, it would not make sense to bring only Awakened to a new world. We would surely die out. Archon believes all psionics have the potential to Awaken. He thinks it is a matter of finding a way to unlock it."

Mamoru grumbled. "I will consider assisting you, as all other paths I have walked lead me in endless circles. However, I require your aid in return."

"You fancy an assisted bath again?" She winked. "I rather wouldn't mind."

"No." Mamoru fidgeted.

"What can I do then?" She raised her mug. Alluring jet eyes hovered behind rising steam.

"If your so-called Awakened friends are as powerful as you claim, I wish them to discover the source of my dishonor."

Aurora set her teacup down. "I am glad to see that you realize it is okay to ask for help when you need it." She leaned forward and winked. "I am sure we can arrange that. Are you sure you don't want to have a romp?"

"I am sure. Do not take my reluctance as a reflection of your appearance. Thank you for the offer."

"Suit yourself." She winked. "We'll be in touch."

Aurora's body melted to glowing vapor within the haori, which draped over the chair as she ceased to be. When he no longer felt another presence in the room, Mamoru leaned back in the chair and exhaled. He flicked his thumbnail against his cup. Caiden's joyous reunion with his mother replayed itself in his mind. Never had he expected to miss having the boy around. He had only known him for a month. At least with his mother in Araphel, he would be safe… perhaps even happy.

He drained the last of his tea, and dropped the cup with a *clink* on the saucer as he thought of Nami.

PIXIE

Rain came down in sheets. Pedestrians scurried about at varying speeds from brisk walk to sprint. A squad of six men in maroon armor, carrying long, black rifles marched the sidewalk outside, oblivious to the downpour. Silver logos on their shoulders bore an angular S with a small C embedded in the upper curve and a small B in the lower curve. Security Corporation Boston, nongovernmental police, seemed to be everywhere he went.

The private sectors within East City had their perks. Almost no gangs, and little physical crime, but they had a downside apart from the horrendous cost. Private law enforcement often let their power get the better of them and made it a routine to harass people who did not appear to be wealthy. It bore similarities to the security forces back home. The familiar routine appealed to him. Here in the UCF, however, he had to hide the bodies when they got in his way. Back home, he would leave their disgrace for all to see.

Another advantage presented itself in how the national police force tended to leave these regions to their own devices. It had been a simple matter to create a false identity, pump up a credit account, and add himself as owner to an unsold apartment on the ninetieth floor of a residential tower. The people here may not have had a proper sense of politeness and respect, but the amenities went a long way to making him feel human again. While waiting for his food, he daydreamed about his giant jade tiled bathtub, and Nami. Sharing it with her as an equal, not a master.

An Asian woman in a passable kimono approached and set a tray in front of him. She offered a polite bow, and retreated. Six steps away, her demure gait returned to a normal stride. *As false as the plastic kamidana.* Mamoru inhaled the rich aroma of nabeyaki udon from the steam plume in front of him. Three hundred credits resulted in a reasonable attempt at food. Sen Kaidan Japanese Restaurant looked the part and even had workers who appeared to be from Japan.

When the din from outside became louder, Mamoru looked up. A woman with short, white hair and ice blue eyes tucked in out of the downpour and collapsed a sad little umbrella. She shot a glance around the room, and it did not take her long to zero in on him. He straightened in his seat as her tall-heeled boots clicked over the pale hardwood floor. Silent doors slid closed, cutting off the sound of the city. The woman stopped at his table, most of her covered by a shin-length white button-down coat. She held her right arm up, knuckles at the shoulder, with a dark handbag suspended from the elbow.

"Mamoru?" she asked, British clear in her accent.

He squinted. This one was much shorter than Aurora and had some color to her skin. Compared to him, she was pale, but not to the point of looking dead. She helped herself to the facing seat and crossed her legs. Despite her diminutive stature, she seemed far less cordial than the blonde demoness.

"Are you another of them?" He poked at his noodles.

"Straight to the point. Brilliant. Yes, I'm Pixie."

After a mouthful, he pondered. "They name you for your haircut?"

Her already dour face darkened further. "No, it's a long story. Look, I've come with a request for a job."

"Your people wish to test me?" He cocked an eyebrow.

"Something like that."

A kimono-clad waitress arrived, offering a heated cloth. "Hello, miss. Would you care to see a menu?"

Pixie took the cloth, wiping her hands. "No need. I'll 'ave the chirashi, please, and hot tea."

Mamoru waited for the server to walk away. "Your associate mentioned an offer of assistance locating the one responsible for what happened in Tokyo."

"Indeed. Before we get to that part, we need to be sure of your ability."

He ate a few bites, thinking. Tea arrived, which Pixie sipped at while making various impatient faces at him.

"So, you go from telling me how impressive I am to demanding proof." Mamoru sectioned the floating egg with his chopsticks, and lifted a piece to his mouth. "I expect you are going to ask for something an ordinary network infiltrator would cringe at."

"Yes. I assume you have heard of The Silver?"

"Perhaps in passing. I have not ventured far out of Japan, virtually or otherwise, until recently." His glare hardened over the last few words.

"The Silver is a data warehousing complex with security rivalling that of government networks. Most net-heads say it's impossible to breach, that it's never been done. There's some rumors about someone getting in once, but no one's claimed it. Most I've talked to think it's a load of bollocks. If anyone could pull it off, they'd be crowing about it all over the net."

"Perhaps they did, and died. You want me to infiltrate this 'Silver' for you?"

"Yes. I left behind a right clusterfuck in London. I need you to go in there and destroy all the records you can find about me." She removed a plastic case from her coat pocket, an inch long and half that wide. A fleck of black perched at the center of a white foam block. "This nodge contains enough information so you'll know what to look for."

Mamoru released the chopsticks and clasped her hand, squeezing the case to her fingers. A lick of white energy danced over the back of his arm as his mind touched the electronics within the ROM nodule.

"Annabelle... You have a pretty name."

The lights fluttered overhead. Every NetMini and table terminal around them erupted in a cacophony of beeping. What little color existed in her cheeks faded for an instant, before they flushed pink amid the sound of half the room saying "hello" to a dead line.

"I..."

Mamoru let go, smiling. "I am no mind reader. Your secrets are your own. This device contains information about you."

"You didn't even plug the nodge into anything." She gathered her composure. "Yes. Yes, of course. It is vital that those records cease to be. If what I've been hearing about you is true, it should be lemon squeezy."

The server returned with a bowl of sushi and rice, which she sent in front of Anna.

He held an eyebrow up until the server walked off. "Lemons have nothing to do with it." Anna suppressed the urge to laugh. Her sudden mirth made her seem much younger, almost teenaged. "I will do this, but your people must honor their side."

"Of course," she said, a piece of salmon held on chopsticks in front of her mouth. "You're one of us. We have to help each other."

She devoured the fish.

PROJECT SERAPH

C louds raced through the indigo sky, luminous, cyan, and unnatural. They twisted and rolled in a wind that did not reach the ground, moving video on fast forward. Eerie light from no visible source illuminated a maze of high-walled white concrete passages that crisscrossed around the perimeter of a wide-open area. The constructed reality was the size of an entire city sector, five miles square, and filled with flat nothingness save for a massive skyscraper at the center. A shard of mirror, the cyberspace representation of The Silver lived up to its name. Toward the top, the building took on a bird-like shape, with glowing cyan eyes and traces of blue light between carved feathers.

The maze was a manifestation of the external security protocol surrounding a network segment separated from the GlobeNet by several layers of traffic analysis systems and gateways. The 'tunnels' teemed with security constructs in the shape of armed men as well as gargantuan German shepherd dogs. Mamoru squinted at the chalk-white expanse. The desolation represented the ease with which a defense operator could spot an intruder traversing the connection. Numerous switchback paths and active signal sweeping left an invader vulnerable to detection during the arduous process of navigating six separate traffic segments on the way to the tangle of storage arrays and security systems the system rendered as a building.

Mamoru observed the pattern of the security teams and shook his head, for a moment feeling a twinge of pity for the ordinary deck jockeys facing such protections. He advanced as far as he could without losing the cover of shadow in the tunnel. His hand, gliding over the wall, brushed an engraving that broke the smoothness of glass. A weak glow outlined words:

Proscion was here.

He tilted his head, feeling nothing from it other than plain text. It did not seem to be a backdoor, an active soft, or anything useful. *What was the point of this? I will never understand deck jockeys.*

Focus on the information he absorbed from Pixie's data nodule sent threads of his consciousness through the network in search of similar patterns. The process slowed, as more than half his mental efforts went to redirecting tracebacks to keep his deck invisible.

Patrols appeared out of thin air, doubling, tripling the number of constructs sweeping the tunnels. The network sensed something happening that should not be, but was unable to determine where it came from. Petabytes of data swam through the forefront of Mamoru's surface thoughts. Images flashed in a dizzying onrush of snapshots: design specs, messages, family pictures, lurid photos of politicians. All of it forgotten as fast as it appeared. The overwhelming stream of information halted on a vision of Pixie, hair wet and looking over her shoulder in a dark, rainy street. Strong glare from the side shadowed her face, as if the image had been captured at the instant of a lightning strike.

His thoughts tuned to the distant gathering of weak electrical impulses. Mamoru pushed himself through his deck, embodying the network hardware on the far end of the connection. His mind swam through layer after layer of neural memory over synthetic strands of nerve-like fibers suspended in white nutrient liquid. The ropey cords pulsed with light as they carried signals. Minutes passed as he flew among the pale grey landscape inside the storage modules. Dendrite threads formed enormous structures through which he glided. Thunder rolled overhead with each impulse. Ahead, a thin line of energy traced across his path and stretched downward to a blinding doorway.

Mamoru went for it. A rush of heat washed over him as everything became blank for an instant. His surroundings shifted. Walls grew around him, liquid silver broken by a black grid that formed discrete twelve-inch square panels as the material hardened. A dark blue door, heavy and armored, appeared on the other side of a modest steel table and solitary chair. Mamoru reached for the cube containing the data he wanted. The realness of his samurai gauntlet flaked off, leaving a green wireframe as he pushed his hand through the secure barrier. A ripple spread out from the point of contact, flooding the room with wobbling reflected light.

He forced his arm through the barrier up to the elbow and withdrew a handful of papers, which he hurled to the side. Eight-by-ten inch panels streaked in an arc through the air, each bearing moving images of the white-haired woman, spanning from infancy to adulthood. Mamoru poked a finger at each page in turn, absorbing the contents as he eradicated the data from The Silver's file system. He hesitated at an image of her about eight or nine years of age, walking down the street with a school bag on her back. A bruise marked the side of her face, and she kept her gaze downcast.

Mamoru sighed.

Annabelle Morgan, also known as Pixie, had been part of an undertaking of the British government under the codename: Project Seraph. While putting on a public face of distrust regarding psionic individuals, MI6 conducted a secret breeding program among those individuals detained under the umbrella of national security. They arrested psionics and charged them as threats to the Crown, holding them without due process. Rather than prisons, they moved them to secure 'medical facilities.' While in custody, scientists harvested genetic material from prisoners of both sexes and attempted to match them with others whose psionic talents were similar.

According to the files, Project Seraph's goal was to find a way to fertilize embryos in a predictable manner with desired psionic talents—and weaponize them. Similarity to his own origin made him shudder. *Is every nation trying this?* The data contained here indicated the project was a dismal failure. Occasionally, a child showed no talent whatsoever, despite both parents having the gift. In no case was the estimation of ability close to accurate. Heather Morgan, Anna's mother, escaped soon after they re-implanted her fertilized egg. She managed to elude them for almost three years before they found and killed her.

Mamoru swiped through site photos of the twenty-year-old telepath lying dead in the streets of London, blood leaking from her mouth. A man in a black coat posed over the body as if a hunter had taken a dangerous animal. Great disdain welled up within Mamoru. *I will kill this man if ever I see him.* He considered his reaction. Her death was a killing without honor. Others of his caste thought little of ending the life of a commoner on a whim, but was he of that caste any more? Aurora claimed him an order of magnitude above it. His beliefs said he had fallen. A ronin is only somewhat more dignified than the women Minamoto had gifted to him.

He lost focus, unsure of where he belonged.

A rush of air drew his attention to the little vault. At the back wall of the twelve-inch cube, beyond more stacks of paper, a whirling portal yawned into a shifting tunnel defined by a honeycomb pattern of blue lines. Mamoru held his hand inside the chamber, feeling around. It appeared to be a hidden point-to-point connection outside of the normal GlobeNet rules. The remaining data tiles yielded information on a number of other British citizens. None had the same long-term observational notes as existed for Anna, but all of them appeared to be prisoners. As best he could tell, they all still lived—none of them had tried to take their children and run.

Mamoru frowned at the electronic rabbit hole. The Silver's internal security was in the midst of going haywire, red lights flashed in the corridor outside the data vault. They could not tell where the breach was, only that there had been one. Since he had teleported in without disturbing the outer door, their defense constructs and living operators had no clue where he was, and fell back on the old standby of a methodical node-to-node search.

He stuck his hand into the spiral and it drew him in. The rest of his armor melted, becoming a stream of white enamel flakes spiraling along in a horizontal tornado devoured by the portal. Azure light engulfed his vision as he plunged through a serpentine tunnel. Radiant bands whipped past every few seconds until the last flash blinded him. When vision returned, he found himself in a huge data storage chamber. It had the appearance of a two-story room with endless rows of refrigerator-sized black cabinets. Behind him, a now six-inch portal swirled on a plain wall.

The hardware in which this virtual place existed felt different. Another manufacturer, different transmission protocols, and even the 'flavor' of the electricity changed. He meditated, sweeping the system for any mention of Pixie. In reality, back in his apartment in Private Sector Boston, Mamoru's eyebrow lifted. His feeler in the room told him his consciousness had reached a server cluster in Britain. Based on data he sifted through, the system was once part of MI6, but now bore the identification of an outfit designated as the CSB.

Clandestine Service Bureau? He grumbled, in and out of reality. *Dishonorable.*

Mamoru's real body broke out in a sweat as he exerted himself in the virtual world. More information than he had ever tried to assimilate at once flooded through him, but only in snapshots. His search came back empty save for a small file pointer lurking in a trash management buffer. Someone had deleted a file containing the word *pixie*.

A momentary query based on the image of Heather Morgan brought up an identification photo of a mid-ranking CSB operative by the name of Allan Charles. He looked older, bald and in his later forties, but had the same self-absorbed smirking smile he'd worn the night he'd murdered Anna's mother.

His concentration ceased, breaking the link between his mind and the Matsushita Oni deck beneath his hand. Mamoru shifted, unconsciously making way for Nami to place tea in front of him the way she always did when he left the network.

At the dark, empty room, he sighed.

STRICTLY PROFESSIONAL

Mamoru narrowed his eyes at the wind, leaning back to watch a half-dozen silver capsules slide up the mirrored face of Interchange Tower to hovercar parking forty stories up. The early morning sky brimmed with shades of amber and blue, the surrounding city too bright to look at wherever it reflected the sun. Distant, dark shapes, other private sectors, loomed like miniature castles perched on a bed of diamonds. East City seemed to favor expansion for width rather than height. In the west, enormous century towers, hundred story buildings, dominated much of the space. For no reason Mamoru could discern, the west did not section off its 'Private Sectors' with walls. On the other side of the country, the rich preferred to use prohibitive cost to create a bubble of exclusivity around their homes.

The thought of it made him long for Japan. These people, separated from the Earth by millions of tons of plastisteel, thought it a rare privilege to set foot upon true ground. *Everything here is artificial.*

He crossed the ledge of the patio café and leaned on the railing. Ten stories down, a nest of elevated roadways ferried ground vehicles as far as he could see. Eight such roads met at this building, each parallel pair ran at different elevations around the octagonal tower, braced to the structure for support. Around where they attached, openings led to a multi-level parking area. Above and below, the tower held some of the most expensive office space in all of East City. It also housed a governmental body referred to as The Interchange, some manner of commerce watchdog. Mamoru grumbled at the thought of 'government.' An extra layer of bureaucracy on top of corporations seemed wasteful and ponderous. Corporations created products and services while all government did was consume.

Clicking boots on sunlit tiles brought his attention around to the rear. Anna, bundled in her white coat, walked up and pulled dark glasses away from her eyes. He gestured to the side and they took a small table at the edge.

"That was fast. I expected you'd take more than one day."

"Their security was impressive, but it was designed to defend against someone who has poisoned their body with metal." Mamoru tapped behind his ear. "They were too focused on trying to *kill* the operator rather than attack the deck. Such countermeasures do not work against me."

Mamoru fiddled with the terminal embedded in the table, ordering a light breakfast.

In a low, clear voice, he explained the bulk of what he had found regarding her. "...Agent Charles was the one who killed your mother. She was younger than you are now."

Anna's eyes reddened, though her expression seemed more taken with anger than sadness. Murmurs spread through other patrons in the café as various electronic devices flickered out and failed. Tiny spiders of blue lightning leapt off her hand and crawled across the table towards the terminal. Mamoru leaned away. Sparks burst out of a console two tables behind her.

She rubbed her face, trying to knead serenity into the bridge of her nose. "You destroyed the records?"

"I erased everything I found inside the Silver. Records on the other side, in Britain, were gone already. Someone named Gordon deleted those years ago." He reined in his contempt at the recent topic, softening his face and voice. "You have my condolences on your loss."

"Was there any mention of my father? My *real* father?"

"Nothing I was able to find beyond several terabytes of medical information on DNA manipulation done on the egg post-fertilization. If they had records of him, it was lost when Gordon scrubbed the files."

"Bugger all." She snarled under her breath, folding her arms and looking away from the hovering bot that dropped off their food. "Mum had shacked up with this spackhead who I grew up thinkin' was me dad. Not sure how those CSB tossers missed me."

"She had assistance escaping... An SAS man, Lieutenant Jack Pritchard."

"Ol' Jack?" Anna's eyes reddened.

"You know him?"

She sniffled, dabbing at her face with a napkin. "He took up outside where I was livin'... I thought he was CSB. He said Heather when I knocked him senseless." She choked up. "I never knew my mother's name."

Mamoru looked off to the side. "It seems unlikely he would work for the CSB after helping her escape. Perhaps he felt shame over her death and decided to watch over you."

A torrent of flickering lights and sparks swept from one side of the café to the other. "I've made such a mess of my life. Damn it all."

"Seems like you managed all right." Mamoru cut his omelet. "I have much respect for your resilience."

"Oh, don't let me fool you. I fell pretty damn far. Archon nicked me from the gutter and propped me up, not for want of me tryin' to fall on my face." She met his stare, sensing his question. "He's the one trying to protect us all."

"Archon?" Mamoru cocked an eyebrow. "Yes, Aurora mentioned him. Interesting parents."

"Oh." A smile crept through her gloom. "He chose that name to represent his commitment to our kind."

Mamoru finished a mouthful. "Sounds like he is full of himself."

"All of us have the right to be confident, Mamoru. The world has never seen the likes of us." She leaned on her elbows, lowering her voice as a fleet of delivery bots visited various patrons, bearing replacement gadgets. "And they'll not take too kindly to it. As powerful as we are, we cannot stand against the whole world. We have to keep our heads down for now. You're not in Japan any more. You need to be careful."

"Let them come. If I am not strong enough to prevail, I do not deserve to."

Anna leaned back, tracking one of the bots gliding off among the clouds. "At least *try* to avoid drawing too much attention to yourself. We need your help again."

He tilted his head, pausing his meal to give her an exasperated look. "More data retrieval? What about our arrangement?"

"I'm sorry, Mamoru." Anna studied her lap. "That last request wasn't official. It was me. I had to be sure I disappeared completely from their records. Your abilities were too great a temptation not to ask. Archon wanted me to verify you could do what we were told you can do. He did not specify the manner in which I was to do it."

For some minutes, Mamoru gazed off to his left at a distant stream of passing hovercars. The sky had lost all traces of amber, leaving a muted sapphire dotted with a handful of clouds. Every so often, a windscreen caught the sun in a painful flash. Beeps from the table came with each touch of Anna's finger on the interface as she ordered a small pastry and coffee. Mamoru forced the image of the dead woman from his mind, still at a loss to explain his feelings at the sight. Omura, his former associate at Matsushita, had killed a man for bumping him on the street. No one batted an eyelash. Of course, such things did not happen everywhere. Sapporo was too progressive, too much like the West. They had not adopted the old ways.

What sort of man would I be if I had lived there? How would I behave if my parents had not died?

"I will do as your Archon has asked. The original agreement is still between us. I require your assistance in locating the one who poisoned Minamoto against me."

Anna offered a curt nod, and slid a small case from her pocket. "Of course. This nodge contains an overview of what we are looking for. Two separate things. We would like you to gain entry to the Division 0 network, personnel files. Aurora's been insisting we look at one of their officers. Some of our people tried to go in, but they're only kids. They *did* make it in far enough to access his evaluation profile." She grumbled. "The man doesn't look the least bit Awakened. They said he's an unremarkable telekinetic. I've no idea why she's got such a keen interest in him, but she's gnawing on Archon's ear about him no end, and won't let it go. He's asked me to see if you can dig up anything deeper that perhaps they're keeping hidden about him. Everything you need is in the nodge." She leaned back as a bot set her order on the table, and smiled at it. "Thank you, little one." It flashed a happy response before zooming off. "The other request may prove a bit daunting, even for you."

Mamoru set his utensils on the empty plate and dabbed a napkin over his mouth. "I would be most impressed if that were the case."

"See, you've got a little confidence too." She winked. "The other data we are looking for is a file reference code. We believe it is in a portion of the GlobeNet owned by the UCF military intelligence group. I've heard stories that people've died from trying to break in there."

"Even if they somehow manage to disable my interface deck, there is no way for them to harm me. The programs have no capability to send a fatal shock over my mode of connection."

"Well, at least you're sure of that. Hopefully, that data is more than a big bag of wank. Shall I meet you here again tomorrow?"

"I will contact you when it is done."

MUD OOZED THROUGH MAMORU'S TOES AS HE EASED HIS WAY DOWN THE banks of the Sumida River. His little sister made faces at him from a few paces ahead where she had gone knee-deep. Her black silk kimono gleamed in the mid-afternoon sun. At the sight of the white orchid embroidered at the center of her back, he realized the dream. The child's teasing little voice sounded distant and muted, calling out to him as if a mile away.

He glanced down where his legs vanished up to the ankles in muck. Back in the apartment, his electronics waited. Why had father chased him out into the world? Mamoru plodded up to the girl, who turned her back on him and pointed at the way the light hit Tokyo's skyline.

"I think it's pretty," she chirped.

"The water's too cold. We're going to get sick."

She held both hands as a visor over her eyes as she turned, grinning. "They clean the river now. The poison is gone. We won't get sick. Papa said you need to meet Suijin-sama." She spun, tracing her fingertips through the surface of the rippling brown water.

He gathered his hiked pants in one hand and stooped to mimic her gesture. "Do you believe in such things, sister?"

"Uh huh. They're everywhere. Sometimes at night, I can hear them whisper."

Mamoru frowned. "How come we never see them? There's a river dragon in *Honor Blade VII* based—"

"You're always playing games." The girl's face twisted with sarcasm. "You're going to get eaten by a computer."

"Technology is our world. This"—he gestured at the water—"is ancient and boring. It's a dirty river that people ruined and now we struggle to fix."

"Shh," she whispered to the surface. "Don't listen to him. He's just a boy."

"Why are you such a brat to me?"

The honesty in the unexpected question chased away her condescending frown. She looked past him at the bank, over the narrow strip of too-green RealGrass where a tiny park clung to existence at the edge of the city. A tiny grunt of exertion came out of her as she unstuck her foot from the river bottom and stepped closer.

"To fool Mother." Her gaze fell to the ripples at their legs.

"Why would you need to fool her?"

"Shh. Not so loud." She put a finger to her lips. "Suijin-sama can hear you. Mother thinks you will go away, and does not want to be sad. Father says you must become a warrior and you will leave us. She said I should not care about you, so if you go away it will not hurt." Grinning, she met his stare. "I like you anyway. I say mean stuff so Mother thinks I don't."

Mamoru stared at his wavering face on the river. "Mother does not love me?"

"She does. She asks the gods to let you stay so she will not cry. She asks them to spare her the pain of losing her son."

The girl reached as if to embrace him, but froze at a distant voice.

"Sadako!" called Mother, "Come in out of the water. It is too cold."

She pretended to trip and hugged him anyway.

SANDALWOOD INCENSE WAFTED THROUGH DARK SILENCE, CALMING Mamoru's mind. The tatami mat beneath his thin hakama did little to soften the floor, but he did not yield to discomfort. He opened his eyes, focusing on a thin strand of smoke rising from the bowl at the center of a square, wood table. Tightness gripped the back of his head from where a servant had bundled and folded his hair. The shadow of a man drifted over the rice paper squares until it reached the wall he faced.

Noiseless, the panel slid to the side to reveal Kutaragi-sensei.

White socks flashed at the base of a charcoal-grey hakama as the elder walked in. Mamoru bowed low, forehead almost in contact with the table.

"I am prepared, Sensei."

He had the voice of a teenager. Mamoru shifted in his sleep as a part of his subconscious objected to this memory.

"You are to present yourself to Minamoto-heika today. I have deemed you ready. This is the day you shall receive your daisho."

"I shall be eternally grateful for your training, Sensei. Minamoto-heika shall have my undying gratitude for all he has done for me."

"It is regrettable what happened to your parents," said Kutaragi, his words preceding a grim sigh.

"Father knew others may come for me. He should have been better prepared. My family made the mistake of not being ready. Mother was too passive." Mamoru shifted in his sleep, wincing. "She should have fought back. Father was too weak to save himself. I was but a boy. It is fortunate that Minamoto-heika had the foresight to intervene and save my life. I live because of him."

Kutaragi emitted a *mmm* sound in time with a short nod. "Continue to center yourself. We will leave within the hour."

"Sensei?" Mamoru asked as Kutaragi turned to leave.

"Yes?"

Mamoru hesitated at the visage of his trainer, long hair spilled like a waterfall over flared shoulders. Both bushy eyebrows raised, moustache twitching in anticipation of an inappropriate question.

"Out with it, boy."

He bowed again. "Sensei, I am possessed of the utmost gratitude for my training and patronage."

"Your tone betrays more. Ask the question in your heart, Saitō-kun."

Mamoru let his gaze fall to the burning coals and flakes of incense. "What became of my sister?"

Kutaragi perched a hand on the katana tucked under his belt as his stance slackened. "I am sorry. It is quite likely she was killed soon after."

"I am grateful for your effort to make me feel no guilt. With utmost respect, if they had desired to slay her, they would have done so without carrying her off."

Ichirō Kutaragi moved around the table and squatted near him, resting one hand on his arm in one of the few moments where he seemed more like a grandparent and less like a master.

"Nippon Shōgyō-Kumiai sometimes takes the children of their targets. Most girls become concubines. Some are trained as ninja. Neither fate is kinder than if they had ended her life at eight."

Kutaragi squeezed his shoulder. "Be thankful you were not forced to carry the memory of such a horrible sight."

Mamoru's face remained a mask of stone. "I shall."

"If the opportunity presents itself, and by some chance she yet lives, I shall ask Minamoto-heika for his blessing to acquire her from them."

Mamoru sat motionless, staring through the smoke as the old man walked out.

"I like you anyway. I say mean stuff so Mother thinks I don't," said a tiny voice in his memory.

The wisp fluttered as if someone walked by, returning seconds later to a calm thread of white winding toward the ceiling. A presence built up at the walls, as if the room was about to implode. Mamoru remembered closing his eyes and trying not to hear the little voice. This time, he left them open. The heaviness built until smoke burst forth with a great roar from the bowl and engulfed the room. The shock of it sent him upright in bed—miles and years from that moment.

He touched a hand to his forehead, brushing the sweat away. His arm fell to his lap, leaving him staring at his pale reflection drawn in moonlight on the black lacquer face of a wardrobe at the foot of the bed. Loose hair tickled at the small of his back.

"She asks them to spare her the pain of losing her son," said child-Sadako in the back of his mind.

The sight of his mother's body riddled with bullets leapt out of the dark at him.

They granted her wish.

"Mother was too passive," said his younger self. "She should have fought back. Father was too weak to save himself."

I have filled my thoughts with deception. They were dead before they knew they were being attacked. Killed by dishonorable ambushers afraid to show themselves to an unarmed woman. My parents were not weak.

He clenched his fists, raging with anger at the same time he cried.

Who had I become that I felt nothing?

"...not forced to carry the memory of such a horrible sight," said Kutaragi from the edges of darkness.

Mamoru covered his face as child-Sadako's screaming faded off to silence.

It is the sights I did not see that haunt me.

BLACK DRAGON

The warmth of dawn nudged him awake hours later. He found himself lying on his side with one arm over the pillow. He considered it strange he had slept past sunrise, and stranger he was not flat on his back. Window blinds heeded a verbal command and closed the room off from the harsh glare of the sun. West or East did not matter. Every building in Private Sector Boston had the same silvery glass that bounced light at all angles.

He moaned and sat up, rubbing at his cheeks to hasten wakefulness. Even through the blinds, the fierce daylight turned the room amber. Mamoru stood and took a step for the door when the lack of any scent of cooking food stood out. He thought of Nami as he peered at the kitchenette, imagining her standing there in a robe.

Do I miss her, or do I miss her cooking for me?

Mamoru chuckled for a second before frowning. "Perhaps I am the one who needs to reveal my true self."

One soft red light winked at the corner of the Matsushita Oni at the center of the dining room table. It, like his agreed task, waited for him, a raven shadow looming over his shoulder. The small space mocked his former dojo. He exhaled and trudged out onto the patio through the automatic door.

Cold morning air woke him the rest of the way as he entered the only area large enough for his morning routine. Putting all thoughts of Nami,

Archon, Awakened, and Minamoto out of his mind, he reached within and sought calm. For an hour, he stretched and worked through three katas until he had covered himself in sweat despite the chill.

Autoshowers offered a far less pleasurable experience than two women bathing him did, but the machine never cringed as if expecting to be hit, and it did not have thoughts and dreams of its own. He tolerated the barrage of soap and hot water with his head bowed. His world had fallen around him, and dragged his stoicism with it. *How large is my part in tearing her from her family?* He had not let on that he had heard Ayame's sobs at night for the first month, before her new reality sank in and became inescapable. With a grunt, Mamoru pushed his way out of the tube and threw on pants and a haori, but left it hanging open.

The food reassembler created a mass of yellow foam-like substance that smelled of eggs next to a cream-colored atrocity bearing a subtle hint of potato and butter. He ate in silence, the scrape of his plastic fork on the plate the loudest sound in the world for several minutes. These people considered the private sector apartment he appropriated to be exclusive and costly, but the accommodations were less than a quarter the size of his home.

Clank.

Mamoru frowned at the plate he had dropped into the cleaning unit as the tray retracted. *The modern world has no need for servants.* He leaned on the counter, letting the subtle thrum of the machinery travel up his arms. *What if she was acting?* His silhouette occupied a square of sunlight on the wall over the sink. Its faceless stare lifted questions from his subconscious and hurled them.

"Why do you care about Minamoto?" *He is my shogun.*

"Was. He ordered your parents killed." *They were not my parents.*

"It was her egg, how is she not your mother?" *Unnatural.*

"Saitō Ichiro engineered your existence. How is he not your father?" *There was no love, only pride in a weapon he made.*

"You feel guilt over Nami." *I… miss her.*

"Forget Minamoto. Bring her here." *I cannot stand this place.*

"These people are not owned by companies." *No, by their government.*

"Minamoto has no influence here. You could be happy." *I gave my word.*

He spun to put his back to the shadow and narrowed his eyes at the deck. "I will prove the deception. If Minamoto does not accept it, I will avenge my mother, I will avenge Nami, and I will leave Matsushita in tatters."

THE DIVISION 0 NETWORK HAD PROVEN EASY, BUT TIME-CONSUMING, A distraction that left a dark cloud over Mamoru's head. He stayed far longer than needed to peruse personnel records, finding their modest database regarding psionic phenomenon most intriguing. Most vexing of all, the talent they had designated 'kinetics' seemed quite similar to what he had long thought of as *chi*. One reassurance was how weak it seemed by comparison. Their documentation had cases where psionics had made themselves much stronger, but none had reached too far beyond the limits of human potential. Certainly, no one Division 0 had yet encountered could tear an armored elevator door off its hinges or accelerate themselves to the point of existing in a slow motion world.

He stood at the end of a narrow span of black glass, which stretched over a square canyon ringing his objective like a moat. At the center of the pit, a building made of the same jet material and covered with millions of luminous gold lines rose from an island. It resembled a cluster of high-tech office towers crammed together in the shape of an ancient fortress.

He expected guards to be walking the parapets.

The structure had no windows, only sleek, glimmering ominousness covered by irregular raised panels. UCF Military Intelligence, nicknamed C-Branch, had established a handful of Priority-Security network locations they referred to as P-SECs. Mamoru focused on the far end of the bridge and the white samurai armor began to appear piece by piece where he desired to go. Interference swirled within his body when it had halfway formed, causing him to abort the teleportation and focus on ridding his deck of an invasive program.

A sensation similar to a snake entering his head through one ear sent a wave of tension down his spine. The C-Branch network bombarded him with anti-intrusion softs the likes of which exceeded all prior opposition he had faced. Mamoru scrambled to catch and kill two dozen separate inbound connections. The hollow armor shuddered in place as he catalogued the deck's neural memory banks. Panel after panel spread open in the sky above him, towering displays fifteen feet high full of shifting numbers and kanji. A long trail of darkness slithered through the white characters, dimming them as a serpentine shape circled around the unused M3 socket hardware.

Mamoru smiled. This was a killer soft, but it had nowhere to put its fangs. He reached one armored glove into his vacant helmet and clenched his fingers around the light within. Waves of brightness banded down through the shifting letters on each panel, shoving the serpent toward the bottom. As the dimming reached the edge of the screens, the gauntlet withdrew, pulling a hissing, thrashing snake out of the armor.

He focused on it, causing it to snap straight as a staff in his grip while its eyes flared with brilliant light. The panels filled with the sequence of code that made up the Death Asp soft, altering it at the speed of thought. *This should give their operators something to play with.* He hurled an onyx quarterstaff to the ground, where it went flexible and slithered away, a blur of black on black streaking at the fortress. It would seek the nearest live operator and attack its former master.

The samurai advanced, walking the bridge rather than risk another teleport. Requesting a coordinate overwrite had opened his deck to invasion once. At the three-quarter mark, a nondescript black man in an expensive tailored suit walked out from the bottom of the narrow span, pivoted up the side in defiance of gravity, and swung over, stepping onto the surface behind him.

He reached for a gun.

Seething orange-white light erupted from the katana as Mamoru whirled and bisected the construct in a single pass. The upper half of the body floated away from the legs and a disintegration spiral of golden numbers spread outward from the slice. The hips and legs fell to one side, exploding in a burst of shimmering crystals before shattering over the ground.

Mamoru resumed his trek, but two more appeared identical to the last, one from each side. He lunged at them, managing to behead both before they could fire. Four more walked up the sides of the bridge in unison, and pivoted vertical at the top. In the time it took him to process their appearance in his mind, another eight joined them.

This must be what Kutaragi-sensei meant by 'discretion.'

Bullets, a cyberspace manifestation of electronic assault on his deck, whistled over his head. A normal operator would have an array of defensive softs they could reach for in a situation like this to do various things: redirect the incoming connection to dead memory buffers, conceal the deck on the network, apply quadruple-redundant virus checking to slow the incoming data and arrest the harmful code. Not Mamoru. It was so rare a hostile network sensed his entry, given his ability to alter programs at the speed of thought, he had not even bothered hiding his connection with a series of false hops.

However, normal hackers also did not *experience* the substance of the incoming program code as he did. As fast as they fired at him, he rewrote their combat routines to harmless detection pings. Bullets shattered as if made of ice against his armor. The effort slowed him to a walk, and then to a trudge as another sixteen identical men swung up onto the bridge. Shots from the ones in back passed without harm through their duplicates and a hornet swarm of virtual bullets converged on him. The exertion of altering so much software took on the form of a headache.

Every two seconds they double in number.

Worry was a new sensation for him. He weathered the hail of irritation, forcing himself forward as if thigh deep in tar under the mind-load of rewriting hundreds of tiny bits of software every second. The last several feet of bridge brought him to a wall of ebon, engraved with glowing circuit lines running in deep grooves. His ornate helmet tilted back as he appraised the surface without a door. Growling low in his throat rose to a roar as he brought his hands together in a detonating clap. A pulse of energy raced in an expanding sphere from where his gauntlets collided.

The defense constructs froze as the wave passed over them, and the amber etching on the face of the fortress turned dull blue. Mamoru slouched from the fatigue of brute forcing a low-level re-initialization of the network node's memory addresses. By fortunate paradox, the insane amount of defense constructs made the node more vulnerable to such a tactic. It would take longer to bring the node online with so many routines to load. One 'room,' the moat chamber, sat outside of network time while the hardware that generated it performed a diagnostic check. In the real world, it would end in six to ten seconds, perhaps four if the hardware was overclocked. In cyberspace, he had a few minutes.

With one hand on the wall, he forced his thoughts into the material. Black stone rippled like fluid, opening in the shape of a door as he struggled to wrench his hands apart. Every inch of progress took great effort and drained his energy. Rather than locate the hidden portal, he altered the node design to create access where there was none. Such a modification to 'dark matter' would take hours for a master deck jockey, not to mention being impossible without a direct connection to the host. Mamoru could manipulate it by imposing his will over the hardware that hosted the network itself. C-Branch had no way to stop a breach that could not happen. All of its defenses were set up on the accessible entry points.

Once the portal opened, he ducked through and stopped fighting the node's effort to restart itself. The spherical opening grew smaller as the goopy substance filled in, but it would not seal before the constructs came back online.

Mamoru ran, cornering at the first opportunity. Once the mass of defenders had no line of sight on him, he stopped. White fire surrounded his inert body in the real world as the hollow samurai grasped the air and pulled the interior network design into his thoughts. Ribbons of streaming letters, numbers, and symbols shot out of holes in the wall and orbited him. It took only a minute to modify his avatar code to appear native to the network.

Now calm, he marched to where he sensed the presence of the data he had come looking for. The nodule Pixie had given him contained reference to a file with the marker: DN-WR-393-EM. Curiosity piqued him to swipe mental threads at the walls. DN referenced a project involving DNA. WR was their code for weapons research, or warfare research depending on which bureau director he wanted to believe. 393 referred to the file creation year, 2393. He found no explanation for the EM at the end.

He walked among rows of storage constructs, tall cabinets formed by thick slabs of shiny obsidian separated by layers of cobalt blue light, stretched to infinity. The white samurai armor glided among them toward his objective, but halted as a resonant voice shook the entire chamber.

"Well now, I haven't had an intruder make it this far in a number of years."

Mamoru whirled about, seeing no one behind him.

"Up here, little one."

He looked up, leaning backwards, and froze at the sight of the ceiling moving. A surface of shining ebon plates slid overhead. He spun to the rear, and stared at two lime-hued eyes hovering in the dark. Each spanned six feet across and bore a tiny samurai reflection in the center like vertical pupils of stark white. Light glinted across long, obsidian teeth as it spoke.

"There is something unusual about you." The face of an enormous dragon covered in scales of glassy onyx loomed out of the sky, its mouth large enough for a man to stand in. "You are most curious, intruder." It blinked, sniffing at him.

The electronic barrage made his deck scream. Phantom pain from a burning hand reached his consciousness. Mamoru shuddered, fighting the instinctual urge to jerk his touch away from heat and lose his connection. *By the gods, all it is doing is scanning me. That wasn't even an attack.*

"I am curious… how is it you are here? How is it you are you doing what you are doing?" Sniffing ended with a snort that knocked virtual Mamoru back a step. "If I find your answer amusing enough, I may not kill you." Clawed hands shrouded nearby data towers as it loomed.

Mamoru steadied himself. He reached for the katana, but hesitated. "What are you?"

"Do you patronize me, human?" It shifted, circling away from the door to the right, never taking its gaze away. "I do not accept that you were able to gain entry here and yet do not know what I am."

It's an AI, that much I know. Dangerous. Grade nine.

"An AI. You're a dragon construct."

The creature put a clawed hand over its snout, chuckling with a turned head as if hearing a wry, off-color joke. Its laughter ended with a flare of its eyes as it lunged within inches of him. "No, simpleton. I *am* the network. This is my domain. I am *Nightwing.*" Hundreds of identical men in suits skidded to a halt at the entrance to the chamber. The dragon thrust itself up on its hind legs and spread its wings, roaring at a ceiling that shattered away in tumbling obsidian chunks sucked upward into a gloomy cloud-filled sky. "You are an insect. You cannot hope to comprehend the magnificence before you. I—"

"Do not know how I am here."

Its head whipped down to stare at him, one eye wider than the other, lip twitching from the insolence. After a momentary pause, it fell forward onto its forelegs, shaking the ground from the crash. "How… dare you."

"You may be the most advanced artificial intelligence I have ever seen."

Nightwing's eyes narrowed, a cat's reaction to a chin scratch. "Indeed."

"Yet, you are still nothing more than program code."

Nightwing snarled. His claws became a blur of black onyx that smashed Mamoru airborne. The samurai avatar slammed through a series of data cabinets, which shattered on impact. With each crash, fragments stopped in midair and collapsed back together after he passed. Mamoru collided with the wall a hundred meters away, stuck for a few seconds, and slid to the floor with an ear-splitting knives-on-glass squealing sound.

Mamoru howled in his mind as his paralyzed avatar twitched; surges of electricity raked through the Matsushita Oni. The Dragon's face loomed out of the shadows in the back of his mind as the AI forced its way into the deck, biting and tearing at the components. Neural memory fried, chips burned out, and a searing thread of pain ran up his back as lightning erupted from the M3 port. *Unbelievable... Black ICE sends just enough current to roast a brain stem. That jolt would have made a user's head explode.*

Innumerable men in suits swarmed around the data cabinets, raising pistols. Before any of them could shoot, eerie lime-green flames filled the sky. A column of inferno blasted from the dragon's mouth. Mamoru crossed his arms over his helmet and sent a psionic spike to his deck that forced it to disavow all I/O processes. The samurai winked out of existence as several hundred dark suits broke apart to pixilated ash. When he reappeared, the jet walls and floor smoked. Cyberspace, so often devoid of any sense of smell or temperature, felt hot and stank of burned flesh.

"Fool!" thundered the AI. "You know not the error of your arrogance."

Mamoru leapt to his feet, drawing the katana as he sprang upward at the descending bite. Nightwing blurred sideways, plucking him out of the air with ease. The katana glanced away without cutting the hardened scales. Conical teeth sparked against white enamel. Mamoru gurgled, crying out as chip after chip inside the deck burst with mini geysers of smoke. The enormous head and neck swung side to side in an agonizing thrash. Mamoru's face warmed in the drip of a gushing nosebleed while he battled with his deck to obey him. This time, the I/O channel refused to turn off. Rather than attack with viruses or precision Black ICE, the dragon tried to flood his uplink path with raw voltage. Fortunately, the Oni connected via wireless link. Frustrated, Nightwing whipped his neck, flinging Mamoru to the ground. After a snarl, the dragon spat to the side. A glop of black tar hurtled forth, growing to a spherical mass with a squid's beak and four tentacles tipped with toothy paddles.

A Devourer soft.

The white samurai armor shattered like porcelain on impact, fragments skidding as far as fifteen feet away. The Devourer's beak opened, and it cried out with an avian screech. Virtual air rushed in to the orifice, and the fleshy mass descended on the broken warrior.

Mamoru groaned in the real world as the hostile construct invaded his deck. It went right for the neural memory, intending on eating every piece of software and burning out every addressable portion of neural-memory it could find. He seized one of the flopping tentacles, dragging the meaty sphere to the floor in the non-space of his deck. Its other toothy paddle walloped him in the back, face, and chest, but he refused to let go. Blood seeped through a spiderweb of cracks in his armor, stark crimson against enamel white. Mamoru growled as he held the struggling, shrieking blob down and forced his will over it. Its beak clapped closed inches from his hollow helmet. The Devourer's skin rippled, flesh replaced by shiny lamellar armor as he rewrote it. Inside the P-SEC, the shattered bits of white samurai slid back together, stacking like a ring of glass chips until he was once again whole.

Nightwing leaned up, raising an eyebrow at the sight of him holding the Devourer as though it were some immense medieval flail. He whirled it overhead and flung it at the dragon. The AI scooted away from the armored tentacle beast, its motion reminiscent of an enormous cat that wanted nothing whatsoever to do with the object flying at it. While the altered Devourer proceeded to chase Nightwing around the room, Mamoru fell over sideways.

Ouch. This deck is almost gone.

He crawled to the nearest storage cabinet, reaching into it in an effort to sneak the data he came for while the dragon was distracted. File after file shot through his mind, shimmering squares of silver and blue. Before he could locate what he needed, the tremendous crash of bending metal overhead announced the end of the Devourer.

"For that, you will suffer long!" boomed a voice, shaking the entire chamber.

Blinded by desperation, Mamoru leapt the data cabinet and struck out with the katana. Nightwing raised an arm, the blade sparking against scales time and time again with little effect. *It is rebuilding itself as fast as I delete it.* He lunged for its belly, hoping to find a backdoor that would give him access to the core of the program's code. For an instant, he thought he had a clear shot at the weaker scales of the underside, but another claw stroke caught him from the left and launched him airborne.

Flaming samurai armor sailed in a comet's arc, landing in the onyx ground and gouging a twenty-meter trench with a spray of shards. Mamoru smelled fire and smoke, in the real world. His deck had reached the point of no return. Only his psionic power held it together, forcing a machine pushed beyond its limits to function. Lines of static banded over the samurai armor as it threatened to vanish if he so much as sneezed.

Nightwing stomped after him, swatting more men in dark suits out of his way.

"Peasant! I tire of your insolence."

Nightwing's great horned head surged forward, jaw opening for the final strike.

This monster is too powerful... I never imagined such a thing. It is only software, yet it is too vast for me to change. A glimmer of insight flashed through his mind. *But, does it know that?*

The room shifted as he used a micro teleport to close with the dragon faster than it could react and plunged a hand into the beast's chin. Glowing eye spots appeared within the helmet and white flames burst forth from the shoulder of the samurai armor.

Mamoru shouted, "You are nothing but a program. You are my domain!"

He forced all the energy he could summon toward his desire to rewrite the dragon. Its self-checking routines continuously repaired it, faster than even Mamoru could change code, but the sensation of being rewritten and repaired had to be something the arrogant thing had never before experienced.

Shiny black scales degenerated to green-line wireframe around where his arm penetrated. Nightwing groaned in agony, stumbling. Patches of exposed crude polygons swam over it as the network's rendering engine searched for a way to represent what was happening.

"Stop. What... are you doing?"

"You wanted to know how I got here. I am showing you." Mamoru turned his arm, shoving it through the beast's hide up to the elbow. "As smart as you are, as advanced as you are, you are still nothing more than a program. I am rewriting you to serve me. I shall make you an enormous dog, fetching sticks and bounding through the grass."

Mamoru's live body shook with spasmodic jerks in the chair, sweat poured over him from the toll of the concentration. In the net, he showed no outward sign of how difficult a time he had contending with such a massive piece of software. The strain of holding his deck together and doing this brought blood from his nose and fire to his nerves. This dragon was hundreds of petabytes of code, far more massive than the largest program he had ever *touched.*

"No. Do not..." Nightwing moaned again, straining to pull away.

Panic rose in the back of Mamoru's mind as he wondered if his ruse would trigger the strongest instinct possessed by any artificial entity—survival.

"I can create program code simply by desiring its existence. My will forms in the neural synapses of the network. I am a psionic unlike anything the GlobeNet has ever seen. Can you feel your vast intellect collapsing, shrinking to become a sub-sentient wretch capable only of urinating on trees? In minutes, you will be little more than an elaborate DataMole."

A blur of wireframe washed over Nightwing's face as it screamed, pulling against him. Man-sized claws dug into the black glass floor, raking gouges amid deafening squeals. "You cannot!"

More suits swarmed through the door. Panic in the creature's voice was Mamoru's signal. He released his mental hold while grunting and reaching at it. The dragon seemed to believe it had broken free of its own will and whirled away, scrambling for the node exit. In its terror, it sheared through the incoming army, shredding them to piles of glowing crystal fragments.

Mamoru allowed himself a moment of rest. Chunks of business suit lost their texture and melted into silver nuggets as the network deleted corrupted software fragments. Laughing to himself at the ever-distancing crashes of the fleeing AI, he put both hands on one of the data towers and pulled.

At his touch, the slab slid outward exposing an open flat tray. A series of eight-inch silver tiles rotated in harmony above it. Each represented individual data folders. Mamoru knew the one he had come for by the way it felt to look at. He lifted one and held it in both hands in front of his face. The mirror-like surface did not display any reflection. He stared at it, smiling when DN-WR-393-EM appeared in glowing letters. He pulled and twisted at the sides. A bright cyan crack split it down the center, stretching to gridlines as he drew the tile apart from itself. Each half reconstituted, leaving him holding two identical copies.

Pixie did not mention he should destroy their copy. He tossed one tile back into the drawer, closed it, and held the other to his chest until it sank through his armor. As far as the network was concerned, he had not copied it—he generated a new file in the Matsushita Oni. Mamoru fought off the weariness in his brain and checked the node buffers to verify they had not logged the file creation. With a wicked grin forming on his semiconscious face, he fiddled with the network ingress buffers, creating evidence that appeared to be a failed attempt to conceal a link trace to the private node in MI6.

CSB Agent Allan Charles seemed like a good name to associate with the breach.

MAMORU CRADLED HIS HAND, BLISTERED AND RED. BLACK BURN MARKS traced jagged across the table from where electrical arcs had erupted from the deck's M3 interface connector. A small fire had started at the far end of the table. He frowned at the charred material, a visible reminder of carelessness. As soon as he had stopped concentrating, the deck shut down, belching smoke. Blood oozed over his face and his body felt as though he had fallen from great height.

He wanted to put the fire out, but his attempt to stand up sent him to the floor and triggered a coughing fit that painted the tiles with more blood. Two paper white feet appeared inches from his face.

"Oh, dear," said Aurora.

The sound of running water fluttered as something passed through the stream. Out of the corner of his eye, an amorphous humanoid shape approached. Aurora tiptoed towards the table and swatted at the burning. The slap of a wet towel striking wood happened several times before the beeping of a fire sensor ceased.

Mamoru groaned.

Hands pulled at his arm, rolling him onto his back. She slid her arms under and lifted him. He tried to reach up to hold on to her shoulder, but managed only an uncoordinated swipe that wound up grabbing a breast.

"Now, now, Mamoru. You're in no shape for that." She swung him to the side to make it through a doorway. "Wot 'appened?"

"Dragon," he wheezed.

Soft material met him from below as she set him on the Comforgel pad. A moment later, her naked torso hovered over him. Mamoru lolled his head side to side.

"For not wanting to, you certainly think of it all the time. You're a bloody mess, and I don't mean that in the British sense of bloody. More urgent things to do than bother with clothes." She tugged at his haori, opening it. "Well, Mamoru, you are one big bruise."

He rasped incoherently as she left him there. Minutes passed in a daze, interspersed with a beeping NetMini, a rush of cool air from an open window, the whine of a tiny hovering bot, and the bed shifting as she climbed up and sat next to him. Mamoru looked at her while she stuck a small, red cylinder in her mouth and bit a yellow cap off the narrow end.

"Relax, luv." She pressed cold metal against his pectoral muscles, which flooded with cool numbness in time with a soft *hiss*. "Looks like you could use another shot." She repeated the process. "There, that should do it." She kissed him on the forehead. "Sweet dreams."

🐁 🦅 🏮 💧 👺

MAMORU AWOKE LATER, UNSURE OF HOW MUCH TIME HAD PASSED. AURORA stretched out beside him with her arms over her head, somehow managing to sleep without touching him or falling out of the bed. For some time, he stared at her breasts, rising and falling with each breath. It was not so much that he wanted to, but it was where his head pointed when he woke up—and moving hurt too much.

A five-count box of Stimpaks, two used, sat on the glowing gel mattress between them. The idea that she gave him two shots of synthetic adrenaline and he *still* passed out frightened him. With a groan, he sat up and swung his legs over the side of the bed, turning his back to her. Stretching made him growl through clenched teeth and consider falling asleep once again.

A white hand threaded under his right arm, crossing his chest and pulling him against her. He was too worn out to protest her touch. His memory drifted to a time when Nami would massage him. One clumsy arm extended back over his shoulder was a poor substitute. *How stiff she had been.* He let his head sag. *She expected I would demand more than a back rub.*

"Are you feeling better?" Aurora slid up behind him, squeezing his shoulders as she tried to work the pain out. "I had a sense you would need some help tonight."

He sat there, unable to resist, making weak grunts and groans.

"Don't get your hopes up too much, Mamoru. I'm not going to cook for you, and the mess in the kitchen is all yours to clean up."

"You have my thanks."

Aurora let her arms fall in her lap. "You're welcome." She slipped past him, letting her chest linger by his face as she got up. "I'll let myself out then."

Mamoru cradled his face in both hands. She arched her back and collapsed in a cloud of fog. A moment later, he felt a sense of being alone again. Two fingers parted so he could see the clock: four in the morning. With a groan, he let gravity take him over sideways.

EMPTY CARDBOARD BOXES LITTERED THE KITCHEN. THE SCENT OF NEW electronics mingled with the horror the reassembler tried to pass off as eggs. It had taken the better part of three hours, but Mamoru managed to get his deck repaired enough to where it would turn on. He wasn't sure how he did it. He only even tried because of what he had found within the Division 0 archives. Most cases of individuals having similar ability displayed their talent as a knack for repairing or working with machines rather than controlling them with their thoughts. He took a chance and it paid off. Without a clue what he was doing, he poked and prodded with tools and a soldering iron at whatever felt *right*.

The deck taunted him. All he had to do was touch it. In seconds, he could know how Nami felt. He replayed the memory of hours ago, of Aurora with him in bed, only he replaced her with Nami. Her scent floated across his memory. His hand pressed on the table, inches short of the device. The last image he saw of her face, broken by lines in the spider-bot's display, flickered through his imagination. *Is she safe? I could know. We could find a life here, free of Minamoto as well as this Awakened nonsense.* His gaze shifted to the bed despite it being noon. Fear curled his fingers away.

He growled and forced himself to his feet. *I am still tired. My thoughts are murky.*

30

SOLACE OF STARS

J ostled about in the PubTran taxi's rear bench seat, Mamoru grumbled with each turn and sudden stop. At least the vehicle's pathetic acceleration left so much to be desired bumping around in the seat didn't hurt much. Nothing came between him and hard plastic aside from a thin layer of cloth bearing a pattern of grey and teal squares. He held on, digging fingernails in as much as he could as the tiny box-on-wheels skidded around a corner.

The last vestiges of daylight slid behind the western horizon as the car squealed to a stop. Mamoru ignored the recorded voice thanking him for using the PubTran taxi service and warning him about the dangerous area around him. Clouds of mist spun in whorls as the sky-blue and silver thing scurried off. Two rows of silver fasteners glinted on the chest of his long, black coat as he strode through the glare of a street lamp.

He stepped off the road, following the sidewalk for a half block before hooking left towards the building Pixie had requested for their meeting location. A handful of younger men and a few women loitered by what had once been a guard station at the front gate. He paid them no mind as he went straight for the fence.

The raised voice of a cobalt-haired man focused the group's attention on Mamoru. "Hey, upsec, you lost?"

"I think he is, Gek. This one looks like he's got some creds."

"Yo, upsec. Why not show a little charity?" A girl with short, violet hair and a glowing azure butterfly tattoo on her left cheek strode up to within a few feet of him.

"You look as though you are in need of a meal. Don't your parents feed you?"

Mamoru clasped the padlock holding the gate closed and swiped his thumb over the chrome.

The girl pulled at the edges of a puffy, red jacket exposing a pistol on each hip—and the lack of a shirt. Shiny, dark material clung to her breasts without any obvious means of support.

Psionic or chi? Mamoru tilted the lock, using the chrome surface to examine the girl. "I do not find pleasure in destroying pretty things. You should return to your home." A wisp of light danced over the back of his hand as he crushed and tore the padlock free.

"Fuck, he's an auggie!" shouted someone behind her.

She went for her gun, aiming the trembling weapon in his general direction. Her eyes said 'stay away from me' but her mouth disagreed. "S-swipe me a t-thousand and maybe I'll go home and be a good little girl."

Mamoru sent a wave of mental energy inward. He spun, drawing the katana in a swing that passed upward through the gun, missing her fingers by a blade's width. He straightened and faced her, the sword back on his hip in its scabbard before the two halves of firearm separated.

No one moved for several seconds. *Tap. Tap. Tap.* Rectangular bricks of blue caseless ammo slipped one after the next out of the gun, clattering around her boots. The young woman lowered her arm, dumping the remaining two dozen rounds onto the ground. One of the men behind her whistled and raised his hands.

"Hmm. I must be getting old. You still have fingers." He winked.

One of the boys waved at her to back off. "Easy, man. We don't want no shit with an aug. We were messin'. Thought you was some no-clue upsec."

She dropped the half-gun and cradled her fingers, as if counting them. Seconds later, she ran. The group fell in behind her, only two risking a peek back to see if he had moved. Mamoru laughed in his head at their faces, though his outer calm did not soften. When the last of them vanished around the end of the alley, he went through the gate. A passage large enough for two trucks to pass side by side skirted the edge of the building, leading in a gradual curve past decrepit cargo containers stacked against the wall. He stepped around shallow standing pools, some striated with rainbow, and entered a courtyard that smelled of rust and chemicals.

At least I no longer taste dirt.

The little figure leaning against the door of a plain white hovercar struck him as another lost thirteen-year-old until she turned. Anna waited in the center of a space defined by the U-shaped warehouse, the collar of her coat up and hands in her pockets. She uncrossed her arms as he neared, shifting her weight off the car.

Mamoru walked up to her. "I expected you'd be inside out of the wind."

"I-I'm not fond of large, disused warehouses. Was it much of a ballache?"

One eyebrow peeked over his mirrored wraparound glasses. "I am unfamiliar with that phrase." He gestured in the direction of the gate. "What is an upsec?"

"Local thing, means someone from an upper class sector." She looked him up and down. "Nice coat. Was it much of a problem getting the data?"

"It was a unique experience." Mamoru moved close enough to kiss her. "You are tense."

Anna glanced about at the roof. "Aurora insisted I bring a case of stimpaks. It's never a good sign when a precog tells you to bring medical supplies."

"Well then, I shall be as brief as I can." He handed her a holodisk in a case. "Here is the information on your Division Zero man. I saw nothing in his records to indicate he has abilities beyond which the government is aware. From what Aurora has explained of... our kind, he seems to be lacking."

She rolled her eyes. "Nothing at all?"

"No. Records and performance evaluations show him to be an unremarkable telekinetic, a few minor commendations and no disciplinary infractions except for showing disrespect to his superiors. The only unusual thing I found was an exemption to their rules that allowed him and his wife to serve as partners. Everything is on that disk. Their own files regard him as 'below average' in telekinetic force, but he appears to have an unusual talent for fine control. He seems normal."

"Normal? Strange. Why would Lauren mention him?" Anna sighed. "I don't understand that woman sometimes. Did you at least find anything useful in the P-SEC? Oh, wait, let me guess... you couldn't get in?"

He took a second holodisk from his coat pocket. "There was a dragon, but I got past it."

"Ooo." She grabbed the box, tucking both into a metal case, which she placed in the car behind her.

"It appears C-Branch was attempting to clone someone. Does the name Ekaterina Myshkin mean anything? The project is dated twenty-five years ago, but listed as failed."

"Did you live in a bubble? Oh"—she made a dismissive wave—"Japan… might as well be another damn planet. Myshkin was a famous psionic who escaped the ACC—a pyrokinetic. After she grew up, she did a lot of speeches and whatnot about how sorry they have it over there."

Mamoru glanced at the roof to his left. "The records had images of a little girl floating in some manner of liquid. It seemed they disposed of her when the project was deemed impractical."

"Was there any mention of where the facility was or what they did with it?"

"As far as the data indicated, somewhere out in a place called the Badlands. There was mention of a river. Mishi… Mossa…"

"Mississippi?" asked Anna.

"Yes, that. Their files indicated the entire compound burned to the ground."

She smiled. "Well, at least she wasn't wrong on that count."

A sense of familiar urgency flooded Mamoru's thoughts as his senses processed a soft scraping noise. Brilliant white light spread over his arms. He leapt the car, dragging her over the roof to the far side. Sharp *pangs* echoed as bullets ricocheted off the plate metal ground where he had been a second earlier. He landed, running at the warehouse, carrying her. Mamoru took four steps before he jumped at the entrance, spinning to shield her. Anna's reaction to the first leap had barely started to show on her face when they crashed through the door, taking it from its hinges.

The impact sent them sliding over bare concrete floor, spinning. She held on, clutching two fistfuls of coat until they stopped moving. A flurry of bullets came through the wall, creating a running line of holes aglow from outside lights.

Anna rolled off him and ducked behind a dead forklift. "Are these for you or for me?"

Mamoru sprang up and moved behind a metal roof support. "I do not know."

A pair of fist-sized orbs, jet-black with dim green lenses, floated through an already-broken window, gliding in a sweeping turn to the center of the room. One pivoted at Mamoru, searing a burn into the column over his head with a bright green laser. Two loud snaps came in rapid succession, resounding through the cavernous building. Hair-thin threads of lightning burned the air between Anna's outstretched hand and the spheres. Mamoru jumped at the gun-like noise, and pressed himself against the post as the metal balls fell to the ground with dull *clanks*.

Anna looked over the top of the cargo loader and locked eyes with him.

You watch that side. I'll get this one.

Her voice in his mind made him jump, wincing from the perceived volume. She sank out of sight behind a stack of plastisteel cargo boxes covered in plastic tarp. Mamoru drew the katana in a loose grip that did not trigger the vibro inducer, and waited.

Shadows slipped over grimy glass as silent bodies seemed to fly from the ground to the roof. Mamoru's shoulders simmered with energy as he drew on his power to bolster his senses. Thinking of it as *chi* had ritualized the process. With the mysticism removed, it took effect in half the time. Creaking ran through the walls from the pressure of the wind. Other sounds filtered through the wind, now an overbearing howl. The distinct sense of people creeping over the roof led his gaze past a dozen broken lamps to an elevated catwalk.

Several spots of molten metal glowed on the ceiling, brilliant in the dark to his enhanced sight. From each two-inch hole, something black slipped in and hit the floor with a *click*, followed by skittering.

"Pixie, small spiders. Poison," said Mamoru as he moved away from the column.

She stood a second before as one came scurrying out of the dark. Mamoru advanced towards the stairs that led to the elevated walkway, body aglow. A mouse-sized metal spider sprang at his face. He moved at such speed time appeared to stretch to a halt around him. The dripping needle-fangs glistened, bearing droplets of pale green liquid. Mamoru slashed it to the side. Another leapt from behind him. He brought his blade across his neck, catching the tiny assassin before it could bite. With a flick, he threw it into the air and cut it in half on the way down

Sparks flashed to the right. One thread of lightning appeared in a jagged arc, vanished, and reappeared in a different shape. Another arachnid flung itself to its destruction against his sword. One ran up a column, turned, and tensed to leap sidelong at him. It never made it off the post, pinned by a stab through its orb-like abdomen. The katana squealed like a quenched blade as the steel beam battled its hypersonic oscillation. A flash of sparks and greasy, black smoke puffed out of it.

A figure in black dropped through a roof hatch, landing on the catwalk with a short rifle at the ready. Hissing drew his gaze up to where several orange melt-circles appeared on the ceiling, arranged around the room. They surrounded where he had been seconds earlier. His rush for the stairs put him right under one.

Anna let off an incoherent shout of rage. Two rapid arcs flashed, connecting wires on the ceiling to her back an instant before an arm-thick shaft of white lightning from her hand launched the catwalk man into the wall twenty feet away. Crackling sparks burst out from the point of impact before he peeled away and fell. The smoking body did not move after landing, aside from erratic twitching.

Mamoru raised an eyebrow at her.

Before he could say anything, five metal discs fell from the ceiling, each ridden by a man on a rappelling line. A burst of kinetic focus launched Mamoru at the one hovering fifteen feet over his head. An upward stab through the chest proved fatal, leaving the assassin dangling on a wire fixed to a harness. The others fired as he landed. A few stray shots spattered the distant wall with the corpse's blood. Mamoru leapt for cover behind one of the roof supports, flattening himself behind it as several tried to shoot through concrete-covered steel.

The room erupted in a flicker of shimmering blue and white. Flashes, screams, and harsh buzzing forced Mamoru to relax his boosted senses. Automatic fire erupted behind him. Anna's cries of "shit, shit, shit, shit" barely made it to his ears over the roar.

Mamoru frowned at the rifle dropped by the man he killed. He rushed out of cover and headed for the gun, shifting the katana to his left hand. Two charred corpses hung from the ceiling, still smoldering while another assassin faced sideways, a wavering flare of blue muzzle fire belching from the front of his rifle. The cargo mover Anna huddled behind flaked away in pieces. Every so often, a geyser of fluid burst from an impact hole. Mamoru dropped to a knee slide when he noticed the last assassin had been waiting for him.

Searing pain lanced through his left shoulder, another bullet whispered past his ear. He skidded to a stop with the dead man's assault rifle between his legs, frozen. The foreign emotion of fear invaded his mind as he found himself gazing at the maw of a gun with nowhere to hide.

The assassin corrected his aim, but plummeted to the ground, trailed by a severed climbing cord. His sudden fall sent his second burst wild. Bullets *clanked* and *plinked* among the rafters in a shower of sparks. Mamoru wasted no time pondering his luck and seized the firearm. He held it as if it were made of animal waste, scrunching his nose while pointing it with one arm toward the man shooting at Anna. His borrowed weapon dragged his arm upward as he squeezed the trigger, raking a trail of bright holes in the wall, but coming nowhere near the target. The shot did however provide enough of a threat to distract the man away from her.

Iridescent flames gathered along Mamoru's arms as a rush of psionic energy permeated his muscles. He tossed the rifle aside with a contemptuous frown and gathered the katana in both hands as he leapt. Gunfire rang out in a series of pops. Individual bullets spiraled through the air below him, sailing at the spot of floor from which he'd jumped.

Mamoru crested the arc of his leap as the man who fell took a firing position. He, too, aimed as if his target was still on the ground. The assassin reacted to Mamoru's charge too late, only starting to look up as the katana took his head.

A distant flash preceded a man's scream behind him, followed by a staccato ripple of tiny explosions. Mamoru ceased concentrating on the tiring boost, allowing time to return to normal, and glanced behind him. The assassin who would have killed him had the cord not snapped twitched and convulsed. His right arm ended midway between elbow and wrist in a spurting bloody stump, and that side of his face ceased to exist. From the look of it, his pistol's ammunition had detonated right out of the magazine. Small bits of fire danced on his chest along the scar of a lightning path.

Anna emerged from her hiding place, staggering. Her left hand, pale and bloody, squeezed her right shoulder. A series of low-intensity sparks shot from her outstretched arm, knocking the last man about like an electric piñata.

"You miserable son of a bitch." She growled. A long-burning tendril of energy connected her hand to his chest.

He shrieked, begging for his life in Japanese.

Mamoru stretched to his full height, picking at a hole near his left collarbone. "I think they were here for me."

Anna splayed her fingers apart, five discrete streams of electricity lapped at the body until bloody foam oozed out of the facemask and he went still. Her anger gave way to disgust, and she stumbled over to Mamoru.

"I... hate that smell. I'm never going to get used to it." She fumbled in her pocket and handed Mamoru three small, red cylinders. "These are—"

"I am familiar with stimpaks. My former employer manufactures stim suits."

Mamoru opened his coat and pushed his shirt aside, amazed that he had not lost the use of his left arm. A bullet had gone straight through him, leaving only a small wound channel. A half-inch closer to inside and it would have shattered the bone.

"They're using indirium rounds, armor piercing." Anna peeled clothing away from her shoulder and stuck herself with three stimpaks, one after the next. "Damn, Aurora..." She winced. "Couldn't have suggested we meet another damn day? No, of course not, that's less fun."

After applying a few autoinjectors to his chest, Mamoru tugged his shirt back into place. "It is not her fault she..." He stared at her with a disbelieving expression. "...sees the future."

Anna smiled. "At least you are starting to come 'round to understanding."

He went from body to body, tearing their masks away. All were Japanese, some with the dark lines of obvious cybernetic enhancements showing in their skin. Dim green light still shone from one man's silver left eye.

"Anyone you know?" asked Anna while rolling her shoulder with a grimace.

"No." He scowled at the holes in the roof, exhaling with relief. "No one I know. You seem pleased."

She gestured at the dead. "This is what we have to look forward to here. I don't mean to be callous, but I made a few *friends*. I keep hoping they don't have the balls to cross the pond... again." After a dire glare at the man who shot her, she put on a smile for Mamoru. "So, whereabouts was this facility that burned?"

"Northeastern Badlands, near the river. They marked the project as a total loss, but there was evidence of some manner of ongoing search."

"Brilliant. There's only one more thing left for you to do. Then we will be masters of our own destiny, no longer hiding like rats in the dark." She took a small case from her pocket, offering it. "This disc contains what information we have thus far been able to gather about the ship."

The sadness in her voice stalled his surge of irritation. "More?"

She put a hand on his arm. "Archon wants to take us away from a world that hates and fears us. There is a military starship, the CSS Angel, that's recently been completed. We are going to steal it, and hopefully find a world where we no longer need to be ashamed of what we are."

Mamoru turned the holodisk case over, watching the light play off the smooth, black plastic. "Why go to all that trouble? Why not migrate to a colony world in the usual manner?"

"Because." She gestured with both hands, as if it was that obvious. "Established colonies come with the same prejudices that exist on Earth. Add to it, some of us don't trust being helpless in stasis tanks for the trip. We can use the Angel as a place to live until we find a planet."

"Planets with natural Earthlike conditions are rare. Most are the result of terraforming. Your plan relies on a degree of optimism I find impractical."

"That's another reason he wants the Angel. It's so large we could live on it for at least two generations if we have to. By then, if we cannot find somewhere to go, we will select one of the smaller colonies. There is also talk of using it as a bargaining chip, trading it back to the government in exchange for sovereignty rights on a small colony. Archon has everything sussed out."

"I do not know about living on a starship for the rest of my life. There is no nature, no spirits." He quieted, gazing at the sky through the holes in the roof. "What about my request?"

"He's looking into it. I assure you, he always keeps his word." She glanced at the door. "I'll be in contact in a few days when the time is right."

"It seems you leave me little choice." Mamoru closed his eyes. "Very well."

The echo of Anna's boots grew distant and stopped with the sound of a car door closing. He did not move, even as the whine of her hovercar moved up and over the building, followed by intense cyan light shifting among the still-smoking portals cut by the assassins. Soon, the ion drive noise faded to silence.

Mamoru waited.

After a minute, he smiled. "Thank you."

A surprised gasp echoed from a few meters behind.

"That line did not fail on its own."

"I did not want them to succeed, but I have killed myself," said Sadako.

He opened his eyes as he spun. She had come within a few steps, staring downcast at a patch of blood. Black material split open as her head covering receded and absorbed into the metal ring at the collar of her suit.

"No, you have not." Mamoru moved to her, cradling her cheek in his hand. "They have no power over you."

She reached up and clasped his wrist. "They have put death in my head, Mamoru. When they realize what I have done..." She sniffled. "Do you even remember me?"

"Each night, I hear your screams as they carried you off." He looked down, eyes watering.

A tear ran from her eye onto his hand, over his fingers. "They were going to train me to pleasure men, but I tried to escape. I was caught, but I got far enough to impress them. They reassigned me as a spy. To be owned by those who murdered my parents... I—" She fell against him, sobbing for a moment. "I want them to set it off. I cannot do this anymore. I cannot live as a slave."

"Sister, you are free. You no longer need wear the name of your captors' clan. You are not Kuroyama, you are Saitō."

She looked to the side, failing to contain her tears. "I know you are not my blood."

"Mother told you to keep your distance, but you did not listen. I regret the circumstances of our first reunion, when they sent you to test our security. I did not enjoy injuring you, but I could not fail Minamoto in such a public way. I am sorry for our third meeting. It pained me to harm you again, but I could not do what you wanted. I could not kill the last family I have." He remained quiet for a moment. "You are my blood, Sadako. She was as much my mother as yours. It is a father we do not share."

Sadako clung to him, ignoring decorum. "It does not matter. They will—"

He grasped her by the shoulders and shook her tears away. "No. Before I left you at the hospital, I burned out the device. They cannot harm you."

Color faded from her face. "I... I've been..."

"Free of them since that moment. I"—he cringed from her watery eyes—"should have stayed with you, told you. I was too focused." One tear glided down his cheek.

A beep made her jump. Sadako pulled out her NetMini, her face twisting at the red Kanji it displayed: 'Shi.' She cradled it to her heart and whispered, "Goodbye, brother."

He waited.

After a minute, she risked a hesitant peek at him.

He smiled.

"You never did believe anything I said." He grasped her NetMini through her hand, turning it off to hide the red symbol. "Death will not find you today."

"Will they—"

"Doubtful. You were one of many tools. One does not dredge the Sumida for a single lost shuriken."

"I can never return to Japan." Her face seemed neither sorrowful nor happy.

"Then do not. It seems we again have something in common."

Hope lit her face. "You have given up on Minamoto?"

Mamoru took a step away; she advanced behind him. "I must know. However, it seems the harder I pursue it, the farther away from knowing I become. I do not think it will matter." He stood in silence for some minutes, showing no reaction when she threaded her arms around him. "I have become involved in something larger than Minamoto."

"It is not important. Let us find our life here." Her voice fell. "For years, I dreamed of you rescuing me. You finally did, but not how I had imagined."

"I asked them to find you. It was my hope that if I impressed Minamoto enough, he would buy your freedom." Mamoru put his hand over hers against his chest. "That is why I was so driven to reclaim my station."

"Forget all of it. We shall make ourselves part of this city."

Mamoru glanced up at light shifting through the front windows. The whirr of a hovercar passed overhead. "It may not be that simple."

31

COUNTER OFFER

B linding glare greeted Mamoru as he emerged from the warehouse, tempered by drifts of fog rolling through the beams of headlights. A single gloss black hovercar sat in the mist, flanked by a man and a woman in matching armor. Both carried rifles, but held them across their chest in the manner of an honor guard. Clear, solid barrels gave them away as laser weapons, and tightened Mamoru's jaw. Pushing himself beyond human speed only went so far. Even with accelerated perception, evading lasers was iffy.

Something familiar about their armor teased at the edges of his mind. As the rear door opened, realization hit him. Division 0 tactical armor—the government's law. Unlike the security forces he was used to, these people supposedly adhered to *ideals* rather than paychecks. *Self-righteous.* He steeled himself, falling back on his recollection of watching Minamoto or his underlings negotiate. The dead men inside had attacked him and he had only defended himself.

An older man emerged from behind the door. His black uniform had a formal design that made him seem more of a bureaucrat than an officer. He walked around, past his escort, but stopped at about twenty meters.

"You must be the one I have been hearing so much about. I would like to discuss your future."

"I do not know you," said Mamoru.

A white glow drifted silent through dark clouds above, chased by flickers of green and red. The soft whine of an advert-bot's engine seemed to echo from somewhere else as it crossed the sky.

The man offered a patronizing smile. "I am Deputy Director Johannes Burckhardt of Division Zero. I trust you are at least familiar enough with my organization after your foray through our data system." His lips stretched to a momentary grin. "Oh, come now. Of all the networks you've infiltrated, how many have been monitored by people with the same gift? We *let* you in. We wanted to see what you could do. I read the reports"—a wave of disorientation rippled through his mind—"Mamoru. I am impressed. There is much we could offer each other."

"How can I know that you are not here to destroy us?"

Burckhardt chuckled. "Us, is it? Have you thrown your lot in with that British lunatic already? Don't let his rhetoric drive you to a foolish conclusion." He glanced up. "The UCF does not persecute psionics. There is nowhere safer for you, despite what that fool has convinced himself."

Mamoru's breath caught in his throat as the older man's eyes turned milk white and glowed. A gurgle came from behind and above, followed by the clatter of a rifle striking the ground. Hand on his katana, he whirled and looked up past several runners of blood descending the wall. A wounded NSK operative clutched the sides of his head, already near death from what could only have been Sadako's work. The man's face reddened as he screamed, an incoherent moan fading to the babble of severe brain damage. His body shuddered and twitched, a tremendous gush of red burst from his nose, and he slumped over the side.

"Your sister missed one," said Burckhardt, as the glow faded from his eyes, not a drop of sweat or ounce of exertion visible. "We can offer her protection as well."

Mamoru faced away from the building, picking at the ito on his katana's handle. "Your files do not mention mind blast can kill."

"All weapons can kill if used correctly." Burckhardt raised an eyebrow. "We don't leave all our secrets lying about. It would be a pleasure to share them with you, after we welcome you to the fold. Division Zero could use a man like you."

"I do not know if I am yet ready for another shogun."

"Think carefully on this opportunity, Mamoru. We can protect you if you become one of ours. The military intelligence community is thrumming like a pack of hornets after an event on their network. C-Branch does not like losing, and they like being clueless even less. I suspect you had something to do with that." He half turned, smiling at the car. "Bear in mind they tend not to be the talking type. If they decide to have a word with you"—he looked into Mamoru's eyes—"it will be with a rifle from about four thousand yards. If you go rogue, I might not be able to protect you from them."

Sadako crept from the warehouse and moved up behind her brother. Mamoru studied the ground between him and the gleaming car. This man offered legitimacy in this place, but at what cost? It seemed too similar to his station with Minamoto, except without the privilege of arbitrary murder, free housing, and servants. The matter of his given word to Anna complicated things further. *What else do I have but my honor?* Tingles swam over his mind, causing an immediate glare at Burckhardt.

"I apologize, Mamoru. I am pressed for time. Please forgive the directness of my approach. I know you were unhappy in Japan. Your nature is at odds with what they forced you to be. You need time, and I can respect that. Do try and stay out of sight until you decide." He walked to within a few feet of Mamoru, offering a small fob. "This has my contact information. I must return to the west coast before I am missed."

Mamoru accepted the miniscule device, turning it over in his fingers. Hair thin silver wires linked one end to a dark pellet, a silicon spider trapped in clear plastic.

"It is most unusual for a man of your rank to pay a personal visit," muttered Mamoru.

The old man smiled. "You are a most unusual psionic, my friend."

Mamoru slipped the fob into his pocket.

Burckhardt paused with one leg in the car. "Do try not to take too long to make up your mind. It would be a shame if the world lost you." He let his weight fall in and pulled the door down.

Clunk.

Sadako squinted at the car as it lifted off, cringing from the brilliant glow at each corner. It floated straight up until it reached a height of about sixty feet, rotated to face west, and streaked off among the hundreds of other lights swimming through the air.

She rested a hand on his forearm, but could not meet his gaze. "I do not trust him."

He let the air out of his lungs, the last third audible with a hum of contemplation. "This place has strange customs. I did not sense deceit in him."

"That man was acting on his own, outside his authority."

Mamoru put his hand over hers. "How do you know this?"

"I was taught how to read subtle cues, for negotiating." Shame kept her downcast. "His rush to return before missed, the nonchalant way he killed Koji, and a man of his station showing up with only two guards." Concern brought her gaze up to meet his. "He is up to something. Perhaps, he wishes to keep you a secret even from his own people."

"You may be correct, but I also do not have the luxury of time. I have made a commitment I must abide."

"I am afraid." Sadako let emotion drain from her face, staring a challenge at the dark. "You have finally given me the freedom I have longed for. I do not want you to die for stupidity. Forget Minamoto. Forget the British man. Remember your family."

Mamoru inhaled through his nose. "We are close to the sea. Shall we visit Suijin-sama?"

Sadako's eyes watered. "You remember the river?"

"Yes." He held her hand and closed his eyes. "And we are still poisoning it."

She cried.

In his mind, her seven-year-old face grinned back at him. They stood in the shallows of the Sumida, now at sunset. The waning light glimmered on the surface, bathing the indistinct shadow of Tokyo in blur.

A year later, her smile would shatter.

He opened his eyes, dispelling the illusion, and wiped a tear from her cheek.

"I am sorry, Sadako. I should have ignored Father. They struck after I had proved my ability."

"That was seventeen years ago," she whispered. "You cannot carry the guilt of a boy's fear. You only wanted to please him. It was Father's mistake to not conceal you."

"I was his work." He shied away from a face no longer innocent and happy. "I poisoned our house."

"It does not matter, Mamoru. You were always my older brother. When the NSK was ready to use me as the instrument they had trained me to be, they told me you were not my brother. They hoped it would break me inside." She clutched a fist to her heart. "They hoped it would make me feel alone. I deceived them as I deceived Mother. A part of me always knew."

Mamoru remained quiet for some time, staring at the ground. "I will not return to Japan. Minamoto be damned." Sadako smiled. "I do not know how fate will play out for me, but I must keep the promise I made."

She sent a somber gaze at the sky, the occasional luminescence of an advert bot dragging her attention through the clouds for seconds at a time. "I understand. Shall we ask Suijin-sama's protection?"

"It would be foolish not to."

Sadako clung to him, looking worried.

He offered a wistful smile and led her by the hand to the pier.

SPARKS

S adako's protests rang through the back of Mamoru's thoughts as he attempted to meditate in the driver's seat. The modest four-person ground car he appropriated ran on automatic, leaving him free to work out his plan. He needed her to remain safe, uninvolved with the aftermath of the situation circumstance had sent his way. Hopefully, she would still be in the apartment when he returned.

"Warning: You are approaching the perimeter of the NavMap system. In four point one miles, manual drive must be engaged."

His eyes snapped open as the pleasant female voice disrupted another attempt to still his mind. Stripes of glare from reflected street lamps slid up the sloped hood, warping across the ovoid protrusions over the front wheels. A dark amber sunset spread out across the horizon, separating two large swaths of black, one ground, one sky. The car sailed down a descending elevated road. The ride had consumed most of the day, bringing him close to the southernmost end of East City.

Transparent holographic signs spanned the four-lane passage, reminding drivers that they approached the Scattered Lands. Artificial light flooded his rear-view screens, hovercars and ad-bots teeming like fireflies on their feast. Even from here, the Orlando Private Sector was conspicuous, off in the distance to the right by virtue of a giant illuminated palm tree. Far ahead, a diamond of white light sat on a bed of inky velvet.

He checked the Navcon, verifying the pin he had placed was still there. Of course, the dotted line connecting the cartoon car to the pin became transparent and flashed once the car icon crossed out of the green-shaded area indicating network coverage. The bottom of this two-mile ramp coincided with the outer limit of the automatic drive feature.

A series of blue LEDs created the effect of a light pulse orbiting the steering wheel.

"Warning: Please engage manual drive."

He grumbled. "Fine. Activate manual."

The steering wheel extended from the dashboard and positioned itself at the angle the system calculated offered the best ergonomics. He took it in both hands, and the car wobbled as he tried to get used to its handling. Since he was the only car on the ramp, his unexpected loss of respect for lane boundaries had no consequence aside from an irritating buzz from the console.

"You insisted I drive. Do not criticize my technique."

Tall floodlights illuminated a tarmac at a point where the driving surface levelled off and met actual ground. A dozen shops faced it, three large warehouses ringed with giant cargo transports, and a rent-a-storage outfit. Hundreds of hologram signs ranging from datapad sized to panels twice the height of a man warned of the dangers ahead and tried to sell weapons and body armor. Others hawked camping supplies and survivalist gear. Animations in the ads were the only signs of life here, not one car sat in the hundred or so lined parking spaces. An eerie 'after-the-world' atmosphere hung over the place, making him feel as if he were the only person left alive.

He drove through, headed for the gate on the far end. A man in a light grey jumpsuit with a rifle over his back emerged from a booth, lifting a floppy-visored hat while waiting for him to pull up.

Mamoru lowered his window as his front bumper stopped inches from the gate.

The guard looked as though he had been here since the dawn of time. His uniform was neat, his weapon modern, but he had a thin, wrinkled face and hair like cobwebs. Dark veins crisscrossed his cheeks, more prominent as he bared yellowing teeth with an odd smile.

"Evenin'," said the man. "Haven't seen you before."

"I have not been here before." Mamoru suppressed the urge to wince at the man's rotten-egg breath.

"You runnin' any sort of delivery? Kind of a small vee-hicle you got."

"I am visiting a friend in the Crawfordville settlement."

"Hmmf." The guard chuckled, narrowing his eyes. "You be careful out there. City law stopped at the bottom of that ramp. We don't get much of the Badlands critters this far east, worst yer likely ta run into is some militia groups. Mind ya, they kin be quite territorial." He hooked his thumbs on his utility belt, rocking back and forth. "Them Fourth Reich nitwits would probably try an' use someone like you for target practice, tho ya look like the sorta fella what kin handle 'imself." He waved at the gate, which trundled to one side. "You sure you don't wanna stop over at Hank's and get some artillery?"

"I have all I need." Mamoru patted his sword. "Thank you." He shifted his gaze forward, waiting for the moving fence to clear his path.

The old man started away, but whirled back. "Oh, if'n you find yourself too far west, careful 'round ol' Eglin. Bunch o' milla-tree types there, don't take too kindly to trespassers."

Mamoru's eyes widened. *There is no way he could know.*

"Course..." The guard sucked on his teeth as he glanced west. "What with the wind way it is, sometimes their sensors go on the fritz." Wrinkles consumed half his face as he winked. "Be wary of road crews comin' out ta fix things. They tend to get trigger happy around strangers."

Something bothered Mamoru, an inexplicable sense beyond the ability to determine what. The way the rickety man walked back to his guard booth, like an old gunslinger, unnerved him. Not since he was a boy had he felt the sort of fear that crawled up his spine at that moment. He struggled to ascribe reason to it. He had thought nothing of close combat with cyborgs, hurtled through the sky in an untested fighter craft, and faced down a dragon, albeit a virtual one. This dread made no sense.

The old man smiled at him through glass when he glanced to the left. Mamoru pushed anxiety out of his mind and stepped on the accelerator. His car bounced over the gate's track, and flooded with vibration as its tires met old paved ground instead of traction-coated plastisteel. The Navcon had gone dark, displaying only the words, *out of range.*

"Stupid thing, no legacy maps?"

Text scrolled along below the range warning, offering a static map download pack for C699.

He scowled. "Your marketing people should humble themselves before their director. That advertisement should show itself *before* the car leaves transmission range."

Mamoru had no sense of the land, but the military starport was obvious enough at night, shining like a beacon in the perfect dark. Aside from abandonment, what little he could see of the countryside here looked livable. It was difficult for him to fathom having so much land unused while the people crammed themselves on top of each other on the coast. They did that back home, but what choice did they have? Japan was miniscule by comparison, and had a large population.

Disbelief and contempt gave way to unease amid the rhythmic *whoosh* of passing utility poles. *No electricity in any of them. These people just gave up. What scares them away?* Something seemed to stare at him out of the black. He gripped the wheel and watched the road, resisting the urge to peer into the night.

Warm countryside passed underfoot. Mamoru did his best to avoid making noise in the untamed brush. He could no longer see the car, stashed along the road a quarter mile or so behind him. Two military crews had set up at the base of electronics towers, making the prospect of driving closer impossible. Nothing had yet responded to his presence. He sensed only weak electromagnetism in the air, not the strong sensor fields he had expected. A strange sense of eeriness sent a shiver down his back. The old man had mentioned road crews. *Has to be coincidence. They must need to fix them several times a week.*

Up ahead, a trio of fences stood between him and Eglin Military Starport. Two electrified wire barricades on either side of a taller green energy wall shimmered between silver pylons. Mamoru had a feeling the wall of light was not as much a physical barrier as a warning of an active laser system. Kinetic energy barriers barely worked in small applications such as a personal defense unit. Something this large would draw far too much power to be practical.

He approached from the south side, behind a row of hangars that offered cover from a tarmac lit like daylight. Thoughts of Sadako's warning made him seek the comfortable familiarity of believing his abilities were the result of focused chi. Mamoru brought his arms up in a wide swing, and pressed his right fist against his left palm. Power flowed from his mind to his body, manifesting as a glow over his back and arms.

He forced the energy to his legs, staring at the white light as he sank to a squat.

"We all have quirks." Anna's words came back to him. "Aurora is... Aurora. I don't get along with machines, and you light up like a wick."

He grunted, the luminescence flared as he released a burst of psionic energy through his muscles and leapt. Annoyed at her calling him a candle, his irritation added extra force to the jump and put him on the roof of one of the hangars rather than the ground behind the field.

"What the fuck was that?" A woman's voice almost stopped his heart.

Perhaps this was lucky. Mamoru flattened as three men and one woman in camouflage came running.

"Not a damn clue," said a tall black man, looking at the fence. "Looked like someone shot off a magnesium flare."

Mamoru slipped away from the edge as the soldier turned, following the arc of his leap with his eyes.

"I dunno, JJ. Sarge, this is Vaughn, over," said the woman. Radio crackle followed. "We got any birds up now? Did anyone report any lost munitions or parts flying loose?"

"Fence is intact," said an unknown male. "Not reading any fault codes."

Mamoru let his cheek touch the cold metal roof, suppressing the urge to snarl. *This is not the way of a samurai. I am hiding like a ninja.* He relaxed, intent on quiet. *What alternative, kill them?*

"Are you sure, Sarge? Roger that..."

"The heck got into him?" asked JJ.

"You heard Sergeant Yost. It's nothing to worry about. We're to resume perimeter."

"Probably some shit we ain't got clearance to know about," said a short man with a Spanish accent.

Mamoru waited until the sound of their walking became indiscernible from the wind. He slid to the edge and lowered himself to hang from his fingertips. Minor focus gave his leg muscles enough resilience to absorb a thirty-foot fall. He remained motionless, both to listen for anyone reacting to the noise of his landing and to catch his breath from the exertion. His last battle with Sadako played over in his mind during his moment of rest. She was right, his ability tired him fast—her mechanical augmentations could run forever. A protracted fight here would not go in his favor. As much as it galled him, he had no choice but to sneak.

Shadow blanketed the space between one hangar and the next, providing an alley packed with old barrels and long cases. They resembled the sort of container used to store missiles, and Mamoru could not help but peek—empty. *At least they are not fools.*

Anna's disk contained schematics for the CSS Angel as well as access codes, systems diagrams, and an overview of the support infrastructure of a secret installation somewhere out in space, well beyond Mars. The transponder data was the most important. All he had to do was appropriate a shuttle. A military shuttle had the necessary hardware to locate the Angel, not to mention would not raise as many alarms as a civilian ship attempting to approach a military installation.

Mamoru crept along the wall, closer to where light invaded the passage between buildings. The tarmac buzzed with activity despite it being close to midnight. On the other side, past several hundred yards of wide-open pale concrete, the ring-shaped heart of the starport gleamed. Any craft capable of achieving orbit would be parked inside. These hangars, according to the files he had invaded, were used for atmospheric craft. If a shuttle happened to be in one, it would not be in any condition to fly.

He climbed the stacked boxes enough to reach a window. Shafts of dusty light pierced the darkness within. Glint highlighted shapes along a row of dormant fighter planes parked at a diagonal to the far wall. All six looked old, as well as tiny. By markings, they belonged to a training squadron.

Mamoru sensed a change in the air, the presence of electricity, in time to avoid being startled when a head-sized orb bot popped up right in front of him. Before it could sound an alarm, he clapped his hand over its lens. Curved sheets of program code appeared in his thoughts, surrounding him as his mind rearranged it line by line. Mamoru was now its friend. When he released the sphere, it hovered away to resume its patrol. A band of green light followed it on the floor and wall, warping over machinery and pushcarts as it glided off through the hangar.

Approaching footsteps hastened him through the window. Among racks of tools and testing equipment, he found six automated armament carts. The sight of medium-sized driverless forklifts with curved tines to hold missiles and bombs gave him an idea. With only the now-friendly orb in the area, he jogged over to the nearest one and crouched. One hand on the side allowed his thoughts to touch the machine. A non-self-aware AI slaved to a master armorer's terminal controlled the loaders from remote. The cart's bulk offset the inertia and weight of what it carried, despite its internal components not requiring a shell that large. He opened a side hatch and stuffed himself into the dead space.

Curled up on a battery unit with his knees in his face was far from comfortable, but still preferable to starting a small war on a military base. Mamoru pulled the panel closed and held on. After a moment's concentration, awkwardness of his body position no longer mattered—he was the machine.

Unexpected disorientation came from sensors giving him full three-hundred-sixty degree vision as well as a proximity sensor granting the inhuman ability to *feel* solid objects within six feet. All four wheels could turn, enabling the cart to spin in place. He acclimated to this new way of seeing and moving within a few minutes, and rumbled out of the berth. The hangar door opened at his approach, unable to discern its operation as anything but normal.

A handful of soldiers moved about on the main tarmac in squads, some with weapons as part of a security detail, others off duty or in the process of changing shift. Men and women passed in front and behind, none paying any attention to the auto-loader whirring across the open space. At first, Mamoru headed in a beeline for a hangar closer to the main starport facility. When he turned away at the last minute and went for the ring-shaped structure, he got a few odd looks.

One of the recent routines run through the loader's memory contained instructions for carting missiles to a waiting DS2, a military dropship that had to land inside the ring. Using the latent instruction set as a map, Mamoru followed the expected route to minimize suspicion. He rolled up to the side of the curved wall, where another automatic door opened as the cart got close. A red stripe followed a path through a low-ceiling access tunnel intended for these carts, a straight passage through sixty meters of building.

An incoming signal startled him as he neared the inside door. Someone was trying to access this loader to find out what it was doing. He halted in place, reaching back across the wireless transmission to the control system. Microseconds later, a process batch existed in the system attached to a random name he plucked from the authentication list. It looked as if someone had made an error entering the date for an ordinance loading, resulting in the sequence triggering now.

As soon as he finished constructing the lure, Mamoru opened the hatch and released his psionic link to the machine. He rolled out of the confined space, kicking the panel closed as the cart re-synced with the network. Motionless, he concentrated on nonpresence so the operator would not be able to see him with digital eyes.

The auto-cart spun in place, electronic motors whining as it accelerated back the way it had come. Mamoru waited for the portal to close and ran to the inner wall. It was a simple matter to fool the automatic door. One finger on the receiver for the weapon cart let him trigger the mechanism. He slipped through the opening and found himself on the landing area. Several dozen platforms, elevated hexagonal pads of dark metal, gleamed from strong overhead light. Around the outer ring, numerous landing spaces large enough to hold a fifty-foot interorbital shuttle surrounded four massive ones in the center.

He peered down a channel between the two largest landing platforms at a transport shuttle. The ship had an overall shape similar to a spearhead, starting at a point and widening in a curve to the rear end. The pad's perimeter lighting caused the craft's olive drab belly to glow. Mamoru waited for an opportunity and crept among the berths. Caustic vapors came by in drifts from Cryomil fuel lines, forcing him to squint every so often. One hand gripped the katana tight. *I do not trust this. I am no master at infiltration. This should not be as easy as it is.* He moved at a brisk jog over the unprotected tarmac, relaxing only when he regained the cover of darkness.

Consoles embedded in the wall flickered with various status updates, standby, or ready indicators. He crept to the intersection at the dead center of the facility, glancing in both directions to ensure his secrecy. A DS2 perched on a pad to the left near the wall, the right passage led toward empty landing areas. Straight ahead, the shuttle beckoned.

Muscles in Mamoru's back tensed at the sight of the long bell-shaped craft. Flying the Fūjin had been awkward, due to its extreme maneuverability. Inhabiting a machine he intended to use to leave the safety of breathable air was another level of danger. He gazed up at the nose, passing under it while circling around the platform in search of stairs. The closer he got, the stronger his trepidation became.

On the next flat face of the hexagon, a gap in the wall contained stairs. As soon as he stepped on the first one, a twelve-inch head appeared to his right. Mamoru's reaction occurred at the speed of instinct.

His katana failed to impress the hologram.

"Calm down, Mamoru," said a dark skinned man in his fifties.

Hearing a British accent come from a UCF military colonel made him raise an eyebrow.

"Oh, I wish I could get a still of that face." The colonel winked. "I've got the security diverted elsewhere, but the false alarm won't keep them away from the pad for long."

Mamoru squinted. "Aurora."

"Innit? Buzz along then, I'm tired of feeling a scrotum between my legs. I honestly don't know how you boys deal with it. S'like 'avin a warm, dead, furless gerbil in my lap." The older man's face twisted in an expression of disgust. "I'd rather toddle off before the colonel here starts being asked questions I can't answer."

"You are not normal." He shuddered.

"Well, you've got eyes like a shithouse rat, haven't ya?" The colonel winked. "Took ya this long ta tell?" A hand floated into the hologram, shooing him off. "Go on then."

Mamoru exhaled as he trudged over to the forward landing pad. He put a hand on the strut, feeling his way among the machinery. Imaginary camera flashes of wirepaths and program code unfurled through his brain as he read the systems. A blast of air came with a loud *hiss*, tossing his hair about and fluttering his coat. Three feet behind the forward landing gear, a slab of hull lowered, revealing a rear-facing ramp wide enough for a person. Mamoru jogged around and bounded up several steps to the pilot's compartment.

Of the two pilot's seats, he chose the left and settled in. After getting comfortable, he rested his hands on the console. Activity drew his attention to the windscreen, where doors around the perimeter opened at once to disgorge a tide of green. Dozens of soldiers swarmed in.

Mamoru closed his eyes and took a deep breath. "This should be interesting."

A moment later, his consciousness melded with the shuttle. Sensors, cameras, and internal systems became his senses. He gathered the intent to fly in his mind, willing his new 'body' upward. Warmth spread through his belly and backside as thrusters roared to life. Soldiers rushed towards him, but he leapt skyward with enough force to swat them flat. Sixty men and women hit the ground and slid away from the downdraft, tumbling over each other like twigs in a hurricane. An uncomfortable sucking coldness at his throat reminded him of the access ramp, which he closed.

He did not look down. An impulse as if he meant to lean backwards tilted the nose up, and he accelerated. The Fūjin had felt as though he walked on a tightrope—one small miscalculation would fling the nimble craft to the ground; the shuttle was more akin to swimming in tar.

Mamoru strained to the point of fatigue from the simple task of getting it off the ground.

The sudden sensation of a warm body in the other seat startled him. Internal cameras opened a separate display panel, which appeared to hover in the indigo clouds a few feet in front of the nose outside. A woman in black leaned across the center console and put a hand on his arm. Panic at being vulnerable roared within, but fear of an out of control shuttle kept his mind where it was.

"Mamoru," said Sadako, "I think you are being used."

SHADOW FLIGHT

Lustrous midnight blue in the windscreen darkened through indigo to black. White points emerged clear from the smog as the shuttle left the atmosphere behind. The touch of outer space on the hull did not come with pain. Going too fast in the fighter jet had burned, despite not being a danger to the Fūjin. Out here, he had expected an agony of ice. Without the burden of a syrupy atmosphere, flying no longer felt as though he had to keep 'running' to avoid falling. In the vacuum of space, the shuttle seemed as graceful as could be.

Mamoru let it drift, bringing his mind back into his body. "What are you doing here? I told you to wait at my home."

Sadako shied away. "I am sorry. The silence… it was so still there, my worry became too great to dismiss. I am afraid we will not know happiness." She glanced at the floor by his seat. "I wanted to be with you for what little time the world gives us. Besides, the soldiers almost caught you nineteen times. You should be grateful I was shadowing you."

He scowled at the console. The shame of having to use the dishonorable tactic of stealth grew heavier, compounded by his failure at it. "I have an agreement to fulfill. I did not want you to get hurt."

Timidity vanished to a scowl. "I've had enough of your *honor*, Mamoru. Your *honor* left me alone, locked in a sad little excuse for a bedroom. I used to wake up in the middle of the night at every tiny sound, wondering if it was you coming to free me." Her voice softened. "One day,

I stopped expecting to see you. I knew you weren't coming. Your *honor* wouldn't let you."

"No, Sadako." He stared at the stars for a moment, resting from the effort of liftoff. "I had no idea where they had taken you, or if you were even still alive. Kutaragi sensei told me you had been killed soon after our parents. He said they wanted to spare me the sight of watching you die."

She pouted, directionless anger dissipating to sadness.

"I did not believe him. They would not have carried you off if they meant to end your life." She went to speak, but he spoke over her. "I feared the worst."

"The NSK does not force anyone to be concubines. They may force the life of a geisha on a girl, but that is not the same thing. That is a rumor. It is up to the girl to choose to take it beyond their normal duties. The women who do are pampered for it. It is not like the criminals you owned."

"Sadako, you said you ran away to avoid that?"

"I did." She shifted, gazing down. "I was a child then, I assumed... The way they treated me, I did not really understand what they wanted of me, but I was terrified."

Mamoru clenched the controls. "It is as much my fault as theirs."

Sadako shook her head. "No, Mamoru. You were a child as well. I could not escape my fate, but I did not allow them to make me a toy for men."

"You did not." Mamoru reached across the console and held her hand.

"I had other talents. Please, brother, can't you see you are being used? That strange woman only wants you to do her master's bidding."

"I have seen nothing to cause me to distrust them. He wishes a new life away from all those who would harm us. We could find peace away from Minamoto, in a place where the NSK can never reach you."

Sadako shivered, pleading eyes fixed him in place.

"What else then? Shall I become a pawn of these psionic police?"

"I do not trust that old man, either." She squeezed his hand. "He is no better than Minamoto. I could see it in the way he looked at you. He wants to control your power."

Mamoru focused on the console and linked with the flight computer. Outer space filled with dozens of streaming amber chains, letters and numbers connected in a swirling flow. The programming flooded his brain as though he had written it himself. Every nuance became known to him in seconds, even a useless piece of remark code calling someone named George an idiot. He set the autopilot for the navigation coordinates in Anna's holodisk, and generated a program construct to emulate a military pilot over the communications channel.

"What was that?" asked Sadako. "The console flashed off and on a dozen times."

"I trust more in this machine's ability to fly itself. Sometimes I question if humanity was ever meant to leave the Earth."

"Do you think the Kami exist out here?" Sadako leaned close to the side window.

The awe in her reflected face made her seem innocent, and filled his head with memories of who she used to be. "It is mostly empty. Perhaps there is a spirit of nothingness."

"Mother did not hate you."

He shot her a pointed stare, which softened as he sighed. "She did not care for me. Despite being harvested from her body, I was a project from father's work."

"You were still her child. She tried not to form a bond, but as she watched you grow, she could not help but be your mother. You never saw it, but she cried many nights, fearing they would take you away. She tried to stay distant, knowing the day would come when you were gone, but could not do it. Does it matter that she did not bear you into the world? She cared for you."

Disbelief took over Mamoru's face.

"It is true. She would argue with Father while you were at school, trying to convince him to take us and flee." Sadako narrowed her eyes at him. "He, too, had much *honor*. Father would not disobey his company."

"I… was too weak to save them. Father tried, but all I wanted to do was play my video games." His knuckles creaked. "If I had only applied myself and trained, I might have saved them." Mamoru forced himself to look her in the eye. "…Saved you."

She moved from her seat, putting an arm around his shoulders. "Do not blame yourself, Mamoru. You were only a boy then. If you had trained as Father wanted, they would have taken you sooner. They had the data, which they thought was far-fetched fantasy. They waited and watched to see if you would prove your power." Her head touched his. "Turn us around. Let us go somewhere far away from all of this."

"I gave my word that I would help Archon. I do not expect you to understand why I must finish this."

"You still care about Minamoto?"

"I do not know, but I will never return to Japan." He hesitated, tapping his fingers on the console. "It would mean death for you."

Sadako stood and folded her arms. "I will not let you do this alone. If you are to die, I will be with you. Tell me what we must do." She glared at the way he looked at her. "I'm not the little girl you remember."

Mamoru studied his lap. "No, you are not. No matter how much I want you to be happy, you are not. In my dreams, you are still a little girl up to her knees in the Sumida, smiling."

Her expression fell to one of regret.

"I am sorry for injuring you in the parking deck. You were trying to force me to kill you, and your skill surpasses mine. Only by virtue of my"—he waved his hand around—"chi, psionics, kinetics, whatever I should call it…"

"You already apologized. I forgive you. I should not have put you in that position, but why didn't you tell me you fried my kill switch?"

Mamoru muttered and poked the button to set the shuttle's autopilot to active. "You were unconscious."

"You left me there." She clutched his arm. "I thought you had forgotten who I was."

"Minamoto wants me dead. Your people would have killed you for failing. I hoped to lead them away from you by making it look as though I had beaten you."

She glared down, trying to stay angry, but could not think of a way to fault him. She flopped in the seat, elbows on her knees and chin in both hands. Mamoru chuckled.

"You haven't made that face since your sixth birthday."

"We didn't have enough land for a horse." She sighed.

The shuttle rumbled from short bursts of maneuvering thrusters as it reoriented itself. Inertia pressed him against the cushions as the main engines came on. Lines appeared on the windscreen, defining the edges of a virtual road on which the shuttle traveled. A green box highlighted empty space, a destination too far away to see.

"I am to steal a larger starship. We must infiltrate a remote construction facility, gain entrance to the vessel, and depart."

"Those ships have crews of over a hundred, how do they expect one person to steal it?"

Mamoru's face was somber. "That is why Archon sought me out."

She leaned forward, desperation in her voice. "He means for you to stay with them to operate the ship. You're going to be trapped."

"No, it is possible for him to find a crew. It is impossible to have a large number of people sneak on board to steal it."

"It is fortunate I am trained to be stealthy." Sadako offered a sad smile. "What kind of security do they have? Did you obtain any intelligence about the facility or are you planning to rush up there in typical samurai fashion?"

"They gave me a disk with information. This is a military facility out beyond Mars. Despite the isolation, their security around this ship is quite high."

Over the next thirty minutes, he went over the schematics of a small military space station.

The console crackled to life, displaying a hologram of a young man in a neat green cap. "Attention Sierra Tango Two-Nine-Nine, you are on approach to a secure facility. Challenge Greenfield."

Mamoru and Sadako looked up. The previously empty targeting box now surrounded a thumbnail-sized speck of bright metal.

"Roger that Crucible, challenge response Wakefern." A man's voice with a pronounced southern accent came out of nowhere. "Requesting approach vector."

Sadako tilted her head at a small screen, and gestured at a caramel-skinned man with a raised eyebrow.

"Program," whispered Mamoru.

"How did it know the answer?" whispered Sadako.

Mamoru smiled. "It's in their database."

"Two-Nine-Nine, your flight is not"—the hologram-head looked up and to the right—"oh, there it is. Damn ground pounders, they never fill these templates out properly. What is your cargo?"

"Crucible, we're on a funerary escort detail, no cargo... We're picking up. Over."

The holographic head leaned away and looked off to the side, seeming eager to get off the comm and cease talking of such things. "Uh, roger that. Stand by for Nav uplink."

Sadako glanced at Mamoru. "That's good, right?"

"Good is often a matter of relativity."

FOR THE TAKING

C rucible station grew to dominate the viewscreen as they approached. Four thick ring-shaped sections orbited a central spindle four hundred meters long. The first and third rings rotated clockwise while the other two moved opposite. Each ring looked tall enough to contain eight levels, and glimmered with thousands of tiny windows. At the relative 'top' end of the main shaft, an enormous starship in gleaming white dwarfed the station. Close to double the length of the spindle, the CSS Angel resembled a giant whale with a bizarre needle jammed in its side.

"That's it?" Sadako's eyes widened. "It's bigger than the station. He wants you to steal *that?*"

"Yes."

Mamoru's program guided the shuttle to a rectangular access hatch along the outer face of Ring Two. The shuttle slid sideways, matching the travel of the rotation to stay lined up with the door. Yellow lights flashed for a second before the flat grey portal split in four sections, each retracting to a corner. The ship slid through, as if rising vertically through the opening with less than four feet of clearance on either side. Mamoru was grateful the autopilot could land the craft. Even had he embodied the ship, the maneuver looked tricky. Brilliant light from the edges shimmered in a black halo effect as the nose end went through the door.

The windscreens, armor-plated electronic displays rather than glass, filtered out the blinding glare.

Inside, greenish-metal walls seemed to writhe as the shuttle's passage through the band of light caused shadows to shift among dozens of pipes and struts. Enormous, square block letters spelled *Bay S2-9C* on a wall that crept dangerously close to the nose. Sadako backed out of the cockpit as their craft slid deeper into the chamber, as if two steps away would keep her alive if it hit the wall. Mamoru's knuckles whitened on the seat as the space between the nose and the station seemed to disappear.

Sadako leapt close and held on to his arm, bracing for a collision that never came. The outer door closed, becoming part of the landing bay floor. Mamoru's stomach fluttered as the shuttle executed a quick vertical drop, and settled on its pads. The initial strike of the landing gear made Sadako stumble. She flailed, keeping her balance for a second. When the craft bounced up on the spring-loaded struts, she fell seated in his lap.

"I thought ninja are supposed to have good balance." He grinned.

She frowned. "It doesn't feel right here. I shouldn't have fallen."

Mamoru lifted her on to her feet and put a hand on the console to initiate the power-down sequence. Once the shuttle's engines went offline, he opened the exit ramp. The shuttle's frame vibrated with whirring motors. It stopped with a heavy *thud* that resonated through everything, and got them moving. Mamoru led the way to the exit hatch, and waited for the flashing red lights on the wall to stop. A few seconds later, the atmospheric sensors turned green and the door opened with a *hiss* and a cloud of fog, revealing the extended ramp.

They flew down the steps, rounding the bottom and sprinting for a pile of storage cartons set against the inner wall. Exit from the docking chamber was on the left, by virtue of a stairway along a raised deck that ran the length of the bay. Above him, the shuttle's nose had a few inches of clearance to the wall. He blinked, captivated at such a low margin for error. Mamoru peered over their cover, watching the door. He ducked when it opened, admitting three soldiers. One wore a dress uniform and appeared unarmed, the other two were in grey fatigues and each had a pistol and a white armband. The trio stopped in the door, waiting.

Several minutes passed in silence. Mamoru put an arm over Sadako, pulling her near. Eyes closed, he focused on nonpresence to hide them from sensors and video feeds.

She squirmed, whispering. "This is not the time to get cute." A subtle white glow danced over his shoulders. She cringed. "Sorry."

After several minutes of silence, a voice echoed in the metal room. "Are you planning to disembark any time soon, soldier?"

"I got nothing on thermal, sir," said another voice. "Shuttle looks empty. Bay looks empty. There's no one in there."

Boots clanked on metal; the pitch changed as they went from catwalk to grated stairs to flat plastisteel tiles. Sadako pushed herself backward into Mamoru, wearing him like a cape, guiding him deeper amid shadow. The sudden activation of her head covering almost made him jump as she shifted to use the black of her suit to hide his face.

The three soldiers approached the entry ramp, the two with pistols in the lead. They had not drawn weapons, but kept their hands on them.

"This is Lieutenant Fuentes. Whoever is on that shuttle, disembark immediately."

All that answered was the lieutenant's voice echoing back out.

"Nothing," said the one on the left, glancing at an arm covered in holographic displays. "There's no one on board."

"I-I don't like it, sir. This shuttle commed in as a funerary mission… and there's no one on board."

"Yeah, sir," said the other man. "This is right outta a holo-vid. Ship of the Dead or some shit."

Lieutenant Fuentes gestured at the ramp. "Check it."

The two MPs gave each other a 'that figures' look, drew their pistols, and moved around the ramp. Sadako tensed. That put them facing forward, right at their hiding place. Fortunately, their expressions gave away how uneasy they were about a scenario of their own imagining. Single file, they went up the stairs.

Sadako disengaged her body from Mamoru, patting him twice on the leg as a signal to let go of her.

"Try not to kill them," he whispered.

She froze as the lieutenant turned at the noise. He looked in her direction, but did not hesitate or seem to notice her. As soon as he had his back turned, she sprang over the boxes. Myofiber augmentation in her legs flung her lithe body through the air in a fifteen-foot arc. She landed noiseless on tiptoe and stole up behind him. In one fluid motion, she pinched his nose and covered his mouth with her left hand while jabbing him in the neck with tiny metal pins that sprouted from the index and middle finger of her right. After a flash of electricity at the base of his skull, she eased a hundred ninety pounds of unconscious officer to the ground. Squatting low, she grabbed his shirt and struggled to drag him.

When it became apparent it would take her too long, Mamoru ran over to help, hauling the inert solider by one arm behind the pile of cargo boxes. She rearranged the unconscious lieutenant to mold with the surroundings a little better, and pressed a small air hypo she took from her belt to the side of his neck.

"He will sleep for an hour or more."

Mamoru ran to the shuttle. With one hand on the landing strut, he sent his thoughts into the machine. A minor program formed, first as an idea, then as a desire, and last as actual code. The shuttle would go dark for two hours, ignoring all commands. The ramp closed and locked, and soon the muted sounds of banging and shouting came from within.

"They'll think it was a ghost," said Sadako.

Rather than jump, Mamoru's reaction to her sneaking up on him took the form of a few seconds of paralysis followed by a dire glare. She winked. He shook his head and jogged across the shuttle bay, up the stairs and over to the panel on the wall by the door.

"This will not take long."

Sadako nodded, flattening herself against the wall at his side and watching the shuttle. Noting the height of the platform, she grabbed his arm. "They can see us."

"No, they can't. The whole thing is dark. Everything's off. Those aren't real windows. They're black painted shapes."

"They'll be telling that story until they're old men."

"Hmph." Mamoru placed both hands on the terminal and focused.

An eerie glow settled over him and threaded around his arms, which the console seemed to absorb. Without a deck between his power and the network, Mamoru experienced visions of digital space as fleeting hallucinations and daydreams superimposed over the real world. He could use the network, but any combat construct or hostile operator could hurt him for real.

Mamoru's online clone walked through the closed door. Tunnels of multicolored light raced past, a fast-forward maze navigated by a disembodied consciousness. Violet, silver, amber, and blue shifted in his imagination. The sense of the station's size filled in as he mapped every wirepath and fiberoptic connection. It was too massive for him to embody in the usual manner, but he did not need to.

Minutes of digital wandering brought him to the part of the network that handled the security system: cameras, biometric locks, pressure sensors, and antipersonnel turrets. The false reality in his mind became more prominent as he tapped psionic power in earnest. Spiraling ribbons of azure light wound together, strings of letters, numbers and symbols took the form of a second digital Mamoru made of light. The program construct, created at a thought, brought its hands together in a double clap, homage to the Shinto spirits. It turned with a spray of luminous hair, and looked up at an array of amethyst crystals—manifestations of CPUs. The construct leapt among them, connected by crackling lightning for several seconds before diving through the opaque surface, which rippled like liquid for a second before becoming glassy once more.

Mamoru released his power, leaning on the wall to catch his breath.

Sadako held on to him, keeping him on his feet. "Are you all right?"

He pushed the button to open the door. "I am fine, just tired. None of the station's security systems will react to us. My program will edit us out of surveillance cameras in real time, and we have full access to the entire facility."

"I thought you didn't like this sneaky stuff?"

Her smile didn't show through her facemask, but was evident in her voice and body language. He jogged along the corridor.

"It is less complicated than killing everyone between where we are and where we need to be. These people do not need to die so that we may steal."

"You are still the same impatient boy in a rush to go back to his room and play games."

He frowned, head down. "I have not played a game since that day."

Sadako hugged him from behind. He clasped a hand over hers. After a moment, they continued down a hallway that circumnavigated Ring Two. The curvature lent a noticeable bend to such a long, open tract, reminding him he was in a place so removed from natural as to defy belief. The passable map of the station in his short-term memory guided him past a dozen other shuttle bays on the left to a round-walled shaft on the right, which led to the inside edge of the ring.

A cluster of tall cylinders, the type used to store compressed gas, sat in racks behind locked cage doors on the left side. Two power-assisted pallet jacks were parked against the other wall. Gleaming white reflected overhead lights, making him squint. At the far end, the passage opened to a cargo elevator. He slid past a pair of heavy-duty loader carts, ducking under the claws made to grip hexagonal one-ton containers, and moved into the forty-foot square lift. Rather than hit the button, he climbed a maintenance ladder and convinced the roof hatch to open with a short mental prod.

Sadako did not question his route. The elevator was far too loud, slow, and confining, and probably only capable of traveling among the four rings. They needed to get all the way to the top of the central spire. Mamoru hauled himself along a recessed ladder, thanking whatever designer had the foresight to afford it enough space to allow the lift to pass without killing him should it begin moving. Shining plastisteel beckoned above, lit every ten feet by a band of white strip-lights demarcating each floor. They climbed four stories before he paused to look around, grumbled, and climbed a little farther to a mechanical protrusion along the side of the shaft.

He examined it, searching for a way to disengage the combination fan/security grate from the wall. It had hinges on the left, but two heavy bolts held it in place on the right.

"How would you get past this?" he whispered.

Sadako climbed up, peering around his hip at the obstacle. "I'd take the fan out and slip through the hole. I don't think you'd fit."

He grumbled, not liking the precarious location for a feat of kinetic strength. Even if he was able to tear the thing loose, the amount of force needed to do it would fling him off the ladder.

Her hand pulled at his belt. "Sometimes tools *are* better than mind powers."

Mamoru leaned away to give her room, and she pulled a four-inch straight-bladed Nano knife from her thigh, severing the bolts with two quick wrist motions. He tugged at the entire fan assembly, swinging it away from the wall like a door. She climbed in first, setting the severed bolts on the bottom of the vent shaft.

A few meters in, she lay flat on her stomach and waved him past. "You know where we are going."

Distinct awkwardness seized him while squeezing over her. Whenever he thought about her, he saw the little girl from the river. To him, she would always be innocent. He swallowed his near-crippling sense of inappropriateness at being pressed against a full-grown woman who was his sister. Mamoru held the image of his angry sensei in his mind as he crawled forward, but guilt came anyway. How many opportunities had he ignored to get her out of the NSK because of his loyalty to the shogun? His eyes narrowed at the thought of Minamoto awarding her to him as a pet. The mere thought of Sadako with a detonator around her neck caused a daydream of him perched on Minamoto's desk, katana rammed through the old man's chest into his throne.

"W-what's wrong?"

Mamoru shuddered at the echo of her voice behind him. "Nothing."

"You seem consumed with rage all of a sudden."

How could she know? "I... have many regrets."

She remained quiet until they reached a ninety-degree turn to the right. When she could catch his eye, she put a hand on his shoulder.

"I forgive you."

He clasped her hand, lost for a moment in a haze. *What the hell am I doing here?* Mamoru stared into his sister's eyes. Her struggle to smile as though everything was fine hit him in the chest. He looked down, fingertips squeaking over the smooth metal conduit.

"I will avenge you."

"Mamoru..." She put a hand on his cheek, forcing him to look at her. "No. Let it go. I would rather they go unpunished than you get yourself killed. Nothing can change the past. You could kill every person in the NSK, raise them from the dead, and kill them again, but it won't change what happened to me. You have Nami and I have plenty of time to make a life. We have no reason to ever go back."

He held her hand against his face for a few seconds of quiet acceptance. "Let us finish what I came here to do, and be rid of the tasks of others."

Sadako withdrew her arm and activated her hood. Black liquid-rubber oozed up and over her face. A wave of matte finish swept over the shiny material as millions of nanobots made it solid. Dark lenses formed over her eyes, showing Mamoru his own face in duplicate. She nodded.

A softball-sized orb floated down the shaft, dark grey with a red ring of light around the central lens. They leaned against the sides to give it room. The sentry paid them no heed, continuing on its route. Several tunnels and two ladders later, the air grew colder and gravity ceased. Heavy rumbling shuddered through the walls, no doubt caused by the mechanism that drove the rings. Based on Mamoru's estimation, they floated through an air conduit connecting the central spindle to the ring assembly. The rotation provided gravity to their sections, but the spire did not seem to move. He grasped the floor, pulling himself ahead in short bursts of floating. The passage connected at a vertical T junction, offering the ability to go up or down. Air rushed from above, tinted with the smell of coffee. Mamoru chose up.

After a twenty-foot section, he glided into a room filled with power management boxes, batteries, and circuit breakers. Red light saturated the area from square LED bulbs in tiny cages. He navigated it by grabbing at the component housings and pulling. Sadako sliced open another ventilation cover. Her blades were mere tools, not sacred like a katana. He led the way in, starting a hundred and forty some-odd meter climb. *I could get used to this lack of gravity.*

When they reached the fourth 'floor' of the pod at the end of the central spire, he diverted to the right down a square-walled duct. Thirty feet later, a patch of light shone on the ceiling ahead through a grating, joined by the fragrance of coffee and the sound of a woman's voice.

"I don't like it, Senator. Not one bit. The Angel has not even had a shakedown run yet, and you want to pack it full of a hundred civilians in some kind of idiotic PR maneuver? Do they drag people into a dark room somewhere and lobotomize them when they win an election?"

A weaker voice, tinted with static and pops replied, "I respect your position, general, but this came down from on high. We don't need a vacation cruise. Take them around the moon and back. Given the size of the Angel, I hardly think 'packing it full' is an appropriate descriptor."

"I don't appreciate the security risk associated with a media stunt. This installation has never been exposed to the public. No civilian has set foot on Crucible Station, and I intend to keep it that way. What is the Senate prepared to do if something happens?"

Mamoru raised an eyebrow. Sadako slipped a small, black tube from her belt. As big around as a light pen, its length allowed her to conceal it in a fist. She crept to the vent slats, and held up a finger.

"We can work around any eventualities, general. The guests can board via shuttle directly from the moon. All we need you to do is fly around out there for an hour or two and make nice with the NewsNet people. This is for morale, for recruitment, and to show those corporate weasels that space belongs to the UCF."

The general sighed, rubbing the frustration out of her forehead. "They have more colonies than we do."

"With all due respect, General Whitaker. Six tents and some half-alive peasants forcibly transplanted to a remote observation post doesn't count as a colony in the eyes of the Senate."

"This is not going to end well, Anders. Never in our history have we waved top-secret advantages in the public eye. Something will go wrong."

"Have a little faith, Jenny." A blurry face on the Vidphone winked. "See you Friday."

"Arrogant son of a bitch." The general seethed for a moment and stood. The room seemed to have some manner of artificial gravity, but weaker than normal. "I didn't put in twenty goddamned years for some bureaucrat to call me 'Jenny.'"

As soon as the Vidphone went dark, Sadako held her fist to her mouth and bit down on the end of the tube. A tiny capsule of pressurized CO_2 ruptured, firing a one-inch dart into the back of the woman's head.

"Ouch, what the—?" The general reached for what stung her, but slumped over her desk before her fingers made contact.

Sadako burst through the vent, sliding like a wraith into the room. She stuffed the general into the hollow beneath the desk and reclaimed the dart. Mamoru pulled himself through the hole, hung on his fingertips for an instant, and dropped to his feet. He crouched, touching a finger to the floor. Some electronic component under the tiles created an effect similar to gravity, attracting matter downward. The effect felt about half as strong as being on Earth.

That must use an enormous amount of power. "A blowgun?" He cocked an eyebrow. "That's a little old-school."

"Hands free." She pantomimed hanging on the ceiling while using her mouth to aim and fire it. "Aside from the pressure capsule, the design has been the same for thousands of years. A tool does not need to be complex to be effective."

He moved to the window and peered through silver blinds at a long concourse. Most of the far wall was viewport, separated in ten-meter segments by bulkheads with emergency blast doors. Outside in space, the hull of the CSS Angel gleamed. Its long, boxy silhouette, wider than it was tall, filled the windows. It had the shape of a battleship, if a battleship did not have to care about hydrodynamics. Multiple batteries of turrets on the fore section were the most startling feature of all.

Mamoru sighed. "Where mankind goes, he brings war."

Sadako tucked the chair in on the General and rounded the desk. "We might encounter aliens one day. No telling how friendly they'll be. I'd rather we had weapons and did not need them than need and not have."

"The main boarding tunnel is forty yards away." He pointed. "Two men and four bots are in the way."

"I thought you said the bots won't bother us."

Mamoru nodded. "They should not."

She leaned up to the window. "I do not see another option but to go through them. They will notice us leaving this room. I would not have time to use my suit."

"Then I shall go through them." He removed his katana from his belt, wielding it with the scabbard on.

He raised the weapon in a two handed grip, closing his eyes as light swam over his arms and back, in time with ripples through muscle. Sadako hit the panel, causing the door to squeak to the side. Mamoru surged forward into the hall and his sprint accelerated over fifty miles per hour. Weak gravity made the task far less draining than he'd expected. The farther soldier crumpled from the blunted sword across his skull before any realization of attack showed on his face.

Mamoru had swung as if to cut the man's head in half, spinning through the stroke and delivering a stepping stroke at the second guard. The other man opened his mouth from shock, fingers flexing as his hand flew towards his pistol. His eyes crossed as the black, curved sheath collided with his forehead. Both sentries were unconscious before the first finished falling.

The quartet of orbs hung in midair as though nothing happened.

Sadako sprinted over, the tilt of her head conveying awe her eyes could not project through dark lenses. With a pleasant beep, the security doors opened on their own as Mamoru took a step towards them. The boarding corridor lacked gravity, and fanned the growing sense of unease in his gut. Only a few millimeters of plastic separated them from a death most horrible. He accelerated himself, hand-over-handing along a heavy blue safety line. Mamoru reached the other side and had the ship's hatch open before Sadako made it a quarter of the way across.

"Nervous?" she asked with a hint of a laugh in her voice.

"I do not like space." He pulled her through and closed the hatch. "Too much can go wrong. They should have left it as it was when it took years of training to leave the planet."

Sadako hugged him. "They said the same thing about pilots when hovercars went mainstream."

"It is not the same. Space is far riskier than flying."

She pushed him inside. "We do not have much time. Someone will see those men lying on the ground."

"Yes," said Mamoru.

A rectangular corridor with truncated corners led perpendicular to the keel. Down the center, a raised central grating covered a shallow trench full of wires in neat bundles. An airlock cluster on the far away port side occupied a room at the other end. At the halfway point, it intersected another hallway of larger size that ran from bow to stern.

"We are below the operational decks in the engineering and cargo areas. We must find our way up several levels."

She nodded once. "I remember the schematics. Left up ahead."

He jogged to the intersection and went left. Several meters later, he entered an elevator capsule and linked with the computer. After closing the door, Mamoru sent the pod up five levels and stopped. Sadako clenched her hands into fists and released, watching the door, waiting for it to open. Minutes passed of nothing before she glanced up at her brother who appeared lost in meditation.

Lights went from white to red and the CSS Angel flooded with alarms.

"Warning: Primary reactor chamber has reached critical temperature. Malfunction detected in control rod assembly one through seven. Secondary cooling loop failure. Warning: Reactor control rod assembly malfunction. Uncontained criticality event imminent."

Sadako covered her mouth with both hands. Mamoru opened his eyes and winked at her.

"It is false. There are a few technicians and workers on board still."

"I am going to hit you for that when we are safe."

He laughed.

They ducked out of the elevator on the upper level among junior officers' quarters. Mamoru went right, towards the stern. Sadako ran behind him, cringing from the blaring alarm, trying to yell something at him over the noise. Mamoru opened a security door leading to the senior officers' quarters, and sprinted to the center of the hallway where a ten-foot wide cylindrical elevator waited.

It took them up to the bridge superstructure, which extended above the highest deck. The door rotated out of their way, creating an opening almost as wide as the elevator itself. Much to Mamoru's pleasure, there was no one else on the bridge. Stark white against the blackness of space, the CSS Angel's hull filled the forward viewscreen. Mamoru stomped with an imperious gait to the captain's chair, spun on his heel, and sat. Almost as soon as his weight hit the cushions, every viewscreen filled with a cartoon caricature of Minamoto: fat, bald, with bright red makeup spots on his cheeks, and clad in ill-fitting samurai armor.

Sadako giggled.

"I modified the ship's AI," whispered Mamoru. "Minamoto-chan, as soon as the workers are evacuated, get us out of here."

The animated warrior snapped to attention, shouting, "Hai!"

Mamoru imagined absolute confusion spreading through Citadel station as the ship broke moorings and powered away. He leaned back, lacing his fingers behind his head. Sadako grinned at him, fluffing her hair out after lowering her automatic hood. His pleased smile faded with a sharp pain in his left thigh where she punched him on a pressure point. It took a moment to rub the paralysis out of his leg.

She turned away from his accusing look. "That's for scaring the hell out of me with the reactor nonsense."

"I thought of it while inside. There was no time to warn you." He shook his head at her before glancing at one of the screens. "Minamoto-chan, find a location where we can hide this ship for a while."

"What is a while?" replied the console, sounding like a bad impression of an ancient samurai video dubbed in English. "Also, I humbly request that you discontinue this ridiculous avatar."

"I will change the avatar once we are done. I need the ship to be hidden for at least a few months."

"There are several debris fields between Earth and Mars, closer to the Red Planet. We could conceal the ship among the Periculum Belt." One of the large display screens on the left wall displayed an image of Mars and a light-grey shaded blob about four planet-widths away. "The Periculum Belt contains a number of massive debris chunks that I could use for cover. In a minimal power state with sensors on standby, it would take close-range exploration by small craft to find us."

"Excellent," said Mamoru, glancing at the plot on the screen. "Since we have about fourteen hours to wait, does this thing have baths?"

Minamoto-chan bowed in a posture of groveling subservience. "Deepest apologies Mamoru-sama. This is a military vessel. The bathing facilities consist of large banks of autoshowers without privacy partitions."

"Damn," muttered Mamoru. "Oh, well. Hot water is hot water."

DESTINY

Fog trailed off in the breeze as Mamoru exhaled. The fragrance of pine needles kept him from focusing on the anxiety gnawing at the back of his mind. He amused himself trying to spot Sadako in the snow, but her suit's camouflage electronics made it a daunting prospect. Light flurries flared violet and blue as they passed through the display above his NetMini. Mamoru frowned at the 'no signal' message. The wind picked up to a howl.

"When are they coming?"

Sadako's question, so sudden and close, brought his katana out by reflex. She committed to a dodge even before he stalled his swing. Each offered the other apologetic looks. He braced the tip on his finger and sheathed the weapon. She stood two steps away, but he found it difficult to differentiate her from the background. Two black lenses seemed to float at the top of a vague woman-shaped outline of ghostly white, flecked with brown and green hints of pine tree.

"He is already late."

She looked down. "It's so cold. Why did you agree to meet here?"

"Scattered Lands…" He shifted, surveying the horizon. "Lawless, yet free of the dangers in the interior, I imagine he did not want to risk spies."

Her hand alighted on his shoulder. "Perhaps he wanted to take you away from technology to keep you at a disadvantage?"

"Why? The one who calls herself Pixie claims he wishes to protect The Awakened from the world. Why would he seek advantage over me?"

"It is the way of men who crave power. Trust is the bedfellow of a fool."

Mamoru put a hand on her shoulder. "I am sorry, Sadako. You are so young to be jaded."

"Am I wrong?"

He patted her arm. "You are not."

An approaching whirr broke the silence. Mamoru shifted, glancing up at the tops of distant pine trees. Needles wavered as cones of headlight in the flurries preceded a dark blue hovercar. The downdraft kicked snow from branches as the vehicle brushed through the treetops, descending to a landing a short distance away. Mamoru let go of his sister, letting his arms hang straight.

"Be calm. At best, they are allies. At worst, employers."

Sadako shifted her gaze to him until the sound of doors brought her attention to a man and a woman emerging from the vehicle. The driver's brown tweed coat and scarf left him looking a bit like an out of work university professor, while his long, thick brown hair lent a hint of anachronism. He hesitated, one hand on the corner of the door while squinting through the snow. At the sight of Mamoru, he smiled and shoved the door closed. Anna, in a dark navy coat and knee-high boots with short heels, rounded the front end of the car and walked at the man's side. They approached to within three steps.

"Ahh, Mamoru Saitō, it is a pleasure. I am Archon." He bowed more with his head than body. "I apologize that it has taken so long to meet you face to face. I have had much to do in the west. You have met Anna. Who is"—he smiled at the woods—"Sister. Alas, not Awakened."

Mamoru squinted at him. *That voice...* "Are you certain we have not met?"

Archon flashed a patronizing smile. "Quite. What have you done with the ship?"

"I reprogrammed its primary artificial intelligence. It is waiting for us in a safe place. Not only would the military have to figure out where to search, the location masks it from sensors."

"Clever." Archon tapped his chin. "I had become concerned since we did not hear from you for a week."

Sadako squinted at Archon, a measuring glance. Anna shot a wary look at her.

Mamoru positioned himself more in front of his sister. "We used one of the life pods to travel to Mars and took a commercial shuttle back."

"Mars... I cannot say I have ever been there. I certainly hope we do not wind up needing to abandon the ship." Archon's chuckle faded to a furrowed brow. "How certain are you they will not be able to track that lifeboat?"

Mamoru remained quiet for a moment, studying the shape of Archon's eyes. "I reformatted the capsule's flight computer. Only those who designed it would recognize where it came from, and only if they stumbled across it out in the middle of the Martian desert. I detest that place."

"I suppose that will have to do for now. Come then, let us get back to civilization."

Archon started back to the car, but paused at the sound of Mamoru's voice.

"You were to find certain information for me in return."

"Ahh, yes, that."

Sadako glanced at Mamoru. *"Keikai suru."*

"Hai." *I am wary, sister.* "I have met you before, haven't I?"

"You are an astute observer." Archon faced him, smiling, hands out in a gesture of apology. "It was a necessary step for the greater good."

"The golden angel was you." Mamoru glanced down and to his right. "I had never felt the presence of a soul within a hologram before. If you were never on Mars..."

"I thought you were some manner of cyberspace guru, Mamoru?" Archon grinned. "You stumbled on that Raziel fellow as a coincidental accident. You overthought it. My connection *was* a simple Vidphone call. Perhaps the feeling of sentience in the image confounded you? No matter. At worst, your wild goose chase on Mars wasted time. I had not intended you to go running off to that dreadful place, merely give you the reason you needed to divest yourself of the man who thought he owned you. We share some similar talents, my friend. I am a telepath of no small ability, and I am able to project my mental abilities through any open connection."

Mamoru's fingers tightened around the katana. "What did you need me for then?"

"Oh, I do not perceive the net in the same way. Think of it like..." Archon paced about, waving his hands as he searched for a metaphor. "I am sending telepathy over the connection in addition to video and sound.

I do not perceive the machines as you do. The line merely carries my psionic ability to a remote target." He stopped with a fatherly smile and arms out as if to offer a hug. "It is not for the sole sake of your skills, Mamoru. You are of the Awakened. Your place is here with us. Even if your talents were not critical to our endeavor, I would welcome you as another son."

Mamoru closed his eyes, searching for calm. "You turned Minamoto against me? You took my honor, and my life. What did you do to Minamoto? What did you tell him?"

"Your life? Your *privileged* life. You were a mere tool, no different from those women you legally owned. What do you miss the most, Mamoru? The power to kill peasants at a whim, the power to own people of a lower class, or do you miss the security of having someone else making your decisions for you?" Archon glanced at him for a few seconds, smile creeping wider. "You were little different than a concubine, my friend. Pampered and coddled for giving your body to Matsushita."

"The white one failed to convince me, so you took my choice away? How is that different?"

Archon sighed, gazing upward as he let his arms fall. "Children and fools often do not know better. They seek comfortable familiarity even if it is in their own disinterest. Your precious Minamoto is the reason the NSK destroyed your family and took your sister." He pinched the bridge of his nose. "Or did you not realize he is the one that paid them to take you? I suspect you are planning to tell me that I have no capacity to understand your 'honor' and you are about to go spare."

"Look, Mamoru," said Anna, stepping between the two men. "That man was using you. Archon was cheesed off that a bugger what's not even psionic was rippin' the piss of ya."

"She means taking advantage of you." Archon continued massaging the bridge of his nose. "Can take the lady out of East End, bit harder to take East End out of the lady."

"Sod it, James." She glared, though seemed as likely to laugh as hit him.

Mamoru narrowed his eyes. *The oni knew all along who I sought.* "It is unfortunate, but I must address your dishonor."

Archon raised an eyebrow. "Do not be a fool, Mamoru. You are better than them all."

"Before you, I was not psionic. I was a master of my *chi* and my destiny."

"You were a master of errands." Archon frowned. "You had not a clue what your potential was, you bowed and scraped to an indolent autocrat, and you had not the weakest glimmer of an idea where your precious sister was." He gestured at Sadako. "Consider that my *interference* has brought you two together."

"If not for your interference, I could have freed her without my entire prefecture wishing us both dead."

"Irrelevant," said Archon, waving at them. "We are leaving this silly place behind."

"I cannot go with one who has deceived me and who has such contempt for my traditions."

Archon bowed his head, once more pinching at his nose. "If it will make you stop whining, I can make Minamoto think you were his great grandfather. Would you care to have him as a manservant? Would you like to own Matsushita? It is all beside the point."

Mamoru boiled inside as rage flared beyond reason. He sprang into an attack, katana gleaming in the twilight moon. For an instant, his slowed time view centered on Archon's dismissive smirk. The ground flashed before his eyes, the brown of trees shot past him as his legs no longer bore weight. Indigo sky and blue-lit snow traded places. Gravity lost meaning as an intangible force crushed around his body from all sides.

Crack. The sound echoed among the wilds, chased by the fluttering of a legion of birds startled aloft.

Mamoru's gut connected with the tree first, and his body wrapped around. The next thing he knew, he lay on his back, staring up through falling snow before the pain of impact reached his brain. Growling, he rolled to the side and got to his feet. After a step, he sailed airborne again. Archon, two fingers raised, flicked his hand to the left in a sharp gesture. Mamoru's body followed suit, careening fifteen meters before landing flat on his chest.

"James… the girl, where'd she go?" Anna put her back to Archon's, fingers splayed and awash with sparks.

"Relax, girl. I do not mean harm toward your brother. I am simply educating him about the folly of rash decisions. He has lapsed beyond rational thought to blind rage. Such a silly construct, his *honor.*"

Mamoru, gasping for air, staggered upright and stumbled against a tree for support. "What…" He pointed the katana at Archon. "What are you doing?"

Archon swiped at his shoulder, knocking snow off his coat. "Your kinetics abilities are impressive, but they are not your strongest ability, correct?"

"How…"

"Do I know that?" Archon smiled, making a 'come here' gesture.

Constricting force clamped about Mamoru's body, lifting him off the ground. He drifted forward a touch faster than a brisk walk, stopping within three feet of Archon. Face red with rage, Mamoru strained and roared, but could not move.

"A little thing I like to call being the most powerful telepath in the world." Anna, behind Archon, rolled her eyes. "Telekinesis is my hobby."

Archon's gaze burned with white light. An instant later, Mamoru's vision blurred as if he had gone snowblind. He floated in weightlessness for what felt like hours. Dreams of the past manifested at random points around him.

He remembered the forest in Japan. Men screamed in anger, charging with rifles spitting fire. His mother fell before she could even scream. His father's chest burst with a splash of crimson.

The NSK came for him out of the shadows.

Archon, dressed as a samurai, walked from the fog and dismissed them with a wave of his hand, smiling at ten-year-old Mamoru. Kutaragi Ichirō morphed into the image of an Englishman. Archon was the man who trained him, raised him, and protected him. The visions came and went, small pieces of his happiest moments shifted to include the man in the tweed coat. In time, he floated once more in silence until Archon's voice pierced the stillness. Sadako, his beloved sister, eight years old, perched on Archon's arm, beaming and waving. She had grown up happy, with a pair of ponies and a large field to ride them in. The image blurred. Sadako, grown, lived in Okinawa, married to a doctor with two girls of her own.

A man's voice pierced the dense fog in his mind. "Mamoru? Are you all right?"

Intense blankness faded to a snowy pine forest. Wet coldness gripped his hands and a steady breeze of icy flakes brushed his face. He blinked, unsure how he wound up sprawled on all fours. He looked up at a man in a tweed long coat. Familiarity settled in through a dull fog in the back of his mind as he sat up and rubbed his head. This man had saved his life.

"Sensei, what happened?"

"You stacked it on a patch of ice," said Anna, sounding less than convincing.

Mamoru stood. "What?"

Archon rolled his eyes and sighed. "You slipped and fell."

"I apologize for my clumsiness, Sensei." He retrieved the katana and put it away. "I am pleased to see you in good health. We should not remain here where we can be detected."

Anna's eyebrows drew together. Her lips formed a thin line. "James, did you"—she wiggled her fingers at him—"zap me like that?"

"A slight touch, enough to get rid of that little habit of yours." He plodded back to the hovercar. "Was a moment of anger, my darling. The sight of you in that bloke's flat was enough to drive me to kill."

Anna looked at the ground, tracing a finger over her left wrist. A small spark danced up the length of Mamoru's sword as he passed her. He eyed the trees, squinting at shadows creeping along the azure-tinged snow. "Archon, I sense someone watching us." He grasped the handle of his weapon.

"The girl," muttered Anna.

"What girl?" asked Mamoru.

"No one who matters," said Archon as he hopped into the driver's seat.

Mamoru bowed and strode to the car fast enough to cause his coat to billow around his legs. "The ship is hidden and waiting, Sensei."

"Excellent."

🐗 🦅 🏛 💧 ♒

SADAKO REMAINED MOTIONLESS AMONG THE LOW-HANGING BRANCHES OF A pine tree. Her suit matched it in color and texture. Her hand slipped under her vest, extracting a tiny, black cylinder. She waited until none of the three looked in her direction and aimed it at the car. A light squeeze at the back end launched a six-legged micro-bot three millimeters from nose to tail. Insect-like wings fluttered to life as it sailed to the car. A small sub-screen popped up in her vision, created by the lenses in her head covering, displaying a view from the drone. She guided it by mental command via wireless implant, piloting the miniscule spy to a landing on the side of the car. It scampered without a sound through a seam, tucking itself out of sight under the body panels.

Sadako narrowed her eyes as the hovercar kicked up a blast of snow, rose off the ground, and shot off to the east. Once it was out of sight, she emerged from her hiding spot—a woman-shaped outline of tree bark, snow, and pine needles. It took her suit only a few seconds to revert to plain white, as she sprinted in the direction of the well-worn land car Mamoru had stolen a day prior. She clutched the wheel in a death grip, kicking up a spray of dirt as she swiveled through a turn and stomped on the accelerator. Unlike the hovercar, she had to dodge trees, though she didn't care about the occasional sideswipe or four. After an hour of bouncing over roots and hills, forest gave way to an ancient paved road that led back to the city. Dodging cracks and potholes, Sadako got the car up to a hundred and twenty. All the while she drove, she stared at a blinking red dot gliding over a map in the virtual heads-up display.

I will find you, brother.

FROM A DREAM AWAKENED

Two bokken crossed with a loud *crack*. Mamoru glared at the intersecting lines of burgundy wood, sweat dripping down his face. As the contest of strength went against him, he shifted his weapon to send the other one sliding away to the side. He ducked the retaliatory strike, using his height disadvantage to his benefit. He circled right, startled by the smooth wood under his bare feet having no discernible temperature. The realization of the porch no longer being cold stalled reality and gave him a moment to think. He glanced up at Archon, clad in a blue haori and black hakama, hair grey and in a topknot. A glimmering aura of gold light highlighted everything: the porch, his bokken, Archon, even his own preteen self.

The Sensei waved a signal to reset. Mamoru adopted a stance with his left foot forward, wooden blade held high. Archon kept his bokken low.

"Remember, Mamoru. Your advantage lies in your power. You may be tempted"—he attacked, Mamoru defended, sliding backwards—"to rely too much on it and not enough on your skill."

Familiarity settled in. He remembered the day, how he had grown tired of his Sensei pushing and pushing. Anger flickered in his heart at constant retreat. Sensei anticipated he would duck again, as he had been doing. This time, Mamoru channeled his *chi*. His small flaming body launched in a vertical leap over Sensei's swinging bokken. His training sword came down atop Sensei's skull a touch too hard, knocking the man loopy. Mamoru landed and knew terror. That afternoon, Sensei had grown furious. He was never to use *those* abilities during this training. He had to learn kenjutsu, not 'swinging a stick.' Sensei had gone after him without holding back. The memory of bruises pulsed through his arms, legs, and ribs. Mamoru tensed, waiting for the onslaught.

Archon-sensei smiled. "Excellent strike."

"Sensei, I am grateful that you have chosen to impart your wisdom to me, but I am confused."

"What confuses you, Mamoru?"

He lowered the bokken to his side. "I know I am dreaming, for I am now a man and this is in my past. You did not smile as you did when I used my power today. Sensei was angry with me. Something is not right."

"Perhaps we have been training too much. It is time for a rest." Archon-sensei waved at a rice paper door. "Go inside and meditate on our practice."

Mamoru stared at him. His brain circled the image like a hawk waiting for a moment to descend on a hapless rodent. Pain gripped the back of his head like a claw. Archon's face flickered, becoming Kutaragi's dour frown for seconds before the placid smile returned. Lines of frigid sharpness traced up and over Mamoru's skull, as if a bone-fingered crone clawed at his scalp. The bokken slipped out of his fingers and he grabbed his head. A young boy's wail split the quiet.

He collapsed to his knees, forehead pressed to the cold wood.

MAMORU PUSHED HIMSELF UP AS THE PAIN LESSENED. HE LET GO OF HIS head and straightened, sitting back on his heels. When he lowered his hands into his lap, they seemed older. His dumbfounded stare lasted seconds before a low throat noise snapped his attention forward. Minamoto sat on a decorative throne crafted in the style of the Tokugawa period. The four samurai behind him fit the scene, save for their modern composite armor and Nano katana.

"Now, Saitō Mamoru, you are a samurai in the service of the Matsushita Keiretsu."

Mamoru bowed, accepting his daisho. The same vibro katana he carried to this day.

Archon-sensei stepped up beside him and bowed to Minamoto. "I am going to bring Mamoru with me to the West."

Minamoto's eyes blazed with anger. Mamoru shuddered at his teacher's lack of decorum. Archon-sensei waved at Minamoto, who slumped unconscious in his chair with a heavy groan. Everything still held the glimmering sheen of a dream world. Mamoru gazed at his Shogun's vacant eyes, rolled back and all white. A thread of drool fell from Minamoto-heika's mouth, stretching to the floor.

Mamoru's chest tightened, dreading the result of the tendril of saliva meeting the ground. This was wrong. This was not what happened. He had been proud that day. Proud he had become eighteen years old. Proud that Minamoto honored him. Proud that he had finally earned respect from an elder.

Proud that he had station.

He screamed. Pain as if iron spikes pierced his skull stole his reason and left him face down in agony. After a moment of rolling about on the hard wooden floor, he seemed to fall forward. The ground became soft, and he plunged into frigid water that had seconds before been wood.

THE SOUND OF A GONG CRASHED THROUGH THE AIR. MAMORU SNAPPED upright, braced on his elbows. A king sized Comforgel pad radiated warmth beneath him. Black silk sheets covered his nakedness from the waist down. The bedroom glowed in the golden aura of dreaming.

Again, the gong sounded. *Doorbell.* Mamoru groaned, moving without thinking. Out of bed, cold floor underfoot, robe tied while stumbling through his home. *Home?* He froze. His Tokyo apartment surrounded him, quiet and as messy as the home of a twenty-six-year-old man living alone would be. He pressed his palms to his face. *I am still dreaming.*

"Saitō-san?" asked a woman's voice, dulled by a closed door.

He looked at his kitchen, his living room, and his beloved dojo. Weak light gleamed across the silhouette of the Matsushita Oni deck, perched on the table where it had been since he first moved in.

The gong rang a third time. A sonic assault fell on him with tangible force, sending his body stumbling against the wall. He cringed, peering up at the speaker a few feet above him. Muttering invectives, he stomped to the door and punched the panel.

Two women stood outside. One in a long, dark coat radiated confidence. The other wore a white kimono and had a silver choker tight to her neck. Her eyes were downcast. *Nami... I did not remember such shame in her eyes.* He squinted at the woman in the coat. Even then, she had looked at him like she wanted to own him.

"Ishikawa-sama. Please, come in. I apologize, I was not expecting company."

Reiko rendered a slight bow, a gesture to someone of lower rank. "I appreciate your offer, but I do not have time. I present you with a gift from Minamoto-heika." She gestured at the other woman.

The woman in the kimono bowed deep. Her voice wavered, indicating great concentration in keeping an even tone. "Saitō-sama, please forgive me for speaking. I am given to you by Minamoto-heika as a token for your loyalty and devotion. I am yours"—she faltered, clearing her throat and shivering—"I am yours to do with as you will."

"What is your name," asked Mamoru.

"Saitō-sama, I am known as Ka..." She fell to her knees, bowing. "Forgive me. I am Nami. I..."

The effort not to turn away in shame and cry made her shake.

"She has no family name," said Reiko. "Her father has betrayed Minamoto. Her family no longer exists." She smirked at the mess. "It looks as though you could use a servant."

Nami shivered, no longer able to hold back tears. She folded her hands at her waist and shuffled into the apartment with her gaze downcast. Mamoru, half-awake, could not put words to an overwhelming feeling of distaste that came over him. This was how things were, but why did it feel so wrong?

"Thank you, Ishikawa-sama. Please tell Minamoto-heika that I am greatly honored by his gesture."

They exchanged bows. Reiko walked away, causing the automatic door to close. Nami jumped at a soft *hiss.* She cringed as Mamoru reached towards her. He touched her necklace, mesmerized by the dream glimmer on the polished silver. It took seconds for him to *know* the device.

"This..." *will kill her if she leaves this building without me. Or, if Minamoto desires her death. I could remove it, but they will kill us both if they discover it.* He let go and put his hand on her shoulder. "Be calm, Nami. Your situation is regrettable. Your father's shame is not yours. Be dutiful to me and you will exist in my eyes as a person, not a possession."

Nami bowed again. "You are most generous, Saitō-sama."

"The last room in the hallway on the right will be yours." Mamoru pointed. "You may spend this day to your own thoughts, and reconcile the emotions you are so poorly concealing."

"Thank you, Saitō-sama." She started in the direction of the corridor, stalled by Mamoru grasping the obi at her back. Nami turned. Her eyes had become fields of electronic static. "Mamoru... What has been done to you?"

Mamoru leapt away from the startling sight, gawking. Her voice changed as well, a touch higher, more earnest.

"Mamoru... Come back to me."

The flickering video snow flowed out over her cheeks in glittering waterfalls as wide as her eyes. Once the streams reached the end of her jaw, they burst into a spray of silver flecks, surrounding him with scintillating light and a deafening hiss of white noise.

He cringed away, shielding his face until silence returned after a moment. When he looked up, the world existed in shades of green. Lines banded upward over Nami's face, so close she filled his field of view. Mamoru attempted to back up, and felt as though he had eight legs.

I'm a spider? He jittered, feeling with electronic nerves, seeing with digital eyes. *I'm in the bot... Nami...*

"Mamoru? I miss you." Her hand grew huge as she reached toward the lens. The drifting slanted bands paused before reversing direction and sliding downward and to the right. "When are you going to come back to me?"

"I..." The metal spider could not embrace her. "I have been busy." *Afraid. What if you lied? What if you only seemed to care for me to protect yourself? I could not face that.* "I... am—"

"Mamoru!" Nami's voice changed again. Louder, higher, more desperate. "I am here. You must come to me."

"Nami?"

"No..."

Loud, wrenching metal came from both sides. The car-sized spider bot shifted right. The old man from Division Zero and a dozen police in black armor had seemingly torn the warehouse doors down. The bot shifted left. Archon, Pixie, Aurora, and the silhouettes of indistinct people behind them had burst through the wall on the other side.

"He's mine," said Burckhardt.

"Mamoru is of a higher order," yelled Archon. "You have no claim to him."

The spider bot twisted back and forth as the two opposing armies converged.

"No!" Nami screamed, but it was not Nami's voice. *Familiar... so familiar. Who are you?*

Bodies charged from both sides, diving on to the metal spider and claiming it part by part for their faction. Mamoru howled as metal legs ripped out of their sockets, and grasping hands dismantled the robot he inhabited.

"Mamoru!" the voice shouted.

Nami pulled at the camera.

Robot parts went in two directions; the optical sensor jerked forward into Nami's arms, and went black.

🐌 🌾 🏮 🔥 ♊

MAMORU SAT UP, GASPING FOR AIR AND SCREAMING FROM PAIN HE NO longer felt. The sound of his voice told him he was a boy. He gazed at shifting trees above him, warm wind lofted his belt-length hair to the side. Birds chirped somewhere out of sight. Mamoru looked down. His spindly legs disappeared amid the voluminous folds of black hakama pants and a white haori jacket covered his chest. He tugged at his clothes, feeling too small for them. His hands came away sticky.

Blood.

His heart raced. He searched around after leaping to his feet. Grass, which had a second before been comforting, felt cold and wet. The bokken lay off to one side, snapped in half and useless. The body of his father lay in a twisted heap off to the right. He could not bear to look left.

"Mamoru!" screamed a little girl, her voice echoing through the forest.

Ten-year-old Mamoru pivoted toward the sound. "Sadako!"

"Help!"

White energy shimmered through his body—chi, psionic power, or whatever it was called, coursed through his muscles. He no longer cared what name it bore, and used it to make the forest around him blur. Wet grass whipped through his toes. Chunks of dirt flew each time his feet hit the ground.

"Mamoru!" shrieked Sadako. "I'm here. Help me!"

He changed course, pushing his body to a sprint that could catch a car. *This is what I should have done. I should not have let them grab me.* A leap over a fallen tree left him tumbling head over heels down a long slope on the far side. Pain came as a root jabbed him in the thigh, a rock caught him in the lower back, and another knobby root got him in the chest.

"Brother!" she yelled. "Come to me!"

He spat out a clod of soil and sprang forward. The whine of ion engines permeated the forest, again altering his course. Such power flowed through him that he had become a white fireball streaking through the trees. The roar of the energy drowned out the distant aircraft and the wind rushing past him pulled his haori jacket open. He shrugged out of it, ignoring the chilly air on his bare torso.

"Mamoru!" wailed Sadako.

"I'm coming!" he shouted, hands cupped over his mouth.

The tree line gave way to a small, round clearing where an approach to an old Shinto temple had been constructed ages prior. A squat aircraft with a dark grey hull perched bug-like at its center. Its fat central body balanced on four long, articulated struts tipped with wheels. Broad but stubby wings rotated to aim their engines down as arrays of segmented vectored-thrust flaps wavered behind them.

Two men hauled eight-year-old Sadako through the side hatch. She screamed and fought as much as a girl her size could. A hand took hold of her hair, pulling her head to the side as an air-hypo approached her neck. At the sight of her brother, she smiled. One hand on the hull, the other on the sliding door, she held herself solid against the NSK strike team. The adults froze in time; even the grass wavering in the thruster downblast ceased moving. Mother's blood, which had spattered her face, faded away.

Mamoru trotted up to her, out of breath and battered from his run. He wanted to say her name, but all he could do was wheeze.

Sadako grinned at him, that innocent, happy smile he longed to see. "Mamoru, you found me."

SWEAT TRICKLED DOWN THE SIDES OF MAMORU'S HEAD. THE DEAFENING roar of the NSK jet evaporated to a room quiet enough to hear the rush of blood through his ears. Cloth-covered Comforgel, glowing dim orange, shifted below him. For a while, he could not tell if his eyes were open or closed. Moonlight fought its way in through shuttered blinds. Rustling came from his right, rhythmic, in time with his breaths.

He sat up, peeling himself out of a lake of perspiration. Shide hung all over the small room, the zigzag paper streamers tacked on to any surface that could allow them to hang. He looked towards the sound of rustling, finding Sadako sitting cross-legged on the ground, waving a haraegushi wand at him. The shide dangling from it made soft papery scratching sounds with each movement. Perspiration caused her face to glisten through gaps in her hair.

"You found me," she said, sounding distant, half-awake.

"Sa... da... ko..." His voice stuck in his throat, reluctant to enter the world.

She looked up, a trace of amber light fled from her eyes. "Do you remember me?"

Mamoru flung the sheet from his body and swung his legs over the side. Sadako set the haraegushi on the floor and jumped up onto his lap. Nose to nose, forehead to forehead, she locked eyes with him, breathing as if exhausted. Amber light glowed again within her pupils.

She squeezed her fingers into his shoulders. "What do you remember?"

Mamoru caught a fleeting glimpse of snow falling amid trees, his hands clutching the ground, Archon smiling. "The woods." He nudged her away from his face, squinting. "How did I get here?"

She put a hand on his cheek. "Do you remember me?"

The sound of her voice pounded his tenderized brain. He cringed, feeling hung over. "Please whisper. Yes, of course I remember you, sister."

Sadako slumped against him, her head touching his chest. "That man did something to your memories. I was praying the Kami would bring you back."

"Your eyes..." He traced a finger over her brow. "You have cybernetic eyes?"

"I do not." She raised her head, glancing off to the side. "I have small abilities. Father tried to repeat his success with you, but it did not work. They had me in the traditional way, but he gave Mother serums. After I was born, he fed them to me as well. I was—"

"Always sick when you were tiny."

She shivered. "A failure."

He held her hands. "You are no failure, Sadako, even if Father ignored you. You broke whatever hold Archon had on me."

"No." Her hair flared out as she shook her head. "I could no more undo what he did than a drop of rain could change the course of a great boat. It was your strength, Mamoru. All I could do was force you to see your memories again and again until you realized they were false."

"Without that push..." He squeezed her hand. "It was as much your doing as mine. I am grateful."

"We should not linger here. I disabled some of his men on the way in. They will wake soon."

Mamoru lifted her off his lap and set her on the edge of the bed, gathering his clothes. She looked away as he dressed. When he drew his katana, she gasped.

"What are you doing?"

He narrowed his eyes at the door. "Archon destroyed my honor. It is because of him I am ronin. He has attempted to enslave my mind. I will kill him."

She jumped up, forcing the sword back in its sheath. "No! You saw what happened last time." Her voice fell to a whisper's equivalent of a yell. "He threw you around like a toy. You cannot defeat him in a face-to-face confrontation. I will do it."

Mamoru bristled. "What makes you think you would fare any better?"

Sadako looked at her feet, her expression apologizing for any unintended insult. "If he sees either one of us coming, we will lose. He is still a man and must sleep. For fifteen years, I was the property of the NSK. They trained me for this."

He advanced on her fast enough to trigger an involuntary combat stance. She gathered herself and clutched his shirt as he put a hand on either side of her head.

"Sister, I do not want you to die for me. He will sense your mind as he did in the forest. He knew you were there. He is too powerful." He slid his hands on to her shoulders. "If we are to do this, we must do it together." He looked into nowhere for a moment. "Perhaps the old man can help."

"Come, we must leave." She pulled away from him and padded to the door. "What old man?"

"Burckhardt."

She stared at him silently for a moment, mouth open. "I do not trust him either."

"Nor do I," said Mamoru. "But, the enemy of my enemy is my ally. Even if Archon destroys Burkhardt, I am certain he will present a threat sufficient to create a fatal distraction. We must travel to the other city, in the west."

"That's where Archon went." Sadako eased the door closed as they slipped out. Her head covering swam up and over her face.

"That is fortunate. Burckhardt is also there." Mamoru gestured. "After you."

Outside of the bedroom, which seemed to be one of dozens in an abandoned motel, a narrow walkway led between the building and a graffiti-covered barrier wall. The speed with which she navigated the often thigh-deep trash scattered about impressed him. Mamoru followed, pausing to roll his eyes at several poor attempts to draw kanji in spray paint. Six or seven people lay unconscious on the second story patios, and three on the ground—evidence of her entry. From the way they sprawled, he felt sure not one of them had a clue she was coming.

Sadako stopped at the corner of the building and peered around. Satisfied, she moved to the wall and climbed a chain link fence that predated the solid metal barrier around the motel. Mamoru remained on the ground, watching her go up and over the top. He closed his eyes in a moment of meditation, focused his power, and leapt the twenty-foot barricade. At the top of his flight, he shifted the nature of his psionic augmentation from strength to endurance to absorb the force of landing, touching down without injury a few paces away from where she waited.

"Show off," she muttered.

Mamoru bowed. "You did say we were in a hurry."

SUMMONED

S hifting light illuminated Sadako's face in the dark car, accompanied by chirps and beeps from her NetMini. Mamoru tapped his fingers on the steering wheel, gazing out over rows of parked vehicles at a huge, shiny plastisteel wall bearing a PubTran Intercoastal logo. A swoosh made of parallel blue and green lines came out from the P, and looped back through the words before they pulled apart to the shape of a cartoony airplane. Tiny points of light drifted back and forth across indigo sky over the shuttleport. A quarter of the size of the one at Eglin, this rectangular terminal existed inside the city, within rifle range of the ocean.

The car went dark as she turned the device off. "There are no scheduled flights until six a.m. We have almost four hours."

"I do not care to wait."

Mamoru got out, cringing at the taste and smell in the air—low tide mixed with human waste and stale liquor from the alleys behind them. He shoved the door closed with a *thunk* that echoed twice, bouncing back from the face of buildings across the street. Sadako jumped at the noise, crouching against the car. Mamoru tucked the katana under his coat, grasping it through a pocket to keep it vertical and out of sight.

"You don't have to hide it here. People carry guns and swords all the time."

He blinked. "What kind of ruler allows such things?"

The parking lot played host to a number of Wharf Rats, a local gang, who congregated on the inland side. Luminous tattoos shifted in the dark as heads turned to watch him. Mamoru ignored a chuckle at an unheard remark, assuming it was some comment made at his expense. He did not have the time to waste on street trash, and went straight to the main entrance of the shuttleport. On either side of the door, holographic posters displayed the PubTran Corporation's intention to prosecute as well as sue any individuals caught defacing company property, especially doll workers.

Inside, no trace of the stench remained. Cool air blew down between two sets of doors, drawn in through slats in the floor. The lobby, even at two in the morning, was blinding. Teal and green tiles made the floor appear to vibrate in the intense glow from hundreds of LED bulbs. Several vagrants slept in a waiting area with rows on rows of bolted down seats to the right. A small kiosk to the left contained an animation of the long history of PubTran, including a feature on this terminal's former life as an ancient airport in a place named Newark. It even advertised tours once a month into The Beneath, to visit the old terminals seventy-five meters below them.

Behind a ticket counter large enough for fifteen workers, a lone woman fidgeted. She looked young, barely twenty, with hair that went from jet at the roots to dark rose-red at the ends. The words *Live Girl* blinked on her plain black shirt by virtue of green neon threads. Dozens of bracelets and random charms covered both arms from wrist to midway up her forearm. Each time a nervous finger tapped the counter, that nail changed color. Mamoru approached, lifting an eyebrow at the remains of six dolls stacked up in a small break room behind the clerk.

"Please don't kill me. I'm really alive." She offered a weak smile and pointed two index fingers at her face. "Living girl here. Not a machine."

Mamoru glanced at the signs by the door. "I am not here to harm you."

"Good. Those damn Jobbers scare the shit out of me." She raked her nails through her hair. "Um, first flight out isn't till six. Did you want me to set up a booking?"

"Should you not be grateful to… whatever a Jobber is? It would seem to me that the reason you are working here at all is they have cost your employer too much money replacing artificial workers."

"Yeah I guess." She fidgeted, twirling hair around a finger. "But, them Jobbers is not the smartest peeps. They get high enough they think I'm a doll and… well, you know."

"Nice shirt," said Sadako.

The girl forced a laugh.

"You seem like a nice young lady. I cannot wait for your company to begin its operation at the usual time. I wish to borrow one of your shuttle craft."

Her fear evaporated in an onrush of confusion. "What? Uh... I don't think we rent them. I'd have to check with my manager Marie, and she's on break right now. Can you wait like twenty minutes?"

"It matters not. If your company desires compensation for the use of their craft, I will address that issue when I arrive in West City. Can you tell me the fastest way to the tarmac?"

"Um, I'm not supposed to do that."

Mamoru reached over and examined her nametag. "Mika. Cute. All right, Mika. I would prefer to omit you from any unpleasantness. To preserve your relationship with your employer, we must create the appearance that you were not involved in my acquisition of one of their aircraft."

Mika slid her hand towards a purse. "Uh, that sounds like it's gonna hurt. I don't really like that."

A tiny dart appeared in her forehead.

"Ow." Her eyes crossed trying to look at it. "I think it's stuck in bone."

Mika went limp and fell out of sight behind the counter with a muted *thump*. Sadako vaulted over and recovered her projectile.

Mamoru glanced at the unconscious teen girl for a moment before frowning at the gang members outside. He touched the booking terminal and linked himself to the building's electronics, locking the front doors. After that, he hunted down and deleted the security video of their entry before he shut off the recorders and added himself to the terminal's employee roster with full privileges to the facility.

Sadako was at his side when he opened his eyes. "I skipped the secondary tranquilizer. We have about ten minutes before she wakes up."

"We will be in the air by then."

He made his way along the concourse past a security checkpoint. A small door marked with *Employees Only* in an armored wall opened on its own at his approach, leading to the monitoring station for the body scanners. The other side continued to the secure terminal area and a hallway that hooked a ninety-degree turn to a long downhill grade. Starting about halfway, the right-side wall gave way to windows looking out over the landing area.

Sixteen non-orbital shuttles parked in a neat row in size order. The largest was half the size of the craft used to go to Mars, the smallest looked intended for about twenty or so passengers. Mamoru picked his stride up to a jog along the downhill. At the bottom, he entered a red-tiled food court lined with closed shops and a handful of sub-sentient cleaning bots. He followed the route he lifted from the computer and headed right for another employee-only door. It opened for him without protest.

"How are you doing that?" asked Sadako.

"For the next two hours, we have full access to this facility."

"You added us to their security system?" She grabbed his shoulder. "Careless!"

"It is a self-deleting program. It will leave no trace."

He smiled and jogged down three flights of stairs through a plain, unpainted shaft. The final door opened inward, allowing a stiff breeze trapped by the walled-in shuttleport to blast him back a step. She held on to his arm to fight the wind, pressing herself against his back as he went for the smallest shuttle.

He touched the landing strut and felt around the inner workings for a moment. Sadako twitched at a *hiss* from above where a hatch had opened. She took a step back, staring up at it before spinning in a cursory search for a portable boarding ladder.

Mamoru let go of the mind link and appraised the door. "Get on my back."

"No need. I have a flea."

He itched. "What?"

She rolled her eyes. "It's a street name for Myofiber boosts in the legs. Synthetic muscle fibers. I can make that jump. It's only two stories up."

"Why didn't you jump the fence before, then?"

"I did not know what was on the other side." She sighed, squinted at the door, and leapt clean through it like a cat.

Mamoru clapped for a moment. She rolled her eyes and backed away from the entry. He concentrated on empowering his leg muscles, glowed, and jumped. His flight was not as graceful, though he aimed well enough to land in the doorway, though he flailed his arms in an effort not to fall backward. Sadako grabbed him by the belt and pulled him in, still smirking at his relative clumsiness. After a brief pat on her shoulder, he walked to the cockpit and flopped down in the single seat.

"Where does the other pilot sit?" asked Sadako

"Here." Mamoru tapped the console. "There is an AI. Only one human pilot, who is technically the backup."

Sadako shivered, folded her arms, and leaned on the back wall. "I don't like that."

"You should take a seat in the passenger cabin. It is dangerous to stand while in the air."

Mamoru placed his hands on the console. Lights raced across the displays and up the walls as readouts, controls, and indicator lights came on.

"Who are you?" asked a genderless electronic voice. "You are not on the pilot roster."

His mind linked to the shuttle, integrating and overpowering the AI. The decaying digital scream echoed through the cabin and sent Sadako running back to his side. He barely noticed her grip on his arm.

"It is fine. Please find a seat." His voice came from overhead speakers. "I am having a word with the onboard AI."

It screamed again, broken electronic noises oscillated from human to buzzing and back again. After another moment, silence.

"Greetings, sir. The shuttle is yours, you have primary control."

Confinement spread throughout his body, a feeling as though he held his arms tucked tight to his chest and his knees curled. His desire to stretch his legs manifested as the engines firing up. A touch over a minute later, roaring ion thrusters pushed the craft skyward. He leaned to his right and the shuttle slipped in that direction, facing west. Mamoru spread his arms, extending collapsed wings.

Such a feeling of freedom. Mamoru lunged upward. While nowhere near as nimble as the Fūjin, this small, inter-coastal craft was far less ponderous than the military cargo shuttle. The ground fell away as the sky embraced him. It no longer struck him as odd that he instinctively knew which way was north or could feel his altitude. The gained altitude and picked up speed. His thoughts wandered amid daydreams of being a crane or hawk, free from the burdens of honor and gravity. The shuttle's night vision system let him look down at the Earth, over passing buildings as East City retreated into the distance behind him.

Words buzzed at the periphery of his consciousness, military sounding voices that demanded he identify himself and his flight plan. He poked the AI with a mental finger, urging it to handle the communication.

City gave way to grassland. From the sky, the skeletons of abandoned civilization appeared clear and obvious, dotted between the shiny web of modern plastisteel roads linking citadel-like settlements in the Scattered Lands. The sight teased Mamoru with an idea. They could disappear there. This place lacked the ever-wandering danger of the Badlands, but offered enough civilization for comfort. He wondered what the technology was like. His life had been a mixture of contrasts. As a boy, he adored technology. As a man, he craved anachronism. Could he accept a life away from the net in trade for his sister's safety? In trade for... Nami?

Thoughts of her brought sadness and a loss of altitude. He snarled at himself, as Kutaragi-sensei's voice emerged from his memory to call him a coward. Only seconds remained before he was too far from the city. A hasty decision launched a text message to Hokama Kiyomi, the identity he created for her.

I must know if you share my feelings...

Her name whispered through his heart as music... Kiyomi.

Boom.

Searing pain wracked his entire body, as if his nerves ignited and burned beneath his skin. Mamoru's scream crackled over internal speakers. His vision turned red amid endless warnings, so many, all he could make out was 'system failure' repeated in a hundred separate message windows. One of the engines had exploded. The AI had smoothed the unexpected takeoff over with the military. Sensors reported no hostile contacts, no incoming weapons fire, yet one by one, every mechanical system onboard his plane shut down.

The AI no longer responded, and the manual controls had become sluggish. Mamoru struggled to fly, a bird with lead weights tied to its feet. Air engulfed him, drowning him, as the inexorable pull of gravity exerted its authority over a hurtling hunk of dead metal.

Out of instinct, his mind clenched in the same response an inhuman leap triggered. *Brace for impact.* He could not stay airborne—this bird had become a stone. He sensed no damage to the skin. It was as though every individual component decided to fail all at the same time. The windscreen grew bright with night vision green as the ground raced up to meet him.

Blackness.

TOGETHER IN ETERNITY

S omething tickled the back of Mamoru's throat. The urge to breathe battled his inability to do so. Pain circled his chest in bands, blood and sweat trickled into his eyes. A great cough burst out of his lungs. His next eye-watering breath drew in the flavor of burning plastic and dust. He reached up to touch his face, and plucked a broken control button out of his cheek. He let it fall with a clatter. Smoke filled the air. No light came in from the windscreen, now a cracked, featureless wall of dark metal and splintered safety glass. A few dangling fragments of clear material glowed with static, while others caught flecks of the sunrise from behind.

Mamoru turned to his right, and his mouth fell open. Sadako lay on the floor at his side, face smeared with blood. He attempted to jump to his feet but could not get out of the chair.

"Sadako!" He reached for her, screaming.

She did not react.

He tried again to stand, this time noticing the harness holding him down. Wind blew over him from behind. He twisted, gazing through frazzled hair at the cockpit door. Early morning sunrise peered over mountains and illuminated six rows of seats—all that remained of the front end. The rest of the shuttle had disintegrated along a debris trail scattered through a long trench.

She left her seat to secure my belt.

He flung the harness off and fell on his knees. His tears created clean spots on her cheek, displacing blood. Her voice spoke in his memory, afraid their time together would be short. He grasped her shoulders and gave her a light shake, but she did not stir. Mamoru lowered his ear to her nose, and felt no breath. He shuddered. Grief peaked with the thought he had only one honorable thing left to do.

Before he did, he sat up and pulled her limp body close in a tight hug to say his farewell. In his mind, she was still the little girl thigh deep in the Sumida river, trying to get a boy who didn't have time for old ways to believe in Kami. Mamoru's composure cracked. Tears streamed down his cheeks as he sobbed. He lowered his head, resting it against her shoulder. This burden weighed too heavily on his honor. His weakness had been her death. He would remain with her here.

Forever.

"Forgive me, sister." He eased her flat and arranged her arms at her sides.

Mamoru grasped his katana. He slid it from the scabbard and held it flat across his belly. For a moment he, meditated on his failures. Had he been patient, they could have purchased tickets and flown in comfort. Had he remembered to secure his seatbelt, she would not have had to give her life to save his. Had he obeyed Father, she never would have been forced into a life of servitude and cruelty. Mamoru drew in a breath in preparation to slice himself open. His fingers tensed on the rubberized handle. If he was quick enough, the vibro blade would cut him in half before he fainted.

"I shall walk with you for eternity, Sister."

A small bubble of blood swelled out of her left nostril, and popped.

She's breathing.

He put the sword back in his scabbard and hovered over her, examining her injuries with a gentle touch. She had a pulse, albeit weak. Her right arm had broken where she struck the console, and her right leg had not fared much better. Mamoru could not tell for sure through her suit, but assumed a few broken ribs as well. He hurried to his feet and climbed through the remnant of the passenger section, squinting at the acrid fumes of burning plastic, as he moved to the shattered end. Glittering metal fragments dotted a desert-like landscape on either side of several hundred meters worth of trench. Here and there, wisps of black smoke rose from the scorched ground. Fleeting memories of thrusters coming back on at the last second returned. He had managed to regain enough control to allow a survivable crash landing instead of a crater.

The Badlands.

Woozy, he stumbled over to a large block of debris, which turned out to be the former cockpit security door. The crash had damaged it, imparting a slight curve that would make for a decent sled/stretcher. He dragged it back to the wreckage and padded it with seat cushions.

A soft whimper issued from Sadako as he slid his arms under her and lifted. She moaned once again as he set her down on the makeshift stretcher and tied her in place with scraps of cloth. He looped scavenged wiring through the top end of the door, creating a pull sled.

Metal creaked as he walked once again through the forward end of the dead shuttle. White energy licked across his arms. He bolstered his strength and picked her up, stretcher and all, and carried her out of the wreck. Once on solid ground, he eased her down and squinted at the rising sun, trying to remember where he was in relation to the map when everything went to hell.

He looked to the dim west, back to the sun at the east, and again at the dark. After moving Sadako to a patch of shade under the broken hull, he rummaged through the wreckage until he found the galley. Mamoru scavenged two cases of trendy bottled water, which he secured to the bottom of the door, below her boots. No edible food existed in any form other than beige goop, OmniSoy that splattered everywhere when the tank ruptured.

He glanced at the arid land and the mountains to the east. *I must be farther from the east.* He gathered the wire and headed west, dragging Sadako at a brisk walk, hoping he was closer to West City. Guessing wrong would send him deeper into the Badlands.

For two hours, he walked. Mamoru flung off his coat, no longer able to tolerate the heat. He paused to open Sadako's suit and give her water. She moved, but seemed out of it and unaware of what had happened. It reassured him when she took the water, aware of the world enough to drink on her own.

His trek continued with renewed determination, gaining speed once he found a stretch of intact road to follow. The improvised stretcher scraped over the paving, making a lot of noise, but it slid with less resistance than over dirt. When the sun reached its zenith, he stopped again to give her water. Sadako seemed able to drink more easily that time, and he poured some over her brow. He removed his white shirt and tucked it around her head, a shield against the burning rays.

The scuff of a boot from behind made him spin. Four men in tattered leathers and jeans clustered on the far side of the road, two with ancient rifles not quite aimed at him.

"Howdy," said the eldest, a Caucasian man in his later forties.

"Hello." Mamoru eyed them with suspicion.

A scrawny dust-covered man, maybe twenty, leaned closer. "Yer wife hurt?"

"She is my sister."

All four smiled.

"She is not available. I must get her to the city as soon as I am able. She needs medical help."

The youngest, a boy of about sixteen, lifted a red cap from his head and put it back on. "Which city?"

"*The* city," said Mamoru. "West City. All the way on the coast."

"Ain't nothin' there but a wall o' fire that'll burn yer ass to a crisp," said the Elder. "You'd best make for Querq. Word is the Prophet's livin' there now. Cain't say for how long tho."

One of the two with rifles used it to tap the oldest in the arm. "Paw, din' you hear? When weez in Littlefield, dey sayin' sheez diffurnt."

"Diffurnt how?" asked Paw.

"She ain't no takin' kind to raiders. Got a whole armee now 'tectin her. Ain't gonna leave Querq."

"Meh," grumbled Paw. "Jes matter o' time fore a big 'nuff group comes ta tek her. You best get on over there 'fore it happens."

Mamoru gathered the sled cord. "Why would I do that? I don't have time, my sister is dying."

"Prophet kin fix 'er. You g'won to Querq," said Paw. "Head northwest from 'ere, you hit path 40 inna bout free hour' an, you just follow it west. Goes right ta Querq. Yew don' wanna g'win from the east tho. Circle it. G'win fromma south. Old city got's bad critters roamin' it. Spesh-lee at dark. Right nasty."

"Yaw, should do it," said the youngest, now at Sadako's side. "She ain' lookin' like ye got 'nuff time what ta get to the curtain' o' flames. Best git 'er to the Prophet if you wanna keep 'er."

Mamoru whirled on the boy, startled at not noticing his proximity. He blamed his aches and pains, crash-addled mind, and worry.

The other man with a rifle lowered it, and tossed a brown lump to Mamoru. "Here, ya lookin' like you could use it."

It smelled like cured meat. The exact kind of meat, Mamoru did not know—or care to think about. "I have never heard of this Prophet." He gave the men each a canister of water in return.

"Best get movin'," said Paw. "Member, tek Path Forty."

The nomads crossed the road, heading northeast. Snippets of conversation between them as they grew distant gave Mamoru the impression they knew where they were going and were not wandering. Incoherent mutterings came from Sadako, as if she spoke to Mother. He dragged her off the road, heading in the direction the old man had indicated. His hands hurt where the wire bit his palms. Whenever the door snagged on a stone or bit of scrub brush, he growled. This was the Kami punishing him for not protecting his sister when she was defenseless. No matter what, he would not fail her this time. No matter how much the wire cut his fingers or the blood made them stick together, he would endure.

Within an hour, his tireless pace brought him to the remains of a major east-west highway. His decision to follow it on faith was rewarded with a shot-up sign in the shape of a blue badge bearing the number 40.

He followed the path for hours. Phantom voices intruded on his thoughts, everyone he could imagine: Nami, Minamoto, Archon, Reiko, Aurora, Sensei, and Anna all nattered at him. A prairie-dog like animal as big as a prize sow stood on its hind legs in a ditch. When it waved at him and said "hello," Mamoru slapped himself. The animal remained, but did not speak again.

He kept on until the sun sank in the distance. Each time she whimpered, his tiredness lessened. Swirls of dim energy appeared in patches here and there over his body as he tapped his psionic power, not for strength or speed, but for endurance.

"Mam..." She whined. "Can't move..."

"Rest, don't try to talk." He pondered a break, but refused to waste any time. His comfort was not worth her life.

He soldiered into the night, ignoring the burn in his legs.

A NEW MASTER

Mamoru trudged until the sun came up, illuminating rotten structures on the side of the road. Dead hulks of ancient wheeled cargo transports collapsed back to the earth, lined up like slaughtered cows along the wall of an old building. Scorpions skittered for cover, seeking places of shadowed cool. He squinted at the cloudless sky, thankful not to see buzzards circling overhead. It was a fool's hope to expect any of the old semis or cars parked in front of the 'Hank's Truck Stop' sign would run, but the building did offer shade.

Weary, he shambled around and removed a canister of water from the pack, slugging it down in one gulp. Another, he took and dribbled in her mouth. At the touch of it, she moved, straining to sit up and drink. He cradled her head in one hand, letting her take the water at her own pace.

Wind rustled through the debris amid rusty creaking and scratching metal. A sense of being watched caused him to survey the area. For an instant, he made out the shape of a black wolf peering around the corner of the gas station office through a haze of heat blur. The huge animal locked crimson eyes on him, and seemed to be smiling.

He blinked, and it was gone.

"I've been walking all night. I'm probably hurt too." He rubbed his collarbone where the harness had bruised. *I do not recall the crash. That is not a good sign.*

Mamoru took a knee at her side, brushing her hair and dabbing sweat from her face. He fed her a little water, but she shied away from the cured meat.

"It is not much farther. Focus on staying awake."

"Mmm." Her head drooped to the side as her eyes closed.

"Sadako!" He shook her, but she didn't move.

The hard *click* of a boot heel on the concrete tarmac startled him upright. A decrepit old man in a brown duster coat, black shirt, jeans, and cowboy boots stood three paces behind him. His skin ran with blue veins. Milky and brittle, it seemed as though the faintest touch would peel the flesh right off him. Wisps of grey hair wavered in the breeze as his lips curled to a smile, baring a ruin of kelp-colored teeth.

I have seen this man before.

"Good day, Mamoru." The man tipped his cowboy hat. A band of silver discs around it rattled.

"Who are you?"

"You wish to destroy the one who calls himself Archon? You wish to avenge your family? The simpleton Burckhardt cannot help you defeat Archon. The Awakened are too powerful."

"How do you know this?" Mamoru narrowed his eyes. "I am supposed to believe you can do something?"

"Look inside yourself, Mamoru. Gaze upon me and answer your question."

This man is strange. His chi is out of balance. Mamoru met his stare. The old man's red eyes radiated energy akin to nothing he had ever experienced. *Power.*

"Your sister is less than an hour from death. I can help, though I require an angel destroyed." He glanced sidelong at the injured woman. "I do have a knack for bending fate, my boy."

"Oni…" Mamoru glanced down.

The old man chuckled, a dry, grating sound that caused the muscles in his back to twitch. "Do you regard everything you do not understand as a demon, Mamoru?"

"Tell me I am wrong."

The old man smiled.

Sadako moaned and coughed. A trickle of crimson leaked from the corner of her mouth and glided down her cheek. She seemed paler now, and her lips looked blue. Mamoru stared at her as desperation quickened his heart. Sadako's skin changed, she took on the color of a day-old corpse right before his eyes.

The ancient man extended a hand. "Sadako does not need to die."

A burp in reality made her look seven years old again, lying bloodied at the bank of the river Sumida, staring up at him with pleading eyes. Mamoru shivered, desperate to get that image out of his mind.

"We can help each other." The old man's voice seemed to come from everywhere.

Mamoru closed his eyes. *I cannot let you die for me, sister. I will not fail you again.* "Sadako lives."

The ancient one cleared his throat. "She lives. The Angel dies."

Mamoru clasped the thick, leathery glove, and shook hands. "I accept."

fin

ACKNOWLEDGMENTS

Thank you for reading Grey Ronin!

Additional thanks to Jackson Tjota for the cover art, Alexandria Thompson for the cover title and layout, and Ricky Gunawan for the chapter art.

ABOUT THE AUTHOR

Originally from South Amboy NJ, Matthew has been creating science fiction and fantasy worlds for most of his reasoning life. Since 1996, he has developed the "Divergent Fates" world, in which *Division Zero, Virtual Immortality, The Awakened Series, The Harmony Paradox, and the Daughter of Mars series* take place. Along with being an editor at Curiosity Quills press, he has worked in IT and technical support.

Matthew is an avid gamer, a recovered WoW addict, Gamemaster for two custom RPG systems, and a fan of anime, British humour, and intellectual science fiction that questions the nature of reality, life, and what happens after it.

He is also fond of cats.

Visit me online at:
Facebook: https://www.facebook.com/MatthewSCoxAuthor
Amazon: https://www.amazon.com/author/mscox
Pinterest: https://www.pinterest.com/matthewcox10420/
Goodreads: https://www.goodreads.com/author/show/7712730.Matthew_S_Cox
Email: mcox2112@gmail.com

OTHER BOOKS BY MATTHEW S. COX

Divergent Fates Universe Novels

Division Zero series

- Division Zero
- Lex De Mortuis
- Thrall
- Guardian
- Harbinger

The Awakened series

- Prophet of the Badlands
- Archon's Queen
- Grey Ronin
- Daughter of Ash
- Zero Rogue
- Angel Descended

Daughter of Mars series

- The Hand of Raziel
- Araphel
- Ghost Black

Virtual Immortality series

- Virtual Immortality
- The Harmony Paradox

Prophet of the Badlands Series

- Prophet's Journey

Divergent Fates Anthology

(Fiction Novels - Adult)

The Roadhouse Chronicles Series

- One More Run
- The Redeemed
- Dead Man's Number

Faded Skies series

- Heir Ascendant
- Ascendant Unrest
- Ascendant Revolution

Temporal Armistice Series

- Nascent Shadow
- The Shadow Collector
- The Gate to Oblivion
- The Queen of Discord

Vampire Innocent series

- A Nighttime of Forever
- A Beginner's Guide to Fangs
- The Artist of Ruin
- The Last Family Road Trip
- The Phantom Oracle
- How Not to Summon Demons
- Ordinary Problems of a College Vampire
- A Vampire's Guide to Surviving Holidays
- An Introduction to Paranormal Diplomacy

Standalones

- Wayfarer: AV494
- Axillon99
- Chiaroscuro: The Mouse and the Candle

- The Spirits of Six Minstrel Run
- Sophie's Light
- The Far Side of Promise anthology
- Operation: Chimera (with Tony Healey)
- The Dysfunctional Conspiracy (with Christopher Veltmann)
- Of Myth and Shadow
- The Girl Who Found the Sun

Winter Solstice series (with J.R. Rain)

- Convergence
- Containment
- Catalyst

Alexis Silver series (with J.R. Rain)

- Silver Light
- Deep Silver
- Silver Quarrel

Samantha Moon Origins series (with J.R. Rain)

- New Moon Rising
- Moon Mourning

Vampire For Hire series (with J.R. Rain)

- Moon Master
- Dead Moon
- Lost Moon

Maddy Wimsey series (with J.R. Rain)

- The Devil's Eye
- The Drifting Gloom
- Dark Mercy

Samantha Moon Case Files series (with J.R. Rain)

- Blood Moon

Immortal Operative series (with J.R. Rain)

- Broken Ice

Four Elements series (with J.R. Rain)

- The Elementalist
- The Black Rose
- The Wakefield Curse

Young Adult Novels

The Eldritch Heart Series

- The Eldritch Heart
- The Cursed Crown

Evergreen Series

- Evergreen
- The World That Remains
- The Lucky Ones
- Nuclear Summer

Standalones

- Caller 107
- The Summer the World Ended
- Nine Candles of Deepest Black
- The Forest Beyond the Earth
- Out of Sight

Middle Grade Novels

The Adventures of Ubergirl series

- My Dad is a Mad Scientist
- Aliens Ate My Homework
- The End of all Halloweens

Tales of Widowswood series

- Emma and the Banderwigh
- Emma and the Silk Thieves
- Emma and the Silverbell Faeries
- Emma and the Elixir of Madness
- Emma and the Weeping Spirit

Standalones

- Citadel: The Concordant Sequence
- The Cursed Codex
- The Menagerie of Jenkins Bailey

www.ingramcontent.com/pod-product-compliance
Lightning Source LLC
Chambersburg PA
CBHW030604180626
46816CB00005B/1675